Novels in the Sam Adams Series by Sarah Shankman

First Kill All the Lawyers *(writing as Alice Storey)*
Then Hang All the Liars *(writing as Alice Storey)*
Now Let's Talk of Graves
She Walks in Beauty
The King Is Dead

Other Novels by Sarah Shankman

Impersonal Attractions
Keeping Secrets

THE KING
IS DEAD

SARAH
SHANKMAN

POCKET BOOKS

New York   London   Toronto   Sydney   Tokyo   Singapore

This book is a work of fiction. Names, characters, places, and
incidents are either products of the author's imagination or are
used fictitiously. Any resemblance to actual events or locales or
persons, living or dead, is entirely coincidental.

POCKET BOOKS, a division of Simon & Schuster Inc.
1230 Avenue of the Americas, New York, NY 10020

ISBN: 1-4165-0307-2

This Pocket Books paperback printing May 2004

10 9 8 7 6 5 4 3 2 1

POCKET and colophon are registered trademarks of
Simon & Schuster Inc.

Cover art by John Howard

Printed in the U.S.A.

For Mary Ann Lynn
and the Full-tilt Kids, Adam and Kim

Special thanks to the many kind people of Tupelo, Mississippi, who shared their time and their stories, especially Detective Ronny Thomas and Detective Cliff Hardy; Gary Bradley for his eagle eye and Jim Gillernan for the electricity; Elaine Dundy for *Elvis and Gladys,* Jane and Michael Stern for *Elvis World,* Phil Brittin and Joseph Daniel for *Texas on the Halfshell.* And love and gratitude to Jane Chelius and Harvey Klinger, my home team, for continuous acts of faith.

THE KING
IS DEAD

• • • • • • • • • • • • • • **1**

Mary Ann McClanahan had been playing leapfrog with the eighteen-wheeler for about fifty miles. He'd pass, then she'd pass him back in her little blue Toyota watching for his big hand to wave Hi there! Once his fingers splayed twice, five-five, warning her to lift her pedal off the metal, Smokey was in the neighborhood.

It was getting on toward afternoon in the northwest Alabama hills. Mary Ann thought it was pretty country. Thick green pine forests climbed up and down rolling hills toward Mississippi, though every once in a while there was the naked slash left by strip mining. Still, it was a lot nicer than where she'd been living, down south almost on the Gulf, a little town called Fairhope.

South Alabama was flat. Mary Ann was tired of flat. A curvy five-four herself, blond and pretty, her latest husband freshly buried, Mary Ann was ready for some ups and downs, some rock and roll.

Which surely wasn't playing right now on the radio. Somebody was singing about Jesus coming to jail and paying his bail, the announcer interrupting to ask anybody in the neighborhood to come on up and bring him a fishing pole, he wanted to go catch himself some perch, gar, benner, buffalo. Then he dedicated a song to a little boy named Gucci. Why anybody would name their kid after a handbag was beyond Mary Ann. She flipped through the stations till she landed on Elvis singing "A Big Hunk O' Love." That had her bouncing in her seat. She loved Elvis with all her heart. He touched her in places no one else ever had, for sure.

Now she was hanging back, letting the trucker up ahead work through his whining gears after crawling through a speed trap of a little town. Slow enough for her to read a road marker that said this Route 78 was called the Bankhead Highway. Named after Senator Bankhead, Tallulah's daddy, she thought.

Mary Ann had seen Tallulah in a couple of old movies on the TV, and she liked her laugh, but mostly she liked what she'd read about her in a *Vanity Fair* article. *Vanity Fair* was Mary Ann's bible, and it said that Tallulah had been a wild girl. Who partied hearty. Was more than a little naughty. Which made Mary Ann right proud to be driving toward Tupelo, Mississippi, on her daddy's road.

Mary Ann's trucker was picking up speed, hauling butt. She let a Buick and a Lincoln slip on in between them. Make the trucker think she had better things to do. Tease him, like Tallulah would. Then over on the right, a sign caught her eye.

ALABAMA SNAKE FARM. One mile.

Mary Ann shivered. Now there was a roadside attraction she could do without.

She honked, then scooted on around the Buick and the Lincoln, both of them full of blue-hairs who glared at her with open mouths. *Lord have mercy, did you see that blond hussy, Mabel, who does she think she is, burning up the road?* She waggled her pink tongue at them, snuggled up to the rear of her Low Ball truck man, thinking about him wrestling that big dinosaur through the long darkness of the Bible Belt, talking about girlies on the CB. The blue tattoo on his left arm said Are You Lonesome Tonight?

Well, yes, she was. And she was thinking about pulling up, holding even with him in the road—which would be tough because the swaying tower of the truck took up exactly one whole lane—then trying to holler above his roar: Pull over at the next truck stop. She hadn't had a conversation all day, unless you counted the one with the waitress at breakfast near Tallahassee who'd read her palm and said she was going to have a great love in her life, which was fine with Mary Ann because she sure as heck hadn't had one yet.

Then the eighteen-wheeler's left rear tire blew and knocked Mary Ann right over into the snake farm.

● ● ● ● ● ● ● ● ● ● ● ●   2

Wen Harry Zack asked Sam Adams if she was
sure she didn't want to drive up to Tupelo Days and
the Third Annual International Barbecue Cookoff,
she'd said, "Are you nuts?"

Harry had pushed Sam's porch swing back and
forth a couple of times and stared off south across
Lake Pontchartrain toward New Orleans where he
lived. "Does that mean no?"

"Means much as I would love to cheer you on at
the cookoff, since you and Lavert opened the Rib
Shack it's been 'cue, 'cue, nothing but barbecue—
which the little dog doesn't eat, and I'm counting
fat grams. Besides"—she hefted a notebook—"I'm
working."

Sam called her book-in-progress *American Weird*
and was enjoying the research, talking with folks like
the Civil War Bungee-Jumpers, who planned to rubber-
band off into the Mississippi River at Vicksburg right
across from where Grant's flotilla had parked.

The work was a relief from her years as a crime
reporter—first for the *San Francisco Chronicle* and
then back home to Atlanta and the *Constitution*, from

4

which she'd taken a leave, probably permanently. She'd about had her fill of people whose notion of good times was inflicting serious damage on one another with guns, knives, sticks, stones, flame throwers, cyanide, ropes, high pressure hoses, and weed cutters.

But Harry hadn't given up. "You could take your laptop with you. I'm staying with Red Holcomb, that man I told you wants to talk to me and Lavert about Q franchising. We met him when we were over there visiting one of Lavert's cousins. He has a big old house, you could work. Maybe even pick up an idea or two. Town ought to be lousy with weird."

"I don't need any more material right now. I just need to hack out this proposal."

Harry took a long slug of his Dixie beer, then held out the bottle and stared at it for a minute. "Cookoff's honoring Japan this year. Samurai hog smokers versus folks like the Chickasaw County Chip Chunkers with the promise of a Mississippi Toyota plant a major factor. Can't you see them big ole bubbas trying to outbow the Japanese? Might come down to an arm-wrestling contest to see who's the most polite first. Might mean *I* have a chance to win."

"Ummm." Sam wasn't paying much attention. She ran a hand through her short dark curls, much like Harry's, and lifted another pile of notes from the porch floor.

"I'd sure love to have your company. Most folks have a whole team, and Lavert's gonna have to stay home and mind the store." Harry paused as a jet flew over, about the same size as a heron in the near distance. "I bet there'll be some good music, too."

Harry Zack was a musician himself, a thirty-year-old Uptown New Orleans society bad bad boy who, after he'd run out of song-writing luck in Nashville had tried process-serving, oil-rigging, insurance-investigating, before he'd opened a BBQ place with his best friend Lavert, an ex-con whom Harry had known since their days at Grambling State where Lavert played football and Harry was The Only White Boy.

"Well, it's too bad about Lavert. Long drive'd give y'all the chance for some superior male-bonding."

"Okay. Okay." Harry stood and strolled the length of the porch with Harpo, Sam's little white Shih Tzu, in tow. "I guess you're going to force me into spoiling the surprise."

At that Sam looked up at his back, at the dark curls just brushing the neck of the gray T-shirt—he needed a haircut again—the hard slim waist, the faded jeans, the right leg ripped where he'd caught it on a snag. They'd gone catfishing the night before, a balmy very-end-of-March evening, had made love in the boat pulled up against some tall grass. Got eaten alive by mosquitoes. It'd been worth it. Everything had been worth it so far with Harry, her boy toy, ten years her junior, turned lover for real. So real she'd left Atlanta a few months ago, rented—on a look-see basis, you understand—this house on the north shore of Lake Pontchartrain to see how it felt to be closer to him. Last night they'd been real close.

"We driving up in a pink Cadillac?"

"Oh, shoot." Harry had a great grin. "You guessed."

"And Elvis really is alive, come home to his birthplace to visit, and you've arranged us a blind date. You tagging along as chaperone."

"Now you've gone and taken all the fun out of it."

. . . . **3**

When Mary Ann came to she was lying on a red plastic sofa in a ladies' room. Two women were hovering over her. Fat women.

"Praise the Lord, she's alive!" said the brunette, who weighed in at about two-fifty.

"Well, we *knew* that," said the redhead. "She was breathing, weren't she?"

Mary Ann tried to sit up, but they wouldn't let her.

"You might have *in*ternal injuries," said the brunette in that tight-lipped voice that some women use when they talk about anything below the neck. "You just don't know. I told 'em they ought to send for an ambulance."

"I swear, I'm okay." Mary Ann was sure she was, except she felt kind of dizzy, and her new jeans were a mess.

"Oh, honey, don't swear," the redhead said. "Not when you've just been saved from the jaws of death."

"Is *that* what it was?" Mary Ann gave herself a shove and sat up anyway. She was okay. See? She held out her hands. Just a few scratches, some little red marks that hurt like the dickens. "I thought it was a Low Ball truck."

"Well, it was. That tire, you know, Velma and me were standing right there in the window, when that big old piece of rubber flew off that tire. It went rolling right at you, I swear it looked just like one of them hoop snakes. You know about them? They hold a stinger in their tails, roll up, and try to stave you with it. They hit a tree instead, it'll die, deader 'n a doornail."

Mary Ann looked around the ladies' room, sniffed, it smelled peculiar. "This is that snake farm, isn't it?" She tried to stand, but she wasn't quite there yet. Or maybe it was the thought of the snakes that was making her weak in the knees. "Are there snakes in here?"

"Oh, no," they both said, staring one another dead in the eye. Then the redhead shook her big hair that was waved and lacquered up about six inches on the top of her head. "They're all out there." She pointed at the door. "Our menfolks out looking at them. P.J. and Lawtey."

"Well, listen, I think I need to hit the road. I'll just sit here a few minutes and collect myself."

"That car of yours, that little Toyota, I don't know as how you're gonna be able to drive it. It looks like it's tore up pretty good. Ran itself up on a gatepost. One of the ones holding up the snake farm sign." That was the brunette.

Great. That was just great. Here she was stuck in Nowhere, Alabama, with no car when where she needed to be was Tupelo. And quick. She looked up at the combined five hundred pounds of woman, not one ounce of it wearing makeup. The brunette was wearing a brown leather jacket over a T-shirt that said BFJ 1989 Fayetteville Rally, yellow on black. Mary Ann asked her if she had a cigarette.

"Oh, I don't smoke."

"I gave it up too," said Mary Ann, "until just recently when my husband died. I smoke when I feel real stressed."

She hadn't meant to say that about Carlin being dead. The words just popped out. But the truth was, Mary Ann had noticed, you take any two or three women in the world, doesn't matter where or what nationality or situation, plop 'em down somewhere like a ladies' room, they'll be talking about the most fundamental issues on earth in about fifteen seconds. Men, it takes 'em about twelve years to get past scratching themselves and football scores. No wonder so many of them are mean and cranky.

"Goodness gracious, you're awfully young to be a widow," said the redhead, reaching around and jerking down her bra that was creeping up on her in the back.

Mary Ann smiled. Well, she was holding her own for thirty-eight, three husbands, two grown girls, and she hated to think how many dumb jobs: waiting tables, tending bar, working the counter in a five-and-dime. At least she'd been able to sit down once she'd married Carlin.

Right now though she didn't look her best. She needed to touch up her roots. That would happen to you when you were on the road, and Mary Ann had been traveling for about a week. Right after Carlin's funeral she'd said to Luci, her partner in the aloe vera cosmetics and lingerie houseparty business, Honey, you just take the wheel of this thing for a while.

Luci'd said sure. Gave her that Hallmark-sympathy-card look. Everybody thinking she was knee-deep in grief, needed to run away from the memories for a while.

Mary Ann had gone to visit her two daughters from

her first marriage—both determined to ruin their lives just like she had—down to Daytona Beach, where they lived. Hung around long enough to get fed up with their squalling babies and the two sons-in-law calling her Grandma, then set out with a stack of AAA maps.

The AAA lady had tried to make her some Trip-Tiks to where she was going, but Mary Ann had said, No, thank you, I appreciate it, but that'd be tough since I don't know.

Actually she'd already been thinking about leaving Carlin, looking around for Husband Number Four, when her October issue of *Vanity Fair* had arrived in a plastic bag along with a separate Calvin Klein Jeans advertising magazine. It had given her a whole new outlook.

The little Calvin magazine was a story, all in pictures, no words, about this great-looking young girl—take Mary Ann back to nineteen, let her natural color grow out, you'd swear they were sisters. The girl rode a motorcycle, wore jeans, of course, and leathers, and was a lead singer in San Francisco with this rock band. The pictures showed her hanging out with these cute guys, but she wasn't riding on the back of anybody's motorcycle. She had her own. And when they showed somebody holding a baby, it wasn't her. It was this blond guy with no shirt bouncing that squalling baby on his knee. What the girl did was whatever she pleased. Just like Elvis used to. She was with them, but she was a loner. Kind of a girl desperado. Riding her bike in those tight black jeans, singing her guts out.

That Calvin magazine plucked a guitar string deep in Mary Ann's heart. It made her think. She'd been married, bing, bing, bing, since she was seventeen in New Orleans, that's where she was born, and her boyfriend, a not-very-good bank robber, knocked her up. She was always putting up with a man because she thought she needed him. Now, why didn't she just strike out, see what she could do on her own?

So she did, once she'd killed Carlin, she hit the road. After visiting Daytona and her daughters, she'd meandered down to Miami, ate herself some Cuban sandwiches, hung out in the dance clubs wearing some new tight Calvins, gave her new outlook a test drive.

She picked up a conventioning meat packer from Alexandria, Louisiana, who said he knew how to show a pretty lady a good time. Yeah, yeah, said Mary Ann. But how do you know what I want to do? So she led the way to dinner in a fancy restaurant that had menus almost bigger than she was, she wore her black chiffon and her red high heels and pointed him at the dance floor. He *liked* being told what to do. So when Mary Ann said, Excuse me to the Ladies', you stay right here, don't move a muscle, he did that too while she slipped out and hailed herself a cab. Gave the driver a big tip from the meat packer's roll.

The next day she sang along with Elvis on her tape deck all the way to Key West, where she met a lot of funny folks, ate her weight in crab, applauded the sunset, decided she liked the independent girl desperado life just fine. It was probably even better than her original lifelong ambition to overcome her white trash background and become a member of the Junior League. Up until now she'd wanted to be a lady, wear big hats and pour tea, go to dances at the country club. But this looked like it was going to be more fun.

That same October *Vanity Fair* had had a picture of Jessica Lange on the cover. Lots of people thought Mary Ann looked like her. And the story inside told how Jessica, who'd had herself more of the world's great manflesh than any one woman was ever entitled to, what with living with Baryshnikov, then Sam Shepard, and before them, a sexy Spaniard named Paco that Mary Ann hadn't even heard of, Jessica said that until she was thirty-two and had her first child, she lived like a madwoman. Said she had lived everywhere and done everything. Didn't give a rip what people thought. Said she, and Mary Ann remembered the words like they were engraved on her heart, *Went down the road full tilt.*

Mary Ann had leaned over the breakfast table the next morning after she'd stayed up till two A.M. looking at the girl on the motorcycle, reading the Jessica article and then one on menopause that depressed the hell out of her—take estrogen and be sane but risk breast cancer or don't and be a raving lunatic—she'd said to Carlin, the pharmaceutical sales manager whose theory was all drugs gave you cancer, "Don't you ever wish you could say you lived your life full tilt?"

Carlin had thrown his paper down and mashed his cigarette out in his egg yolk. "Just proves my theory it's a shame they ever let women learn to read, and a crime some of them get paid to write for stupid women's magazines. Now where's my blue suit?"

Mary Ann had said, "Carlin, do you mean the magazines are stupid or the women are stupid?" and then she ducked.

It wasn't too long after that, the day after they'd visited the Elvis Hall of Fame in Gatlinburg, that Carlin had gone flying headfirst off that big old rock in the Great Smoky Mountains National Park, and she didn't have to worry about him anymore or his damned breakfast or his blue suit—which she'd buried him in. All she had to worry her pretty little head with, as far as she could see, was waiting for Carlin's life insurance to chunk in.

That was, until she'd called home a couple of nights ago. She'd been in Boca Raton hanging out in a tonk with a beer-drinking young real estate developer who'd been wearing lots of gold chains when the evening started. Luci told her on the phone about the insurance company and a Tupelo lawyer calling. Mary Ann kept waiting for her to say April Fool! but she never did, so yesterday at dawn Mary Ann had aimed her Toyota straight at Mississippi just like it was the pearl-handled Colt she'd inherited from her second husband, the dirty cop.

"You know, you look a lot like that actress, that blonde who was in that picture show *Tootsie,*" said the redhead watching Mary Ann, who'd discovered her purse and her lipstick still intact beside her on the ladies' room sofa.

"Oh, I do not," said Mary Ann. But there it was, that Jessica thing.

"Now you know you most certainly do. What color is that?"

"This lipstick? Fire and Ice. I've been wearing it for twenty years." Then she bit her tongue. If she was going to act like the Calvin girl, she was going to have to drop a few. But what she'd said about the lipstick was true. Mary Ann was a firm believer in brand loyalty. She told her cosmetics customers that, even if it didn't help her aloe vera line. You find something you like, you stick with it, and it'll be good to you.

Now, it was too bad Carlin hadn't felt that way, wasn't it?

Mary Ann reached in her bag and pulled out her comb, started fixing the front of her hair.

"Is that natural?" asked the brunette. "That color?" Then she slapped her hand over her mouth like she wished she could snatch back the words. "I'm sorry, that's rude."

"Honey, don't think a thing about it. I sure don't. I started bleaching it when I was fifteen. I always use Lady Clairol Sunbeam Blonde." Mary Ann was staring at those red marks on her hands again. A few on her wrists too. They had a funny pattern to them and they hurt something awful.

"It's really pretty," said the brunette. "You know, you was saying about your being a widow. I bet if I was to lose P.J., my hair would turn whiter than that overnight."

"Well, it wasn't that way with me and Carlin. He died, it made me give some serious consideration to dyeing my hair purple." Mary Ann giggled. "But I got over it."

The two women cut looks at one another like they didn't know what to do, then went ahead and laughed.

"I *did* go out and buy myself some bright red high heels and a couple of pretty dresses. Got one in black chiffon, it's cut real low and draped across the bosom." Mary Ann gestured. "I wear it with lots of rhinestones when I'm feeling trashy."

"Honey, was he not nice to you? Your husband?" the redhead asked.

"Nice? Are you kidding? The way he treated me after I washed his clothes and cooked his meals and picked up his underwear? Wouldn't let me eat tunafish because he didn't like the smell on my breath. That's exactly like Elvis did with Priscilla, that tuna thing, but I'll tell you, if Carlin had been as cute as Elvis I wouldn't have minded."

Just then, somebody pounded on the bathroom door. "Did that blond girl die in there or did y'all fall in?"

"Come on," said the redhead. "That Lawtey, once

he's decided it's time, there's no stalling him. Honey, do you think you can walk out—"

"I'm fine." Mary Ann grabbed her purse. She was ready to hit the road. But if her car was totaled, she'd have to think about hitching a ride.

Outside two fat men lounged up against big chopped Harleys. Well, do tell. Those two old girls sure didn't look like biker mommas to her.

"Well, look at you!" one of them called. He was wearing neon green suspenders. Mary Ann turned around to see who he was talking to. "No, you!" he laughed, he was missing a few teeth, pointing right at her. "I tell you, when we picked you up out of that pen—"

"Now, be careful, P.J.," cautioned the brunette.

But Mary Ann couldn't hear the rest of what he was saying as a big truck was roaring up into the driveway, which wasn't all that wide. They scooted. Sure enough, it was the Low Ball man waving his tattooed arm out the window like she was his long-lost love.

"All them beauties hanging off you."

Beauties? What was this P.J. person talking about?

The Low Ball man jumped down from his truck. He was older than Mary Ann had thought, but bigger and better looking too. "Ma'am," he was saying, coming right up to her, so close she could smell his Brut, "I can't tell you how sorry I am about that tire. It took me another mile and a half to stop, I'm telling you I thought I was going to jackknife, that empty trailer bouncing all over the place—"

"I bought one of them very king snakes we pulled offen you," P.J. was saying. He patted a screened box on the back of his motorcycle. " 'Course they ain't poison. But I like 'em anyway."

Pulled off of her? Pulled snakes off of her?

"Can we give you a ride somewheres?" P.J. was patting the seat of his bike, right in front of that box. Something rattled inside. "It'd be a tight squeeze, but—"

That was the last thing Mary Ann heard before she pitched over into the dirt.

Harry's Aunt Suzanne's 1963 Cadillac *was* pink, and it sported tail fins, a rag top, and wraparound sound. Hitched to the rear was a trailer carrying a fifty-five-gallon crude oil drum on wheels—Harry's smoker. The Caddy's trunk was stacked with oak and ice chests full of pork, including a 125-pound whole piglet especially raised for the cookoff. And handed down from Lavert's grandmother, the ingredients for Rib Shack secret sauce.

Friday morning, Harry was leaning on the horn with one hand, trying to comb his curls into a DA with the other. He'd been pressed to choose between his *BBQ Is My Life* and his *Elvis Lives* T-shirts. He'd gone with the King.

Yes! Sam said when she stepped out on her front porch and saw him. A tall pretty woman of forty with high cheekbones, a bright red mouth, and an aristocratic nose, Sam was wearing a plain white cotton sweater that advertised nothing but her curves, a pair of old khakis cinched with a brown woven leather belt, loafers, and a bright scarf twisted through her short dark curls. Yes! yourself, he answered.

"Get over here, bubba, let's start this weekend off with a big kiss."

Harpo rolled his eyes. It was going to be a long ride for a small dog who didn't care for kissing or loud or road 'cue. And didn't know from Elvis, though they shared the same birthday.

"Little darlin'," Harry sang at the top of his lungs, doing his Jack to the King routine on the interstate all the way to Jackson. No time for Delta back roads, Harry wanted to get there before dark and set up his rig, but at Jackson they turned onto the Natchez Trace, the parkway following the path of Indians, hunters, and boatmen who'd sold their boats as well as their goods in old New Orleans. The two-lane ran a long diagonal through nothing but green—pasture land, forests, fields, and swamps from Natchez to Nashville—without a word of advertising.

"Bandits." Sam was reading from the Trace brochure they'd picked up at a rest stop.

"Wild Indians," said Harry, who'd driven the Trace before.

"Oprah Winfrey."

"I beg your pardon."

"Didn't we just pass by Kosciusko? That's where Oprah was born."

"You know the weirdest things."

"That's what I do for a living, sweetheart. Now fill me in on little old Tupelo." Sam imagined it to be a village, a wide place in a dirt road peopled with Faulkner's Snopeses—chew-spitting white trash living in houses with no doors who'd just as soon shoot you as walk around. After all, Faulkner's Yoknapatawpha County was only fifty miles west, and Philadelphia, Mississippi, a hundred miles south, where they'd buried the murdered civil rights workers Chaney, Goodman, and Schwerner in a dirt dam.

"And a quarter of a century ago," said Harry. She could tell he was irritated. "God, you sound like a Yankee. You lived in San Francisco too long, think anybody outside of Atlanta or New Orleans is going to bite your head off, suck your blood like iced tea. You been watching double-feature reruns of *Deliverance* and *Easy Rider?*"

"So you're saying Tupelo's like everyplace else in the U-S of A? Main Street dead, lousy with Jack in the Boxes, satellite dishes, and shopping malls?"

"Actually, it's a pretty little place, prosperous, set in rolling farmland and forests, and downtown's still alive around the courthouse. They're doing some gentrification. But mostly it's your average twenty-five thousand middle-class New South consumers, a van and a Honda in the carport. Even Massas in the Big Old Homes are mostly concerned with paying off their Gold Cards, don't have time to hate nobody else no more than any other God-fearing Amuricans."

"Shucks," said Sam. "Here I'd been hoping for some real trash to sink my teeth into." Then she went back to reading aloud from a pile of books about Elvis to put them in a Tupelo mood.

"Unconscious twice in one day. I don't think that could be good for you." Dewey Travis had just shifted into sixth gear.

Mary Ann could hardly hear him over the roar of the engine and the banging of the empty trailer. But sitting so way up high, would you look at that view? Had to be Mississippi up ahead. She said, "Well, it's not been the best day I've had lately, I can tell you that."

"You mean what with the—"

"Don't say that S-word!" Mary Ann didn't ever

want to hear *snake* again. Nor think about them. In fact, she'd borrowed a pair of Dewey's driving gloves so she wouldn't have to look at her hands and those little punctures that still smarted something fierce. They'd assured her when she came to that the snakes that bit her weren't poisonous, had struck only because she scared them. Now she conjured up this mental picture of herself flying out of her Toyota and into that snake pit and her teeth started chattering all over again.

"You ever driven one of these things?"

The trucker had a nice voice. Kind of country, but deep and sweet. He blurred some of his words. What had he just said?

"Do you want to drive this truck?"

"You mean now?"

"Well, better be pretty soon. 'Less you want to go with me to Holly Springs. That's where I live, half-way between Memphis and Tupelo. I came from there just yesterday, did a quick run down to Birmingham."

Mary Ann slid him a look. Dewey was around fifty, she guessed, maybe a little more, but holding. A handsome six feet, about two hundred, two-ten, he could lose a pound or two. Lots of light brown hair, graying at the temples. Nice straight nose. Dimples. Then there was that voice, smooth as Black Jack over ice. His eyes were another matter. Blue, which she usually liked, but there was ice in them too. On the other hand, his smile, more like a grin, was so warm it could break your heart. Hot and cold, cold and hot, that was Dewey.

"Well now, it's gonna cost you," he was saying, "you wanta drive."

Damn. Why did men always have to do you like that? Well, he could have nookie on his mind all he wanted to, she still had her second husband's little pearl-handled Colt in her bag, and she knew how to use it. Except that if she shot him going—she looked over at the speedometer—seventy-five miles an hour, it was for sure they'd both be roadkill, but on the other hand, how was he going to rape her and drive this truck at the—

"Your best secret?"

"Say what?"

"Woman, did you land on your ears? I said, I'll let you drive if you tell me your deepest most awful secret."

He said those words and inside herself, Mary Ann felt strangely moved. Then her mouth followed suit. "Well, lately I've been doing a little stealing." Then she slapped her hand over her mouth. Mary Ann McClanahan, girl, have you lost your mind?

"It happens," Dewey said, then gave her that slow grin like he wasn't the least bit shocked, which in itself was pretty shocking if you stopped and thought about it. "You gonna knock me in the head, steal my truck?"

"I don't think so." Mary Ann laughed. That was the way to play it, like it was a big joke. But she was nervous that she'd laid herself wide open like that with a complete stranger. She watched her Fire and Ice fingertips tapping on the window. "You have anything worth stealing?" There, that was the right attitude.

"Nope. I'm a poor man." He turned and gave her his full grin. "I hope that don't mean you won't have a Co-cola with me in Tupelo."

"I thought you were going on home."

"To Holly Springs? I am. But then I'm turning right around and coming back on my bike. There's a barbecuing contest this weekend. Music. Some other stuff, interests me. Pretty exciting for this neck of the woods."

So Dewey was going to be around, and she could tell he thought she was cute. Well, he might come in handy, you never knew. Especially if he'd been up to some naughty, too. She knew he had. Her second husband, the cop, had taught her that, you poke around long enough, there ain't nobody's Mr. Clean. "What's the worse thing you ever did, Dewey?"

He shook his head. Wasn't telling.

Now she was the one grinning. "I bet it was awful."

"You showed me yours, now you want me to show you mine, is that it?" He was holding that mother of a truck even in the road while looking straight at her. He had big muscles in his forearms, big for an older guy. Maybe, she wasn't sure yet, muscles where his brains ought to be too.

"I ain't shown you nothing yet." Mary Ann licked the Fire and Ice on her bottom lip, playing with him. She bet he'd do anything she asked him to, until he had what he wanted. That's how it usually went.

"Oh, yeah?" Dewey said, then pulled the Low Ball truck across the center line, passed a Mayflower moving van, and headed straight on into a sky blue BMW. "Oh, yeah?" he repeated it, giving her that steady look again. "What else you got to show me?"

He thought he was scaring her—and he was. But Mary Ann, having decided she'd be intimidated by no mere man, guessed she'd die before she let on. "No way. I told you what I did bad. Now it's your turn." Smiling like butter wouldn't melt in her mouth, all the while that Beemer was barreling straight at them. Dewey's breathing was perfectly even. Okay, so maybe he wasn't a wuss. "Tell me, Dewey," she asked, smiling sweetly like she was pouring at one of those country club teas she used to dream of, *"you* ever robbed anybody?"

"Nu-uh."

22

"Killed anybody?" Not that she intended to make a habit of it, but on the other hand, she wasn't walking away from Tupelo empty-handed. No matter what it took.

"You mean like now?"

"Is *that* what you're doing?" It sure as hell was what it looked like.

"Nawh." Then he jerked the wheel of the high-balling rig, clearing the Mayflower moving van by inches. The BMW took to the ditch. The Mayflower's horn ripped a hole in the air. Before Mary Ann had a chance to feel relieved they hadn't crashed head-on, Dewey said, "But I have though."

"Have what, killed somebody?"

"Yeah, most recently was a couple of weeks ago, unless you count—"

Mary Ann slid him a look, he was kidding, right? Putting her on.

"I was hauling, everything running on schedule even with changing a flat, just like today, when this woman jumped up on her high horse. I was carrying a load of fruit from Miami to Memphis, going to stop for a minute in Lauderdale, leave the rig in a truck stop for an hour tops, go visit this woman who had the biggest collection of Elvis stuff in the whole world, outside of Graceland, of course, and the Elvis Museum in Nashville, but they didn't have the one thing I was looking for and I thought she might."

Mary Ann nodded, unh-huh, like every day somebody told her a story about killing somebody, cool as they were giving her a recipe for chicken salad.

"I was barely in the door when she went huffy with me, right in my face, said she wasn't interested in selling the likes of me a thing and certainly wasn't no museum for every Tom, Dick, and Dewey. That made me mad, and the next thing I knew she was lying on the floor, her neck funny, little trickle of blood coming out the corner of her mouth."

"You mean you killed her? For real?"

He shrugged. "That's what it looked like to me."

Nobody would tell you that if that's what they really did, would they? They'd be b.s.ing. Then Dewey said, "How about you? You killed anybody?"

"Sort of," she said, fluffing up her bangs. She'd show him two could play at being cool. Except what she was saying was the truth. She had sort of killed Carlin.

Dewey snorted. "Is that like being a little bit pregnant?"

She grinned. "Now I answered your fool question. Do I get to drive your truck?"

Dewey turned and stared into Mary Ann's big brown eyes as if he was just figuring out they hadn't left all the snakes behind them at the farm. "That next stop, up about five miles," he said. "We'll pull over. See if you can hold 'er in the road."

5

The land was beginning to roll as Sam and Harry left the Delta behind and headed toward Appalachia's toes. But enough already, said Sam of the pristine Natchez Trace Parkway. Enough green, enough scenery. I want to see a Burma-Shave sign. A McDonald's. Give me Rock City.

Finally there was the Tupelo exit and they cloverleafed onto West Main Street on the outskirts of town. To the north stood open fields and a little airport. To the south they'd cut down the trees, poured concrete in cul-de-sacs with names like General Hood, Breckinridge, Stonewall Court, Rebel Drive. Never let it be said that the glory of the Old South ever died: it lives on in expensive tract housing.

Warehouses loomed in an industrial park. There was a lot of furniture manufacturing around Tupelo said Harry, the expert, who'd visited once before. They passed a spanking new mall, two barbecue pits, crummy and authentic-looking, another older mall that had seen better days.

Six minutes off the Trace they were in the old Tupelo amidst a covey of Protestant churches, three blocks of quaint two-story buildings still bustling with hardware stores, ladies' clothiers, a stationer's, a cleaners, an art museum, antique shops on Main Street. Sam could see the copper dome of the old courthouse a block away. Then they rumbled east across the railroad tracks toward what looked like the poorer side of town. A forgotten shopping center foundered in acres of weedy parking lot. They made a right into the fairgrounds under a banner that welcomed them in brilliant blue to Tupelo Days and the Third Annual International Barbecue Cookoff.

This was the very place, Harry announced, that Elvis made his professional debut.

"Go 'way," said Sam. Not this shabby fenced field scattered with trucks, tents, campers, and a few outbuildings, though the dusty old grandstand looked like it might seat a couple thousand.

"Hey, he was only ten. He stood on a chair to reach the microphone and sang 'Old Shep.' Won second prize in the talent contest, five dollars, and free admission to all the rides."

Sam threw her mind back to county fairs of her childhood. The thrill of it, the Ferris wheel, the merry-go-round, the Tilt-A-Whirl, bumper cars. That would have been something, a kid not having to beg for just one more time. Especially a poor kid.

"Howdy, howdy. Can we help y'all?" A large, blond, friendly looking man in a red-and-white checked shirt, overalls, and a straw hat that proclaimed him to be a Holy Smoker leaned down to the Caddy. "I'm Cooter Williams, your official," and then he stopped, put his hands to his mouth, and yodeled, "Sooie, sooie pig," then resumed his normal drawl, "greeter and I have to tell y'all this is one fine-looking pink Cadillac. Y'all here to sip some whiskey, get down with the hogs, smoke, and wallow?"

Sam shot Harry a look as he stuck his hand out the window and grinned. "Cooter, I'm Harry Zack, this is Sam Adams, and we sure are." Five minutes later Cooter had them signed up, backed in, and unhitched. Harry's plot was a staked-off area about twenty by twenty—one of a hundred and twenty-five in four double rows.

"Not many folks here," said Harry looking around at the sprinkling of cooking rigs already set up. He pulled a diet soda out of the cooler for Sam along with two cold Dixie beers.

"Don't mind if I do, thank you kindly," said Cooter. "Nawh, most of 'em'll come in tomorrow. Be ready to party hearty by sundown. Don't take all day to do the ribs, you know. Get them done, then the shoulder, Sunday's the whole hog and the final judging. There'll be more folks than you can shake a stick at by then."

"Well, I'm looking forward to it. Is Red Holcomb around?" Harry asked. "He said he might meet us here."

"Nawh. He was here earlier. I reckon he slithered off somewhere."

Harry winked at Sam, then said to Cooter, "Guess Red's not your best friend."

"Well, you could say that." Then Cooter seemed to remember his manners, tipped his beer at Harry. "Hope I didn't mash your toes."

"Actually, I don't know him very well, but we're talking about the possibility of doing a little business. Sam and I are staying with him for the weekend."

Cooter took a long pull on his beer and killed it, belched, begged their pardon, then squashed the can flat with one huge hand. "Well, you know what the lady said. Diamonds are a girl's best friend. Red ain't no girl, but he's got plenty of diamonds and gold and silver and cars and buildings and land and you name it, he's got it, or he's about to buy it or trade it, but the one thing he don't have in this town is a single friend."

"Great." Sam punched Harry. "Bubba, you've done it again. I can't tell you how happy I am I left my work and my front porch to spend the weekend with Mississippi's Hitler." It had been a long time since her last meal, fat-free at that, and she was more than a little cranky.

"Well, ma'am, I wouldn't go that far," said Cooter, nodding thanks as Harry handed him another beer. "Though there are those who've said him and Saddam Hussein, you couldn't tell 'em apart in the dark."

Harry nodded. "That's real interesting. Listen, Cooter, what kind of wood you using in your smoker?"

Right, Harry. Change the subject before your girlfriend goes and turns this car around and/or registers you both in the nearest Ramada, Hyatt, or Holiday Inn. Sam let the guys debate the virtues of hickory versus oak versus mesquite while Harpo lapped up his second bowl of water. Then she leashed the little dog and was about to take him for a stroll when something caught her eye. "Excuse me, Cooter? What is that?" She was pointing at an object under a blue tent that looked like an old Coca-Cola machine lying on its side with a stove pipe sticking out one end. Smoke was blowing out of the pipe. It smelled good.

Cooter scratched his head under his hat and asked, "Ma'am, is this your first Q-off?"

Sam nodded.

"Well, that is a smoker." Then Cooter pointed at an old butane tank in the next space. "And that is a smoker." Across the way was an aluminum beer keg that was also a smoker, as was something that she had taken to be a mobile home. Cooter shook his head as he pointed out the latter. "Now we discourage those big guys," he said. "For a rig like that, you need some kind of sponsor, and you do that, next thing you know, you'll be like the contest up in Memphis. I don't mean to criticize anybody, they produce some mighty fine smoked meats up there, but it got to where your ordinary feller felt like a pine tree in the middle of a bunch of redwoods, you know what I mean? The bankers and the lawyers and the Pepto-Bismol and Wonder Bread folks, they have the kind of funds behind them, put on such a show, bands, parades, costumes, crystal chandeliers hanging over million-dollar rigs, well, that's why we started this 'un in Tupelo, try to keep it to just folks."

Then from somewhere behind them, there was a clanging and a couple of shouts. "What the hell was that?" asked Cooter, who had wheeled and was headed toward the sound when his portable phone, hidden by his stomach and his overalls, started ringing.

"Earl? What? Son, slow down, I can't make out what—well, did you call nine-one-one? Then hang up and I will!" Cooter's fat face was grim as he punched in the three numbers. "Hello? This is Cooter Williams over at the fairgrounds. We've got a man just turned on his rotisserie and it blasted him halfway to East Jesus. No, no. I don't know. Yes, I'll do that." Then Cooter stuffed the phone back in his overalls and, still holding his beer, took off running toward the back of the lot faster than you would think a fat man could.

Sam threw Harpo in the Caddy, yelled Stay, then she and Harry took off after Cooter.

Mary Ann was sitting in her room in the Tupelo Ramada Inn on North Gloster touching up her Fire and Ice manicure and evaluating her afternoon.

She had found a wide variety of things to hold her interest in that truck stop she and Dewey had pulled into. She'd fingered Jockey shorts and undershirts, cowboy boots, motivational tapes that would teach you how to become a salesman if you wanted to drop off the long haul. Tacky lace undies to take home to your lady, let her know you'd been thinking about her on the interstate. Hundreds of dirty cards, only a few of which were funny, all of which were sexist, lots of Preparation H, Campbell's soup in little plastic tubs, beef jerky, potato chips, and other not-so-good-for-you foods. No fresh fruit. But the most surprising thing was the area marked TRUCKERS ONLY.

After you, ma'am. Dewey had smiled, opening the door for her with a little bow like she was a lady. Like he didn't intend to take her into the white-tiled shower, lock the door, strip her of her black French lace teddy from her own lingerie line, one heck of a lot nicer than the $19.95 jobbie for sale outside, soap her up six ways to Sunday, then take her likewise.

"You've got a great body." She'd said that afterwards when she grew tired of waiting for him to. But she meant it. Nicer than a lot of younger men.

"Karate," he'd said, staring at himself in the mirror right next to the machine that dispensed rubbers, razor blades, shaving cream, deodorant. "Keeps me in shape." Sliding his comb just so through a heavy coat of brilliantine.

"Is that where you learned those moves?"

"Country boy like me sure don't know what you're talking about, ma'am."

Then he'd kissed her and they'd done it again nice and easy, like they'd done it lots of times before, would do it even more before they were through.

Uh-oh, she'd said to herself, back on the road. That's what happens to women, Mary Ann. A little good loving and their brains turn to mush. Men, they just look at it for what it is. Sex. Plain and simple. Girl, she lectured herself, keep your eye on the goal.

"Hey!" Dewey had grabbed the wheel, back on the road. "Watch what you're doing."

It had turned out to be a lot harder than she'd thought, wrestling that monster down the blacktop. There was absolutely no leeway. Not an inch on either side. Ten forward gears, five high, five low. One reverse, not that she had any intention of going backwards.

Then Dewey had said, "You never told me why you're going to Tupelo. To visit Elvis's birthplace?"

"Uh-huh. That and see a girlfriend."

He'd laughed.

"Well, I am." He couldn't prove she wasn't. And she wasn't so sure she wanted anything else to do with Dewey, other than what she'd already done. A little burst of passion like that, it cleared your sinuses, helped you focus. Now she had business to do.

"Tell the truth," he said.

It was so weird. It was like he could make his voice suck the real story right out of you. And the next thing she knew, she was telling Dewey about how right before Carlin died, he was up on that big rock . . .

"And he starts talking this trash about how would I feel if I found out I wasn't the only woman in his life? And I say it wouldn't surprise me one bit. Nothing he would do would surprise me one bit. And he says, Well, what if it was more than seeing? And I say, You mean like kissing? Being silly, you know. Like he wouldn't be screwing her. Like he hadn't screwed jillions of women, for all I knew. After all, he was a traveling salesman. I just assumed, given what a generally rotten human being he was, he did that too, and I must say it made me nervous, once this AIDS business started. He says, More than kissing, more than screwing? I say, You mean like loving? Carlin, you never loved anybody in your whole life except your own selfish self.

"And then—" Mary Ann had stopped. They'd listened to the bumping of the truck and the whooshing of the wind for a couple more miles.

Finally Dewey said, "So that's the woman you're going to see, the one he was talking about?"

It was so strange, that he knew that.

"Why do you care now, if he's dead?"

"You want to know why I care? I'll tell you. Because this Lawyer Rakestraw who called, he said to my friend Luci that his client, this woman in Tupelo, was married to Carlin not only *first*, but *still was*, and therefore, we had not even been legally married and *furthermore*, I could go whistle you-know-what if I thought I was entitled to a penny of his hundred-fifty-thousand-dollars-worth of pharmaceutical company accidental death life insurance."

Now Mary Ann screwed the top back on her Fire and Ice and said aloud, practicing, in the empty motel room: Well, we'll just have to see what we can work out about that, won't we, Ms. Dixie McClanahan? Mary Ann narrowing her eyes, looking real tough.

Back at the fairgrounds, three men in jeans and cowboy shirts stood and shuffled in a circle in front of a banner that read HOLLY SPRINGS HOGBOYS. A tall, elderly white-haired man lay very still facedown in the dirt. He looked like he'd been flung to earth from a place high up.

"Is he breathing?" Sam asked as she elbowed in. Nobody said anything. "Any of you try CPR?" She knelt down.

"Nawh," one of the men finally drawled in a slow sad voice. "Ah think Floyd's dead. Ah sure do hate to have to call his new wife up and tell her the bad news. I never seen anybody electrocuted like that. He said, Boys, look at this rotisserie, how I got it working, and the next thing we knew—*kerplow.*"

Floyd was going to have severe brain damage if she didn't shut this man up and start moving. "Help me roll him over, fellows," she said as calmly as she could.

"I don't rightly think we ought to move him," said another. "They say you ought not to move 'em when they felled."

"If your friend Floyd doesn't breathe in four to five minutes he'll be dead for sure if he's not already," she said. Then she looked up. "Harry?"

At that, the men nodded at one other. Then without saying a word, they knelt and rolled the old man over.

Sam lifted Floyd's neck, tilted his head back, lowered first her ear and then her cheek to the man's mouth. Nothing.

She pinched his nose shut and started mouth-to-mouth. Two breaths into him. She waited to see if his chest moved, if she could feel the exhalation. Not a peep. Two more. Nope. Two. Wait. Two. No. Again, again, again. Breathe, Floyd, come on, baby, Sam said to herself. She breathed into him four more times. Don't die on me, Floyd, there are your ribs to cook. Again, she breathed. Floyd, you ornery son-of-a-bitch, I only did this once before, and I'm going for two for two. Don't ruin my record. Again, again, and again she breathed. The man was dead. Then she pushed two more into him, waited, and heard the exhale. Yea! the men cheered. Shhhh! she hushed them. She needed to hear. Two more, another exhale. Then none. Two more. Nothing. Then it was like a cold car engine catching, turning over, yes, no, yes, yes, yes. Floyd was still unconscious but breathing steadily when the orange-and-white emergency van, siren going, bucketed in following Cooter Williams who'd run back and met it at the gate. Two paramedics jumped out, kits, oxygen tank in hand. Sam scooted back out of the way on her heels. She was high as a kite, her adrenaline pumping. As the paramedics lay hands on him, Floyd Morgan moaned and opened his eyes. They were an amazing blue. The orange-haired paramedic whose name tag read Alma West gave Sam a big smile and a thumbs-up. Lady, she said, you done real good.

"Did so good," said Harry, his arm around her in the Caddy, snuggling close on the wide leather seat as they turned onto Main headed back toward the main part of town, "I'm going to take you for a Quarter Pounder and a cup of coffee."

"Hey, big spender. Don't put yourself out." But she was teasing. Exhilarated and exhausted at the same time, she didn't care where they went.

"Nothing's too good for my baby." He turned and kissed her on the cheek. "Saved *my* life for sure. Rescued me from Heartbreak Hotel."

"Awh, hon, it weren't nothing." But it was good to be back in the car, in the circle of Harry's arm as the sun began to drop in a pink and gold sky. There was the ghost of the full moon already sailing overhead. Then she reran the scene back at the fairgrounds, stepped off and saw herself bending over the old man. She saw herself trying and trying and trying—and failing. What if she *had* failed? What if she hadn't remembered the technique? What if Floyd Morgan had died anyway? Was this how Harry had felt when he'd pulled that kid out of the pool up in Atlantic City? He'd never talked about being scared, having doubts later, but men didn't.

"It was something, all right," Harry said now.

"You're something. That's why I'm taking you for a surprise right this very minute."

"McFries are no surprise. Besides, I can't have them anyway. Remember fat grams, Harry."

"It's better than McFries."

"Better than chocolate?"

"Nothing better than chocolate. Well. Maybe one thing." Then Harry gave her another kiss and wheeled off Main at the crosstown intersection onto South Gloster—into gas-station, fast-food, one-story, strip-shoppingland. Two blocks more, and he pulled in at the golden arches.

He really was taking her to McDonald's, where there was not a thing she could eat except a salad. Shoot.

But once inside, Harry grinned as Sam's mouth dropped. For every available surface, except behind the counter where it was Big Macs as usual, was wall-to-wall Elvis.

The Elvis Memorial McDonald's was hip-deep with thousands of plaques, clippings, photos, record covers, mementos. Three Elvises were etched in bas-relief on the glass panels behind the highchairs, napkins and straws, salt and pepper, and sugar and nondairy creamer: a hot young full-length Elvis with an acoustic guitar, a close-up, then the King in his jumpsuit and cape.

The spell was broken when a young girl behind the counter called, "Sir, you can't bring that dog in here!"

It was Harry who hadn't wanted to leave Harpo in the car after they'd dumped him like a sack of potatoes at the fairgrounds. "Here," he said to Sam, "hold him, stay here and look, I'll go lay some N'Orlins charm on Miss Sweet Pea and rustle up some coffee. Then we'll go find something real to eat."

Sam didn't notice the couple of young bubbas at a table nearby checking her out. She was too busy rating the burger emporium. On a scale of weird, she'd give it an eight. Maybe an eight and a half.

It was probably even better if, like Harry, you were a true Elvis nut. She'd never been. Sam glanced over at him at the counter ogling a record jacket. A light stubble of a beard, his *Elvis Lives* T-shirt, faded jeans, he was bouncing up and down like a little kid. Oh sure, he had some distance, but because he was a musician, Elvis wasn't a yok to him. Not someone you pointed your uptown forefinger of irony at and wrote up as Weird. She was going to have to watch that she didn't poke too much fun at the King this weekend and hurt Harry's feelings.

"Ma'am." Miss Sweet Pea was talking at her over the top of Harry's head. "You have to take that dog out *now*."

When Harry came back with the coffee, Sam said, "This is truly terrific, but let's come back another time, take the coffee out to the car, and find some real food. I'm famished."

"I hear you." Harry knew how frazzled she could get when she was hungry, and the yogurt they'd grabbed for lunch was wearing pretty thin. "Just *one* minute." He took her arm and pulled her over to a wall of inscriptions behind a block of orange booths.

My crushing ambition in life was to be as big as Elvis Presley. John Lennon.

My daddy said, you should make up your mind about either being an electrician or playing a guitar. I never saw a guitar player that was worth a damn. Elvis.

I believe I will see Elvis in Heaven. Billy Graham.

I didn't know a lot about music. In my line I didn't have to. Elvis.

And from Sam Phillips, who first recorded him:

THE KING IS DEAD

If I could find a white man who had the Negro sound and the Negro feel, I could make a million dollars.

"Sir!" Miss Sweet Pea behind the counter was fresh out of patience. "You *said* you'd take the dog out."

Sam whirled toward the door.

"Wait a minute." Harry grabbed the little dog out of Sam's arms. Harpo glowered up at him.

She said, "He's trying to remind you Shih Tzus were imperial dogs of the Tibetan court, transported reverently in the flowing sleeves of silken robes on satin cushions and fed on demand."

Harry wasn't even listening. "Isn't this the greatest?"

Sam sighed. So they died of starvation. So they were arrested by the health department. She stared at Harry, staring at Elvis. And then, maybe she was hallucinating but . . .

"Son," she said, "it's the family resemblance that's grabbed you. Why, you could be the King's first cousin."

"Go on."

"No, really. Look." She backed Harry up against an early black-and-white photo of Elvis, 1955, 1956. The King looking more like the Prince then, lounging in a blond wood fifties chair, his hips slid all the way down just grazing the edge of the plastic cushion, a tired young man, spent after a concert, a round of interviews, his light brown hair dyed dark, one hand on the upper thigh of his black pants leg, maybe on his crotch, the other arm flipped back in a window-pane plaid linen sports jacket. But, Sam thought, it's not just the languor of his body that gets you. It's the open mouth, the relaxed bottom jaw, and the hooded eyes, fringed with heavy lashes, focused out of the frame on something you can't see and never will. The young Elvis was bad and beautiful and innocent. The tenderness breaks your heart.

It wasn't that Harry, at thirty, looked like the even-younger Elvis. Though you could make a case for something around the eyes and that full mouth. But the similarity was more one of feelings. Her bad little boy had that same way of looking at her from up under his long lashes, the lazy left eye drooping just a little, that made her warm inside. When he gave her his slow voluptuous grin, she knew that whatever he had in mind, it was going to be very naughty, and she was going to want to eat it with a spoon.

"My folks gonna be awfully upset you mistaking me for common." There it was, his grin.

Miss Sweet Pea was still on her high horse. Sam took Harry's arm and started toward the door. "The Love Me Tender McDonald's has been an A-Number-One hit. Now, let's go find somewhere I can have some pasta and veggies before we head over to your Mr. Holcomb's and see if he really is a Hitler clone."

Just then, a very large redheaded man, fleshy, well over six feet, with the kind of ex-pro body you saw most often at Hall of Fame dinners, roared out from behind the counter. "Wanda June, point me at the trash came in here with a hound!"

With that, the long day crashed in on Sam. She grabbed up Harpo and wheeled on Harry. "I told you and I told you."

"Hold up there, little lady. Where do you think you're going?" The big man was closing in fast.

Harry said, "You lay a hand on that woman or that dog, you're deader than a Quarter Pounder." The giant of a man was going to snatch his head off.

But he didn't. Instead, he threw his arms wide. "Well, kiss my grits!" He sounded like a bubba, though in his starched white shirt, brown jodhpurs, and knee-high riding boots he was dressed like an English lord—if you overlooked the diamond pinky rings. The big man jerked Harry into a hug, pounded him on the back, then kissed Sam's hand. "Here I was about to order the help to grind up this cute dog into McNuggets."

Harpo gave the man a fishy-eyed look. He wasn't crazy about loud. Or blustery.

Harry said, "May I present Red Holcomb, Esquire, gentleman, entrepreneur, bon vivant—"

Red interrupted Harry. "Scalawag, junk dealer, rag picker, prospective owner of this burger joint—"

"And our host for the weekend."

"Harry didn't tell me that he'd made away with the belle of New Orleans," said Red. "But I can see why he'd want to keep that information—and you—to himself."

Well, for a scoundrel, if what Cooter Williams had said was true, Red had himself a silver tongue. "Actually, I'm from Atlanta—" she began

"Even better, Miss Scarlett! We country folks up here in little ole Tupelo, we'll have to work some to see if we can entertain the likes of city slickers like y'all."

Red's wave included a couple of dozen customers who no more wanted to go to Red's house than they wanted escargot for supper. Then, done with the pleasantries, Red turned to Harry. "I'm thinking of buying this place next month. Snapping up a couple of others over toward Grenada, Oxford, serving catfish too, after all this is the Gret Stet of Mis'sippi, them cats our number one export!"

Sam thought he sounded a lot like Uncle Earl Long, of the Louisiana Longs, who'd once been locked up in the looney bin not far from her rented house in St. Tammany Parish. Minus the charm. But then, when she was really hungry, she was very hard to please.

Red said, "One of the things I was thinking about for the franchising, is what if I did a theme for each of 'em?"

"You mean like the Satchmo Rib Shack?" Harry smiled as if Red had said *we* instead of *I,* which would have been the politic word choice.

Sam gave Harry credit for that. He was always willing to overlook human frailty while she was ever ready to classify and label it, tie it up with a red ribbon and leave it in front of the owner's doorstep.

"Hell, yes. Or it don't have to be music. You know. Whoever people like. I was thinking about doing a Miss America one in Atlantic City."

"We were there." Sam nodded.

Uh-huh, said Harry who'd gone along with Sam when she'd covered the Miss America Pageant, against her will. "Those folks could use some good Q. A person could starve to death in New Jersey."

"I'm thinking about doing local heroes around Mis'sippi. Like Ross Barnett, George Wallace."

Hell, why not throw in James Earl Ray, the assassin of Martin Luther King, Jr., we're talking old-timey racist heroes? Sam thought it, but she didn't say it. So far, except for Red's perfunctory pretty words during the introductions, Cooter's evaluation of the man was good.

Harry read her mind and said, "Or go back to music, the Aretha Franklin Rib Shack. Michael Jackson. Hell, Mick Jagger likes Q."

"What makes you think these people are going to let you use their names?" Sam asked.

That stopped Harry. "You mean we'd have to use just dead people?"

Dead people was exactly what Dewey Travis was thinking about. He'd made a flying trip up to Holly Springs after he'd dropped Mary Ann at her motel, and now he was sitting out in the Elvis McDonald's parking lot thinking about people who were dead—and well-done hamburgers.

The first thing he always did when he drove down to Tupelo was come here and have himself a Big Mac, large order of fries, ketchup please, king-sized Co-cola. The Big Mac would be well-done of course, the way Elvis liked them, the only way you could get a burger at McDonald's.

This was the starting point of his Elvis pilgrimage. He did it the same way every time. He started here to fuel up, both on the burgers and on the museum. He thought it was fitting that the Tupelo Elvis Museum—which was how he thought of it, the collection of framed pictures, albums, citations, awards—should be in a burger palace.

Then he'd go over to The Birthplace, where the twins Elvis Aron and Jesse Garon were born that frosty morn, just like it said in that song about the ghetto. He'd sit outside for a while, studying the little two-room shack Vernon Presley had built, borrowing $180 to do it, then lost the house when he couldn't make the payments on the loan.

Once a Birthplace tour lady had told Dewey that Vernon never had had a head for money, even though Elvis let him manage his affairs, which maybe hadn't been such a good idea, but that just went to show you how much Elvis loved his daddy.

But, she'd said, waving her hand around the tiny house, Vernon was good at building. The Birthplace was a sturdy little thing that stood up to the winds of that awful tornado of 1936. The lady showed Dewey a story about the tornado in a book, it killed over two hundred people in Tupelo—no Presleys among them, praise the Lord. They'd gathered in Uncle Noah Presley's house, the tour lady said, the men lining up against the south wall to try to hold it up against the winds—which they did. Gladys and Elvis, who was just a babe, huddled in a corner.

To think that Elvis could have died right then! It was enough to make you puke. But there was a lot about young Elvis's dirt-poor life here in Tupelo that turned Dewey's stomach. He hated to think about little Elvis, from the wrong side of the tracks, teased to pieces by the kids at Milam School. That's where he had to go when his family was kicked out of their house in East Tupelo. They moved into a shack on Mulberry Alley inside the city limits, the neighborhood called Milltown right next to the fairgrounds, near the dump, across from colored quarters. The Milam kids teased Elvis because he was a hick, because he didn't have the right clothes and precious few of the wrong ones, and because he liked to sing and show off like he knew he was good—even then.

Yes, those memories hurt Dewey, but he bore the pain willingly, though sometimes, like now, he popped a few Valium to smooth it out. That constant aching in his gut, he thought of it as his Elvis stigmata. It was part of the process of becoming Elvis, feeling his anguish, thinking his thoughts, walking in his shoes. Take a walk in my shoes, Elvis said that a lot. Sang it, too. Dewey looked down at his blue suede boots.

Then he stared in through the big plate glass windows. There was a lot of Elvis, *strong* Elvis, inside. He took a few deep breaths. And a lot of Red Holcomb. He'd been coming down to Tupelo to look at Holcomb, and the others, for the past few weeks. Refining The Plan.

Dewey hadn't picked Red to go first. He wasn't sure about the timing of Red's Big Date. He was working on that. He might save the biggest and best for last, like eating chocolate-covered cherries, biting a little hole, slowly sucking out the creamy sweet until the walls collapsed, then closing down on the round red prize, *ka-chunk*.

He'd thought about that, the proper order of things, adding up Red's numbers. The number of his big old fancy house up off Highland Circle with the garage full of fancy cars. Their license tags. The street numbers of Red's warehouses, his pawn shop, his office on the courthouse square, Dewey wasn't sure what it was for. Dewey followed Red right to the door of the Coffee Pot and Orleans Deli off the square where Red grabbed a cup of joe to go. There were two groups of men—bankers, lawyers, bondsmen, pharmacists, funeral directors, stock brokers—who met every weekday morning to drink coffee and jawbone, but Red wasn't part of either one so Dewey didn't add the street number of the coffeeshop to his total. Dewey knew numerology just like Elvis. Elvis's magic number was eight.

Dewey also knew this trip was very important. The signs were right. The numbers and the planets were lined up. If he did things right, in their proper order and at the proper time, his life would change forever.

Which was why he maybe wouldn't go back and visit with Mary Ann at the Holiday Inn where he'd left her. Women could stand in the way of your plans, really screw them up. There were more men doing time because of some sweet piece, and Mary Ann was that all right, than because their getaway car choked. Dewey knew that for a fact. On the other hand, she might come in handy, depending on how things went down. You could never tell. And then there was the matter of the way she looked that drew him to her like a bird to a snake. It wasn't that she was that beautiful, though she was cute and he was awfully taken with the way her little behind looked in those tight jeans, it was who she'd look like, if she wasn't blond. Color her brunette and he thought she'd be a dead ringer for Priscilla, who'd been a carbon copy of the King's high school girlfriend.

Just then another motorcycle drove up, gunning its engine, and the sound blew Dewey's picture show to smithereens—which was just as well. He needed to concentrate on Red.

Red. He'd watched him pull in a while ago in a Lamborghini, a little bitty expensive thing, the big man had to heave himself up out of it. Dewey made a note of the numbers in the license plate, to add them to the numerology. Dewey knew a lot about cars too, just like Elvis. He'd watched Red stroll in the back door of the burger joint like he owned it. Maybe he did. Wouldn't that be something?

Dewey squinted and imagined the shootout with Red here. He'd seen it lots of places before. He looked up at his ceiling at night and saw it playing there like a drive-in movie, but it was always set in the old part of town, not out here.

In front of the Birthplace on Old Saltillo Road in East Tupelo, now Elvis Presley Drive in Presley Heights, still the wrong side of the railroad tracks, no matter what you called it.

On the sidewalk on Main Street outside the Tupelo Hardware where Gladys bought the King his first guitar.

Or maybe in Long's Dry Cleaners, one of the places Vernon used to work. Before he served time because Red's . . .

But lookahere. How would it go, him and Red about the same age, mid-fifties, Red more bowed-up with that old football-playing muscle, but Dewey tougher, meaner, sleeker. The two of them head-to-head, Dewey with his black belt in karate. He knew the moves.

Dewey was tempted to just walk inside right now, let this Red Holcomb take a good long look at him, then say, You know what I've come for. Let's go get it, and while you're at it, hand over all the cash. And oh, yeah, a couple burgers, make those super well done, the way he liked 'em, I don't wanta hear you don't do special orders.

Yep, maybe he would. Maybe he'd do that. Or maybe he'd just go in and check out Holcomb close up. Big Red Holcomb yakking with the not-bad-looking tall brunette with the curls, the younger guy, *what* did that T-shirt say? Dewey was walking toward the door knowing nobody would notice him, just another Big Mac, large order of fries, ketchup please, king-sized Co-cola.

He was almost there when this young pimply dude with too-long hair jumped out of a little truck that was pulled right up in the door. Dewey had noticed him out of the corner of his eye sitting in that silly little baby pickup truck—Dewey ran 'em off the road for fun sometimes.

Now he pushed right in front of Dewey. Son, he thought, you're a stone fool, you messing with me. I may be getting older, but I ain't slow and *definitely* ain't to be ignored.

Then Dewey took a deep breath. Meditate and be calm and still your mind and body. It was part of the practice the King did everyday to improve himself—as if he needed to.

When Dewey felt better, when he felt he'd regained control, he reached back and pulled the wire cutters out of the back of his pants thinking he'd whack the young dude upside the head one good with them, teach him some manners.

Then he noticed the boy was jerking a ski mask up over his face.

Who the hell skis in Tupelo, Mississippi?

Nobody, that's who.

6

Oh, cripes, said Harry when he saw the boy with the bright blue mask headed right at him behind Red Holcomb.

Harry was absolutely sick to death of fast food stick-'em-ups.

The first one had been a convenience store, a Pic'N'Pac in New Orleans, and it was his partner Lavert who was there, not Harry, but anyway a lot of food—ice cream, garbanzos, cans of SpaghettiOs—had gone to flying before it was over and Lavert talked about it more than once.

The second holdup had been not too long ago, the first week they'd had the Rib Shack open, both of them working the counter, a young brother, just about the size of this boy now, had jumped up in their faces.

"Gimme all y'all's cash!"

"It ain't Saturday night," Lavert had said to the dude, who'd jumped back. Lavert had learned a lot about dealing with stupid people who were easily confused when he was doing his nickel for hotel burglary in the Louisiana State Penitentiary at Angola.

"Whaddyu mean?"

"I mean, why you waving that Saturday night special in my face it ain't but Tuesday?" And then Lavert had smacked the kid so hard he was already in lockup when he came to.

Now this one is dancing around like he has to go to the bathroom, besides, the whole mess of them— Sam, Red, Harpo, and himself—are filling up the space right in front of the boy so he can't decide whether to kill 'em with the pistol he's stuck down in his pants or go 'round.

So Harry made up his mind for him with one of those moves big bad Lavert had taught him.

He leaned over and screamed right in the kid's ear: "Hey, son! What the fuck you think you doing?"

Sam hit the deck, Red cleared the counter, and Harpo bolted for cover.

The kid jumped like he'd been shot, reaching for the gun, and Harry grabbed it and twisted it out of his hand. The gun went skittering across the beige tiles and landed beneath a framed picture of Elvis, that heartbreak look in his eyes, wearing a white jumpsuit with a three-inch gold belt buckle. Harry and the kid both dove for it. The air was thick with people jumping and diving and running and smashing into each other.

Then the kid seemed to remember some Bruce Lee moves he'd seen on a video, tried to kick Harry in the crotch with his white Reebok with the fancy red trim. Harry grabbed onto that foot and almost wrenched the kid's leg from the hip socket. But the kid had the pistol.

He's got the gun! He's got the gun! someone was screaming, Harry didn't know who, but he knew they didn't mean him, so, still holding on to the kid's foot, he stood and, with that kind of superhuman strength you read about in stories in the *National Enquirer* like "I Lifted a Pickup Off My Baby Girl," whirled the kid around and around over his head as if he were a helicopter and the kid was his propeller.

The kid was screaming a lot of things like Oh shit! Let me down! Help! Help! Help! He was into the Do Jesus! the words that he'd heard as a kid when his momma's housekeeper used to take him to the First Corinthians African Baptist Church for the singing, when Harry whirled him around and around and around, then just like in crack the whip, turned him loose. He went flying right out the front door which opened when some little kid who'd been playing outside in the McDonald's playground had had enough amusement without french fries.

At the crash landing Red Holcomb jumped up from behind the counter swinging a baseball bat, a little too late, but that didn't slow down his momentum as he whirred out the front door, bent over the boy crumpled up against the swing set, reached down, and ripped off the ski mask. The boy's freckles stood out like mud splattered in a pail of milk.

"Well, I'll be hogtied!" Red said. "Walter Barnes, boy, your daddy is gonna kill you! When you get out of Parchman, that is."

"He is not! You're the one ought to die!" The kid was screaming, tears and snot running down his face with a good deal of blood. "You nasty old bastard! My momma—you ought to be ashamed of yourself."

Hmmmm, thought Sam, right behind Red. Interesting. Score two for Cooter.

"You watch your mouth, son!" Red screamed.

The kid was fighting his way up out of the woodchips that filled the playyard. "And you watch your ass, old man. People are mad as hell about what you're doing!"

"I ain't doing shit!"

Now who ought to watch whose mouth, set an example for Tupelo's youth?

"So that's why you came to hold this store up? You mad about that silly business?" That was Red again.

"You stupid old geezer! I'm not robbing them! I'm scaring you!"

"Well, who's scared now, son?" Red's mouth settled into that kind of self-satisfied smirk people wore when they thought they'd scored a big one. The kind that made you want to slap it right off them.

In the distance sirens screamed as the police responded to the call placed by some good citizen. An ambulance bawled like a cat in heat. Sam looked down at her watch and thought, Well, we've been in Tupelo about an hour and a half, already party to two 911's. Then she checked out the parking lot like any decent about-to-be-ex-reporter: a biker, a couple of Hondas, a van, and a low saloon of a car, maybe a Lamborghini, filled with small white yapping dogs.

Dogs. Sam whirled. Harpo! Where was Harpo? She ran back through the glass door.

Red came stomping behind her, shaking his head, saying to anyone who cared, "Can you imagine, varsity football player, a senior at Tupelo High, his daddy sells more luxury autos than anybody in the South, these kids have every advantage on earth—"

Harry was holding out the kid's gun, staring at it. Uh-oh, he said.

But Sam wasn't listening. She was looking under chairs and tables calling, "Harpo? Harpo? Sweetie, where are you?"

A woman who had picked herself and her son up off the floor out of the middle of a chocolate shake pointed at the door. "Was that your little dog? He followed somebody was heading for the hills out the side door before that boy got hisself flung out there."

"He ran *out?*"

Sam's heart stopped. A man electrocuted by his smoker was one thing. Practicing a little CPR was another. Holdups were no big deal. Gunplay, she'd seen plenty of times. Whirling bodies, flying glass, people screaming, diving, scrambling. She'd seen it all. Harry was safe, probably going to win some kind of Mississippi State Medal of Heroism. But Harpo? Harpo was her baby. Her dearheart. The love of her life. If anything happened to him—

She flew back through the side door and raced into the parking lot, ignoring the growing knot of people around Walter Barnes, Jr., still lying inside the high playground fence.

She was trying to focus on one thing at a time. If Harpo were out here and those emergency vehicles came roaring in, he hated loud noises, he'd bolt and one of them would squash him for sure. Her heart was pounding so loudly the sirens and the ambulance faded into white noise.

"Harpo! Harpo! Harpo!" she called. She should go back and grab Harry. She needed help. But what if somebody backed up and—*"Harpo! Harpo! Harpo!"* she screamed.

Then over at the edge of the parking lot close to the street, the biker she'd noticed before with the Darth Vader helmet stood and jumped his motorcycle. The Harley roared to life. Was the man cradling something in one leather-jacketed arm? Was it Harpo? *Was it?*

"Stop! Stop! Give me that dog!" She raced toward the bike. The man turned and faced her for a long moment, eyeless, faceless behind the dark Plexiglas, a slash of gold on his forehead. Then the bike laid rubber out of the parking lot.

Inside the Elvis McDonald's, Harry and Red Holcomb were trying to explain to Ollie Priest, Tupelo PD, exactly what had happened.

But the part that Detective Priest—who'd responded to the call along with a dozen uniforms, because the town had been pestered recently with a rash of armed robberies and the word had come down from the top, Stop those suckers before somebody is kilt—was having trouble keeping straight was that *a*. Walter Barnes, Jr., had never said Stick 'em up, and *b*. Exhibit A here was a facsimile .45 automatic with a CO_2 cartridge that fired beebees. A toy.

"Stop! Stop, you son of a bitch! *Stop!*" Sam was screaming, running, falling, scrambling back up, she'd never catch the bike. There were people all over the place, jumping out of their cars, heading back toward the door of the McDonald's, people determined to stand in her way. But she dodged and bobbed and smashed and ran and then she stumbled and fell again, twisting her ankle and losing her loafer.

"Harpo! Harpo! Baby!" She was still screaming, face down into the asphalt.

And then there was a roaring again, and it wasn't just inside her head as a Harley circled by her and a voice said, "Can I help you, ma'am?"

She looked up, and there sitting on a fat bike, not the one she'd seen a minute ago, was a heavy-set man in Day-Glo green suspenders over a baby-blue T-shirt holding out a wriggling Harpo and a pamphlet. The pamphlet said, in big black letters on yellow: JESUS WAS A BIKER.

• • • • • • • • • • • • 7

Lovie Rakestraw loved everything about her house. She loved the fact that it had a name, Oakmont, which she'd remembered from a novel about a bunch of English lords and ladies she'd read when she was eleven years old in Miz Tarver's class at Milam School. She loved that her house was on Parc Monceau Drive West in North Tupelo. That neighborhood, in the section of town near the old Country Club, was only three miles away from Milltown, where Lovie had grown up dirt poor.

Oakmont, the house that Lovie's lawyer husband, Will Rakestraw, built for her, was a red brick French chateau with fifteen thousand heated square feet, as Lovie was wont to say, which meant she wasn't counting the six-car garage, the pool cabana, the groundsmen's barn, or the little changing and equipment room off the tennis courts.

Lovie loved her sweeping expanse of rolling green yard, which the landscapers had installed in one week like a mammoth emerald carpet. She loved the fan of beveled glass over the double front doors and the rainbow of light it cast onto the Aubusson she'd

bought in New York City. She loved the twin stair-
cases that rose like grace notes to the second-floor
landing. She loved the room after room filled with
French and Italian antiques and English oils, the acre
of wall-to-wall cream wool carpet, the dining room
that sat twenty-four. She loved the blue-and-white
kitchen by Smallbone where her cook Tiwillda held
forth, sneaking in her old cast iron skillets.

Lovie loved to laugh about that at her Ladies'
Legal Auxiliary luncheons while passing Tiwillda's
tiny cranberry muffins. "Tiwillda pretends she bakes
these in silver-lined copper tins we bought in Paris.
She thinks I don't know."

Lovie loved the king-sized tester bed that she had
had a local black carpenter construct from a matching
pair she'd found in a shop in Natchez. "From an
old cotton plantation near Greenville," she'd told the
carpenter, who'd swallowed his disdain because he
needed the work. She said the same thing to The
Ladies when she took them upstairs to tour her latest
treasures—as if her people on both sides were landed
gentry rather than sharecroppers since before The
Late Unpleasantness, as the Daughters of the Confed-
eracy labeled what everybody else in Mississippi
called the War Between the States.

But most of all what Lovie Valentine Rakestraw
loved was her bathroom. The three-room frame house
in which Lovie had grown up on Spring Street in
Milltown hadn't had indoor plumbing. There had always been enough chicken and rice and beans and
tomatoes and greens on the table and lots of love
among the Valentines—her ma, her pa, and her three
older brothers—but what Lovie had thirsted for
throughout her girlhood was tap water.

Now Lovie was fifty-five years old and she'd
known cool white porcelain fixtures for forty years.
Ever since she'd hitched a ride on a wagon over to

Oxford to wait tables in a coffeeshop and snag herself
an Ole Miss boy—the only ticket she could imagine
to the good life where people didn't bathe in the
kitchen in washtubs of galvanized tin. The snagging
wasn't something that the blue-eyed, bountifully
chested Lovie with the headful of pale blond curls
had any trouble doing—in the time-honored fashion.
Danny Rakestraw, Lovie and Will's first son, was
born in married student housing when Lovie was six-
teen. Lovie had painted their tiny bathroom bright
blue and soaked herself and the baby in the tub till
their fingers and toes shriveled.

When Lovie and Will, a founding partner of Tupelo's Rakestraw, Smythe, and Kitchens, Attorneys at
Law, decided to build their dream mansion eight
years ago, the first thing Lovie said to the architect
was this: I want the biggest and fanciest goddam bathroom in the entire state of Mississippi. The architect
grinned. There was nothing he loved more than building for white trash with bushelsful of money and high-
falutin aspirations.

Now Lovie sat wrapped in a plushy white terry
robe at her cream and gilt glass-topped desk in the
dressing area of her six-hundred-square-foot warm
beige marble bathroom. Her pretty face and curves
didn't look a day over forty—thanks to the very skill-
ful ministrations of Dr. Joe Weaver, a friend of Will's
and the most expensive cosmetic surgeon south of
the Mason-Dixon line. Before Lovie was spread a
quadrilled floor plan of Oakmont's first floor drawn
by her Memphis party planner, a sheaf of possible
menus, and a notebook filled with names written in,
crossed out, a few in ink, most in pencil. When plot-
ting a social coup there was no better place, thought
Lovie, to think than in one's drop-dead, Venus Rising
from the Half Shell bathroom.

That was what Lovie called Botticelli's glorious

painting, *Birth of Venus,* when she first saw it in Florence with Will when they began to travel and broaden their horizons. Will had said he thought the Venus looked exactly like Lovie, and though she knew that was an exaggeration, Venus being a lot longer in the leg than she, he did have a point and she took the Venus for her mascot. Lovie had Venus cocktail napkins, Venus needlepoint pillows throughout her formal sitting room, and a Venus in mosaic tile on the bottom of her swimming pool. Naturally, a life-sized copy of the painting was the focal point of the bathroom. The shell motif extended into the shape of her warm beige marble lavatories, her bidet, and her huge soaking tub cum whirlpool. The walls of her roomsize shower/steam were lined with actual rare seashells from around the world imprisoned under glass.

Lovie's bathroom had been featured in a story in *HG* that had been the talk of Tupelo for about a month three years ago, the general consensus of the buzz being that Lovie Rakestraw's was not a Christian bathroom.

Nothing could have pleased Lovie more, except she *was* pleased as punch planning her party. For Lovie was about to throw the very first of what she knew would be a lifelong line of June Fetes, a benefit for the Outreach Clinic of the Medical Center.

Lovie stepped over to her gigantic pinky-beige shell of a soaking tub to see if it had filled. This was her very favorite part of her very favorite place in the entire world, and she wanted to slide into it to work on her very favorite part of the fete, the guest list, before she had to go over to Martha Jane Gardener's for a bridge party.

Could there be anything more delicious imaginable, if you had grown up poor, than picking and choosing who you would allow the privilege of ponying up a thousand bucks a couple to come to your house?

If there was, Lovie didn't even want to know about it.

Her colors would be gold and white. String quartets would play minuets, and ladies in long gowns with panniers and plenty of décolletage and their consorts in knee pants and powdered wigs would dance under billowing tents over the tennis courts and the covered pool. Lovie planned to hold dance classes for a month for the invited guests.

She threw off her robe and her gold lamé mules, climbed the three steps to her bathing platform, then lowered her pink and white body into the pool.

Yum. She closed her eyes and floated for a moment. She had plenty of time. It was only four, and she didn't have to be over at Martha Jane's for a while yet.

She was thinking about the biography of Marie Antoinette she'd been reading for research. She'd also been studying up on the famous chef Carême, who cooked for Talleyrand, Tsar Alexander I, Lord Stewart, King George IV, and the house of Rothschild. Carême was famous for *pièces montées*, constructions of Greek temples, Roman ruins, landscapes, imaginary cities made of lard, spun sugar, or chocolate, on and over which elaborate dishes of truffles, crayfish, and turbot were presented.

When she'd spoken with her cook Tiwillda about this, Tiwillda had said that June was when she was having her gallbladder taken out, but Lovie knew that was just an excuse and she'd been planning on using a fairy caterer from Dallas anyway.

Lovie switched on the whirlpool. Rub a dub a dub. Oh, God, how she loved her bathing tub.

Now. She dried her hands on a fluffy white towel from the pile on the platform and picked up her notebook. Five hundred was the number she was aiming for. An even five hundred would mean a contribution of a cool half mil to the Outreach Clinic. She liked the sound of it. Just like she liked the idea of her name on the plaque they'd have to put up.

Not that there were five hundred suitable people in Tupelo. Jesus! Even if you invited all the lawyers and their spouses—well, that would give you only about half. The doctors and the bankers—well, that'd be about right. But, if she did that, just blanket invitation by profession, what would be the fun of it?

The fun was, well, like inviting a favored flirt who knew how to shake a leg and tell a good story, but not his hideously fat wife.

Inviting old Miz Tarver from Milam School (gratis, of course, Lovie would put in for her) because the old lady had been so kind to her and showed her books and pictures filled with possibility.

Not inviting Red Holcomb for whom she had nothing but disdain, but inviting his mother, Miss Estella, who was nuts, but fun.

Inviting Dixie McClanahan. By herself. With no little guest card. She hated the younger Dixie, who was her chief rival in Tupelo. Lovie had spent years maneuvering her way toward the presidency of the Ladies' Auxiliary, and the gavel was within her grasp when Dixie moved to town (a child bride!) and they just handed it to her. Putting Lovie in her place, white trash who had to try harder, while Dixie, who'd been born to power and money, had only to breathe. Lovie had done lots of evil things to spite Dixie over the years, but this party would be the frosting on the cake.

Lovie felt like she needed that. Dixie had done her a favor, in a backhanded kind of way a while ago— and if there was one thing she couldn't stand it was the notion of Dixie being one up on her.

The warm water churned around Lovie's pink-and-ivory lifted and tucked and sucked and otherwise surgically enhanced curves. The swirling water made her so happy. It felt so good. Now if she could only add her favorite scented oils, but the whirlpool folks said no. It gummed up the works.

Lovie tapped the notebook with her gold ballpoint pen. Maybe she'd invite that radiologist from New Orleans whom she and Will had met in Aspen, and then maybe they'd invite the Rakestraws down for Carnival.

Lovie smiled. Word about the Fete was already filtering out and here it was only the third of April. The calls had begun. "Darling, Lovie, George and I would just love to have you come to dinner." That sort of thing, from people who'd never had them before.

The part she liked best was when people asked straight out. "Well, Lovie, are you inviting us or not?"

And she'd drawl, "Maybe I will, and maybe I won't."

She said it aloud now, the words echoing off the warm beige marble. *Maybe I will and maybe I won't.*

Suddenly there was a blip on her horizon of perfection as she remembered another voice, she must have dreamed it, saying *You bitch! Who do you think you are?* She must have had a nightmare—but when? Last night after her lover had gone? Will was out of town and she hadn't seen her tuck-away sweetie for a while, they'd had a little disagreement, so when he called, it was late, she was already dreaming. *Breaking my heart?* Whose heart? Her lover didn't have one, as far as she knew, he was just for fun. And spite. *Do you know who I am? Do you, Miss Milam? Do you? Do you? Do you?* Milam? That was so long ago, junior high school. She could almost place the voice, it was on the tip of her— Just then the outside grounds lights switched on. Lovie saw them through the big uncurtained bathroom window. No one could see into the back of the house, especially the second story. But Lovie didn't have time to wonder why the lights had flipped on early because when they did, their timing switch, which had been jiggled along with the main ground wire to the house, sent 110 volts directly into the water system of Oakmont. The live energy surged through Lovie Valentine's cream-and-pink body and electrified her red heart, which seared to well done, then stopped. The blue bolts of electricity, almost the exact blue in her Venus on the Half Shell painting, continued to dance a strange galvanic minuet around the giant shell of a bathing pool until finally someone came and shut the power off or the outside lights switched off at ten, whichever happened first.

• • • • • • • • • • • • • • *8*

Over at Shoney's Mary Ann McClanahan was trying to get her waitress's attention but wasn't making much headway. The restaurant was filled to the brim with barbecuers yelling at one another across orange vinyl booths.

"Q ain't worth a damn iffen the old folks cain't eat it. I say they ought to be able to suck on it like ice cream, even if they ain't got no teeth."

"Then, son, I say you ought to be working for Gerber. Me, I'd rather have *my* pitman than a hundred shares of IBM. Hell, I done traded two wives for him."

"Unh-huh. Named Spot and Rusty, I bet."

"Named Headache and Tired."

The man who said that last had a face that looked like a bear's behind and Mary Ann didn't need to hear any more of that kind of talk. She'd been hoping for a little decent dinner-table conversation. She waved for her check again, being through with all-she-could-eat from the salad bar and ready to hit the road. She had Dixie McClanahan's street marked in red on her map. Then an old man in the booth beside her said, "You know, I told your momma straight off she was the best-looking seventy-nine-year-old woman I'd ever seen. But that didn't mean I intended to do anything that wuddn't honorable."

Dixie McClanahan could wait another few minutes. "A cup of coffee, please," Mary Ann said to the waitress.

The old man, his still-strong tan forearms showing beneath the short sleeves of his pearl-buttoned blue cowboy shirt that matched the color of his eyes, was talking to a man in his fifties. Both of them had the words *Holly Springs Hogboys* embroidered on their backs and chests.

"Unh-huh," said the younger one, sipping his coffee. He sported a red Allis-Chalmers tractor hat that didn't quite hide all his graying cowlicks. "I know that, Floyd."

"I told her that I wuddn't gonna come calling on her till Miss Minnie Lee had been gone for six months."

"Unh-huh."

"And I waited that long, even though during that time you know my daughter Veralynn and her daughter Tiffany both up and married and left me all alone."

"I know."

"I liked to starved to death. I don't know how to cook anything but 'cue."

"Unh-huh."

"Roy, I just don't think a man was meant to live alone."

"I don't either."

Well, I do, Mary Ann thought. I think we'd all be one heck of a sight better off if every man in the entire world was required to do for his ownself for a good long while before he could even *talk* to another woman after he and his sweetheart split up or she'd worked herself to death. None of this taking his dirty laundry from one woman's clothes hamper to the next, not even bothering to learn how to run the machines in the Sudsy Washateria in between—or do anything else for that matter.

"And I courted her a good two months before I asked her to marry. Took her to the movie show. Took her fishing a bunch of times. Mowed her yard, I mean I had a grandson do it."

"I know you did, Floyd."

"I showed her every single room in that big old house I have. Biggest in Holly Springs. Took her over to Grenada to visit the family before we had the ceremony."

"Unh-huh."

"It was then, on that trip she started asking me about the money."

The younger man named Roy just stirred his coffee.

"And I told her I would give her anything she wanted. She said she wanted a new car. I bought her one. Not brand new, but you know, I thought it was good enough for a woman who's seventy-nine, don't need a Corvette."

"She ought not to even be driving."

"Well, she's pretty spry. You'd be surprised."

Roy looked like he'd just as soon not hear about that part.

"Said too she wanted me not to play the violin in the house, it chewed on her nerves. So I went out in the backyard, played for the dogs."

"I know."

"I told her I used to be a stinker, everybody knew that, but I'd changed."

"Unh-huh."

"Went to church twice every Sunday, since that time I fell out of a tree and broke my neck. That turned my life around. Made me see my life hadn't been worth spit up until then. God, I was a *mean* man."

"I know."

"But it wuddn't two weeks after we tied the knot, she started writing checks on me."

"She was standing right in my face, wearing about three thousand dollars' worth of New-York-store-bought clothes, calling me names I told her I didn't think a lady knew." That was the taller of the two black men who'd slid into the next booth, both of them wearing nice slacks and sports jackets, white shirts, ties. He had one of those deep black baritone voices that made you wonder why white singers even bothered to roll out of bed in the morning.

"So what'd she say then?" asked the shorter man who was not bad-looking, but Mary Ann thought he didn't hold a candle to the taller man who looked a lot like O. J. Simpson.

"She unloaded a whole bunch of trash on me. I was about to tell her I was gonna have to seriously consider handcuffing her—"

They were cops. Mary Ann sat up straighter. See, girl, that's what happens when you have a guilty conscience. She tried for a more natural posture, relaxed her backbone.

"—when that husband grabbed hold of her, and just about then Poochie Hood—"

"Oh, shit, Ollie."

"—yep, the good sheriff came strolling up, you know that pimp walk he learned watching *Miami Vice*, man looks like he ought to be dealing crack up on The Corner—"

"Said, What's the problem, here, men? Anything I can give you some he'p with?"

Ollie, the good-looking cop—they must be detectives, look at the clothes—leaned over and slapped hands with his friend. "That's it. Exactly the Big Cracker's words. So there we are, I tell you we're still in the ER? Doctors and nurses and orderlies pushing us all around, I tell you, Grippa, man, next time around I'm gonna be a doc, they the ones holding the *real* power."

"They pushing that Mr. Barnes around too? Man with that much money?"

"Oh, yeah. Those ER docs, they shove anybody around, break your arm trying to stick a tube down your nose, save your life, don't think a thing of it. I'm telling you, they are *bad*. Though they were having themselves a time trying to push Miz Barnes. That woman ought to enter herself in some pit bull fights, she'd come home with some trophies.

"Anyway, there's Poochie, trying to impress on her that he's the Chief Enforcement Officer of Lee County—the fact that he's up for reelection not hardly being the issue—asking what it is he can do for Mr. Number One Luxury Car Dealer of the Southeast. Saying Oh, my Lord, is that your sweet son Walter, Jr., lying there, has he been in a car accident? When Miz Barnes grabs hold of me and says she wants to press charges against *me* for pressing charges against her son for attempted robbery. And wants to hit that man from New Orleans who whirled Walter, Jr., out of the McDonald's with attempted murder. And Red Holcomb with accessory. Not to mention that she wants Red locked up on g.p.'s."

"Hell, you think there's anybody in Tupelo hadn't wanted to press charges against Holcomb for one thing or another?"

"Don't think so. Every time we grab a homicide call, I point my car right over to his house. Always amazed when it's not him."

*　　*　　*

"So what does the total amount to?" That was the white man with the red Allis-Chalmers hat.

"Well." The old man leaned back in the booth and looked at his hands. "She ran it up to five hundred before I told her I was going to have to move out, she didn't stop."

The old man moved out on his bride over five hundred dollars? Puh-leeze, Mary Ann thought.

"But you know, now that this thing happened today, being brought back from the dead, it makes me think. When I was lying there on the ground, still buzzing with the jolt of that electricity, I had another one of those out-of-body experiences you read about in *Reader's Digest*. First one was when I broke my neck. That's the one that saved me from being an out-and-out son of a bitch the rest of my days, but I think maybe I was slipping back to the old ways here lately, being uncharitable to your momma. I mean, it wasn't like she was asking me for much. And she's such a sweet woman, putting up with me, I ought to give her the Taj Mahal if she wanted it. Sometimes, I just don't know what comes over me. I tell you one thing. The minute this 'cue cooking is over, I'm going over to that Barnes Imports and I'm ordering your momma that new Italian car I saw. In red. Power everything. All she'll have to do is think it, that sucker'll make a left turn."

"You had one of those out-of-body things?"

"I'm telling you, it was as real as anything. There's somebody motioning me on through this tunnel of light, but then there's your momma standing at the other end, saying Come on back, I love you, Floyd."

"So how'd y'all leave it?" That was the short cop Grippa again.

"You mean did we leave Poochie there with his head up his patoot?" The O. J. Simpson cop had a gorgeous smile. Mary Ann was partial to men with great teeth, no matter what their color. Then grab ahold of yourself, girl, she reminded herself. It's men that got you sitting in this burger joint in Nowhere, Mis'sippi, ought to be having tea at the Plaza Hotel, New York City, right on the park. "Nawh, we just laid a bunch of mumbo jumbo on Poochie till he figured out he ought to back off or he was gonna have to duke it out with the Chief, and even dumb as he is, he figured it out, and said he'd be calling on Mr. and Miz Barnes tomorrow."

"Like they were gonna invite him in for iced tea."

"Well, you know those country club folks. They just might. 'Course, then they'd sterilize their glasses and long silver spoons, like it'd been you or me."

"I hear that."

A two-way radio that was sitting right by the sugar shaker suddenly squalled. "Tupelo Blue, three-oh-two." The cop named Ollie said something into it. The radio answered back, "Detective Priest, sir, there's a—"

But Mary Ann couldn't hear the rest of it as the real radio blared out into the Shoney's dining room. "This is Sister Demetrius Holy Woman of the Church of Visible Bliss. I heals by touch. I removes sickness and sorrow from your body. I removes all pain. I removes spells. I rewrites the story of your life."

Mary Ann was planning on doing that last thing all by her lonesome, thank you very much, or at least part of it. The two cops had tossed money on the table and were already rolling. Mary Ann waved her right hand hard. Check, she said, and I mean now!

9

Over in the old substantial part of town, on Woodall Street, a little cul-de-sac off Highland Circle, Dixie McClanahan's good friend Lucille Phipps was sitting at the table with Dixie drinking a cup of tea. She ought to have gone home hours ago.

Dixie was telling her that. "Lucille, I don't want you coming over here and cluttering up my kitchen when I come dragging in bone-tired from a hard evening of bridge. Don't feel like seeing your ugly face."

"Shut up," said Lucille. "You ought not to be out on the streets anyway. Walking advertisement for why they used to keep pregnant women locked up."

They were crazy about each other, had been since Dixie wangled herself a doctor's excuse from Memphis society a dozen years ago. Lucille, a golden-skinned, generous-figured woman of color, as she called herself, lived right up Woodall on York Drive, an even smaller cul-de-sac. Except she called hers a dead end.

Next door, the dogs started barking again.

"That's it," said Dixie, standing and opening a kitchen cabinet. "I'm not in a good mood anyway.

My stomach itches. I can hardly breathe. Then that damned Lovie Rakestraw screws up the bridge. Maxine Barnes, at least she had an excuse, her son Walter went crazy and tried to shoot that son of a bitch next door at the McDonald's.''

"What?"

Dixie was feeling around in the cabinet with her right hand amidst the sugar and the flour and the grits. She waved at Lucille with her left. "I'll tell you about it later. I don't know who Lovie thinks she is, didn't even call. We had one and a half tables. That meant three women yakking their heads off while three others were trying to pay attention to the cards. It was a mess. Martha Jane Gardener—that's where we were, at her house—she called Lovie, Lovie didn't even answer. Martha Jane said she was going over there later, give Miss Marble Bidet a piece of her mind. God, I wish Walter, Jr., had killed Red. I told him last night that was my very last, and I meant it, warning about those mutts.''

"Lovie Rakestraw. Those airs she puts on. *What* are you looking for?" Lucille didn't even glance in her direction.

"Just never you mind." Dixie moved on to the cabinets over the washer and dryer, having to heft herself up on a little stepladder.

"You fall off that thing, kill those twins, those prolifers, and then me, twins' stand-in grandma, gone be swarming over you with both feet.''

"Very funny, Lucille. Does that mean you think Slaughter's the father of these children? I mean, Slaughter's cute but . . . ah, ha! Here it is. I knew it was.''

Lucille chose to ignore the remark about her son. "I don't know how you think you'd know where anything was, you ain't lifted a finger for yourself in about thirty-six years.''

"I'm *not* but thirty-five, twenty years younger than you, thank you very kindly." Dixie passed for twenty-five. She had a very pretty face, a turned-up nose, widely spaced dark brown eyes, a porcelain complexion, the whole framed by a whirl of dark curls. But that small face looked misplaced above her eight-months-gone balloon of a body. She grunted her way carefully off the ladder and slapped a tiny box on the kitchen counter. Then rummaged around some more. "Where have the damn pitchers run off to? Did you sell 'em off as Elvis's through your mail order?"

"I said *about* thirty-six. You'll be that in a month. One of us don't kill the other one first."

"The pitchers, Lucille?"

"Woman's got so much stuff she don't even know where it is. Last time I noticed one's in the fridge full of OJ. One's got milk for you and the babies. One's water."

"And one's got planter's punch you brought over here to keep yourself company."

"You lose at bridge today? That's what's wrong with you?"

"Oh, hell." Dixie opened another cabinet, scrabbled for a minute among the blue flannel bags of Tiffany sterling she inherited from her maternal grandmother, bone china swaddled in plastic cleaning bags, mops, brooms, the vacuum cleaner, and pulled out a silver pitcher. "There. That'll do just fine."

"Is that Rit? What color *is* that?"

Dixie held the package out and gave it a long look. "It says carmine."

"That means red."

"Thank you, Lucille. I don't know what on earth I'd do without you."

"Hard time, prob'ly."

Dixie poured the dye into the silver pitcher, mixed it with a half-gallon of hot water, then leaned back in the long tall cabinet and snatched up her dead husband Carlin's old hunting rifle. "Well, toodle-loo." She waved at Lucille as she headed gingerly for the door, carrying the rifle in one hand, the pitcher in the other.

Lucille reached in a fold of her aquamarine Indian sari and pulled out a pack of Kools. She always had had exotic taste in clothing from back in her younger days when she moved up to Memphis and lived on Beale Street. Recently her wardrobe picked up again, ever since that little Fleishacker girl came back from California and opened a shop on West Main full of pretty things. Lucille lit her cigarette, she let herself smoke two a day, dropped three cubes of sugar in her tea, and said, "What's the rifle for?"

"I figure Red comes out and catches me dyeing his yappy little Maltese dogs carmine"—she put a lot of English on that last word—"a week before that Jackson Kennel Club Show he's dying to win—could you open that door for me, pretty please and thank you— takes ugly with me, I might have to shoot him."

"Oh," said Lucille, blowing a double smoke ring.

Now that she was here Mary Ann wasn't sure that she wanted to get out of the rental car. This was a lot fancier neighborhood than she'd expected Carlin to be living in. Certainly a lot fancier than where they lived in Fairhope, which really burned her, to think Carlin was up here living high on the hog while she was busting her butt, selling aloe vera and lingerie door-to-door to help meet the house payments on their three-bedroom ranch that could use a new roof. These were great big houses set back from the sidewalk in rolling green yards, and this street was a dead end, the houses even larger than the ones she'd just passed. People were bound to notice her, a stranger walking around by herself in the gathering dark. Too late to pretend she was out for the exercise, especially in her cowboy boots.

The house that went with the address that the phone book gave for Carlin McClanahan looked like it ought to be in New Orleans. Four big columns marched across the front of whitewashed brick. Balconies on the second story had that lacy kind of ironwork you see on those houses down there when you go to take falling-down-drunk for Mardi Gras. Mary Ann had only been once, though it wasn't that far from Fairhope. Carlin had griped the whole time, saying New Orleans stole the Mardi Gras from Mobile, they didn't need to drive all that way.

Mary Ann sat in her car listening to the yapping dogs next door trying to imagine grumpy old Carlin living in this huge fancy house with the cherry red Mercedes in the driveway, the vanity plate read DIXIE, when suddenly a side door opened. A pretty brunette—Mary Ann would put her at thirty, five-four, it was tough to guess her weight in that big mauve dress—was floating in and out of the chest-high shrubbery. Then Mary Ann figured out what was under her left arm—and ducked.

Harry was worried about Sam. She hadn't eaten anything since lunch, which was a *long* time ago, and now she'd barely picked at her dinner.

"Honey, it's over. I'm safe. He's safe. Look." Harry pointed to Harpo curled up asleep on the rug under the big round oak table in Red's pine-paneled kitchen, which was awash in antique copper pots, china, and silver, chockablock with two porcelain stoves, three breakfronts, two tables, a freezer from some restaurant that had gone out of business. There must have been twenty-five paintings hanging on the walls. "Here, at least try the banana pie. Whipped cream. Chocolate sauce."

"Fat grams, Harry. I couldn't. It's just the thought of Harpo's being squashed—or stolen, I thought that biker, the first one, had nabbed him, and then that other one, that Jesus biker, could somebody please tell me what the heck is a Jesus biker anyway, the man just handed me Harpo and that tract and I don't even think I thanked him, I was so glad to see the little dog again, much less ask him about his religious affiliation—and you could have been shot, you didn't *know* it was a toy, taking chances like that—Harry, I'm way beyond hunger."

Red was smoking a cigar. "That's why you passed on my prime rib I had Buddy cook especially for y'all? 'Cause you worried about that dog? Hell, I have a whole yard full of dogs out there. Folks around here call me the dogcatcher—among other things." He laughed, by himself. "That little thing had been squashed, you could just go out there and pick yourself out another one. They're all the same."

The look Sam gave him didn't even say thank you.

But Red didn't notice. "Hell, *I'm* the one would have been killed, Walter, Jr., hadn't been fooling. Don't see me shirking my dinner plate. Got to toughen up, little lady." He held a big hand straight out. "Nerves of steel." Then he reached over and slapped Harry on the back, hard. "Thanks to my new partner here."

"It was nothing, really. Actually, it was dumb." Harry shrugged. Dumb, that's what Lavert was going to say when he heard about his McDonald's trick.

"I tell you, son, it was *something*. Even if they did let that kid right out on bail. I tell you, I think that's a shame, that's what I think. Ought to put him under the jail, threatening folks like that. Why, he could have given one of the customers a heart attack. And you know who'd be liable?" He pounded himself on the chest. "The owner, that's who. Not that I am yet,

but I will be soon. You have to think about things like
that, you dealing with the public. Always covering
your butt, looking out for Number One. Just like y'all
with that dog in the store. Now, no offense, but that
little girl behind the counter, she should have taken
care of the problem just like that." He snapped meaty
fingers.

"Well, now," said Sam, "that was our fault. We
shouldn't have—"

"Nawh. It's hers. She let that situation get completely out of hand. I was standing back there watching. First thing, I take ownership, I give her her
walking papers."

"But, Red, she told us—" Sam tried again.

"Nope. No question about it. She can't handle the
situation, I don't want her. Don't like to hire girls
anyway, no offense intended, they just don't have
guts."

"To sell hamburgers?" Sam was growing unhap-
pier by the minute. If Red wasn't their host, not to
mention Harry's prospective business partner (though
that was looking to her like an increasingly bad idea),
she'd have already given him what for.

"To be in business of any kind. I don't think the
gentler sex has the wherewithal to make good business decisions. The drive. The stamina. I've seen it
happen time after time, you give women a little of
that power they're always whining they've been shut
out of, they fumble the ball."

"Red," said Sam. She was too mad for manners
now. "Are you aware of the numbers of women in
this country who have—"

"You're going to go spouting statistics at me. I
don't care about statistics. What I know is that
women in business are just too much trouble. You
can't win with them. Either they're trying to boss
you around or they're screaming that you're using

unfair advantage, sexual harassment, that kind of rot, to boss them, half the time their hormones've got them het up or they're crying in the john."

"Well now, Red," Harry said. "I think I'm going to have to beg to disagree pretty strongly with you there. Actually, I think we ought to talk some basic philosophy before we go any further on this barbecue business."

"Awh, son. I didn't mean anything. 'Course"—he gave Harry a wink—"if I was sitting here with that pretty little woman, I'd feel like I had to come to her defense too."

"You just don't get it, do you?" Sam snapped.

"Red, I'd say you've raised some issues that my partner and I'll need to think about." Maybe he and Lavert ought to forget about this franchising thing after all if it meant this kind of compromising. Dealing with jerks. Maybe they were doing fine by themselves. He squeezed Sam's knee under the table.

She turned. "I think our friend at the fairgrounds was right, old son."

What Harry couldn't figure was how he and Lavert had been so wrong about the man that time they'd met him. The two of them had been up to see a pig grower in Tennessee, spent the night with Lavert's cousin here in Tupelo. Maybe it was that sippin' whiskey. Maybe. Could be. The whiskey and the music they'd been listening to in Cousin Slaughter's bar when Red had wandered in for a few. Ambience had stepped in the way of character evaluation more than once in Harry's experience.

Then Red said, "Awh, hell, Harry, let's don't get mad at each other talking about womenfolk. Reasoning ain't what they're best at, is it?"

Red was saved from banana pie in the face and Harry was saved from punching Red when someone out in the yard racked a cartridge into the chamber of a Browning 380 automatic, aimed and fired through Red's big kitchen window, blowing the dinner table conversation to hell and gone.

Martha Jane Gardener was talking with her mother, Alfreda Spoon, on the phone. "I'll tell you what," Martha Jane said, "if Lovie Rakestraw wasn't one of my very dearest friends, I'd cut her dead in the middle of West Main. I swear, that woman has just about pushed me to the brink. She absolutely ruined my bridge party."

"Now, darling, calm down," said Alfreda, her seventy-seven-year-old mother. Then Alfreda took a deep breath because the hippie reflexologist/masseuse who came through town once a month in his van with the sign that said ROB THE ROOTER/CLEAN YOUR DRAINS was doing her toes. It felt so good it was all she could do to keep from moaning, but then Martha Jane wouldn't have heard her anyway. Martha Jane never gave anybody else a chance to talk, she might as well pick up the phone and chat with the dial tone.

Martha Jane said, "This is the third time Lovie's done this. Stood me up for bridge. I don't know what it means. Do you think maybe this is the first sign that Howard's practice is on the skids? The president of the Ladies' Legal Auxiliary starts standing me up?"

"Oh. Oh." Alfreda couldn't help herself. Rob was working on her arches now. His hands felt so good she wanted to cry.

"*What,* Momma?"

"No. I said, no, I don't think you have a thing to worry about. Maybe Lovie's just busy."

"Hmph." Martha Jane, who wore a foundation garment even under her bathrobe, jerked it up. "Well, she *hasn't* been attending the Board of Sessions meetings at the church every time either, and people are beginning to wonder about her commitment."

"Ummmmm." Rob was doing her ankles now. Alfreda still had trim ankles that she was very proud of. "Well, I know she's awfully busy planning that benefit for the hospital."

"Mother! Whose side are you on?"

Mine, I'm on my right side, thought Alfreda, as her reflexologist with the magic hands stretched her full length on her dining room table. Alfreda hadn't stepped into that stuffy brown dining room for almost ten years until he came along. Now everytime she walked past it, a little shiver ran up and down her old bones. "Martha Jane, darling," she said, "did it ever occur to you that maybe you and Howard ought to step out a little more, go up to Memphis, kick up your heels, have a little fun?"

"Fun! I don't have time for fun. I'm the first vice president of the Ladies' Legal Auxiliary, an elder in the church, I have Howard and this house—"

"Well, that's what I mean. Oh!" Rob'd turned her full over on her back and was slowly working up to her knees. Every time he touched them, it made Alfreda want to do the shimmy. Not that that dance wasn't before her time, of course, but she always thought it was the cutest thing, next to the Charleston.

"Fun!" said Martha Jane. "That's what I think Lovie Rakestraw is having at my expense, is fun. Making me look like a fool. Well, she think she's so high and mighty, everybody remembers where she came from. And furthermore, there's been talk. I've heard things, I could tell you."

"Now, Martha Jane, you know the Lord does not love a viperish tongue." Then Rob the reflexologist leaned over and flicked his long pink wet one behind each of Alfreda's knees. He'd never done that before.

"Darling," she said, "listen, I've got something needs seeing about on the stove."

"That's okay, Momma. Don't worry about me. Howard loses his practice, we'll just come over to your house, put our feet under your table. But I'm telling you, I'm calling Lovie one more time, and if she doesn't answer, I'm going over to her house and break her door down if I have to. I'll let her know there are still standards in Tupelo, Mississippi, and people who do not hold with, and furthermore will not abide, rude!"

Ollie Priest had just finished a call to North Green, in the vicinity of The Corner, the intersection that was the heart of Tupelo's drug traffic.

Drugs weren't Ollie's beat—he left that to the hotshots who fancied dressing like bums, hiding and sneaking. The star of this particular domestic scenario was a naked woman out in the yard screaming her head off. Her husband had come home early, shot up her and her lover. The latter was lying out in the yard still as a corpse, which Ollie assumed he was, until the man snaked out a hand, caught Ollie's ankle, and hissed, "Man, is he gone?" Ollie'd almost wet his pants. Then a neighbor came out and turned a water hose on the naked woman who, in her opinion, was making entirely too much noise.

Ollie had climbed back in his midnight-blue police-issue Oldsmobile and headed back down North Green a few blocks to where the neighborhood started to be mixed again. He was waiting for a red light to change when Slaughter Phipps came strolling out of his bar/pool hall/blues club/art gallery which served barbecue on weekends. A toothpick stuck out of his handsome mug.

Slaughter was the one who was always so smart when he and Ollie were in school. He was the one everybody thought was going to be somebody, maybe a famous painter, until his daddy was killed up in Memphis.

"Mr. Phipps," Ollie called, then pulled the Olds over.

"Mr. Priest." Slaughter's oiled curls took a bow. Slaughter Phipps was a man of many enthusiasms, including long hair, red leather, hot meat, cool blues, pale women, and paintings of the latter, some of which he executed himself. Slaughter's girlfriend, Turquoise, who could pass for white if she chose, which she didn't, was partial to monogamy and sharp knives—which kept Slaughter's reflexes quick and highly tuned. "What you doing over here?" Slaughter smiled. "Come to lock up some folks?"

"Actually, I was about to drive over towards your momma's house. I ran into her earlier in the street, promised her I'd go talk with a man about some dogs."

"Well, if it's Red, you tell him Momma said Dixie said she's gone poison those mutts he don't make 'em shut up. They start in at five in the morning, Momma can hear them all the way up at her house. People need their rest."

"Well, I hope Dixie doesn't play cute into a tight spot with Red. That man remembers more ways of revenge he learned from his pap than his dogs have fleas."

Slaughter shrugged. Fancy little pups didn't mean much to him, hunting dogs were more his style, unless—"Hey, Priest, tell Momma to tell Dixie to shoot 'em instead. She does it clean, I can put 'em in the chopped Q. Folks won't know no different. Or maybe I'll sell 'em back to Red, hear he's buying the McDonald's. Serve 'em up as Big Macs. Wouldn't that be something?"

Ollie laughed, then continued down Green to where

it turned white and monied again, when Rita Molina jumped on the radio fast and loud. That wasn't like Rita, who'd come to Tupelo from Houston to slow down, fed up with bubbas shooting each other out of their pickup trucks. Rita's Spanish accent crept up on her when she was excited, and she was pretty excited now.

There'd been a shooting reported at 78 Woodall. Red Holcomb's house. Ollie sighed, called in and grabbed it.

Nine o'clock. Another hour and he'd have been home with his sweet Diane. It was definitely time to get serious about a different line of work, one where he didn't have to pretend he, his johnson, and his .45 automatic were one and the same, have to practice life-saving techniques once a week, *twice* today, on this greedy-gut piece of trash playing like he was a gentleman, Red Holcomb, in addition to which booking a perfectly good young football player gone nuts because Holcomb was such a pissant.

Ollie rolled down his window. Just look at this beautiful spring night. The air was heavy with honeysuckle. A full moon, sky strewn with stars, perfect for the citizenry to be home making love to their wives and girlfriends, if they had the sense God gave a duck.

Lucille looked out the window and saw Dixie hit
the grass. Oh, Lordy, she's dead. Dead. My Dixie's
dead. But if I move my butt maybe I can save those
babies. Move, Lucille. Move. But her extra-wide size
nines were glued to that tile Dixie brought back when
she went down to Cuernavaca. Or was it Oaxaca?
One of those Mexican places.

Woman, what difference does it make? You better
run out of this house, into that yard, stop pretending
you don't know nothing 'bout nothing, your momma
the biggest midwife Shakerag ever saw before they
tore those pitiful houses down. And where'd that get
'em? Moved folks up to the hill, to the projects, that
old mall standing empty now—Move, Lucille! Move!

She looked back out the window. There was Dixie,
risen from the dead, no gun, no pitcher, standing out
in the yard in the moonlight chatting with Red's mom
Miss Estella like they hadn't heard any gunshot.

Now, everybody knew old Miss Estella was pretty
strange, and Lucille knew that more than most, but
what she wondered, looking at the two of them, was
if Miss Estella knew that Dixie had another side to

her, honed sharp as a tack those years she spent at U of Alabama she talks about when the two of them sit down and set out on a toot—before Dixie got in the family way, of course.

Dixie talking about drinking, hollering, drinking, and more drinking, had no use for anybody who wasn't one of those first-class fraternity boys, talking about the drunken runs those boys do, stealing cars, holding up banks, pretending they were outlaws. Dixie, the only girl, smarter'n all them little lilywavers put together, right up at the front of the pack— kind of like that Patty Hearst when Patty was wilding, then had the nerve to pretend she was drugged the whole time.

Dixie, Dixie, Dixie, wild child Dixie. Lucille shook her head. 'Course that wild part was a long time ago, before Dixie married her Tupelo doctor, Dr. Stuart Hardy, the one who started the Medical Center, Dixie was practically his child bride. She had herself several years of playing lady, country-clubbing, getting right back in the swing of the life she was born to up in Memphis, when the doc up and died—leaving her boocups de bucks but no children. Dixie said she'd thought she couldn't have any. Since then, well, she looked like a lady, she talked like a lady, she walked like a lady, but even when it looked like she'd settled down again with that Carlin, well, Lucille knew better.

Lucille reached over and without even glancing at it grabbed the bourbon bottle and took another little tot.

Wasn't life strange, she thought. Herself, growing up in Shakerag, her daddy, a preacher on Sundays, doing the hot dirty work over at the lumber mill, hat in hand the other six days, Yes suh, bossing, till he'd come home, take drunk, punch that same hand through the wall 'cause he couldn't do it to Mr. Charlie Boss Man, who treated him like a dog? Her momma birthing most of the babies in Shakerag, half of 'em in East Tupelo, those poor white folks, Momma never saw a cent, was paid in flour, piece goods, hogs, who'd a thunk one of them'd grow up to be Elvis? And who'd a thunk, black folks'd vote, much less hold office, or like that Ollie Priest, *be* the law?

Lucille herself'd gone full circle, around and around, poor child became a grownup woman with three kids of her own but never let those children slow her down, running up and down the roads, in and out of Memphis tonks with handsome men, wearing pretty dresses, riding in big fast cars, leading the fancy life, now—well, when she looked in the mirror, she didn't even recognize herself, a middle-aged lady who owned two houses over on York, one to live in, one chockful of her mail-order Elvis business. She hung around Dixie's house for the amusement value, fussing at the help—the cleaning lady, the yard man and his son, the laundry lady, the girl who did the fine ironing. And she kept an eye on her kinfolks. Her son. Her ex-husband. No grandchildren, though she was crazy for some, her twin daughters both killed in a fire out in L.A., teenagers, she didn't like to think about that. Of course, she did, every day.

Lucille took another little nip. Things had changed so much in her lifetime, sometimes Lucille just couldn't wait to see what was going to happen next. Here she'd grown up too poor to have a radio, as a girl listened to live blues in broken-down clubs you took your life in your hands to walk through the door. Now she had forty-two channels on the cable TV.

Wasn't anything for keeps, for forever, though, that was for sure. Take for example that Carlin. He came from who knows where a few years ago, smooth like one of those *L.A. Law* actors, charmed

Dixie right out of her drawers. Lucille never could see it, but then, nobody knew what went on between two people in the dark. Besides, when it came to men, well, you had to use different standards. You judged 'em like women, wouldn't ever be any children born.

But, and this was what puzzled her, why'd Dixie let him stay so long? And, big question, how come she let herself get knocked up? Seeing how it was plain, after a while, he wasn't keeping her pleasured and was gone half the time. Dixie had that down-in-the-mouth look about her. Of course Lucille had asked. Dixie'd said, I can't talk about it. Best friend, she knew better than to push.

Lucille herself didn't know how to talk about Carlin now. Folks asked, what happened to that man? Lucille wasn't sure. Somebody called up, said he was dead and already buried down in Fairhope, Alabama. And Dixie not saying a word about moving him, not grieving a lick, it was almost embarrassing, wearing that Mona Lisa look that wasn't just because she was pregnant either. Lucille had grown up with pregnant women in and out of her momma's house every five minutes, they didn't look like that. Dixie knew something Lucille didn't know. What was it? Being on the outside of a secret drove Lucille fairly wild.

Then about a hundred million police cars drove up for real, not your *In the Heat of the Night,* not your *Law and Order,* but for real for real, in Red Holcomb's yard.

Sam, Detective Ollie Priest, and Alma West, the persimmon-haired paramedic from the fairgrounds, were all talking at the same time in the back of the orange-and-white emergency medical services van. Harry was still out cold. Alma raised her eyebrows when she recognized Sam. Twice in one shift?

Ollie was doing the questioning. "You say you were sitting there after dinner? No warning, only the shot. Then a little bit later the lights went out? How much later?"

Sam wasn't positive. She closed her eyes and ran it again. "Thirty seconds. Long enough for me to see nobody was hit." Though Harry almost killed himself flying through the air to cover her. Now she squeezed his hand but got nothing back. Well, at least he wasn't hurting.

Ollie asked, "And you didn't see anything outside before the blast?"

Sam shook her head. It was hard to speak over the words repeating in her head: "Hold on, Harry, Harry, sweet Harry. Serenity Prayer or no Serenity Prayer, AA or no AA, she was going to have one hell of a time accepting she couldn't change this one, if he didn't wake up.

"I'm sorry, I know this is hard for you, Ms. Adams." Detective Priest had a soft warm voice for a cop. Kind eyes.

"Sam," she said. *Hold on, sweet Harry.*

"Ms. Adams?" It was Alma West. "I know you're worried, but he really wasn't hit. I think all we have here is a concussion, maybe a cracked collarbone, definitely a broken arm." That would be from where her hero slammed into the counter, flying like Superman. "And Tupelo has the finest medical facilities in the whole state. Hundred and fifty docs in this town, most of them top-notch."

Harry groaned. He was coming around.

See, Alma grinned, told you so.

"Hey." Sam leaned close. "I love you, son."

Harry heard her, but he was looking at Ollie Priest, and for a minute he thought the big black detective was his friend Lavert.

Ollie Priest was smiling at him, saying, "Harry

Zack, you look like you've seen a ghost. You remember me from earlier—at the McDonald's? I'm the one who took your statement. Decided you were the good guy.''

Harry managed a grin. "So I'm not dead?"

Ollie said, "Nawh, just banged up. Not gonna be playing any basketball for a while."

"Hey, sweet baby." He smiled up at Sam, thinking she looked like an angel. "Guess we better give you a quick and dirty course in smoking 'cue."

Mary Ann ran three red lights heading back to the Ramada Inn, a ticket for sure if the TPD had been around. Once she was within shouting distance of the Ramada, she'd slowed, then stopped at the Rebel Package Store, picked up a pint of Southern Comfort, a Coke, and a bag of peanuts to steady her nerves.

Good Lord have mercy. She slammed the door to her dark motel room, then double-locked it behind her. What the hell was going on? Police sirens wailing like it was the end of the world, ambulances all over the place. The woman she guessed was Dixie tromping out in the yard with a rifle, blasting away at the neighbors. Blowing away the lights. Scaring the dogs. Setting folks to screaming. God! She shivered, it was cold in this room, and it stunk of cigars.

Then from out of the darkness over by her bed, somebody breathed: *Welcome to the end of Lonely Street.*

Mary Ann was a pretty good screamer herself.

Now Martha Jane Gardener was really mad. She'd been ringing the bell at Lovie Rakestraw's side door for five minutes. She knew Lovie was in there. All the outside lights were on. She'd peeked into the garage and Lovie's car was there. She'd stomped around to the back of the house, and there on the second floor, probably the bathroom, a light. What was Lovie doing in there? Sitting in that tub she was so proud of, laughing at her? Laughing because she'd ruined another bridge afternoon. Well, she needn't think she was going to get away with it.

Martha Jane Gardener was simply not going to put up with this behavior. She was going to give Lovie a piece of her mind if she had to break in to do it.

But how was she going to do that?

The side door was locked, of course. And the front door. She tiptoed around to the back of the house through the thick grass that rolled across the entire yard like a green carpet. Lovie was almost as vain about that grass as she was about her damned soaking pool. Maybe one of the French doors on the back was open. Nope, no such luck. Well, hell. The most daring thing Martha Jane Gardener had ever done in her life was turn down an invitation to serve punch at Grace Nell Carpenter's daughter's wedding because she was mad at Grace Nell. Well, she was even madder at Lovie, and passion called for drastic action. Martha Jane dug a brick from the border around Lovie's caladium bed, pulled back and tossed it with all her might through a low breakfast room window.

Then she gingerly undid the catch, raised the sash, and climbed inside. "Lovie!" she called. Not a peep. Well, that was just like Miss High and Mighty, ignoring a crash that could raise the dead. "Lovie Rakestraw! It's Martha Jane Gardener!"

Nothing.

Well, she'd march upstairs and beard the hussy in her den, or however that went. But before she did that, Martha Jane, who abhorred dirt, and that was an awfully dirty brick, wanted to wash up.

She stepped into the kitchen and up to the sink, carefully removed her diamond and emerald engagement ring and her wedding band and her diamonds-all-around anniversary ring, and reached to turn the water on.

When she made contact with the chrome faucet, which was still energized, as was all the plumbing in the house, and would be until the outside lights switched off at ten, she took a shock that punched her across the room.

Martha Jane was still lying in a heap when the security service, responding to the silent alarm that had tripped when she threw the brick through the window, let themselves in, revolvers drawn.

Now Sam and Ollie were standing in the hall right outside the hospital room where Harry was flying on a cloud of Demerol. Ollie had some more questions.

"Were there any phone calls before the gunshot?"

"You mean like a warning?"

The detective nodded.

"Not that I know of."

Then Ollie asked her to run through what happened after they'd arrived at Holcomb's house, after they'd finished at the McDonald's.

There hadn't been that much. Red'd shown them the guesthouse out behind the pool. An old sharecropper's cabin, two rooms on either side with a dogtrot through the middle, it had been dragged up onto the property, be-cuted, antiqued, and Ralph-Laurened to a fare-thee-well.

They'd freshened up, then walked back over to the big house for the dinner Sam hadn't wanted—

"Is there a phone in the guesthouse?"

One in the bedroom, probably another in the living room, it was hard to see with so many gewgaws. The bedroom phone didn't ring while they were there.

But, wait, there was a call in the middle of dinner. Red didn't take it in the kitchen, but excused himself and stepped down the hall, to his study, she thought. She couldn't hear what he'd been saying.

"Detective Priest." He said call him Ollie, everybody else did. "Ollie, do you think that business at the McDonald's this afternoon had anything to do with this? The kid, Barnes, said his father was threatening to kill Red."

"You're assuming Red was the target."

"I don't think we've been in town long enough for anybody to want to shoot either of us, that is, unless Mr. Barnes sees Harry as the instrument of his son's downfall." Which would be an interesting case of projection, but one thing Sam had learned in her years as a newshound was never to underestimate the ability of humankind to pass the buck.

"Well, I'll tell you," said Ollie. "Wally, Sr., might have been riled and he'll spout off at the mouth, but it'd be hot air. He'd be more likely to arm-wrestle you over a trade-in on a car than shoot you. Now his wife, Maxine—there's another matter."

"Wally, Jr., said something out in the playground about Red and her, said Red ought to be ashamed. Does that mean what I think it does?"

Ollie laughed. "No way. Not unless Maxine meant to screw him to death, pardon my French. Red Holcomb is the kind of man who has half of Tupelo ready to kill him on sight at any given moment. We ought to keep him in protective custody."

"I'm not too taken with him myself."

Ollie raised an eyebrow.

"So far I'm not crazy about the way he talks about women or dogs, or the way he does business."

"Man's selfish. Long hungry, we call it around here. Red would take bread out of his children's mouths, if he had any. Confirmed bachelor. He knows what he wants, doesn't give a hoot about anybody else. They say he inherited that from his daddy, the stingiest *and* meanest man ever lived in Lee County."

History aside, what specifically had Red done to Mrs. Barnes?

Ollie gave her the choice of short or long. She chose the latter, then watched Ollie's face as he went back to the beginning. He explained how Dr. James Ireland, OB/GYN, woke up one morning and decided he'd had it with Tupelo's long hot summers, mosquitoes, everybody's nose in his business. He was selling his practice—which he'd inherited from his daddy, old Doc Burma Ireland—and moving to Pebble Beach where he intended to play eighteen holes each and every day for the rest of his natural life.

Ollie could have been an actor. His face was full of light.

Dr. Ireland did the best he could to sell his practice, but there were no takers. "Then seeing as how he had already closed on his new house in California and needed to be on his way, he put his old place on Jefferson Street up for auction." It'd been his home and his office. Red Holcomb won the bidding. "He'll buy *anything,* if he thinks he can turn a profit on it."

"That's why his house is packed to the gills. I never saw so much stuff."

Ollie nodded. "Plus he has three or four warehouses full down in Milltown. South of Main, near the old cottonseed oil mill. Red's the kind of man who likes others' misfortunes. It's an ill wind that blows me no good, he's always saying that. People don't want to hear it when he's snapping up farms that have been in their families since their great-great grans, their tractors, their scrubboards."

"Like the doctor's house?"

"Well, it wasn't that that gave folks the mean reds, excuse the pun. Folks have been gentrifying those old downtown houses for the past few years, and it's good for the town, most say. I'd agree with 'em, I like old things. It was buying the practice that burned 'em.''

"Red wasn't pretending to be a doctor all of a sudden?''

"No. But here's where it gets funny. He bought the whole shebang. The house. The equipment. And then, as a separate item, Dr. Ireland's medical records. Paid five grand for them.''

"You can't sell medical records. That's privileged information.''

"Well, see now, that's what everybody thinks. And that's what everybody's telling Red, including the docs who were right there on the scene bidding against him for the equipment. They said, Whoa! when that auctioneer started in. And Red's no sooner won them, than he turns around and starts trying to sell them on the spot to those docs. They're backing away like he's trying to hit 'em with an ugly stick.''

Sam laughed. Ollie was good. You could see all the parts he was acting out. "So did anybody call the appropriate agency, report him?''

"Sure did. A woman from the American Medical Record folks said, Well, it could happen, though it never had before. She said hospitals have tighter rules, but a private practice, dissolution or the death of the doctor, those folks are up the creek concerning what happens to their confidential medical information.''

"I can't believe that.'' Sam was thinking about her own gynecologist, what they'd discussed in addition to the usual litany of ailments. There'd been her depression after her parents' deaths, her alcoholism, a long-ago back alley abortion in Mexico. Would she want those items on the auction block?

"Red advertises the office and the medical records in medical journals, but in the meantime the town's women are in an uproar. He's holding secrets back through his daddy's practice, probably five thousand patients over the years. Women are threatening to kill him. Little old ladies are hollering that next he'll be printing news pictures of 'em stark nude. Didn't make any difference that Dr. Ireland wasn't in the picture-taking business in the first place. Women in this town haven't been this upset since the Clarence Thomas hearings. Oh, it's been a mess. I'm sure that's what Wally, Jr., was all het up about. Listening to his momma, who was one of Dr. Ireland's patients, sitting around the dinner table hollering the past month or so.''

"So Red still has the records?"

"He does. I don't know what's going to come of it, but if that's what Wally, Jr.'s problem was I can tell you he's out on bail, back home in bed right now. He'll go for a hearing, get a slap on the hand from the judge, maybe Wally, Sr.'ll have to come up with a few bucks. It's not going to amount to more than that.''

Ollie shifted his weight, readjusted his trousers. He was a snappy dresser in a light-weight tan wool suit. Good laced brown calf shoes. Green and brown striped shirt. Green tie with a brown and cream paisley. No jewelry except a simple gold watch and an equally plain gold wedding band.

"Sam, I guess, back to the shooting, what I'm telling you is if we lined up every man, woman, child, and dog in Tupelo and asked 'em if they had some reason to want Red Holcomb dead, three-quarters of them would be lying if they said no.''

"So you're not going to press on this shooting too hard?"

"Did I say that? What do you think this is, Possum Holler?'' Ollie was tired. It was late. Diane had long since gone to bed. He was definitely working OT and had just run out of pleasant. "What do you think I'm doing now? You're an interesting woman, but I'm not visiting with you for my health."

Sam raised a hand, palm out. "Sorry, sorry." Sometimes her mouth didn't connect with her brain. This was obviously one of them.

"You can be damned sure the state lab's been out there already, put a laser on the bullet entry, traced the trajectory. We'll know exactly where the shot came from, the probable height of the shooter. They'll have roped the scene for any other evidence, cast footprints, if any. Canvassed the neighborhood for witnesses."

"Yes sir, I read you," Sam backpedaled. "Look, I'm a jerk—"

He shook his head. "No, no, you're not. You've had a long bad day—well, we both have. First the McDonald's, now this. There's lots of gunplay with the youth gangs up in the projects, but among the general population, a doubleheader's rare. It gives a man pause."

Sam was still explaining. "It's hard to lose the habit of being professionally nosy." She knew the natural antipathy most cops have for the working press, rating them somewhere below necrophiliacs and child molesters, but fessed up anyway. "Until recently I was a reporter with the Atlanta *Constitution.*"

"How recently?"

"A few months ago. I'm on leave, probably not going back. I've been doing free-lance magazine work."

"What kind?"

Sam laughed. "What's it to you?"

"Try me."

"Crazy stuff. Men who wear their wives' clothes. Faith healing. Trainers for beauty pageants. Tractor pulls. I'm collecting them for a book I'm calling *American Weird.*"

"A book?" Ollie's voice perked up. "Do you have an agent? Listen, could we talk?"

It was then that Sam realized she'd missed her guess on what it was Ollie Priest wanted to be when he grew up.

Mary Ann had had about all the excitement she could handle for one day. "Dewey, you like to have scared me to death! How'd you get in here, anyway?" She was staring at the thermostat. Fifty-five, it read. No wonder she was so cold. She flipped it up twenty-five degrees.

"Man drives a truck has to be handy," Dewey was saying by way of explanation. "Ain't no Triple A comes to help you out, you and forty-one tons stranded on the road. I wanted to tell you something."

"So you just let yourself in? Haven't you ever heard of knocking? Or using the phone?"

"Well, that'd be kind of hard, wouldn't it? Since the last time I saw you, you were a blonde standing with your suitcase in the check-in at the Holiday Inn." Now that she was a brunette, she *was* a dead ringer for Priscilla, who in turn had been a carbon copy of the girl Elvis had fallen in love with his eighteenth summer when he was driving that Crown Electric truck, right before he became famous. The very thought made Dewey weak in the knees, except Lookahere, what was this woman trying to pull?

Mary Ann knew he had her dead to rights. The minute she'd heard his truck pull out, she'd registered at the Holiday Inn as Georgia Thompson, which was her mother's maiden name, headed for her room, then called the rental car folks at the GMC-Cadillac dealership to come pick her up, Mrs. Velma Hightower, Room 1301.

Not wanting Dewey able to say who or where Mary Ann McClanahan was if she found herself between a rock and a hard place. And she didn't want the Holiday Inn people to know either name, if push came to shove.

Anyway, Velma Hightower was the name on the fat brunette's driver's license in the wallet she'd lifted out of her purse back at the S-farm ladies' room. Which was pretty fast thinking on her part, if she did say so herself.

Actually, she'd been thinking, right before Dewey blew her off the road, that she ought not to use her own car or her own name for running around once she was in Tupelo. Especially since she hadn't known how long it would take her to find Miss Dixie and do what she had to do to get her money.

For one thing, she hadn't known how big Tupelo was. Looking at it on the map it was in big and little red letters. The dumb legend didn't explain about population, but she could figure out Tupelo was smaller than Mobile, which was in good-sized red capital letters, but bigger than Fairhope, which was in real little upper and lower red. The point was, she didn't want to be standing out in a tiny little town like a sore thumb.

Anyway, while she was waiting for the rent-a-car people, she took a shower and dyed her hair back to its natural dark brown. So it'd match Velma's. But she'd have done it anyway.

Yes indeedy, she'd been thinking ahead in more ways than one. She'd stopped back in Montgomery at a drugstore—one of those big chains where they wouldn't remember her, clerks in those places were about nineteen and either studying their boyfriends or half-high on crack cocaine—and bought herself some Miss Clairol Smoky Brunette and a wig the same blond as she'd been for the past twenty years, it couldn't hurt. Next she'd stepped next door to one of those stores where they sold ugly clothes for women who had given up or never had any hope in the first place and bought herself a loose red plaid dress like a nightgown, a big beige sweater with a popcorn knit, some white socks, and some Keds with no rhinestones.

But when it got right down to it, she thought the hair was enough. So she put on a clean pair of Calvins and a white shirt, her cowboy boots, and then after the car people came and picked her up and she'd signed the papers as Velma Hightower, she drove back and registered as Velma at the Ramada Inn, right across from the Holiday. So then nobody in Tupelo knew who she was or where she was or even exactly what any of those women looked like.

Now she took a closer look at Dewey, who seemed to be done up in a disguise himself. He was head-to-toe in a leather outfit. Actually, he looked a heck of a lot like Elvis in his black leather jacket and pants, the spit and image, unless she was mistaken, of the outfit He'd worn in the '68 Comeback Special on TV. The one where He was on this little stage that was like a boxing ring lighted from beneath. Sitting around the edges had been these women with great big hair and tons of mascara, and you could tell they were about to *die* from the experience. One woman completely lost it, cried her eyes out when He sang "Are You Lonesome Tonight?"

Which, now that Mary Ann thought about it, was the same thing Dewey had tattooed on his left arm, under that black leather jacket. And it dawned on her what he might be up to. Among other things. You could not trust a man who would track you down and break into your room.

"So," she said, "are they holding some kind of Elvis imitators contest, part of these Tupelo Days I see these banners for up and down Main Street?"

"I reckon as how that might be."

"You didn't tell me you were one of them." She took a closer look. She'd be John Browned if Dewey hadn't bought himself some Miss Clairol too. She said that to him.

"L'Oréal Excellence Blue Black. That's what Elvis always used."

"Is there some kind of imitators' Bible y'all follow? Make sure you get it right?"

She knew she was being snotty, but she was nervous, never having forgotten that story about Connie Francis in that motel room, those awful things happened to her. And who *was* this guy?

"Who's *y'all?*" Dewey asked, trying to look at her from up under his lashes the way Elvis did, but he wasn't even close.

"You Elvis imitators."

"I never said I was one. I said I might be thinking about it. Try it out once, for the experience."

"Dewey." She put her hands on her hips. "Don't play games with me. You're getting on my nerves."

"I don't know who you think's playing games. You're the one's gone and dyed your hair, changed your name, and moved across the street to the Ramada. A fellow could think you were avoiding him."

Mary Ann didn't miss a beat. "Well, I most certainly did register at the Holiday, but then I went and saw that room, and I tell you, I wouldn't have asked a hog to stay in it.''

"You don't say?" Dewey leaned back in his chair, make that *her* chair.

"How did you find me, anyway?" He gave her a big grin. She didn't like his attitude, not one bit. And wasn't that part of the point of this whole thing, her new outlook, not having to put up with men's attitudes? "So I went back down to the desk and said, Excuse me, I cannot stay in this pigpen, could I have my money back? And then I came over here.''

"And dyed your hair. Used a different name.''

"You know, Dewey, just because we had us a little fun back at that truck stop does not allow you to garnishee my personal life.''

"Oh, yeah?" He slouched down a little further in her chair. "What you been up to this evening?''

"Visiting my girlfriend I came to see. Now, if you don't mind, I have some stuff I'd like to do. Maybe you could go to wherever it is that you're going.''

"I bet you'll change your tune, you hang around me long enough.''

"Why, what're you gonna do?" she sniffed. "Hold up a 7-Eleven? Bring me a box of Almond Joys?''

"Something lot bigger than that.''

"Well, why don't we let it be a surprise? I'll read about it in the papers.''

"You don't believe me, do you?''

"Believe what, Dewey? I don't even know what you're talking about. And I'd like to get on with my life here, if you don't mind.'' Mary Ann turned her back, started playing with her hair in the dresser mirror. She'd been bleaching it so long she'd forgotten what she looked like as a brunette.

Actually, she looked a lot like that woman Carlin had married, or at least the one Mary Ann thought was her, she'd seen out in the yard. Wasn't that funny? You'd think Carlin would try for a little variety. She always had.

"So, did you kill that woman that's trying to steal your life insurance? Or'd you scare her to death?" That was Dewey.

Mary Ann whirled. "What on earth are you talking about?"

"Well, I don't think you came all this way to sit down and shoot the breeze with her. Hoping she's gonna say, Oh, sure. Here, I don't want this money. Why don't you take it home with you?"

"That doesn't mean I'm going to kill her. I don't know where you get such ideas. You definitely ought not to go around saying things like that about people."

"Well, didn't you kill your husband?"

"I did not!"

"Couldn't prove it by me. I'd have to swear in a court of law, they asked me, that's what you said."

"I said I *sort* of killed him."

"You want to explain that, Mary Ann?"

"I most certainly do not."

Dewey stood. But she wasn't afraid. She still had her second husband's, the bad cop's, pearl-handled Colt in her purse. She snaked a hand over to it. If he touched her, she'd shoot him dead right through the purse, claim self-defense, after all, he did break into her room—

"Well, I think I'll take myself on down to the *po*-lice station, have a little chat with the boys, see what they think about that—" He half-stood, playing with her.

"Now, wait a minute, Dewey." They couldn't prove a thing, but it wouldn't exactly be good timing, if he was to do that, and the cops were to start asking questions. It'd be hard to explain what she was doing here, her hair dyed, Velma Hightower's driver's license in her wallet, along with those gold chains from that young real estate developer, the meat packer's cash and traveler's checks. This is what happened when you put yourself in a compromised position. She bet that Calvin girl on the motorcycle never did that. "Just wait," she said.

"Why don't you climb off your high horse, sit down, and tell old Dewey about it? Like I said in the truck, I'll show you mine, you show me yours."

Mary Ann narrowed her eyes and gave him a look like what she'd really like to do was throw up. But she sat down.

"Now, tell me, Mary Ann." He was staring straight into her eyes, using that soft voice again. Using that grin that would melt your heart, along with your resistance. It was like he worked some kind of spell, she swore. "Tell me about killing Carlin."

From his study Red Holcomb could still see policemen out tromping around in the yard when he settled in his favorite chair, lit another cigar and picked up the phone.

"I know what you been doing," he said when she picked up on the second ring.

"Who is this?"

Red laughed. His laugh was not a nice sound. "Come on, old woman. That stuff didn't work even back before the flood."

Alfreda Spoon said, "Red Holcomb, you don't know what you're talking about."

"We'll just see."

"I'm sorry, I have to go."

"Yeah, well, you do that. Go on back and sit back down at your dining room table and think about what you and Doc Ireland discussed. What old ladies can or can't do. Should or shouldn't. And with a younger man! Alfreda, I'm ashamed of you. You might also give some thought, while you're sitting there, at that dining room table, to selling that piece of property you own out by the airport."

Alfreda Spoon, despite the fact that she was a Southern lady, hung up.

And then Mary Ann was doing it. Was she hypnotized, she asked herself, or what? She watched the words come out of her mouth like those little balloons in comic strips. "I didn't *exactly* kill Carlin. Though I'd been planning to."

"Uh-huh."

"It took me weeks of begging to get him to go up to the Smokies."

"The man didn't like to travel."

"He said that's what he did for a living. Came home, he'd plop down in front of the TV. What about me? I said. He said, What about you?"

"Now that's no way to talk to a pretty lady."

Well! It was about time. Mary Ann smiled the little thank-you smile she used when people commented on her looks. Which plenty of them did when they hadn't even seen her naked.

"He never appreciated a thing I did. And he bossed me from get-go to get-down. He was one of those controllers, you know what I mean?"

"Wanted his way."

"Was the *only* way, according to him. No discussion. Just like with my first husband, he was the one said he knew when it was the safe time of the month, I should have known better, but unh-uh, I was young and hot and there I was found out I was pregnant on my senior trip to New York City." She could hear her mouth speeding along, but she couldn't seem to find the brake.

"It happens."

"I *loved* the Big Apple. I would have moved there in a New York second, you know how people say that, well, it means that place *boogies*. Things are fast there." She snapped her fingers. "And I like fast. You ever been down in Fairhope, Alabama, where I've been living?"

"Been everywhere, driving. But I'm seriously thinking of giving it up. Taking up my trade."

"Well, Fairhope's a really pretty little town, just east of Mobile, overlooking the bay. But I want to tell you, pretty ain't everything. Fairhope is slow. As in dead." As in Carlin, which reminded her. "Carlin, I was telling you about his being a controller—I never knew that that was a whole category of people, with a name, until I saw a bunch of them on Sally Jessy Raphael. Do you watch her?"

"I don't have much time for TV. Are we sliding off the point here, Mary Ann?"

"Well, if you wanted to sell things to women you would, watch TV that is. That's all they talk about, that and the way their husbands do them, at my lingerie houseparties. Did I tell you that's what I do? Sell lingerie and aloe vera cosmetics at houseparties?"

"You mean like Tupperware? Except it's underwear?"

"Not *underwear,* Dewey. Real special things. Why, I've got gold lamé bustiers, cream chiffon bras and panties—"

"I've always been partial to white cotton my ownself."

"You're no fun, are you?"

"That ain't what you said back at the truck stop."

White cotton indeed. No wonder he hadn't said anything about her teddy. He still hadn't said he liked her body. Said she was pretty, but nothing about her body. Maybe he thought she was too old. Things moving south. Even men his age liked eighteen-year-old girls. It made her want to jump up and down on their tiny little brains.

"Anyway, I was saying, you're doing business with these women, you have to know about Sally Jessy, Geraldo, Phil. That Oprah. I don't care too much for Oprah. Nothing to do with color, my momma didn't bring me up that way, I just think that woman, for all her putting on how awful she feels about those people she drags up there and makes them spill their guts, is underneath it all, cold as ice."

"There are lots of people like that. Treat you like dirt."

He had the funniest look on his face—almost like he was going to cry. Well, she hoped he didn't mean her. She felt like she cared a lot about people. It's that most of them weren't worth the effort, when you got right down to it. Just looking out after Number One. Like Carlin.

"Anyway, Carlin, that's who I was telling you about, he knew everything. Knew the best way to drive to the Safeway, not that he'd ever gone shopping, you understand, but he knew the route I ought to take."

She looked at Dewey staring at her. She wasn't sure he could find his butt with both hands, much less the Safeway. Why was she telling him this? But there she went again, just like he'd put a spell on her.

"He would check up on me, too. Once I had a flat, going *my* way to the store instead of his, I thought he'd bust a gut. Carried on for days, then didn't speak for about two weeks even after he got home from his business trip. Only way I lived through Carlin, he was on the road about half the time. He was a district sales manager, all of Alabama and Mississippi, for a big drug company. He traveled constantly. Always did."

Then Dewey said in that blue velvet voice of his, "Did Carlin ever hit you?" The words floated.

"Oh, yes." Mary Ann's mouth was suddenly so tight you couldn't see the Fire and Ice. "He'd go on a tear, about once a month."

"So that's why you killed him?"

"Well, it's like I was saying. I'd planned to kill him because I couldn't make him leave, and he said if *I* did, well, have you ever seen one of those bumper stickers that says: IF YOU LOVE SOMETHING SET IT FREE, IF IT DOESN'T COME BACK TRACK IT DOWN AND KILL IT? That was pretty much Carlin's philosophy. I figured sooner or later it was him or me. So my plan was to take him up there in those mountains where we didn't know a soul. And then, after we'd been to the Elvis Hall of Fame, I—"

"Where?" Dewey said it so loud it made her jump.

"Oh, I guess you've been there too, seeing as how you're such an Elvis fan."

"I've been everywhere he ever went." Dewey's bottom lip quivered. "I'm serious as death about Elvis."

"Well, I am too. And so first I wanted to make sure I got to go to the Elvis Hall of Fame. I was dying for a copy of His grocery list, you know the things He insisted that the Memphis Mafia—"

"He didn't call them that."

"Oh. Anyway, the things that He wanted kept in Graceland at all times. Every day."

"Pepsi. Orange drinks. Brown 'n' Serve rolls. Canned biscuits." Dewey rattled them off like that.

Mary Ann was amazed. But she could do it too. "Hamburger buns. Lean ground meat. Pickles. Potatoes and onions."

"Fresh fruit. Sauerkraut. Wieners. Milk and half-and-half."

"Thin lean bacon. Mustard, peanut butter, fresh-squeezed orange juice."

"Banana pudding."

"Makings for meat loaf."

"Brownies."

"Ice cream."

"Vanilla *and* chocolate."

"Coconut."

"Fudge cookies."

"Spearmint, Doublemint, Juicy Fruit."

"Cigars."

"Cigarettes."

"Dristan."

"Super Anahist."

"Contac."

"Sucrets."

"Feen-A-Mint gum."

"Matches."

Mary Ann took a deep breath. "Well, you sure know your Elvis, all right. Do you think He was constipated, He didn't eat enough green vegetables? I'd have told Him that, if I'd ever had the chance. I tried to—hung around afterwards a couple of Vegas shows, I saw Him three times with my second husband, the cop, he could get tickets to anything—hoping they didn't mean it when they said Elvis has left the building."

"Elvis is the only thing that matters."

"Well, I wouldn't go that far."

"I would."

Red's cigar was half gone when he picked up the phone again and dialed the number of his neighbor next door. "You know, Dixie," he was already talking when she answered, "you read these doctors' notes, well, there's some right interesting stuff a man can pick up even if he's not in the doctoring business.

For example, I'm looking right here at these notes Doc made, second or third time you came into visit him after you found out you were in the family way, y'all chatting on about when that might have been, the ultrasound, genetics, and some amazing possibilities an old bachelor like me never even thought of, and I was wondering if you'd given any more thought to that offer I made you on your house—"

"Shove it, Red." Dixie slammed down the phone.

Mary Ann turned and stared at Dewey. His eyes were so hot she bet if she turned the lamp off they'd glow in the dark.

"That's what I'm doing here," he said, "in Tupelo. Taking care of business."

"Taking care of business," she repeated. TCB, it was Elvis's motto. His coat of arms. TCB with a lightning bolt. Taking care of business in a flash, that's what that meant. TCB it said on His eleven-and-a-half-carat diamond ring, on the tail of His jet *Lisa Marie,* named after His daughter. TCB on badges and pendants worn by the Memphis Mafia.

And Dewey. He opened his jacket one button so she could see. There they were, on a gold chain around his neck, the letters and the lightning bolt, flashing in solid gold.

"Wow!" Mary Ann was amazed. "Wow! Where'd you find that?"

"My brother gave it to me."

"God!"

"And now I'm going to take care of his business. It's the least I can do."

His? Oh, he meant his brother's business. Not Elvis's.

"Yeah? And how do you do that?"

"Shazam!" Dewey stood and ripped his leather

jacket all the way open. Under it he was wearing a blue T-shirt slashed with a gold lightning bolt.

Mary Ann couldn't help but laugh. "Who're you pretending to be? Batman?"

"Batman, shee-it. Shazam!"

"What do you mean?"

"I mean I have the power!" Dewey jumped up, *stood* on the bed. Some people would never get over being white trash. "Oh, my boy, my boy, my boy." Dewey was jumping up and down on the plaid bedspread saying the words over and over.

That was Elvis's refrain, He said the words a hundred times in that '68 Comeback Special, Mary Ann knew that for a fact. She must have watched that video a thousand times, had a copy of it with her in her duffel bag, played it when she was lonesome in the night.

"My boy, my boy, my boy." Then Dewey took a big shuddering deep breath and seemed to get ahold of himself. He leaped off the bed and grabbed her up, flung her around about a dozen times, then gave her a big juicy. "You're something special, Mary Ann," he said in a real sexy voice.

Mary Ann felt like she'd been nabbed by a tornado, spun dry, and dropped. "Wow!" she finally said. "That's something, all right."

And then Dewey turned the full force of his smile on her. It was like sunshine after the storm. He ought to do really okay in the imitators' competition, though Mary Ann thought he was too old for the black leather stuff. But who knew? Maybe if Elvis had lived He would have gone full circle, gotten over the gold lamé and glitter, which Mary Ann never much cared for, and returned to the Basic Elvis. The Man, The Moves, The Guitar, The Song.

"I'm filled with the power of the heavens." That was Dewey. His grin stretched wider, showing off his dimples. "And this is only the beginning." He raised his arms high and wide, his head down, chin tucked, your basic Elvis move. "By the time this weekend's over you're going to see magic!"

"Wow!" Mary Ann said, clapping her hands, swept up.

"You're going to see miracles!" Now he did one of those karate stances, one arm forward, one back, legs apart. "You're going to see lightning bolts streaking the sky!" That forward arm pumped. "You're going to see healing!" The arm rose to the ceiling. "It's going to be *amazing!*"

Mary Ann shook her head. Dewey Travis was one weird, totally insane, though real good-looking and not bad in the shower, truck driver/Elvis imitator. But this shazam stuff, he had to be kidding, right?

• • • • • • • • • • • • 12

The phone rang. Sam jumped up, out from under a handmade quilt, not sure at first who or where she was. In her nightmare, her loverman Sean had been flying up up up in the air. If she just kept watching, maybe he wouldn't come down again. Maybe he wouldn't die.

No, no, no. That wasn't right. Oh, Christ, it was Harry. He was shot. Dead.

"Harry? Harry!" she screamed into the phone, so she didn't hear someone pick up on an extension.

"Sam, it's Ollie Priest. Hey, I didn't mean to scare you."

She sank back, switched on the lamp. Okay. She was Sam Adams, soon-to-be-ex-reporter, sitting up in bed in an overdecorated room in a sharecropper's shack/guest cottage in Tupelo, Mississippi. Her BBQ boyfriend was slightly broken, but fine. Her once-lost but now-found Harpo, who *hated* being disturbed, was glaring at her from under his bangs.

"So what's up?" she said, trying to sound normal.

"I was wondering if y'all been taking any more fire over there."

Sam squinted at the clock. Almost midnight. The man woke her up, frightened her out of her wits to ask her that? "We're just hunky-dory," she said, then reached for the glass of water on the bedside table wishing it were a cigarette.

It used to be so nice to lie in bed late at night, smoke, and talk on the phone. Eat chocolate ice cream till she couldn't anymore. Smoking was out of the question, but maybe Harry was right about she didn't need to lose five pounds. And she never did have any supper. Maybe there was chocolate in her future.

Ollie was saying, "Right after the shot was fired into the kitchen all the lights in the house went off. Like there was some kind of electrical problem, right?"

"Right." What did this man want?

"Hey, did I wake you up?"

"No, no, I was lying here reading."

"Well, about this electrical thing, tomorrow some guys from the lab'll check out Red's wiring, see if they can find anything queered."

"Hey, great." Somehow she thought the gunshot was the main event, but she'd learned to humor cops. Especially male cops. She stared at Harry's bag across the room. Inside of which, unless she missed her guess, were their favorite chocolate bars, Lindt dark with hazelnut.

"Considering Lovie Rakestraw."

"Who?"

"Mrs. Will Rakestraw. A prominent local lawyer's wife. She didn't show up for a bridge party late this afternoon, early evening."

"Unh-huh." The man had lost his grip. And she was famished. She crawled out of bed holding the portable phone. Yep. Under Harry's blue denim shirt she felt a zipped plastic bag, his stash. "That's pretty suspicious, all right, not showing up for bridge. Did she have it in for Red, too?'' She took a little nip of the chocolate, then shuddered it was so good.

"We don't know about that. But a couple of hours ago the hostess for the bridge party the Rakestraw woman stood up, a woman named Gardener, went over to the Rakestraw house, Miz Rakestraw's car is in the drive, lights on somewhere in the back, nobody answering, she finally breaks in a window. At least this is her story. She stops in the kitchen to wash her hands—''

"A proper Southern lady.''

"You bet. Turns on the water and gets knocked up against the wall.''

Now this was more interesting. "The plumbing's live?''

"Yep, throughout the house. One of those big, I mean big, new houses built to look like they're old out on Parc Monceau West. Security service finds Miz Gardener still out cold.''

"And the lady of the house?''

"Miz Rakestraw's turned the help loose, her husband's off somewhere at a meeting, she was home alone, decided to take herself a nice long soak.''

"We're talking electricity here? Her whirlpool?''

"You don't give a man a chance, do you?''

"Well, hell, you were leading right up to it. Wasn't I supposed to guess? But I thought those things were wired so you couldn't fry yourself, assuming she's dead.''

"They are, and she is. I don't imagine it'll take the guys long to figure out how it was done.''

Now he had her full attention. "So who's your prime? The husband?''

"Sure, the spouse is always the first suspect. . . .''

"But then you have the spurned bridge hostess, this Gardener woman, and you're trying to make this electrical connection, as it were? Trying to put this Lovie and the shooting at Red's together? Why'd you want to do that?"

Ollie laughed. "You're implying I'm trying to make it easy on myself, look for one guy? Look, I know I woke you up."

"Or woman. Ms. Gardener seem like the type who could jiggle the wiring, then make it look like she shocked herself on purpose?"

"Hardly. Though they're pressing her pretty hard. I want to make sure I've got this straight, you're saying I'm slacking here. Or nuts."

"Ollie, I don't know you well enough to say a thing like that. But keep in mind, you called me for this little chat."

"Yeah," he laughed again. "Next thing you know, I'll be what-ifing it all on Walter, Jr."

"Why not? You've got him dead to rights on the McDonald's thing. Few hours later somebody takes a potshot at Red. Is the kid out on bail, he could do it?"

"Scooted right home. *Could* have loaded up, hightailed it back over to Red's with the real McCoy, lobbed one through the kitchen window."

"So?"

"Not a chance. We've already been over there. Wally, Sr., and Maxine Barnes swear the kid's under house arrest, locked in his room till he turns twenty-one. We looked, he was down for the count. When Harry whirled him around, he was banged up enough they ran him by the ER before they booked him and docs slipped him a few painkillers. We'll ask their neighbors and around over by you tomorrow, first thing, see if anybody saw the kid out and about, but I don't think so. Plus, they pretty much put the fear of God in him down at the jail, gave him a little tour of his potential roommates, with a four-hundred-pounder making kissy noises at him, the kid almost wet his pants.''

"That'll usually do it for the amateurs. So let's take Wally, Jr., out of the game. But when this Rakestraw woman turns up dead, electrocuted, you remember about the lights going out over here. I'd say coincidence, Ollie. The *shooting* was the deal, don't you think?''

"Who knows, you're dealing with crazy people?''

"You think this is a nut, maybe two, running around loose?''

"Hell, I don't know. It is a full moon. Plus people starting with spring fever, sap rising, couple days after April Fool's.''

"You pay attention to that stuff?''

"Why not? Our clientele, the killers and crazy people, do. Plus, I'm not thrilled with a major crime wave, all these folks in town for Tupelo Days.''

"You worried about your fair city's image? Or you mean you think it's one of the barbecuers gone mad? Or how about the Elvis impersonators? Harry said there were a bunch of them around, too. Then there's your musicians come to play, the crowds here to see the whole thing, take drunk . . .''

"You trying to make me feel worse?''

"Actually, what I'm trying to figure is why you're calling me, I'm not a cop, in the middle of the night to tell me all this. To try out what-ifs. Not that I mind, you understand, I'm not doing anything real important—''

"Well, what I was wondering was, do you see this as a true-crime book, depending on how it turns out, of course, or—you know, except for Walter Mosley, there's not really anybody writing with a black private eye. Or, do you think I ought to do it heads up, black cop, police procedural?''

• • • • • • • • • • • • 13

S am went back to sleep and dreamed that Elvis was a spokesman on TV for General Electric, opening and closing a refrigerator over and over like Ronald Reagan used to do in GE commercials before they let him play like he was the President and run the country off into a ditch. Stuffed inside the fridge was a man who looked a lot like a pig, or Ed Meese. Take your pick.

Actually, Meese would have done a lot better as a pig than as attorney general. "Of course you would have had to knock him in the head a couple of times a day to pull him away from the trough," she said to Harpo, curled up against her bottom, giving her a dirty look. Harpo considered morning a personal insult. "I know, I know, you don't care about politics. What you want is for me to rise and shine, ankle over to that kitchen and rustle you up some doggie breakfast pâté." She would do that very thing, that is if the cops hadn't declared the kitchen off-limits.

Before somebody'd shot up the place last night, she'd been thinking about saying to Harry they ought pack up and move out to the Ramada or the Holiday

Inn, seeing as how their host was such an oink. But now that Red's house was looking like Action Central, maybe they'd stay put.

She pulled up the shade, and sure enough, there in the yard was a whole clutch of men standing just outside a yellow crime scene ribbon. Men in plainclothes, men in blue uniforms, then a bunch in tan, all of them jawing and pointing and hitching up their drawers. It looked like the TPD and the sheriff's department had both sent their teams. She wondered if they'd tossed for the kickoff.

Poking around started early here in Mississippi, seven-thirty. Too early to call Harry? She did it anyway.

"Sammy? Hey, sweetie pie. Listen, today's ribs, tomorrow's shoulder and the whole hog." Harry was already mid-sentence when he picked up the phone. "Shoulder could go ten, twenty hours, but we can talk about that later."

"This is your way of telling me you're feeling fine, right?"

"The first thing you need to do, you'd better take notes, is take those ribs out of the ice I packed them in. Rinse 'em off and let the meat to room temp. Then rub them all over lightly with the mustard. Mix half-and-half Dijon and Zatarain's Creole."

"Have you lost your mind?"

"Wait now. We have a long way to go." Then he paused. "You don't think anybody's listening in on this line, do you?"

"They've bugged the phone to steal your rib recipe? Call the nurse, son. You're running on your rims."

"Never underestimate the lengths Q freaks will go to, Sammy."

"Well, I can tell you that *I* for one am going to no lengths. You're fishing with a rotten line and an empty hook if you think I am."

"Ain't doing links, hon. I have no respect for them what barbecue sausage."

"Don't make wise with me. I'm having breakfast in the middle of an attempted murder investigation."

"Whose?"

"Yours. Mine. Red's."

"Sammy, don't be silly. I'm right as rain, come pick me up at nine, we'll drive over to the fair-grounds. I can't lift anything with this broken wing, but we'll work it out, and I need you to start now. So, are you taking notes? After the mustard, coarse-grind some fresh pepper—I brought tellicherry—over the slabs, both sides, then dust 'em with a lot of that Hungarian paprika."

"*And* an honest-to-God murder."

"Then the slabs go back in the pans, cover them with plastic wrap. The hard part's hauling them out to the fairgrounds, building your fire so it'll go low and slow. But once you come pick me up, we can do that together." Harry paused. "You know, I bet I can find somebody to help us. Don't know why I didn't think of this before. Be a lot more fun too. I'm gonna call him as soon as we hang up."

"I said murder, Harry. Somebody died."

"Somebody else had his collarbone crunched and his arm broken and *died?* Was he a Q-er?"

"Harry, I'm serious."

"Listen, babe, me too. Really, I need those ribs to start warming up."

"She was *electrocuted,* Harry. Lovie Rakestraw, a lawyer's wife, electrocuted in her own bathtub."

"Wow! That's *lots* worse than having her Elvis T-shirt cut off her, I'll tell you."

Mary Ann had had snake nightmares, one after the other. Crawling snakes, hissing snakes, leaping snakes, rolling snakes, kissing snakes, snakes flying across the room.

She woke up screaming, afraid to reach out and turn on the lamp, afraid there might be snakes on her bedside table, too.

She lay there, her teeth chattering for a good long while, then she gave herself a little lecture. Girl, she said, you have not come this far to spend your whole adventure screaming and fainting, fainting and screaming. Now shape up, get your act together, and make a plan of attack on that Dixie McClanahan. *Or* climb in that rental car, drive back to Fairhope, and spend the rest of your days selling aloe vera and underwear to fat women.

With that, Mary Ann snuggled down and was drifting off for a little last snooze when she reached out, felt Dewey, thought *he* was a snake, and screamed, which brought him up out of the bed swinging. He connected with Mary Ann's left eye, just like Carlin used to do. Which is who, in the confusion, Mary Ann thought he was.

"Carlin, you son of a bitch," she yelled, "you ever touch me again, I swear I'm going to kill you."

"You already did, woman," growled Dewey.

Was she sleeping with a dead man? Then Mary Ann remembered who he was and switched on the lamp. She sat up, wondering why the heck it was she couldn't seem to keep these men out of her bed and get on with her life as a single girl desperado, when she caught a glimpse of herself in the dresser mirror and screamed again.

She'd forgotten she was a brunette, thought there was a strange woman in her room. Well, if that's what Southern Comfort chased with peanuts and Co-cola mixed together in the bottle would do to you, she was giving up the Co-cola.

Then once she'd grabbed ahold of herself, what the

heck, he was *there,* she'd grabbed ahold of Dewey too for a nice sweet spell. Afterwards, she lay there thinking. If this woman Dixie was the kind who stomped out in her yard with a gun, blew the bejesus out of her neighbor, maybe killed his dogs, Mary Ann wasn't sure what all had gone on, maybe she ought to consider revising her game plan. Not that she'd ever had much of one anyway other than going and saying: Look here, woman, I don't intend to take the giving up of this insurance money lying down. Maybe she ought to take advantage of the muscle that was right at hand. Crazy muscle, that didn't give a hoot.

She reached over and ran one finger down Dewey's thigh.

He twitched. "Unh-uh."

"Dewey?"

"Leave me alone. It's hard for me to fall back asleep."

Now he was claiming insomnia, which Elvis suffered from too. Next it would be sleepwalking. Would the man go to any lengths to imitate the King?

"Dewey?"

He rolled over, smashed his face deep down in the pillow. "Whunt?"

"You know that woman I told you Carlin was married to? I went to see her, and she's gonna be a lot tougher than I thought."

"Unh-huh." At least he'd rolled back over and was face up, but she wasn't sure if he was really listening to her. Of course, with Dewey, she wasn't sure how'd you'd ever know, his being lost in the World of Shazam half the time.

"So, you know what?" She traced a finger upwards from his thigh. It was only a minute before he started to show some interest. Wasn't it funny, she hadn't ever been with a country boy who still had his original wrapper before. But what was it they said about variety? It wasn't bad, just different. *And,* that was another thing he had in common with the King. Now that was kind of spooky. Once she had his attention, she said, "I was thinking maybe you could give me a little help."

"Like what?"

"I haven't figured that out exactly yet. But I have a few ideas. Sit up a minute. Let me run 'em by you."

Unh-huh, unh-huh, unh-huh, that sounds good, and my cut's half? He said he'd think about it. Then after a while he said, "You know, I forgot to tell you who I saw yesterday, after I rode back into town."

Somebody had taped a big sheet of plastic over the shattered kitchen window, and there was an orange circle drawn on one cabinet door where it looked like they'd dug out a bullet, but other than that, it was just another Friday morning chez Holcomb.

When Sam walked in the kitchen door, a short black man, sixtyish, wearing black pants and a white shirt, said in a rich rumbling bass, Morning, I'm Buddy, how you want your eggs, sugar? Red was sitting at the breakfast room table reading the paper. Morning, Sam, he said. I talked to the hospital, understand Harry's fine, they're springing him this morning. Sit down and have some coffee. Not a word about the shooting, the investigators keeping him up asking questions, stomping around half the night.

Well, Mr. Greedy Gut Misogynist Cool, she thought, I can just sit and drink my coffee too. She sat down and poured herself a cup, then things began to pick up almost immediately.

"Sonny, I'll tell you what." The little old lady was running her mouth as she stepped smartly into the room. "You good for nothing dirt-dauber, you almost stepped on me climbing out of bed this morning. You trying to kill me again? Why don't you go on and shoot me? Better'n trying to crush me to death."

Red peered over the tops of his reading glasses. "Now, Momma. You're gonna give Miss Adams here the wrong impression."

Sam couldn't take her eyes off the tiny old woman in the dark blue boy's lightweight three-piece wool suit complete with a pin-striped shirt with a wide white collar, a red silk bow tie, tiny black spectator lace-ups—and false eyelashes. She looked like Charlie McCarthy with a touch of Marlene Dietrich.

"Don't know how anybody could do that. Don't know what wrong impression there could be of the meanest man in Mississippi. Second only to his daddy Arvis, who's dead, praise the Lord, and I pity the Devil who has to be real sorry he took that sucker in." Then the little old lady, whose snowy hair was twisted up in a perfect imitation of a cowpat on top of her head, plopped down in a chair next to Sam, reached over and grabbed herself the largest of the biscuits, poked a hole in it, pushed about a quarter of a stick of butter in the hole followed by a half-cup of sorghum syrup, and dispatched the entire business, along with a cup of hot black coffee, in about thirty seconds. "Now then." She turned and gave Sam a grin. "I feel like I'm going to live another day. May make seventy-six after all." Then she gave Sam's hand a rock-firm shake. "I'm Estella Holcomb who spawned that good-for-nothing egg-sucker, I call him Sonny, sitting at the end of the table. I'm pleased to make your acquaintance, I'm sure."

Sam's own grin went wide. "Samantha, call me Sam, Adams. I'm certainly pleased to meet you, ma'am. Could I pour you some more coffee?" It was news to her that Red had a mother, much less that she was living in the same house.

"Thank you. Thank you kindly," Estella said

sweetly. Then she turned her head and screamed, "Sonny! I'm speaking to you."

Red didn't even lower the paper. "Yes, Mother?"

"What are those po-licemen doing out in the yard? They the law come to lock you up, something else you stole from the citizenry? And why'd the power company come and turn the power off last night, I was trying to read my new *People* magazine, see what kind of devilment the world's up to this week? Was that 'cause you offended the power folks, too? They made one hell of a lot of noise tromping around in the yard. Heard 'em stomping around in the house, too, knocked on my door, I didn't answer 'em. Too late to be talking to strange men."

"Mother, you're not making a very good impression on our houseguest here."

Oh, yes, she was. Sam thought Estella Holcomb, the septuagenarian cross-dresser, was a pip and a half.

Then she asked Estella what she meant, Red was trying to crush her to death? As if Red weren't sitting there.

"I sleep on the floor, right beside his bed."

"Now, Momma." Red was gritting his teeth.

It was interesting, Sam thought. Your mother got on your nerves, it didn't matter how old you were, you sounded about thirteen. She said to Estella, "Isn't that uncomfortable?"

"It's pitiful, that's what it is," said Estella, lighting up an unfiltered Camel.

"Estella, you gonna want some eggs 'fore you start stinking up the room with that smoke?" That was Buddy from the kitchen.

"Thank you very kindly, Buddy, I do not. But I will take my tot, get myself kick-started."

Sam watched as Buddy cruised into the room with a snifter of cognac on a silver tray. "Princess, I was only waiting for the word." Then he winked at Sam and waltzed back out through the swinging door.

"Why do you sleep on the floor, Miss Estella?" She also wanted to ask her why she dressed like a man, but that seemed a little rude.

Red rattled his paper, but didn't say anything.

"In case Sonny needs anything in the night."

Well, nobody ever said family matters were simple, did they? Especially Southern families, which tended toward the baroque Monday through Friday. Saturday nights and holidays, Katy bar the door.

"It's the duty of a Christian mother, see that her chil'ren have everything they need. *Especially* when they're in danger of eternal hellfire." Estella waved a tiny forefinger in Red's direction.

"Momma, *please.*"

"You know how it says in the Bible, Matthew nineteen-twenty-four, It is easier for a camel to go through the eye of a needle, than for a rich man to enter into the kingdom of God. Well, Sonny, here, is one big fat camel. Going to spend eternity in the desert of desolation, crying for the water of salvation. Just like his daddy Arvis before him. Can't get enough of the earth's goods. Greedy. That's what his daddy taught him, to be a greedy gut."

Sam wondered about Estella's religious affiliation, Bible Belters not usually holding with transvestism or cognac and Camels in the morning. Didn't hold with lots of other things, either, did they, but that hadn't stood in the way of the likes of Reverend Swaggart or Reverend Bakker. Like most people, they lived with the parts they could—let the Devil take the hindmost.

"My ownself, I've winnowed my personal possessions down to one hundred and twenty. One hundred's my goal," said Estella. "I'm trying hard, but clothes are my weakness."

"Why don't you get shut of Buddy?" said Red. "That'd help do the trick."

"Buddy is not a personal possession, Sonny. Now you know that."

"Way he drags around after you, I thought you bought him at an auction."

"No, Sonny, that's the kind of thing *you* do." Then she turned to Sam. "He's been jealous of Buddy ever since he came to help me out after Arvis died. Then Buddy and I moved over here five years ago, when my house burned down. I think Sonny torched it for the in-surance."

"Mother!" Red threw down the paper. "Now that's enough. Let's let Sam here get on with her morning. We've all things to do."

"Actually," said Sam, thoroughly enjoying Red's discomfort, "I was thinking of having another cup of coffee before I go over and spring Harry."

"Who's Harry?" asked Estella.

"He's my boyfriend," said Sam while reading the paper on the table upside down. The story about Lovie Rakestraw's death had made banner headlines. PROMINENT TUPELO WOMAN ELECTROCUTED. Mrs. Will Rakestraw, Attorney's Wife, Meets Grisly Death, read the deck. She'd hate to make the papers that way, not the electrocution part, though that wouldn't be her number one choice of ways to die, but as somebody's wife. Like she didn't have a name or a life of her own.

Estella said, "Your boyfriend, huh? Is he still asleep?"

"No. He's in the hospital," said Sam, ready for Estella's next question, but the old lady was reading the headline too.

"Does that say grizzly? Did a bear eat up poor Lovie Rakestraw? And just when she told me she's going to invite me to her big shindig. I was fixing to dig out my old tux for it. She invite you, Sonny? I bet she didn't.''

Red didn't answer.

Sam said, "It's my understanding that she was electrocuted in her whirlpool."

"You mean one of those things makes the water in the bathtub go around?" The little old lady leaned back in her chair and laughed so long and hard Sam was afraid she was going to stroke out. Then Estella started patting herself on the back. "I'm sorry," she said. "That's not funny, is it? I always liked Lovie. Even though she did put on airs."

"I heard it on the radio this morning," Sam said.

"Huh," said Red, shifting his weight around in his chair. "It doesn't say that in the paper. It says electrocuted but it doesn't say how."

Sam gave him her Mona Lisa smile. Let him figure it out, he was so smart.

Estella said, "They probably didn't say because those whirlpool people'd jump all over 'em like fleas on a pup. Which reminds me, Sonny, have you taken a close look at those animals of yours this morning?"

"Nope." Red lit up his cigar. "Buddy fed 'em, didn't he? Unless he's got so finicky he couldn't manage that. You trying to tell me my dogs out there starved to death?"

"No," Estella said brightly. "Just thought you might want to see about 'em later."

"Anyway," Sam said, about to choke on Red's cigar smoke. "I'd better go on over to the hospital. Unless"—she turned to Red with a tight little smile—"you find we're in your way here. What with the commotion, I mean, it might be easier if we moved into a hotel."

"Oh, please, don't." Estella grabbed her arm. "He'll say it was my fault. I'll never hear the end of it. He'll beat me with a stick. Please stay. Pretty please with sugar on top."

"Now, Momma. Don't be so silly. Sam, I wouldn't hear of such a thing."

"Good." Sam stood and threw her napkin on the table. "Now, Miss Estella, do you think it would be all right if I asked Buddy to help me bring those coolers in from the car?"

Next door, Lucille took her coffee cup and Dixie's and tossed them in the sink. Hard.

"Lucille, what in the hell is wrong with you? You get up on the wrong side of the bed?" Dixie was sitting at the kitchen table, or as near it as her belly would allow.

"I did not."

"Then why does it sound like the Battle for Atlanta in here?"

"Maybe I'm trying to awake your conscience, must still be piled up in the bed."

"My conscience is the property of the First Presbyterians."

Lucille hooted.

"I swear, it's trying to be held up for judgment day after day."

"That's what you better pray for—a sympathetic judge—help you out of your situation."

Dixie stood, placed her arms akimbo on her hips, but that didn't make her back feel any better. "I don't know what you're talking about, Lucille. When these babies are on the outside of me, that'll be all the situational assistance I need, thank you kindly. I can't wait to feel like a normal human being again, instead of a Trailways bus."

"*That* is not the situation I'm talking about."

"If you don't go ahead and say what's on your mind, I'm going to stab you with this fork." Dixie was holding the piece of her grandmother's silver she'd extracted from a slice of French toast.

"See? That's exactly the kind of thing I'm talking about. Woman eight months gone, behaving like a criminal." She wanted to add, And not mourning her dead husband a lick, which is not only embarrassing, but awfully suspicious. But she didn't.

Dixie rested her back against the wall with her knees slightly spread. "Is it your opinion, Lucille, that pregnant women are supposed to behave with some kind of extra-special morality? All the books I read said that this is the one time it's okay if I go ahead and be crazy. So that's what I do. I go over to the club and have dessert first, before my dinner. You know, around Tupelo that's the height of eccentricity."

"So that's why you threatening me with a fork? You blaming it on chocolate cake? Blaming it on sugar?"

"Lucille, I think this conversation has become too convoluted. Could we back up?"

"Plain and simple, I think you ought to be ashamed of yourself, traipsing around the yard *shooting* at people, then lying about it."

"Well, I'll tell you what. If I had shot somebody, I sure as hell wouldn't be yapping to the cops about it. What would be the point? But I didn't shoot anybody."

Harumph, Lucille snorted.

"Okay, tell me when I did that."

"Last night. You went right over there and shot out Red Holcomb's window."

"Now you were here, you heard me tell that policeman who dragged me out of bed this morning that I was out in the yard with a rifle, but I didn't shoot not one single solitary thing. Exactly the same thing I told them last night, they were out there till all hours tromping around, bright lights, doing God knows what. I told 'em twice, last night and again this morning: I went out there, exactly like I said I was going to do, was in the process of dyeing those little yappers, when somebody blasted the bejesus out of Red's kitchen window. I came back in, you'd skedaddled. You know, I forgot to tell them that. They ought to come back and talk with *you*."

Lucille glared at her. "It's going to be a shame. Brand new babies, no poppa, momma in jail. Guess we'll have to find a wet nurse for 'em, like back in the old days."

"Lucille, I gave the policeman the rifle so he could look at it. The thing hasn't been fired since last fall when Carlin went hunting."

"And then you told him you didn't see anybody last night either."

"Well, I didn't." But Dixie's gaze took a hike.

"Look me in the eye and tell me that, girl."

"Who do you think I saw, Lucille?"

Now it was Lucille's turn to stare at the black-and-white tile. She wasn't going to tell Dixie that she saw her chatting with Estella Holcomb. Unh-uh. She'd thought about it last night and had come up with some possibilities for that chat that made her real uncomfortable. Nope. She wanted Dixie to know she knew *something* was up, but now that she'd stepped this far into it, she was looking for the exit sign.

"I thought I saw you talking with somebody."

"What did he look like?"

Trying to trick her, that's what Dixie was doing, this *he* business. Estella may have started dressing like one at her husband's funeral, but underneath there, well, they *thought* she was still a woman anyway. She hadn't been off on one of those extended vacations that people take when they undergo a personal beautification project. "The person was not a man and you know it," Lucille said.

Just then, the front doorbell rang. Lucille and Dixie stood staring at one another.

"Well, I guess I'll go answer that," Dixie finally said.

"Sit down and shut up. All this lying's bound to hurt those babies. They need to rest."

"You know, Lucille, you've come to be a crotchety old church lady. Judgmental as the day is long. You think I don't know the fast life you used to lead, what you told me? You burning up the roads looking for the perfect pulled meat sandwich—and the perfect man? As if there was such a thing." Dixie lowered her voice on that last line, did it gravelly, the way Nina Simone sang "Mississippi Goddam."

Lucille waved her hand behind her, swatting Dixie's words away as she opened the front door.

There stood another white woman, dark brown hair, big brown eyes, about the same size as Dixie when she wasn't blown up. Wearing a navy blue spring suit, white blouse, red pumps, the whole outfit looked to Lucille like she must have borrowed it from some other woman who didn't wear semi-big hair and so much makeup.

"Hi!" the woman said, just as perky as if she didn't have a black eye. The right one—which she'd tried to camouflage, but Lucille knew the signs of a woman being on the losing end of a right hook. Then the woman stuck out her hand like Yankees do. Lucille stared at it.

She knew this was going to be a bad day from the get-go. All night she'd dreamed about her poor dead momma, bless her heart, two of her three ex-husbands, women giving birth to dead babies, flying snakes, Slaughter in jail, lightning zagging through the sky, the head of one of those ex-husbands rolling down the street like a bowling ball. It had been like going to one of those malls that had eight movie theaters, sneaking from one to the other on one ticket. Behind it all a soundtrack of Elvis singing "Love Me Tender."

Now the woman in the suit was talking. "How do you do?" She handed Lucille the rolled-up morning paper, which Lucille and Dixie always read together over their second cup of coffee, swapping sections and hooting about the good parts. Then they did the crossword puzzle. Next they'd open Lucille's mail orders, people begging for Lucille to send them, among other things, little plaid swatches of cotton material for $19.95 sworn and bona fide to be cut from an Elvis baby quilt. Which they actually were, Lucille not being a crook, but those fools had no way of knowing that. "I'm Velma Hightower and I wonder if Mrs. McClanahan is home?"

"No, she is not. She's out and won't be back till late afternoon." Lucille started to shut the door. Whatever it was this woman was selling, that little suitcase in her hand, they didn't need any. They had more than enough of everything right here, including whatever it was happened last night that she intended to get to the bottom of before Dixie went and had those babies, they'd be so busy she'd never find out.

"Lucille?" Dixie called in her ladies' luncheon voice that made Lucille want to wring her neck. "Who is that?"

On second thought, maybe Lucille'd shoot her.

Overnight the fairgrounds had been transformed into Camp Cookoff. As far as Sam could see, bright flags and banners fluttered through billowing smoke. All hundred-odd plots had been spoken for by large hairy men wearing T-shirts proclaiming them to be Swine Swizzlers, Pork-a-Dots, Q-Man-Chews. They huddled around fireboxes fueling their flames with mostly hickory or oak, some mesquite, and themselves with a river of beer and precontest barbecued shrimp, ham, ribs, brisket, sausage, and bologna. The talk was rowdy. "My wife won more trophies than that changing diapers," offered one man, about the size of Paul Bunyan's ox Babe, to another who had been standing tall before his display of barbecue trophies, each topped with a small hog. The latter said, "Yeah, well, you come on over and throw a lip on these ribs, see who ought to be chunking rocks."

"I thought you said the rigs here were simple," Sam said to Cooter Williams, the man who'd offered them the right hand of barbecue fellowship the afternoon before and had come to offer it again. Sam was pointing at a 1965 Studebaker with its windshield removed and grilling racks where its front seats once stood. Its chimney was above the dash, and beneath the hood a pile of coals smoldered.

"Well, I didn't say some old boys aren't carried away in the spirit of the moment." Cooter was wearing a red-and-white checked apron that would have been fine on a table for four. "But mostly, it's home-folks doing the best they can. Speaking of which, Harry Zack"—he stood back and looked at Harry's cast—"what the hell happened to you? And more important, what does the other feller look like?"

"Like a corner cabinet and a countertop of yellow Formica." Harry grinned.

Anything was possible in the fields of Q. "You gonna be able to smoke?"

"Well, that's what we brought Sam's new friend Buddy along for. I called somebody else I know, he wasn't home, but now I think Buddy's my main man. Says he might throw some additions into my sauce he learned from a Mongolian general, died in his arms in the very last campaign of the European theater. Man had walked across the Alps with the recipe tattooed in code over his heart."

"The Big War." Cooter was serious.

"Yep," Harry nodded. "And my sauce was already within four-and-a-half molecules of being the most perfect sauce anybody ever gave mouth to."

Sam snorted, but nobody paid her any attention. And nobody heard her when she said that today the fairground reminded her of a cross between a football locker-room and the first circle of hell, if they let you have Budweiser in hell.

"Where is this Buddy you're bragging about?" Cooter asked.

"Oh, he'll be here any minute," said Harry. "I think the man likes to make an entrance."

And indeed the man did, as he came rolling up over

the grass to the back of Harry's smoker in a black 1932 Oldsmobile hearse. Then Buddy Kidd pulled the brake and stepped out, his small dark frame, which Sam had seen only in his breakfast-time garb of white shirt and black pants, covered in zoot-suit glory.

Buddy's high-waisted baggy pants of beige gabardine were nipped in tight above his black-and-white spectator lace-ups and sheer black socks complete with clocks. The matching jacket was long, wide-shouldered, and draped. His shirt was black. His tie, wide and elaborately knotted, black, beige, and white. He had a pocket handkerchief to match. His felt fedora, a slightly darker tan than the suit, sported a black band and brilliant plumage.

Harry and Cooter gawked. Sam whistled between two fingers. Buddy turned full-circle, then saluted smartly. "I trust you approve of my smoking apparel."

"You trust right," said Harry. "I think we may have to rename our team."

"You definitely have to buy some new threads," said Sam, eyeing Harry's faded jeans and the blue denim workshirt slit down one side to accommodate his cast.

"Buddy Kidd! Is that you, man?" said Cooter. "Known you all my life, almost didn't recognize you."

Buddy looked around at the banners and badges and wild costumes, then back at Harry's plot, which held only Harry and the smoker. "And what're we calling this team?" You could tell he thought he'd signed up with a scrub and wasn't too happy about it.

Harry shrugged. "Well, our place is called the Rib Shack. I entered under that."

Buddy shook his head. "No music. No poetry. No style. Do you *see* these folks around here?" Buddy waved his hand at a band of Spiffy Porkers strolling by in their tuxedos.

"Red Holcomb said to keep it simple. Said it was the meat that counted." Harry drew a circle in the dirt with his sneaker like a little kid.

Buddy's voice was weary with experience. "Red Holcomb is a lying son of a bitch."

That having pretty much settled that, Sam left the gentlemen to discuss the finer points of smoking and venting, the efficacy of prayer versus bourbon vis-à-vis barbecue sauce, and took Harpo on a little stroll toward the tent where the Elvis impersonators were registering. It was time for some serious Weird research. The crowd caught her up for a while in front of the Samurai Smokers and the Tokyo Twisters, only two of the invited Japanese teams who were dazzling the locals with barbecued sushi and teriyaki. Four sumo wrestlers each consumed an entire roast pig in a race against the clock. Betting was hot.

Sam almost slipped past a Holly Springs Hogboy, but he caught sight of her and gave a Yippie-ky-yea! that made the little dog jump. "Floyd, bubba!" he shouted, waving his cowboy hat, "here comes your angel of mercy."

Sam looked for a place to hide while Harpo crouched between her sneakers. But there was no escaping the old men in cowboy boots, jeans, and fancy black cowboy shirts with their team name spelled out in rhinestones.

"No, ma'am!" The silver-haired man on whom she'd practiced her CPR the afternoon before rushed over and threw his arms around her. He was strong for an old man. "No, ma'am, don't you be shy. Why, you saved my life! 'Course I almost lost it again last night after they turned me loose from the hospital, we didn't have any cooker, went to this hamburger place for dinner. *That* was almost fatal." He couldn't seem to stop hugging, squeezing, and patting her. People turned and smiled. It embarrassed Sam that at forty she still blushed. And the more she blushed, the more she was embarrassed, and the more she blushed . . .

"Darling, you and that little dog just come over here and sit down and have a beer and let's visit. Now that you're an honorary member of the Morgan family not to mention a Holly Springs Hoggirl. Now tell me this doggie's name, and let's make him an honorary Hogpup." With that, he produced a black bandana with rhinestone trim from his back pocket and tied it around Harpo's neck. The little dog, who'd been known to keep a party hat balanced for hours, sat tall.

Then Floyd produced a rocking chair, and Sam had no choice but to sit and sip a Coke while Floyd pulled up a wooden crate and proceeded to catch her up on the Morgans from Holly Springs to Tupelo for the past three quarters of a century.

Finally she said, "You know I'm responsible for you, don't you, Floyd? That's what the Chinese say."

"Why, what do you mean, darling?"

"They say if you save somebody's life, you're responsible for them forever. So you better be careful up there in Holly Springs. I can't be running up there every week to make sure you're safe."

"Oh, my new missus, she does a pretty good job of that. She'll be insisting you come and see us. We've plenty of room. Holly Springs is full of gorgeous old houses, and we live in the biggest and the prettiest of 'em. I know I look like a hick, but I'm a retired country lawyer, makes me a hick and a crook too. Missus's gone want you to come stay with us for a good long time."

"Well, I'd love to do that, one of these days,"

said Sam, who was raised to be polite before being truthful.

And then, it struck her like a bolt of lightning. Damn! Why hadn't she thought of this? Floyd was almost electrocuted, too. And as far as she knew, the police didn't know a thing about it.

She tried to slide into the subject with Floyd. "I'd love to come visit. But, you know, it might be dangerous."

"That's right," laughed one of his friends. "Floyd's been known to charm the momma birds off their nests. Floyd'll win anything that's female. You better watch out, Miss Sam."

Floyd shrugged. "What do you mean dangerous, honey?"

"Well, I was just wondering if you had any ideas why your smoker gave you such a jolt. Had you been having electrical problems?"

"Well, you know, we've been talking about that. Never seen anything like it. The rotisserie'd been giving me some trouble, mechanical not electrical, and I'd been working on her. But I tried it out last week and she worked like a charm." He leaned in close. "There's those that think it's another team, you know, somebody thinks we have a good chance to win ribs, who rigged that smoker."

He sounded like Harry. "Oh, come on, Floyd. People don't take this cookoff business *that* seriously."

"Seriously? Don't take it seriously?" Floyd looked around at his friends for confirmation that his ears hadn't deceived him. They all shook their heads. "Young lady, do you take *history* seriously? Do you think it's serious that Cro-Magnon man ate saber-toothed tigers crisped to a fare-thee-well by God's own lightning? Is it serious that your Native Americans were smoking meat in pits generations before Columbus was a twinkle in his daddy's eye? Do you

give a hoot that the first whole pig was smoked in this region by a European-type Caucasian in 1638?"

"You sure that wasn't 1639, Floyd?" A man in a red Allis-Chalmers hat passed Floyd another beer.

Sam said, "Well, I thought probably Q was pretty serious when LBJ took it to the White House. But I never heard of anyone *killed* over it."

"Just goes to show you don't know *nothing* about government."

"Now that I think about it, I bet you're right. The things America's killed people for—why Q would probably be the least of it."

"Damned straight," said Floyd. "Q's always been an important component of combat."

"Right," Floyd's friends chorused.

"I don't quite follow you," said Sam.

"You mean you don't remember that time on *M*A*S*H* when Hawkeye called his favorite Q place in Chicago from Korea and asked, 'Do you deliver?' And they did."

Sam laughed. "You got me there, Floyd. You're right. I'm absolutely sure Q is not only necessary to American combat, and the source of many wars, but could easily be the reason someone would want to bump you off." Hell, maybe it was. Who knew?

"Well, now," the old man said, holding up a cautionary hand. "Wait up a minute here. Now nobody said *exactly* that."

"I knew it, Floyd. I knew it. My uncle George is a retired lawyer too, and he'd do *exactly* what you're doing if he were here."

"What's that, sugar?"

"Argue me over to his side and then jump ship."

"Well, all I'm saying is, if the competition did try to blow me up, I don't know how they did it. We'd just pulled in and set up our rig right before the thing happened. Couldn't have been here more than half an hour, we're standing right here that whole time, getting ourselves unpacked and disorganized. I was moving toward cooking us some weenies and beans for supper, but I wanted to show the boys how my rotisserie was working, turned it on, and thar she blew. But I don't know when the competition would have rigged it, if they did."

Sam said, "Probably was some kind of freak accident." But the itch at the base of her neck told her that wasn't true. "I don't suppose you talked to the police about it."

"*Po*-lice? Honey, we ain't got time for police. We got to get to cooking some Q. They try to attack us again, we're armed. We can defend our perimeters."

Sam didn't want to know about that. What she did wonder was if they still had the smoker.

"Nawh, my son-in-law Roy said to haul the thing off. Didn't want to see it again. I think Cooter or one of his gang did it." Floyd scratched his head. "Now, what *I* think is there's three important things to look at here."

"One is that you're still alive," said Sam.

"Nawh. I'm too mean to die, though I don't want you to think I don't appreciate the effort you put in. One is that Elbert had time to go on back home, hitch up his rig, and drive back here in time to start cooking this morning." Floyd patted their replacement smoker. "This sucker cost Elbert a thousand dollars, cast-iron, custom-made. It's been blessed by every minister in Holly Springs, and we're gonna win with it, for sure. Now, two is that the blast didn't touch our bustin' sauce."

"Bustin'?" It was time for folderol again. Which was fine. She didn't want to alarm the old gent unduly.

"Busts right on through the surface of that meat and socks the flavor to it."

"What's *in* your sauce, anyway, Floyd?"

A hush fell over the Hogboys as if she had passed wind in the middle of the preacher's sermon. Forget war. Forget attempted murder by hot-wired rotisserie. Forget pestilence. She was talking serious business.

"Well," Floyd finally said after staring at her mournfully for a good long while, "I was going to say that the third important thing that came out of this whole event was that we met you, Miss Samantha Adams, and had this little visit, but I can see now that you're a spy for another team." He narrowed his blue eyes. "I saw you with that curly-haired young man, that old black gent. I reckon this whole thing was nothing but a plot y'all hatched up, almost blew me to smithereens, to snuggle up to us and steal our recipe."

"Why, I never—" Sam protested. The men's faces were grim. She *thought* they were fooling.

"Well, here's the deal." Floyd stood again and tossed his empty beer can at the garbage. "Y'all went to all that trouble, we're gone tell you exactly what you want to know."

It was the *exactly* that let Sam know that he wasn't going to do any such thing, not that she'd really wanted to know in the first place. But she was beginning to get the drift that exaggerating and boasting and lying, big-time lying, along with drinking and dressing up in silly costumes, were part of the barbecuing game. As, perhaps, was just a smidge of violence. A barbecue cookoff was simply an extension of being white, male, and Southern. Which meant once the fever took hold of them, they'd claim no responsibility for their behavior.

Floyd's voice was serious. "Everybody cooks pretty much the same, low and slow and don't ever let the meat feel the kiss of the flame. We're talking *smoke,* not fire."

"Go on, Floyd, quit fooling around and tell her the secret ingredient in the sauce," urged Elbert.

"You mean the chocolate?"

"Naw, the Tabasco."

"We didn't use that this time. Fred said you mix four tablespoons of cayenne in a six-and-a-half-ounce bottle of Co-cola, throw that in, it wasn't the same as Tabasco, but better."

"How about the pineapple juice?"

"Nope. I think it's the wine. Want to tell her the vintage, Floyd?"

"Well, it's red. Santa Cruz County. Southeast slopes. From there you're on your own."

Sam hadn't grown up a Southern girl to be a fool. "I think I got it all," she said, serious-faced as the Hogboys. "But I was wondering?" Then she leaned in even closer to them. "Y'all know the secret of the shoulders?" Shoulder was one of the three categories of pork in the contest. If you wanted to cook beef, you needed to turn left and head for Texas.

"What?" they breathed in unison.

"You know, the thing about *which* shoulder?"

"Why, honey, what do you mean?"

"Well, y'all know hogs sleep on their left sides, which means that left shoulder's tougher. My boyfriend Harry only uses the right one. That's *his* secret."

With that she thanked them kindly for the Co-cola and the visit, picked up her little dog, gave them a big smile, and strolled off in the direction of the Elvis impersonators where she'd been headed in the first place, stopping in the process to place a call from the pay phone over at the main building to Ollie, who wasn't in, but yes, ma'am, if it was important, they'd make sure he knew about it.

• • • • • • • • • • • • • **15**

The Tupelo Police Department, along with its jail, is housed in a one-story blond brick building on Front Street right along the St. Louis–San Francisco railroad line that contributed to the town's early vitality as a center of commerce. However, the Criminal Investigation Division was tucked in the rear of a new, nondescript city services building on Court Street, which itself stood behind the community theater.

At least that's where the cops at the main office said it was to P. J. Hightower, the fat biker with the gaps in his dentistry, the chartreuse glow-in-the-dark suspenders, and the whorl of frizzy gray-and-brown hair which he valiantly combed over his bald spot: You'll find 'em right behind the community theater.

P.J. walked all around the corner of Court and North Broadway, back and forth in front of the old Lyric, which was a little Art Deco beauty with octagonal windows, a facade of tiny blue and red and beige tiles, and a bright red ticket booth. He crossed the street and stared up at the gray marble monument to the Confederate dead on the corner of the courthouse square and read the words, "the love and gratitude and memory of the people of the South shall gild their fame in one eternal sunshine," and tears sprang to his eyes, for P. J. Hightower was nothing if not a son of the South, not to mention a mightily religious child of God, in addition to which he was getting to be one highly impatient son of a gun, he said to himself, and he wasn't going to be responsible for what happened next if he didn't find that detective's office soon and find out what had happened to his wife Velma's wallet, her driver's license, and her credit cards.

"No, I don't think we need any beauty products," said Lucille to the woman who called herself Velma Hightower. "Today we're just about as pretty as we can stand to be."

"Well, how about Mrs. McClanahan?" asked Mary Ann, who was being held at bay in the foyer of the great big house by the woman she took to be the help. Mary Ann was more than a little surprised at the way the place was decorated. Take those faded old red-and-blue Oriental-looking rugs on the hardwood. Mary Ann would have thrown those things out and laid some wall-to-wall shag in a New York minute.

"Mrs. McClanahan is not at home."

"Oh, really, but I thought I heard—"

"What you heard was the upstairs maid who better," and then Lucille raised her voice, "run her skinny butt back upstairs and get busy with those beds if she knows what's good for her."

Upstairs maid, thought Mary Ann. Good Lord have mercy, what kind of fancy had Carlin married into? Maybe she ought to revise her estimation of what Mrs. Carlin "Dixie" McClanahan was good for. Then she asked, "When do you think she might be home?"

"Miz McClanahan?" Lucille shook her head. "There ain't ever any telling. You might try back next week."

Mary Ann didn't plan to be here next week. She'd

have to figure a way around this heifer. But in the meantime, there was no point in wasting a perfectly good house call. "Do you mind my asking your name?" Lucille didn't mind a bit. "Well, Lucille, I notice that in addition to being pretty yourself, you like pretty things, and myself, in addition to representing this aloe vera line . . ."

The next thing Lucille knew she and the woman called Velma were sitting down in the living room on Dixie's yellow chintz slip-covered sofa fingering some of the most beautiful lingerie Lucille had ever seen. And when it came to your silky and your lacy, Lucille had some first-hand experience. But would you just look at this nightie of lemon-colored crepe de chine with the black lace insets above and below the bosom? The rose-colored satin brassiere with the ecru chiffon straps? And how about that dressing gown, it looked like something a movie star would wear, cut like a man's bathrobe but of the very palest violet satin jacquard woven with little violets and petunias in purple and green? Lucille couldn't put the dressing gown down. How much was it?

Well, said Mary Ann, it was three hundred dollars. Lucille threw a hand to her chest. Do Jesus! However, said Mary Ann, inspiration striking her as she spoke, what she *really* did, instead of this door-to-door, was houseparties. That's where you had a whole bunch of women over and you had little refreshments, tea and cookies, or beer and dogs, depending on the crowd, of course, and the lady who hostessed the event had her choice of a free item, though usually it wasn't something as nice as this—Mary Ann gently took the dressing gown from Lucille's hands and spread it across her own knees, stroking the soft satin, then picking it up and rubbing it across her cheek. But seeing as how she had just come to town and was anxious to start networking with the Ladies of Means, and she was sure Lucille and her Mrs. McClanahan knew who that might be, if Lucille could arrange to have such a party on the spur of the minute, like tomorrow or the next day, give the ladies something to do, she winked, while the menfolks were out tromping around the fairgrounds getting hot and smoky with this silly barbecue thing, the ladies could be spending some of *their* money on pretties. Then Mary Ann sat back and gave Lucille her best big smile.

Girl, Lucille thought, you're real good, ain't you?

Dewey was fit to be tied. First of all, the impersonator contest people had said you had to be here at this blue-and-white striped tent in the fairgrounds from noon to one to register, then and only then, and he had this other business he needed to tend to, not only his errands but Mary Ann's too, that woman was a bossy little thing, but so far she was worth it. And here he'd showed up on time, and the impersonator sign-up person wasn't even here yet, and he was standing around with these other impersonators, and they were seriously getting on his nerves.

If there was one thing Dewey couldn't stand, it was horn-tooting, and it turned out that was the one thing these turkeys were good at.

Take this one. His name was Shawn Magoo, and he was short and fat, the man was fat as a pig, and come to think of it, he had this turned-up nose, he looked like a pig, he talked in this real loud bleating voice like a pig, fast and loud like everybody wanted to know him and his business, and Dewey wasn't risking stepping close enough to see if he smelled like one too.

He had coal-black hair, you could tell it was dyed, but then every one of the eight or ten contestants standing around in the tent did that. You had to. But Magoo didn't have to wear this black jumpsuit with gold metallic trim that did nothing for his pig gut and *brag* about it.

"I just flew in from San Diego," he said, "where I wore this outfit" —he gestured with fat fingers covered with cubic zirconia imitations of three of Elvis's rings— "and did three shows. I tell you, I sang, they almost ripped my clothes right off me."

"In a nightclub?" asked a taller one named Obie Vaughn, who was heavy, but not as heavy as Shawn. He had these kind of buggy blue eyes that looked at you very seriously, frizzy hair, and his smile was all gums. But you could tell that he thought *he* was God's gift and wasn't too thrilled with Magoo.

"Not exactly," said Magoo. "I was working a convention. I do a lot of them."

"Fan conventions?" Vaughn asked, like fans weren't something he wanted to cozy up to, they might get something on you.

"Sure. I do them all over the country. 'Course, then, I'm always a headliner at Tribute Week. This was a convention of dog groomers, though. I'm always asked. I used to be a poodle clipper before I moved into show business."

Vaughn nodded and allowed as how he was a furniture stripper in his pre-Elvis life. Now he was really into fine food and great wine, he and the missus. They lived in a trailer park in Hot Springs. He pulled out a picture of the woman who looked to be about six-foot-four and ugly as unadulterated sin standing in front of a double-wide mobile home. Dewey felt sorry for him, for about a nanosecond. Then Vaughn asked Magoo, "So who makes your costumes?"

"My momma used to make 'em. She's a lot like Gladys, you know, always has been real interested in my career, stood right there beside me, but since I hit the big time, I've gone full out. I've had Paul Mantell Studios Special Creations make me ten different replicas of the King's jumpsuits. My act is completely seventies Elvis. I do the exact concerts. That convention I was telling you, three women fainted.''

"Oh," said Vaughn, "I've seen your act. You're good. Yeah, man, you're real good. Of course, I do the earlier stuff. Mostly fifties, the real rock and roll. It's been a calling for me. I mean, I would have never had the nerve to think I could do the King, but one day I was singing 'Hound Dog' in the shower, a neighbor came and almost knocked my door down, thought it was the King come back to life. Since then, well, it's been something. You know, after I was in that story they did on imitators in *Newsweek,* well, sometimes I have to beat the fans off with a stick. I've had women come right up to me after a show, said they want to have my child.''

"I know." Magoo shook his head. "It's tough, ain't it? But it's the price you have to pay for being talented and carrying the torch, memorializing the King's spirit. Just think what it must have been like for him.''

"Sometimes"—Vaughn shrugged his shoulders like the weight of Elvis World rested on them—"I'm out there on the road, and like I've done Dallas, then Houston, then Dallas again, them bookers, they don't know what they're doing, I think, dear God, I don't know where Elvis found the strength to go as long as he did. You just have to be determined and iron-willed.''

And loud and full of shit, thought Dewey, who'd never entered a competition before in his life and had no idea there was so much crap to it. He thought he'd just dye his hair and sideburns, pick up his guitar, open his mouth, curl his lip a little—and sing. That's what he thought Elvis was all about—the singing. He could see now, listening to these two carrying on with their pissing contest, he couldn't have been more wrong.

Ollie and his partner Grippa had shared an office for the better part of seven years, their two desks facing, his obsessively neat, Grippa's a pigpen. In that time, little in it had changed, neither the fake wood paneling that Ollie hated, the overhead fluorescent fixture that blinked, nor the constant chatter from the squad room next door, though he did give full points to the powerful air-conditioning. Now Ollie rocked back in his green office chair, picked up the homicide case folder and pulled out the reports on Lovie Rakestraw.

The quick-and-dirty autopsy findings showed that she had died of electrocution which had caused her heart to stop, plain and simple. A short time prior to her demise, she had ingested a beer and some cheese and crackers. Cheddar, the medical examiner thought. He could have also told Ollie if the beer was Bud or Amstel Light if he was pressed, he said, but Ollie wasn't sure that it made any difference. That wouldn't have been his precise choice of a last meal—he'd lean toward a big rare T-bone, baked potato, green salad and tomatoes straight out of his garden, and Diane's chocolate-chocolate cake.

What else? The one thing that stood out, other than the fact that Mrs. Rakestraw seemed to have had a good deal of cosmetic surgery, was the semen found in her vagina. The ME was hoping, of course, that the intercourse was very recent and the man involved was a secretor, which would give them his blood type.

All of which was interesting in that the lady's husband, Will Rakestraw—who had seemed appropriately shattered, grief-stricken, and otherwise torn-to-pieces when the Atlanta PD found him at a legal seminar at the Hyatt Regency on Peachtree and informed him of the tragedy—hadn't seen his wife, nor apparently enjoyed marital relations with her, unless they did it by phone which wouldn't explain the semen, in at least fifty-six hours.

Mrs. Rakestraw's cook, Tiwillda Simmons, and her housekeeper, Margaret Leonard, and her gardener, Lucius Broadwell, had all left at four that afternoon and had not seen anyone, no repairmen, no salesmen, no nobody, except each other and Mrs. Rakestraw. And no, neither they nor the neighbors had seen anyone they could remember other than the help. But then, the houses were far apart.

It would be noon before the electrical expert out of Jackson would be in to determine exactly if and how the house's wiring had been fiddled.

The guys who had dusted the house for prints were of the opinion that anyone who had a house that big *a*. deserved to die, and *b*. was probably done in by the servants who had to clean it. The help had been interviewed and printed. They said Miz Rakestraw was crazy for that bubbling tub, seemed to spend half her time in it. They knew for sure she bathed every evening, though sometimes she bathed in the morning too.

All of which was very interesting but nothing that led anywhere specific. Unless Mr. Rakestraw knew who might have been having sex with his wife with her consent, for there were no signs of a struggle. It was going to be interesting discussing that topic with Lawyer Rakestraw. Ollie looked down at his watch. Rakestraw's plane was due in soon. Grippa was meeting it, would drive the widower to the funeral home, then interview him.

Suddenly, in the squad room next door, there was a sound like a tornado.

". . . already *been* over there," a man was hollering. "Sent me halfway around Jack's crabapple to get myself this far, now you telling me I'm in the wrong place? Man, I'm gonna have to think about having myself a piece of . . ."

Ollie jumped up out of his creaky chair. Whoever the citizen outside, he was about to get himself blown to East Tupelo in about half a second because Cedric "Wyatt" Earnest—the biggest hot dog on the TPD, who was not only trigger-happy but an active drunk who'd proved it again last week by shooting a cow that a demented Vietnam vet who lived in a refrigerator out by New Albany was more than passing affectionate with—was sitting there in the squad room alone with his nonissue six-shooter.

"How you doing, sir?" Ollie said as he extended a hand to the snaggle-toothed fat man in the T-shirt, suspenders, and jeans who was P. J. Hightower. "Come on up here to my office, let's see what we can do about your problem."

It didn't take but about two minutes of listening to P.J. for Ollie to realize that what he had on his hands here wasn't in his bailiwick, but was indeed a prime example of what Ms. Samantha Adams, his literary adviser, whose call he'd been trying to return, was looking for. Genuine weird.

"No, she is not here," said Miss Estella to Ollie on the phone. "I imagine she'll be back directly. I like that woman, I told her to come home for lunch so we could sit down and have a visit. Now, Ollie Priest, while I have you, I want you to come over here and help me with these dogs."

"Miss Estella, ma'am, I am not the dogcatcher. But I'll be happy to give you his number."

"I know you're not, and I know you've plenty on your mind, what with somebody electrocuting Lovie Rakestraw in her bath." Then Estella tee-heed. She couldn't get over the picture of Lovie in that tub. "You know, Ollie, it *could* have been her bidet."

Ollie held out the phone and stared at it for a minute. He couldn't think of an appropriate response.

"I know what you're thinking. That's only because no one ever realizes that we're only more of the same when we age, and I was a pretty juicy young lady, if I do say so myself, should have left Arvis a thousand years ago, found myself a *cute* man. Now, can you see the *Daily Journal* trying to explain a bidet to those Baptists? It was bad enough when Lovie's bathroom was in that magazine, but then the Baptists didn't have to read that with their corn flakes." Then Estella went off into a fit of giggling.

"Well, Miss Estella, I see you've recovered just fine from somebody taking target practice through your kitchen window."

"Shoot. I don't care about *that*. But I do care about those little pups I'm trying to convince you to do something about. They're yappy, but I like them. Actually, come to think about it, *I* bought that first bitch, so if we got rid of her, I'd be closer to exactly one hundred items, which is my goal, and I've been over it for some time, but anyway they're sweet dogs. Sonny doesn't care about that. He only raises 'em for show and now that Dixie's gone and dyed them red. At first I thought it would be funny, to make Sonny mad. But now I'm having second thoughts."

"I beg your pardon, Miss Estella."

"Have you gone deaf, Ollie? Last night—I thought you police knew everything—Dixie came over here and threw red dye all over the pups. Didn't you know that?" Well, maybe he did and he'd forgotten. The shooting had slipped down a notch in importance since Lovie Rakestraw had been found dead. Estella said, "I don't blame her, I know she'd warned Sonny about the noise, they don't bother me when I turn my hearing aid off, but Sonny's gonna be mad as a wet hen when he finds out, and you know how he is when he's mad. He'll go over there and scream at Dixie and upset her, poor thing, pregnant with those fatherless children. Now I'm looking at Dixie right this minute through my window into her kitchen, she and Lucille are jabbering at one another sixty miles a minute pointing so hard at the morning paper they're going to poke a hole in it, just read about Lovie Rakestraw would be my bet. People rose at a decent hour, turned on the radio, they'd get a jump on the news, but those two, they like to lie around in their beds, not that I'm saying that's wrong, so that that woman who was here last night creeping around in the yard, she was back just a while ago, took their paper into them."

"*What* woman who was creeping around last night?"

"The little brunette in the jeans and the cowboy boots, of course she was dressed real nice today, looked like a saleslady."

"Miss Estella, did you tell any of the officers about this woman?"

"No, I did not. And before you ask me why, I'm going to tell you. *A*, they did not ask me. And *b*, they talk to me like I don't have good sense. You don't, that's why I mentioned it to you, though I wouldn't have if I'd thought about it for a minute. Now, Ollie, are you going to come over here and do something about these pups before Sonny comes back home and finds them dyed red right before that Jackson Kennel Club Show and goes over there and has a fit and puts Dixie into premature labor with those poor fatherless twins?"

• • • • • • • • • • • • • • **16**

Dewey had popped a Seconal to calm down the Benzedrine he'd popped to get himself up before he stepped into the registration tent. Now the drugs were wrestling it out in his brain. He thought the upper was winning because he still felt pretty jazzy. He slipped his gold Elvis sunglasses on against the bright spring sunshine that was struggling through the smoke and the haze. "Come on over here, Elvis, and have a beer," one of the barbecuers called, and Dewey was headed that way when this tallish brunette stepped right in his face.

She was wearing big gold hoop earrings, a yellow cotton sweater that her curves did a nice job with, and a pair of faded plaid slacks. Madras, that's what they called it. Old beat-up sneakers. Had a little bitty white dog on a blue leash. Dewey squinted. There was something familiar about the two of them, but he couldn't place it. He nodded and tried to scoot around them because the woman was standing between him and his beer.

"Oh, excuse me," she said. "Here, let me move out of your way."

"Thank you kindly, ma'am." The bubba with the words SMOKE IS FOR REAL printed across his chest gave him the beer along with a big wink. Yep, lots of Elvis groupies showed up at these things, that's what Dewey'd been told. And this one was a prime example, unless he missed his guess, dying to speak to him. "You an Elfan?" he asked her, thinking he'd give her a foot up into the conversation.

"I don't know," she smiled. He liked the way she looked. He'd put her at thirty-five or so, somewhere around Mary Ann's age.

"What's an Elfan?"

"An Elvis fan, they call 'em Elfans."

"I'm sort of one, I guess."

Dewey shook his head and gave her The Smile. "Ma'am, pardon me, but I don't think there's any such animal."

She gave The Smile right back to him and said, "You mean either you're an Elvis fan or you're not?"

"That's pretty much the size of it." And then he shifted himself, threw one foot up on a wooden box that someone had left by the side of the tent. Turned and gave her his profile.

"You really do look a lot like Elvis," she said.

"Well, I try to."

"Do you mind talking with me a few minutes?" Then she pulled a little notebook and a pen out of her back pocket and handed him a card. Dewey squinted at it. Between the sunglasses and the drugs, it was tough for him to read. Then she stuck out her hand just like a man and they shook and introduced themselves, though he didn't really catch her name. "I'm a journalist," she said. "Working on a book. I thought I might do something with impersonators."

See. It was happening exactly like he thought it would. Here it was, tonight was the first eliminating round, and he hadn't even done that yet and already he was standing right on the edge of fame. He knew it, knew it, knew it. Knew that once he stepped forward, the whole thing would fall into place. Now she was saying something about Atlanta, a newspaper, or maybe it was a book. It didn't matter. Soon, they'd all be lying at his feet like little dogs.

"I've talked with some of the other contestants, and they have some pretty interesting stories. One's the mayor of a town in Illinois. Another is a preacher." Now she was grooving on it, made her cheeks flush. "One is black, one is a woman, and there's a little kid. One man told me that when he heard on the radio that Elvis was dead, he pulled his car across two lanes of traffic and almost died in a head-on collision. He decided that Elvis's spirit saved him and this was his mission."

Dewey spit in the dirt. "You talk to that Magoo and that Vaughn?"

Sam nodded. "They said they'd show me some trophies later."

Dewey spit again. "They don't know nothing. They ain't ever even been in Tupelo before."

"And you?" She looked up at him while she was scribbling.

"I was born here."

"Really?" And then he could tell she was staring at the name tag they'd pinned on him. It said his name and his town. "I live in Holly Springs now, it's about fifty miles up the interstate, toward Memphis. But I was born here."

"You don't say." Then she narrowed her eyes, probably trying to figure out his age. "I met some other people here at the cookoff from Holly Springs."

"Yeah. There's probably some smokers. It's like a whole world of Q, here to Memphis over to Arkansas. I eat a lot of it myself."

"I understand Elvis liked barbecue. If you were born here, did you by any chance know him? Is that why you're an impersonator?"

"You might say that." Dewey gave her his other profile, reaching back to make sure his collar was still turned up. He'd always hated his long neck, just like Elvis.

"You did? You knew him? What was he like?"

"Well, he was like a kid. Any poor kid, except he was kind of intense in a way even back then."

"What do you mean intense?"

"I don't mean strange. It's that he played music, he wanted to play music. He used to follow around this guy called Mississippi Slim who picked and sang on the local radio station. Followed him like a pup. But Elvis left here, you know, when he was thirteen."

"And why was that?" Now she was scribbling like crazy.

Dewey frowned. His face grew dark. His long blue-black hair flopped lower on his forehead. "Because Vernon was fired again."

"Vernon was his daddy, right?"

Dewey rolled his eyes. If she didn't know that, what point was there in talking to her? But then he tried to get ahold of himself. Come on, old son, he said. She's gonna start you on that road to the bright lights, be patient now. "People were always taking Vernon's jobs, his houses, his dignity away from him."

"What kind of job was he fired from?"

"Driving a delivery truck."

"Oh, really? Elvis drove a truck too, before he made it, didn't he?"

Dewey nodded. Well, she knew *something*. "Vernon was delivering hooch for a bootlegger."

"You really do know a lot about Elvis. Do you go

to Tribute Week at Graceland? I understand those people are experts."

Experts! "What do *they* know? They're ghouls! Bloodsuckers! They don't know! They don't know nothing!" Dewey could hear himself getting loud, but he couldn't help it. His head was starting to ache, the strain of listening to those fools back in the tent piled on top of the drugs. He dropped his foot off the wooden box, started pacing back and forth in the dirt. "*They* never walked in his shoes. *They* don't know how it feels, your daddy having to pack up and leave town and move up to Memphis, accused of selling off a stolen pig!"

Dewey was talking a *lot* louder than he meant to. A little crowd was gathering. Amen! a man shouted. And then Dewey got the feeling, the one that used to come over him when he was a little kid in church. The preacher would say, "Melt the sinner's heart, oh Jesus!" and the thrill ran right through him and he knew that it was his turn to speak. His duty to testify. Just like now. He wheeled on the audience, taking a karate stance, his legs wide, that right hand pushed forward like a knife. "They don't know how it feels, your daddy shipped off to the penitentiary when you're three, a man telling lies on him about *another* pig! Your daddy shipped to Parchman, the pea farm. They work you sunup to sundown, chopping cotton in Parchman Penitentiary. Did you know that? Did you know that Vernon was sentenced when Elvis was only a pup?"

"Tell it like it is, Elvis," a woman in the crowd screamed.

Dewey struck another pose. This was *great!* He was filled with the power. He could feel it brimming, splashing over on the people. "Man said he sold that hog for four dollars, then added zeros to the check! Like he was that stupid!"

The crowd laughed. "That *would* be stupid!" a bubba said slapping his knee. Dewey rolled an eye over toward the writer woman. She was taking notes like crazy.

"Vernon wasn't stupid! He had a long run of bad luck, like most poor people do. You think people are poor because they want to be?"

"No way!" the crowd answered.

Dewey was pacing up and down. Sam thought he looked like an old caged lion she'd seen once in the Atlanta zoo. She watched the crowd, open-mouthed, swaying, and this wasn't the real thing, and he wasn't even singing. It was pretty amazing.

"Well, they're not poor because they want to be! They're not poor because they're lazy! They're poor because they started out poor and it's hard to get ahead when all you can think about is putting food on the table!"

"I hear that!" The crowd was clapping now to the rhythm of Dewey's words.

"Vernon and Gladys's folks both, you know they was poor for generations! Sharecroppers! Working for those who had, could never get ahead themselves! Gladys's momma had a whole passel of kids, *and* TB, then Gladys's daddy died!"

"Preach it, Elvis," said an old man who looked like he'd hoed many a hard row himself.

Dewey didn't even pause for breath. "Gladys slaved in the fields, cleaned houses, sewed in a shirt factory for two pitiful dollars a day, right over *there*"—he pointed a block away to where the old factory buildings still stood—"and was *grateful* for it! They lived in the slums in Memphis!"

"Poor, unh-huh. Those folks was poor." That was an old black lady, holding her hands like she was praying, rocking back and forth to the music in Dewey's words.

"Did you *know?*" he shouted. "Did you *know* that up in Memphis Vernon loaded paint cans for eighty-three cents an hour? Gladys cleaned up other people's cafeteria slops? Elvis drove a truck? About to make that first recording for Sun, right then, on the verge, they didn't have nothing! They was broke! Do you *know?* Do you *know* what I mean?" Dewey was screaming. The crowd was clapping its hands. Yes, yes, yes. Sing it, brother.

"People born with means, *they* don't understand," said a woman standing right behind Sam.

"They don't," said Dewey, "they don't. They don't know the feeling. Feeling. Feeling. *Ah* know the feeling. Feeling."

And then Dewey hit the wall. Inside that black leather he was wet to the bone. The drugs in him had waged a mighty battle, and they had won. He needed to lie down. He didn't think he'd slept more than three hours all night. He never slept. Or when he did, he walked. Walked in his sleep like he walked in the King's shoes.

Now he staggered off from the crowd, back over to that wooden box he'd thrown his foot up on when he was showing off to the writer woman. He couldn't remember why he needed it, but he knew he needed it. Something to do with Mary Ann. He picked up the box and stumbled to his motorcycle, leaving the applause of the crowd behind him, someone yelling, "You gonna take it, man! Gonna win that there contest."

Dewey believed that. He was, he knew he was. He jumped on the bike, and it roared to life, the power now between his legs, and in that moment it came to him. He knew who that writer woman was. Brunette, Mary Ann had said that. A dog, Mary Ann said something about dogs when she went to see her. The right age, and rich, but not dressed rich, that was a trick he'd learned rich people played. That woman, what did she say was her name? Sam, Sam, that was it. Mary Ann had that funny look on her face when she talked about her, playing cute, never said the woman's exact name, but said something about the country, patriotism, Uncle Sam, that was it, this was the very woman Mary Ann had come to Tupelo to find. And rob.

17

So what did she look like?" asked Dixie.

"Didn't you sit right there and listen to me tell Ollie Priest all about her? And I already told you once." Lucille was fast running out of patience.

"Heard you say she was brunette, five-four, one-twenty, pretty, if you overlooked the black eye, carrying a suitcase full of sexy undies."

"That's her, all right. Did you see how Ollie got excited 'cause I remembered as much as I did?"

"I wish you hadn't."

"Yeah, well, you wish that and I'll keep hoping I don't go to jail for withholding evidence. At the very least I bet I lose my notary public, they come take my stamp away. Why'd you shake your head at me when he asked if she said her name or we knew where she might be staying? We know exactly who she is and where she is and her room number."

Dixie ignored all that. "What you were looking at was that purple dressing gown you were telling me about when that cute young policeman Ollie sent over roared up in the driveway, missed her just like Ollie did five minutes later."

"Well, Miss Nancy Drew, what exactly was it you wanted to know?"

"Tell me this, Lucille," said Dixie with a look on her face that made Lucille wonder what the hell was going on, "forget these babies making me resemble a double-wide mobile home, does your Miss Velma favor me even slightly?"

"I always said good timing's half the game," said Sam, riding shotgun in Ollie's midnight-blue Oldsmobile, the two of them taking a ride out to the Elvis Presley Campground.

Ollie saying what luck it was he ran into her, he pulling out of Dixie McClanahan's driveway, she pulling into Red's next door. A man had to eat lunch sometime, take a break, there was something he wanted to show her, and wasn't it nice she happened to be carrying a big sample of Floyd Morgan and the Holly Springs Hogboys' ribs she was going to share with Miss Estella who'd come to the door in a navy blazer and gray slacks and waved her off, saying, Child, don't think a thing of it, go have yourself a good time riding around with the *po*lice even if they won't do anything about helping a poor old helpless woman with her dogs. Ollie saying Golly gee, Miss Estella, I clean forgot, could we talk later, I'll give you a ride too sometime if you'd like that. She said she would indeed, but only if there was gunplay and she could wear a uniform.

They headed north out of town, then east into the piney woods, Sam telling Ollie about Floyd Morgan's rotisserie almost jolting him to the Great Cookoff in the Sky. Ollie was holding a rib with his right hand, steering with his left. "Well, I'm glad he lived, 'cause he makes some *good* Q. Juicy, not too hot, not too sweet. You find out what happened to his cooker?"

"You mean after it shocked him? Cooter Williams had it dragged over to the dump."

"We'll have somebody go take a look at it." Ollie picked up his phone, and before he'd finish his potato salad, one detail would be questioning Cooter's workmen and Floyd, then taking Floyd over to the dump, where another detail would have already begun the search.

Sam said, "So you think it's worth looking into?"

"I don't know what I think, except I've never seen so much hullabaloo go down in one twenty-four-hour period in all the years I've lived in Tupelo." Ollie chewed for a minute. Then he told her the boys hadn't found anything amiss with the Holcomb wiring. "Yep. Looks like two separate incidents. No connection between the shooting and Lovie Rakestraw's death. At least not that one anyway, and I'm fresh out of guesses."

Then he told her about Lovie Rakestraw's little indiscretion.

"So you think Lovie's husband found out she was fooling around, set the timer on her whirlpool, left town, and bye-bye Lovie?"

"I'd like it a lot, except she ought to have fried the night before, unless, of course, she skipped her bath and didn't lay a finger on any of the plumbing. Which is pretty unlikely."

"A woman who was as fond of water as you said, I doubt she'd go to bed without brushing her teeth. So now you're looking at the lover. How about other enemies? Beneficiaries?"

"Husband gets what's hers. Enemies?" Ollie waggled a hand. "Lots of folks thought Lovie was a little too big for her britches for somebody who grew up dirt poor in Milltown."

"Married up?"

"Way up."

"All in all, I'd say you have your hands full. Raft of people to talk to."

Ollie shook his head. "Not so much confusion in these parts since the tornado of thirty-six. 'Course I wasn't around for that, and it was an act of God anyway. I don't think God had anything to do with this mess."

"Me either." They both chewed for about half a mile, then Sam said, "Bad tornado, thirty-six?"

"Real bad. We have a lot of them in this part of Mis'sippi. Actually, this weather today, I guess that's why I was thinking about it, you notice how it's been getting hotter and more oppressive—could be tornado weather. It's the season."

"I hope not."

"If it is, it'll be pretty thrilling. They whomp up, sometimes practically out of nowhere, pick up houses and cars and pigs and people, set 'em down in the next county."

"In funnels."

"They do that way out on the plains. Around here, there's not enough room for them to form like that. I heard this writer, a man named Nordan from over Itta Bena way, read a story once, it had a tornado in it. He said it looked like a bullfrog. I thought that was perfect."

"Sounds like you're a weather buff."

"I've always been crazy about storms. Maybe I like the smell of ozone. But that one I was telling you about, April fifth, 1936—why, tomorrow's its anniversary—it was a killer. Two hundred and thirty-five died in Tupelo. It injured three hundred fifty. Five minutes start to finish, it leveled forty-eight city blocks. Wiped out the entire black community over at Tank Hill, picking up people and throwing them into Gum Pond. Tore up nine hundred houses, President Roosevelt sent help and the Red Cross was at the train stations, set up in boxcars."

Then Ollie pointed at someone's side yard. They were driving through woods down a two-lane road past a few scattered suburban ranch-style houses, set back from the road on two-acre plots. "See that little hump, covered over with grass, those two doors? That's a storm house. Most folks have them, or cellars, to run to when storms are coming. They've saved many a life."

Sam said, "Now you're scaring me."

Then dead ahead of them in the road was a little gatehouse where a young bearded man waited to tell them they could drive down to see Lake Elvis Presley if they wanted to, but the campground and its facilities were full up. "Yep," he said, stroking his mustache, "I'd say the Good Lord Himself'd have a hard time fitting another one of His bikers in here. Even with a shoehorn."

"Alfreda, I am so glad that you could join me for lunch on such short notice. Now, you're sure you don't mind leftovers? We could go out someplace." Estella Holcomb was standing in her kitchen slicing cold beef. Her friend Alfreda Spoon was wearing a powder-blue velour warmup suit that was nice with her bright red hair. Estella was still in her navy blazer and gray slacks.

"Don't be silly," said Alfreda. "I swear, that is some bullet hole, there in your cabinet. Hon, do you have any beer?"

"Coming right up."

"Put plenty of horseradish on mine, pretty please. Lettuce and tomato, too, if you have it."

"My, my, we certainly do have a healthy appetite today. Was that Rob the Rooter's van I saw parked by your house yesterday?"

Alfreda shot her a look. "You want to hear about Martha Jane finding Lovie Rakestraw or you want to sit around picking on me?"

Estella brought the sandwiches to the table along with her cognac spritzed with soda then leaned so close their heads almost touched. "I'm sorry," she said. "Now tell me."

"Well, Martha Jane is all to pieces. You know, I always told you I'd failed her as a mother. I taught her manners, but I didn't seem to give her a lick of common sense. She thinks if a lady wears white shoes after Labor Day that's a reason to call out the National Guard. You can imagine what kind of state this Lovie thing has put her in."

"Well, she is a little prissy."

"She's a snot and a pain in the rear end is what she is and you know it, Estella. I've always said it was a shame she didn't marry Red, the two of them could have taken turns driving each other to the nut house."

"That's why I can't imagine her breaking into Lovie's. Can you, Alfreda?"

"No, but that shows you how upset she was that Lovie stood her up for bridge and then didn't answer her phone. I think she was afraid that Lovie wasn't going to invite her to the Spring Fete."

Estella took a long swig on her cognac and soda and then stuck out her bottom lip. "Now, that's a shame, isn't it, with Lovie gone I guess there won't *be* any Spring Fete. And I was so looking forward to it. I haven't seen such a display of tacky as that fete promised to be since—well, I guess since that time, you remember when Violet Ann had that houseful of Yankees down when her niece married that man from Chicago and they chewed gum and waved their diamonds and talked about their husbands' money? And then that one in the red dress with the blond hair that was too long for her age got up and walked across the room with a cigarette in her hand like a prostitute?"

"Estella, I swear."

"I know. Wasn't it fun?"

"What I think is that Howard may have to put Martha Jane in the hospital for a couple of days to pull her nerves together. The part she can't stop talking about is how awful it was when the security service came and took her for a burglar. And then the police came and acted like she was a murderer. She said they questioned her for hours, but you know how she exaggerates. Anything to stay in the limelight with her poor-me's. I haven't seen her so worked up about something since Violet Ann told her she thought Chantilly wasn't nearly as pretty a silver pattern as Grand Baroque."

"So what does she say about Lovie?"

"She hardly talks about that part at all. You know, Martha Jane always was jealous of Lovie. I don't think she's even sorry Lovie's dead."

"I swan. Of course, I feel that same way about Sonny. Though maybe I wouldn't, if he was gone." Estella paused and thought about that for a minute. "It's hard to know. I'll tell you this though. The minute his daddy Arvis breathed his last, I was turning cartwheels. Couldn't wait to jump on the phone, share the good news. I called his sister, she took to singing and dancing. I could hear those feet clogging, right on the telephone."

This was a field that had been plowed many times before, so Alfreda went right ahead. "You know, every once in a while Martha Jane lets something slip, accidentally on purpose, about how she knows some dirt on Lovie. I always say, Either tell it or shut up about it. Nobody likes a tease."

"Good for you, Alfreda, *now,* before I forget it, Dixie's called a meeting. Tonight, six-thirty, her house. She called me a little while ago, right after Sonny came home, yelling at the top of his lungs just like I knew he would because Buddy wasn't here to fix his lunch. I told him Buddy does it out of the kindness of his heart, since he works for *me* and Sonny doesn't exactly have the best disposition in the world—''

"What's the meeting about, Estella?"

"Well, Dixie said she had a new idea about moving things along."

"I think she's anxious, those babies coming."

"And Sonny stomped over there and hollered at her about those dogs, just like I knew he would if Ollie didn't help me out with them, threatened to sue her, he is the meanest man, Sonny, and she said, Oh, yeah, we'll see about that, and that's when she said she decided to call the meeting. She said to bring your checkbook or boo-cups cash, she'd provide the supper and the entertainment. I said, Does that mean we're having go-go boys? She said, You're real warm."

Dewey was sitting on his motorcycle in the parking lot of the Elvis Presley Playground on the little rise up behind the Birthplace. The King himself drove down here from Memphis when things were weighing heavy on his mind, sat in his car in this very spot looking down to the little house where he was born.

This was a sacred place. Memories shimmered up out of the earth.

To Dewey's right was the swing set and jungle gym for the little kids and the swimming pool, to his left the baseball diamond. Four boys were tossing a ball around, two of them black, two of them white. Dewey smiled. Elvis would have liked that. He grew up friendly with black folks. Borrowed a lot of their music. Stole some of it.

Down the slope on the left was the Elvis Presley

Memorial Chapel, where fans from around the world came to meditate and gaze in wonder at the stained glass mosaic. In its center is a cross, and if you squint, those arcs of color radiating out from the cross are exactly like Elvis's cape with his arms outstretched. The window behind the pulpit points you right at the Birthplace.

Graceland was one thing, but the Birthplace was the Holiest of Holies. The little two-room shotgun house—that meant you could stand on the tiny front porch and shoot in the front door, the slug'd go straight through and out the back door—Vernon had built it with his own hands, two rooms about fifteen by fifteen, the plain board walls flossied up with wallpaper now. There was no running water in the kitchen, no electricity, a fireplace to cook in, an icebox, a couple of tables, the only closet was also the pantry. An outhouse used to stand out back.

But it was the front room—now fitted out with a chenille-covered double bed, a rocking chair, a treadle sewing machine, a chamberpot sitting on the worn linoleum, the fireplace where the Presleys had burned kerosene because they couldn't afford coal—where the Miracle occurred. On the wall hung a picture of Jesus as an angel hovering over two children. Twins.

Of course Dewey had been in the room hundreds of times, dropping his dollar in the basket, exchanging a few words with the guide for the day, but most times, he could only stay a few minutes. He always felt that he was going to be overcome, like that first time he visited. When he swooned.

It was embarrassing, a great big man fainting dead away. But it was a gift, too. A gift to be so moved by the Spirit, and in that moment, To Know. To Know who you are and what you were put on earth to do.

Dewey closed his eyes. The Birthplace dropped away. He saw his momma's face. Janice. The woman he'd *thought* was his momma, who'd raised him as her own.

He never saw his pretend-daddy's face. Wyatt Travis had been gone for more than fifty years, died cutting down a Christmas tree when Dewey was only a little thing. Janice had raised her baby boy all by her lonesome—though she said she'd never been. Lonesome, that is. Not with having Dewey to herself to keep her company.

Dewey'd never married. Never met a woman who could hold a candle to his own sweet precious momma, he called her *his* baby. The same thing Elvis called Gladys and Vernon—his babies. And Elvis took care of them, the same way Dewey took care of Janice. Her home had been his whenever he wasn't on the road hauling tomatoes, electronic equipment, radiators from one coast to the other. He kept her house fixed up real nice. Hung around fooling with his motorbikes. Played his guitar. Did some wiring for neighbors, picking up a few extra bucks—when he wasn't being hassled for something that wasn't his fault. Now, that had happened more than once. Dewey had a real sensitive nature. He took things real hard. Some would say he overreacted.

Like that woman down in Fort Lauderdale a couple of weeks ago. She puffed up, all huffy, that wasn't his fault. People ought to treat you with respect, they didn't, well, they got what's coming to them.

He didn't feel the least bit bad about it, leaving her lying there on the floor. He climbed back in his rig and drove on to Memphis, delivered the bananas, was thinking about making another stab at penetrating Graceland without the $8.95 ticket, do a little overnight, see if he could finagle Elvis's Aunt Delta Mae who still lived there into cooking him up some grits. That's what he'd been thinking about, eating supper in the Piccadilly Cafeteria where Priscilla used to

model clothes when she was still in high school—
Priscilla, who looked so much like the girlfriend Elvis
had in Memphis in high school, nobody ever wrote
about her, but Dewey knew, oh, yes, he knew. He
was eating a Piccadilly vegetable plate—fried okra,
summer squash, black-eyed peas, a cornbread stick—
when he read an item in *The Commercial Appeal*
about this auction that had happened back down the
road in Tupelo. How folks were all upset about it.
That was only a few weeks ago, when Dewey received The Calling sitting right there in the Piccadilly.

There were several parts to it. He had The Plan
laid out in his mind like a solitaire deck, but the first
part hadn't gone so well.

Floyd Morgan's cooker hadn't done its job like
Dewey had rigged it to do back in Holly Springs.
He'd run a hot wire from the terminal block and
attached it to the grounding screw in the junction box
so the whole frame of the smoker was energized. He
hadn't counted on the fairgrounds having ground-fault
circuit interceptors at the panel where the service
comes in. That's what had screwed him up. That's
why Floyd was still alive.

Tears filled Dewey's eyes as he thought about
Floyd and what he had done. It didn't matter that it
was a long time ago. In fact that was all the more
reason that Floyd had to die. Too many years he'd
been living high off the hog after tearing the Presley
family to bits. Dewey was furious that smoker hadn't
killed Floyd Morgan on the spot, hadn't torn Floyd
Morgan apart the same way he'd ripped at the tiny
Elvis's life and broken his momma's heart.

Well. There were other parts to The Plan, and he'd
gotten one of them right, that was for damned sure.

Dewey wiped his eyes. He always felt better when he
made a pilgrimage to The Source. Now, up and at it.

• • • • • • • • • • • • • • 18

The kid at the gate was right. As far as Sam could see, motorcycles of red, silver, and black were parked in a maze of tents in blue and yellow and green. The Elvis Presley Campground looked like a medieval carnival, updated.

Sam figured there must have been almost a thousand motorcycles. Lots of old Harleys, they were her favorite, but an equal number of new monster Kawasakis and Suzukis about the size of a walk-in deep freeze with storage bins for tents, sleeping bags, Coleman stoves, lanterns, ice chests, and other accoutrements for those who like to sleep on the ground and picnic. They had wrap-around-sound consoles complete with AM-FM and CD as well as CB.

Bikes for sissy couch potatoes, thought Sam. One of her fondest teenage memories was riding through Atlanta's Piedmont Park on a Harley, summer nights so hot and still you could hardly breathe, holding on to the back of a sweet sweaty blue-eyed boy who popped that suicide clutch and took the curves lean and mean. Rushing through the tree-bowered lanes, they'd felt the air drop fifteen degrees.

These bourgeois hogs, you might as well stay at home, fat ass on the sofa, glued to the tube. Which is exactly what it looked like many of these bikers did. They were so hefty the encampment seemed even more crowded than it was.

These were bikers without leather. Without chains. Without slut mamas and kick-ass attitude. Sam watched big-hipped women in white pullovers and pastel polyester pants chase swarms of screaming kids. Up a little rise stood a huge tent sporting a flag which read JESUS IS ALIVE AND WELL IN TUPELO.

"Ollie," she said out of the side of her mouth, "what the heck is this?" But she was beginning to get the drift. The Biker for Jesus at the McDonald's had to come from somewhere.

"Weird." He grinned. "Just a little American weird."

"I thought this was a murder investigation."

"Nope, this is lunch." All the time they're walking through the encampment, smiling, nodding. "We're visiting with some slightly strange folks. Gathering you some material so you'll be beholden to read the little story I left back in the car, tell me if you think I've got the goods."

So that was it, the writing again. "Ollie, I'd be happy to read your story anyway. You didn't need to do this." Which was a lie. She despised reading wannabes' manuscripts, of which she received an amazing number considering she was a reporter, because most of it was so bad, and then what did you say?

"Watch your mouth, don't jive with a cop, we can smell a lie before it even crosses your—"

Before he could finish P.J. Hightower spotted them, waved and hollered, "Praise the Lord, y'all just in time for dinner! Come on over here!"

Sam grabbed Ollie's arm. "That man, that's the

very same man who saved Harpo in the Elvis McDonald's parking lot!''

"They're saving dogs? I thought they had their hands full bringing salvation to human beings.''

Sam narrowed her eyes. "Saved as in rescued from being squashed. Harpo'd run outside. This man scooped him up, and I never even had a chance to thank him.''

"Well, see. Now you can.'' Then Ollie raised his voice and stretched his right hand toward P.J. "Mr. Hightower, sir, so good to see you.''

"Amen, brother. Amen. Now, you and this pretty lady come sit yourself down over here''—P.J. ushered them toward a heaped picnic table—"and let's offer up the blessing before the fish gets cold. Though I don't think that's likely in this heat. Y'all think it's gonna rain?''

P.J.'s thanks to the Lord were long and enthusiastic and included about thirty people he recalled by diagnosis, prescribed cure, probable outcome of their affliction, and first, middle, and last names. When he shouted Amen at the end, the dozen folks sitting around the picnic table joined in, then toasted P.J. and the Lord with glasses of presweetened iced tea. P.J. hefted his own blue plastic pitcher, which in his paw looked about the right size.

Little lake fish, perch and bream, battered in cornmeal and fried, were heaped on platters along with french fries coated in the same batter. Coleslaw studded with raisins and pineapple chunks glistened with sweet salad dressing. White bread was thick with butter. Strawberry shortcake smothered in jellied glaze shimmered beside German chocolate cake. It was a good thing Sam had stopped counting fat grams because she'd left her calculator back at the house. Not to mention she was full of Floyd's ribs and this stuff looked a tad unappetizing, but a lady had to be polite.

"P.J., this looks great! Now, I know you don't remember me—"

But he did. "I *told* Velma I'd seen you somewhere before when you stepped out of that car there with the detective. Velma, this is the lady with the little white dog at the McDonald's."

When Sam had finished thanking him, P.J. introduced her and Ollie to Velma, his best friend Lawtey, and Lawtey's red-haired wife Pam. Everybody else was too busy eating to do more than nod. "Now what you saw there in that parking lot," he said, piling Sam's plate high with cholesterol, "was a prime example of the kind of ministry we do. My being there, that was no accident. There's no accidents when you've put your faith in the Lord. Now, what I *thought* I was doing there was grabbing us a bite to eat, we drove in, set up, didn't have time to cook up anything before the service, and passing out a few tracts."

"Amen," said Lawtey around a mouthful of fish. "Doing the Lord's work."

Tracts. Like the pamphlet he'd handed her along with Harpo. Sam remembered the words, black on yellow, JESUS WAS A BIKER. But she hadn't read it then in all the excitement and didn't know what she'd done with it.

"Yes, ma'am. You see what happens, we Bikers for Jesus, we have these motorcycles"—P.J. waved a great paw at the campground—"and folks are fascinated by 'em. Why, I bet even you yourself'd stop by a big old Kawasaki like that 'un." P.J. pointed at a red and silver hog about the size of a six-cushion sofa.

"I would indeed," she said.

"That's right, 'cause people love bikes, like we love bikes. And we love people, and we want to see them right with the Lord. So what we do is, we drive up where there's likely to be sinners . . ." He paused for the laugh that he knew was coming from his friends. ". . . which is right near anyplace there's human beings, and when they stop to look at the bikes, we give 'em the tracts, which grabs their attention."

"I think it would," she agreed.

"That's 'cause you think bikers are devils, not angels, not that we're them either." P.J. took a long swig of iced tea and wiped his mouth on the back of his hand. "But you expect big old hairy men riding bikes to have drugging and drinking and raping and pillaging on their minds, not the Lord. Am I right?"

"You're right." Sam realized she was being sucked right into his rhythm, which was the rhythm of every southern Protestant preacher she'd ever heard who was worth his salt. It was the rhythm of the Old Testament. It was the rhythm of Martin Luther King, Jr. It was the meter of Elvis, rhythm and blues, down and dirty rock and roll.

"And we used to, we used to."

"Amen to that." Several of the men grinned. "Used to have plenty of that on our minds."

"All of us here used to be outlaw bikers." P.J. waved a ham of a hand at the men around the table.

"You're kidding." They didn't look like it. They were rednecks, but clean rednecks.

"Nuh-uh." To prove it, P.J. rolled up the sleeves of his plaid cotton shirt. On one huge forearm were tattooed the words BORN TO RAISE HELL, on the other HELL'S ANGELS, OAKLAND, CA. He gave her a wink. "I was chief enforcer for the Oakland club. I had my fun. At least I thought it was fun then. Now I rejoice in the Lord."

"And this?" Sam raised a hand at the encampment.

"We gather together, as many as want to, there are *thousands* of us, several times a year. For rallies like this, or runs. 'Cause we love bikes, bikers, and Jesus. For most of us, the bikes came first. Then we found the Lord, but you know, there are lots of folks in churches, they think if you got long hair or a beard, wear jeans, and ride a bike, you're going straight to hell. What we think is, not only does the Lord love everybody, and welcome them to His blessed name, but if He was here today? We think He'd ride too.''

Sam smiled.

"Go on. Go on and laugh. Lots of folks do. But think about it. The church thought He was a weirdo. Folks in power didn't like Him. Didn't have a lot of friends. Those He did have, when push came to shove, turned their backs on Him. He was persecuted by hypocrites, exactly like those you see dressing up in their fancy clothes and furs and traipsing down the aisle of many a First Baptist Church taking a front pew like the Lord loves them more than he loves you. Jesus didn't hang around with folks like them. He didn't hang around with any sucker-uppers.''

"Well, you have a point there.''

"And if the Lord were on earth today, He'd be riding right beside us, telling us He died for our sins.''

"And you'd be making Him a good deal on a Suzuki, wouldn't you, bubba?'' teased a man with white-blond hair who was tall and thin as a young pine tree.

"That's about right,'' laughed P.J. "That's just about right.''

"What exactly do you do at these rallies?'' Sam asked.

"You finish up that grub, Sisterwoman,'' said P.J., chug-a-lugging his pitcher of iced tea, "I'll take you on a little tour.''

Dewey had cruised back to the Ramada, changed out of his leathers, grabbed a quick shower, closed his eyes for about ten minutes, and was ready to roll when Mary Ann came bustling in the door, hot as Hades.

"Well!" she said. "Look at you, fresh as a daisy, and here I am worn to a frazzle with trying to see that McClanahan woman. I'll tell you, Dewey—why the hell is this air-conditioning turned down to fifty-five again, you could hang meat in here—this thing is going nowhere fast. The only hope I seem to have here is lingerie, and I'm not even sure about that. I think we're gonna have to go ahead to Plan B, Dewey. Did you do what you were supposed to?"

"I'm on my way right this minute."

"Now, Dewey!"

"Don't you *Now, Dewey* me, woman. If I wanted that I'd marry me a wife. Besides, I did more than you did."

"Oh, yeah?" Mary Ann was staring at herself in the mirror. She hadn't realized her black eye showed so much. Well, when aloe vera failed, there was always pancake. Now, where did she put that Max Factor?

"At least I saw her."

"Saw who?"

"That woman who was married to your husband." Mary Ann whirled. "Where?"

"Out at the fairgrounds. I talked with her."

"You *did?* When?"

"Little over an hour ago." Dewey considered telling Mary Ann that the woman was going to write an article on him, but then he thought better of it. Girl as ambitious as Mary Ann, she might go horning in, you never knew.

"Well, I'll be. Maybe that was the upstairs maid after all. I was sure that colored woman was lying to me."

See, thought Dewey, that was the kind of mind Mary Ann had. Suspicious. Like most women. Always thinking you're trying to pull one over on them, when lots of times you're going along, minding your own business, not giving them a thought. But they're giving you one. Yes, indeedy. Women giving you thoughts all the time, trying to figure what they can finagle out of you. Well, he just might be the one doing the finagling here, Miss Mary Ann better watch her *p*'s and *q*'s. He didn't have any intention of being used, and on the other hand, when *he'd* used a woman all up, well, there was no telling what kind of fix she might find herself in. Maybe. You couldn't tell. You couldn't be sure. It depended on Dewey's mood.

Then the telephone rang, and Mary Ann jumped on it like it was the buzzer on a quiz show.

"Yes, it is. Yes, I most certainly can. We'll start at six-thirty, but come over to your house early? One-oh-five York? Off Highland Circle? Well, that certainly was fast work. Oh, no. No, it's not too quick. I'll freshen up some and be over in a little while. Why, certainly, it's my pleasure. See you soon."

Mary Ann hung up the phone and gave Dewey a thumbs-up.

He growled, "Who was that? That woman your husband married?"

Mary Ann answered with her sweetest smile—and that's all. Dewey wasn't doing his part, he better not be thinking he was getting any sugar tit. Or any other reward.

Out at the fairgrounds, Team Blue Pig was engaged in its tenth knock-down drag-out of the afternoon. Things had been cool, Harry and Buddy agreeing on the distance the ribs should be from the fire, the proper angle of backdraft, the exact amount of hickory, when Slaughter Phipps drove up on the scene and everything went to hell.

Slaughter Phipps, Harry's partner Lavert's second cousin, had finally received Harry's call for assistance. It had taken him a while to get his girlfriend Turquoise out of his face and pull his outfit together—all white, shoes to chapeau without stopping for Go at the white-on-white hand-stitched suit, which Harry thought fit right in with the blues/barbecue theme, Buddy Kidd and Harry having agreed those were two of their favorite things in the whole wide world, why not go with it? But Buddy took one look at Slaughter's snowy threads and snorted: Just told you something about how much dirty work Slaughter intended to do.

"Old man," Slaughter sneered, "I guess you think you've gone and made yourself a hero 'cause you know how to cook the onions sweet. Well, I'm here to tell you we don't need onions in the sauce anyhow. You planning on giving the judges bad breath?"

"Whyn't you breathe on them? Do the same thing," Buddy snapped back.

"Hey," Harry said. "Wait up, guys. We got a problem here?" Maybe it was the heat. It was awfully hot for so early on an April day.

"I have no problem," said Buddy. "I was here first, doing my thing with these ribs. Just like you asked me to."

"Except he asked me first, old man. Probably you jumped up waving your trembly hands, acting pitiful the way you do, begging Take me, Take me, 'fore they put me in the cold, cold ground."

"You two know each other?" Harry ventured, wondering what the heck he was going to do now. He needed some help, but he didn't need help that was going to chop each other in little pieces and throw them in the Q.

"You might say that," said Slaughter around the

gold toothpick that Harry remembered as a semipermanent feature of his face. "Know him as much as you want to know a stone killer."

Great. Incredible, in fact. Harry wondered if anybody had ever won a barbecue cookoff with a sauce of cold blood, bitters, and rue.

• • • • • • • • • • • • **19**

P.J. was giving Sam and Ollie the ninety-nine-cent tour while his wife Velma tagged along. They'd inspected bikes, kicked tires, had the right hand of Christian fellowship extended to them by a motorcycle evangelist who rode sixty thousand miles a year in the western United States alone spreading the Lord's word. They'd each ponied up five bucks to a woman in a lemon-yellow seersucker pants outfit that was not the least bit becoming who was collecting for Bikers for Jesus in the World to send horses and cows and bikes and Bibles to foreign countries. Now they were standing under the biggest tent Sam had ever seen outside the circus. It was filled with folding chairs, each of them holding a sheaf of song sheets.

"You didn't get all this here by motorcycle?" she asked P.J.

"Nawh. We lease trucks for rallies. Now this is where we hear the preaching and the healing and the singing every night. Y'all ought to come. The Lord Jesus'd be mighty happy to see you."

"Well, we just might," said Ollie. "But let's go back to the story you were telling us. You think this woman you picked out of the pit at the snake farm is the one who stole Velma's wallet?''

"I'm pretty sure she was. Velma can't remember any other opportunity anybody had to do it. Can you, Velma?''

Velma shook her head, which they took to mean no, she couldn't.

"And you say she climbed in this truck with the trucker whose tire had blown her off the road?'' Ollie asked.

"She did that,'' said P.J. Velma nodded again. Sam was beginning to get the drift that maybe in this particular neck of the woods wives were seen and not heard.

"That's where the band sits.'' P.J. was pointing at a place up by the side of the pulpit. "At rallies we use drums and guitars and banjos, and an old boy from near Waco, Texas, brought his saxophone. I'll tell you, it sure makes a joyful noise unto the Lord.''

"What time's the service?'' Sam asked. Harry might like the music if she could drag him away from the fairgrounds.

"Gets started about seven-thirty. When it gets good dark.''

"And lasts till?''

"We'll go as long as the Spirit moves. Or the rain catches us. Y'all see those clouds coming in? Hope we don't get washed away.''

"And you say the woman looked like Jessica Lange? That's what you said, Velma? You mean she's a pretty blonde?''

Velma nodded her own dark bouffant, the likes of which Sam hadn't seen in a long while. It was a special look, closer to Marie Antoinette than country and western, that you only found on Southern women of the Apostolic faiths. They let their tresses grow and grow and grow and then teased and shaped them into waves and crests and tidepools. Older women too, sometimes they looked like they had giant snowballs on their heads.

"And she never said her name?" Ollie said.

"Not that I remember. Do you, Velma?"

Velma's nod said no.

"Did you see what kind of truck it was?"

Neither of them had.

"And you don't know where it was headed?"

They didn't. But they had canceled the credit cards, though it'd taken them a while to discover that the wallet was gone, the Good Lord Himself only knew how much the woman had already charged. It wasn't the wallet, the cards, or the little bit of money they were concerned about. It was a picture of Velma's maternal grandmother, the one she was named after who'd raised her after her mother died, that was breaking Velma's heart. The only picture Velma had of her granny. She carried it with her always.

"Well, we sure thank you for the dinner, but I guess we ought to mosey on back into town and let me get back to work," said Ollie. "Y'all coming in for the cookoff?"

Well, originally, P.J. said, they were just here for the rally. It was a coincidence that the cookoff and Tupelo Days were here this weekend. They hadn't even known about it. Of course, now that they did, they planned to take advantage.

"Eat you some good Q, huh?" said Sam.

"Nope." Ollie shook his head. "Do some witnessing. Distribute some tracts."

Well, there you were. Ollie motioned Sam along. He needed to see if Grippa had come up with anything else on Lovie Rakestraw, the two of them heading up the case, along with the Chief of Detectives and the Chief of Police, that is, breathing down their necks and wanting the business closed—like yesterday. It didn't look good, wife of a prominent lawyer parboiled the day of the opening of Tupelo Days. Not good for Tupelo Days. Not good for the Chamber of Commerce. Not good for the hundreds of volunteers who've worked their fingers to the bone for months to put this thing together hoping to impress the socks off the Japanese who had to put that Toyota plant *somewhere*.

It was clear to Sam that Lovie Rakestraw was the most pressing thing on Ollie's plate, which made sense, the woman was dead. The shooter at Red's and the Velma Hightower business could wait. However, P.J. had saved Harpo and she owed him a big one, and suddenly she'd had an inspiration.

"Velma?" she said. "Could you point me at a ladies' room?"

Velma did. It was in a low cinder block building.

"Would you like to come with me?"

Velma would.

"I don't want to talk about it," said Slaughter. He and Harry had piled into his gold 1977 Buick Riviera, a model that Harry had always thought was particularly hot. It looked like a car that belonged to a man who might be partial to bending the law in an interesting and glamorous fashion. They were headed over to Slaughter's mother's house to pick up Harry an outfit for Blue Pig. Slaughter said she had closets full of them. Harry didn't know why she would, but he figured he'd find out. In the meantime, he was trying to learn more about Buddy Kidd, the murderer.

He said, "Somehow Buddy just doesn't strike me as the type. Flashy, yes. I'm crazy about the man's style. But murderer, nawh."

"That's just 'cause he's old. You don't see many old killers, except in gangster movies. Most of 'em are dead. But I don't want to talk about it."

"Well, what should we talk about?" Harry pulled one out of his hat. "Elvis?"

"He's dead too."

"You think so?"

"Ah, man, don't tell me you're one of those freaks who thinks he's still alive and well in Detroit."

Harry laughed. "Nope. Why would he want to go to Detroit?"

"I saw that TV show they did last year, those people who swore they'd seen him. A woman had this tape of him talking to her on the phone. You notice how those people always seem to have a tape recorder or an answering machine that was on the blink, just that one time when Elvis called?"

"Yep. But you know, the picture they showed that man took just last year of somebody sitting right inside the back door that overlooks the pool at Graceland? It *did* look like Elvis."

"Yeah, well, lots of folks do. I saw one of those imitators yesterday are in town here for the contest, riding a motorcycle, you'd have sworn it was him." Slaughter turned on the radio, and a preacher declared, "Remember when your back was against the wall, His was against the cross." Slaughter punched the button until he hit Ray Charles singing "Georgia" and they both felt better.

"You ever been to Graceland?" Harry had been twice, couldn't believe what he'd seen the first time.

"Yeah. It's pitiful, ain't it? Man had all that money, his taste in his mouth."

Harry shook his head. "The Jungle Room. That knotty pine Kon-Tiki crap. Green shag on the ceiling."

"But you know—" Then Slaughter interrupted himself, pointing at the angel in front of the courthouse, they were taking the route through the heart of old downtown. "Guess what that pretty thing stands for?"

Harry didn't have a clue.

"Women's Christian Temperance Union put it up in memory of Mississippi prohibition. 1908. It's always been a joke, drinking in this state. All the counties around here are still dry, so folks come to Tupelo to take drunk, carouse—which I don't complain about, you understand, since it makes me a pretty penny at my joint. 'Course there ain't a place in the state you can't find yourself a taste, you know the right people. But back to Graceland, I have a theory on that."

"I'd love to hear it."

"It's simple. You know the Presleys were real poor. Country people. Had been white trash for years, both sides. My momma knew 'em, my granny, her momma, well, the Presleys, the Smiths, the Mansells, they were sharecroppers, some of them poorer than *we* were. You can ask Momma about that. When the Presleys moved over from East Tupelo to Mulberry Alley, that was right across Main from Shakerag, the old quarters they've torn down, and Momma, who was a year younger than Elvis, you know my granny *delivered* him, well, Momma said Granny felt sorry for the Presleys, they were so hard up. 'Course, it wouldn't do to let on."

Harry nodded. He knew about that, that delicate dance. *If you ain't better than a nigger, who are you better than?* is a philosophy that many a desperately poor white man has killed to disprove, not realizing it was poverty, not race, that was gnawing on his gut.

Slaughter continued, "But you see, the point is, white people, poor like that, they'd never been in a nice house. Houses like these." He pointed out the window. They were driving on Jefferson Street where some of the old guard still lived in mansions that had been standing since before Elvis was a boy. In fact, the very house that Slaughter was pointing at was the one that Red Holcomb had bought at auction from Dr. Jim Ireland. *"We* had—been in lots of nice big white houses."

Harry nodded again. As help, of course.

"So think about it. The Presleys still don't have a pot to piss in up in Memphis when Elvis all of a sudden hits big. First thing he did, bought his mom and dad a ranch-style house in a rich neighborhood, furnished it with new junk."

"Red rhinestone phone," said Harry, who definitely knew his Elvis. "Lots of big lamps."

"The boy didn't know any better. He'd never seen quality, and then where'd he go?"

"Hollywood," Harry nodded. Slaughter had a point. "Las Vegas."

"That's right. That's right. And that's what Graceland is. He went from poor white trash to rich white trash."

"You think he knew it, somewhere deep down?"

"I *know* the man knew it. Those rich white people, *quality* white folks up in Memphis, you think they were nice to him? Weren't laughing at him and his tacky house and tacky clothes and his child bride?"

"They asked him to play charity benefits."

"That's right. They'd invite him in, just like they always invited *our* musicians in, play the music, play the fool, but you see them having us over for dinner?"

Harry winced. It was *his* folks in New Orleans that they were talking about here. Same people. Uptown folks, generations of blue blood. Filled with the arrogance of old money and a racism that ran so deep nobody was even aware of it. "Why, darlin', that's the way things have always been," his mother would say, truly puzzled and hurt when he called her on the issue which was one of their major bones of contention, one of the reasons he'd been such a rebel, a dropout musician, a cab driver, oil rigger, insurance investigator, now ribs smoker. He hadn't left New Orleans, because the city was his heart, but he'd left Uptown, for good.

"Well, listen," Slaughter grinned, pulling up before a neat little brick house, "enough about white folks. We here. Come on in and meet my momma, let's see if she invites *you* to dinner."

"Yuk!" Sam shivered. "Right into a snake pit?"

"I know," said Velma, who'd found her tongue once she and Sam crossed the threshold of the Ladies'. The cool in here was a relief. "Them snakes were all over her. Of course, she's unconscious, having been flung out of that Toyota when it hit the gatepost, and it was a blessing, too. I don't reckon it'd made any difference we yelled it was the harmless snakes she'd flew into. Them rat snakes, they coil and strike, their tails going ninety miles a minute, and the racers, Lord Jesus, they sound exactly like rattlers, and them bites *hurt,* but they're not poison. I think she might've died of a heart attack, she'd come to in the middle of it. Even though she's pretty young."

"Twenties?" Sam pulled out her notebook and pen.

"Nawh. Thirty-five, maybe a little older. Good skin. Dyed her hair Sunbeam Blonde. Lady Clairol. That's what she said. I guess she was a natural brunette, had brown eyes."

"You remember a lot," Sam said.

"Oh, I have a photographic memory. Always have. I keep wanting to go on one of them game shows in Hollywood, but P.J. says it wouldn't be fitting to use a gift God gave me thataway."

"Really? So what else?"

"Well"—then Velma ticked off the details on her fingers—"she wears Fire and Ice lipstick, is a new widow, though she didn't seem very upset about losing her husband who was named Carlin, said she thought about dyeing her hair purple when he passed."

Sam laughed.

"Me and Pam thought that was ridiculous, but we didn't say so. She said she went out and bought herself a dress in black chiffon, cut real low and draped across the bosom"—Velma gestured across her own generous chest—"and bright red high heels. She must have been partial to red. She was wearing a fancy pair of red cowboy boots with white and silver inserts with her Calvin jeans. And she was an Elvis fan. I think that's it."

"Well, that's a lot. Maybe if she's an Elvis fan she's here in town for the imitators' contest."

"Could be. Oh, and she said her husband Carlin wouldn't let her eat tunafish, didn't like the smell on her breath. Like Elvis wouldn't let Priscilla, for the same reason."

It was absolutely amazing, the things people knew about that man's life. "But nothing about the truck driver?"

"Well, sure. You didn't ask me that. I just said I didn't see what kind of truck it was. He was a good-looking man, fifty–fifty-five, light brown hair, gray sideburns, blue eyes, six feet, probably go two hundred, dimples, nice voice. Said yes ma'am and no ma'am. Awfully apologetic about his flat knocking the woman off the road."

Bells were beginning to go off. This man was sounding very familiar, except for the hair. "Did he look like anybody to you?"

"Well, sure. Oh, I guess I didn't say that. I thought about it later, and I decided he was right."

"Right?"

"Well, he had one of them vanity plates, you know, I mean he had a regular Tennessee commercial plate too, MD12243, but in addition to that, he had a plate said PRSLEY. He looked enough like Elvis, older, of course, to be his brother."

"That's his commercial plate number?" Sam read it back to her from her notes and Velma nodded.

It was the same man, Sam just knew it, the impersonator she'd interviewed at the fairgrounds, the one who'd done that weird routine. He'd dyed his hair black, since Velma had seen him. Of course, they all did. She flipped back through her notebook.

"Does the name Dewey Travis ring a bell, Velma?"

"No. He didn't say his name. There is one more thing, though. He has this tattoo in big letters running up his forearm, so if he was propping it up on the window of his truck like this"—she held her arm at a right angle—"I bet you could read it going sixty. It said, ARE YOU LONESOME TONIGHT?"

It was too bad she was about to give up reporting. Otherwise she'd take on Velma as her sidekick. The woman was better than an Instamatic.

Harry stepped out of the dressing room of EP, Tupelo 38801 which was both the name and the address of the mail order business Lucille ran out of a little wood-frame one-room house next to the larger brick one where she lived. The room was filled, floor to ceiling, with hanging racks of clothes and shelves of boxes with hand-written labels like *Blue Moon Tour, 1954, Black and white shoes*.

Harry was wearing his own white shirt, open at the collar, the left arm slit to accommodate his cast, a long pink sports jacket, pegged trousers of black flecked with pink, black socks, and white bucks. He threw his good arm open to Slaughter and Lucille. "What do you think?"

Mother and son exchanged grins, and Slaughter said, "Ma, you've done it again!"

"Go on." Lucille ducked her head. "I didn't do a thing, except hold on to it. It was Bernie Lansky who designed that outfit."

Harry stepped back. "Bernie Lansky of the Lansky Brothers of Beale Street?" He didn't need to add of Memphis, Tennessee. They knew what they were talking about.

"That's right," Lucille said. "The very one. Open up that jacket, check the label."

"Designer for the King," said Harry.

"And for Rufus Thomas and Little Milton. That's where all the R&Bers bought their threads. Those Lanskys, they got hip quick selling clothes on Beale, the black heart of the blues," said Slaughter.

"You talk like you were there," Lucille teased her son. " 'Course, I guess you were for a while, when you were too little to enjoy it."

"Uh-oh. Back up. Old lady's about to tell us about her hell-raising days." Slaughter threw Harry a wink.

"No, I am not. I wouldn't give you the satisfaction. I'm just going to fit this young man up, and then I need y'all to get. I have things to do. *Otherwise,*"— she smiled at Harry, who she thought was nice-looking, for a white boy—"I'd ask y'all to stay for supper."

At that, Slaughter and Harry slapped high fives. "Man, you in like Flynn," laughed Slaughter.

"Lucille?" Harry started then stopped. He didn't want to know it if the answer was no.

"What, son?"

"Did this outfit, I mean, was it, did it—?"

"You want to know if the King himself wore them threads? Of *course* he did. What do you think this is?" Lucille gestured with an arm robed in purple velvet with a trim of crystals on the ruching at the wrist. She'd fashioned her gown after one she'd seen on TV on Jessye Norman, a good old Augusta, Georgia, girl, even if she did talk funny. "That's what my whole business is, selling things that belonged to Elvis, pre–August 14, 1958."

"The day Gladys died," said Harry, gingerly running a hand up and down the lapels of his jacket as if they were filled with stardust. Then he looked back at Lucille. "I don't understand. Why that date?"

"It's simple, just small town doings. My momma and her family did Gladys some favors when the Presleys needed help bad. They were about to starve. Momma asked her cousin, who made deliveries for a black grocer, to give little Elvis a job, and he did. Gladys didn't forget. When it started looking like Elvis was going to hit, Gladys, who was not the stupid woman people made her out to be, started packing up all her son's old things. And I mean *all*. That woman never threw away a thing. You don't, you know, you grow up that poor. Elvis moved 'em into that first nice house in Memphis and bought 'em brand new furniture, Gladys saved every stick of their old stuff, packed it in the den. I still have some of it over in the house, you want to see it. It's pitiful." She paused and grinned. "But it's valuable."

"So Gladys gave everything to your momma and she passed it along to you?"

Lucille nodded. "She did, said she didn't have a head for business, and that was the truth, though she was a powerful healer and midwife, she birthed more babies—" Somebody was knocking on the door.

"Hello? Hel-lo?" A pretty brunette wearing a white polka dot on red suit, the jacket with a little peplum effect which was nice with her small waist, stuck her head in, then when she saw Lucille had company, backed up. "Oh. Excuse me. I didn't mean to interrupt."

"That's okay, honey," said Lucille, crossing the room and taking her by the arm. "Come on in here and meet my son, Slaughter Phipps." Slaughter bowed at the waist and gave her his very best smile. "I love your shoes," he said, looking at her scarlet high heels. Lucille shot him a look. "And his friend Harry Zack from New Orleans. This is Velma Hightower from—"

"Waycross, Georgia," said Mary Ann, smiling. That's what it said on Velma's driver's license, and she was doing her best to keep her story straight.

"Velma's going to entertain us this evening," said Lucille, "some of us ladies."

"Well." Mary Ann dimpled. "I'm not sure how entertaining I'm going to be. I'm just a saleslady."

"What do you sell?" asked Slaughter, taking a silver dollar out of his pocket and flipping it in the air. "Heads or tails?" He smiled at Mary Ann.

Well, *he* was something, wasn't he? And the other one was cute, too. Tupelo looked like it might be *full* of handsome men. Maybe she'd settle down here. Right, Mary Ann, she caught herself. Maybe you could move in with the other Mrs. McClanahan and the two of you could hang out at the bar at the Ramada, that's where the woman at the registration desk had said the action was.

"Heads," she said to Slaughter. Then she giggled. "I don't mean that's what I sell, I sell lingerie." That line always slayed them—except, of course, it hadn't worked with Dewey. But then Dewey was weird.

Slaughter opened his hand. "You win. Lingerie, huh?" He said it staring straight into her eyes. Then a big grin cut across his handsome face and he pressed the silver into her hand. "You put that on that shiner tonight, it's gonna take the blood away. You'll be right as rain in the morning."

"Well, gentlemen," said Lucille all of a sudden, herding them toward the door. "I think y'all said y'all had to be someplace, like tending your fire, am I right?"

"You're right, Lucille," said Harry, taking Slaughter by the arm. "Got to go *on* that fire. Got to tend to some ribs."

"You need me?" Slaughter asked Harry, lingering. Then to Mary Ann, "I'd be happy to help you with y'all's party."

With that, Lucille shoved them through the door and slammed it. Slaughter turned on the porch, tapped on the window, and waved. Lucille shook her head at him and snapped the blinds shut.

• • • • • • • • • • • • **20**

If there was one thing Dewey hated, it was following directions. Not that he was a complete fool about it. Like he knew he couldn't ignore road maps, he didn't mean that. He meant like some woman telling him something that started, *Now, Dewey,* with that tone in her voice, hands on her hips.

So now, instead of heading out to get the equipment for their stunt with the McClanahan woman like Mary Ann had told him to, he was calling on one of his lady friends.

You'd be surprised how many of those he had in Tupelo.

It had been so easy. A couple of other truckers had said to him, Boy, you want to fall into some stuff, just clean yourself up, throw on a little Brut (which was what Dewey wore anyway), pull into Bogart's at the Ramada Inn Wednesday through Friday nights, Thursday's the best, about eight. You'll have to beat the women off with a stick. From northeast Mississippi, southwest Tennessee, northwest Alabama, they can't get enough of the traveling men stopping through Tupelo. What's funny is that a lot of the married ones, their men are traveling too, keeping company with some other women in another place like Bogart's, somewhere else along the traveling man's route.

And those old boys had been right.

The very first time Dewey had walked into Bogart's, he hadn't even cruised past the fake palms when he'd been waylaid by a big blonde with huge hair and a beauty mark on her cleavage peeping out of a keyhole in stretchy black lace. He'd barely taken in the half-acre of pink and green tables, bentwood chairs, circular bar so big you could work up a thirst walking around it, band pumping "I Heard It Through the Grapevine" through speakers the size of a stepvan, than she'd dragged him over to a fountain with colored lights, reminded him of Graceland, whispered in his ear: You wanta try to lick it off? He'd guessed she meant the beauty mark. So he gave it a shot there next to the tinkling water and the colored lights and later in her room. The beauty mark was real, which was more than he could say for other parts of the blonde, including her name. Marilyn.

It didn't take him long to figure out that most of the women didn't use their real names. In fact, it was kind of a game they played, seeing who could be the most outrageous. They used the names of movie stars and singers, but sometimes—Dewey guessed they called each other on the phone and agreed on the date—they'd come in makeup and costumes really trying to look like the stars.

He'd spent the night with Julia Roberts, Madonna, a bad Elizabeth Taylor (though he wasn't sure there was a good one anymore), and Ann-Margret.

Eventually he'd hooked up with a local woman whom he saw on a regular basis, and then things got pretty interesting.

She, Lovie, was actually the second local woman.

The first one, who said her name was Melanie, but he didn't think it was, met him only that once at Bogart's, that'd have to be eight, ten months ago. She'd been pretty loaded, upset about something, her husband probably. He'd seen the kind before, looking for a way to get back at the old man. They'd done it in his truck. Then about a month later he'd been picking up some Co-cola and Nabs at the Fast Lane convenience store when Melanie walked in. All dressed up. Looked like a lady. Acted like one too, real polite, except he could tell she didn't really want to visit, there were no reruns in their future. Then this second woman, that was Lovie, cruised in for a quart of milk and started being cute. Like, Hi! Who's your friend? Like she wanted to make something of it. Melanie, cool as a cuke, turns to Lovie and says, This old boy? This's Dewey. And since you always want everything I've got, I'll tell you what, I can recommend this studhorse to you, Lovie. Triple A guaranteed, bonded, four stars. And one hell of a fuck. Then she stomped off.

The little girl behind the counter at the Fast Lane dropped a whole roll of quarters at that one, they're rolling all over the floor and in the time that it took Lovie and Dewey to help her pick them up, Lovie brushed up against him a couple of times in a way that let him know that backtalk from Melanie had turned her on.

Now Lovie wasn't exactly Dewey's type. Melanie was. Melanie with her big blue eyes and dark hair, pale skin, Melanie looked like Elvis's high school girlfriend. Dewey had gone to a lot of trouble and expense tracking down a photo of the girlfriend when she was young. She'd be about fifty-three now. He'd written her a letter, too, found out her married name and her address, but she'd never answered him.

Whereas Lovie was blond and round and peaches

and cream. She lied about her age, but every once in a while she said something that let him know she wasn't that much younger than him. But she was well preserved, and then when she got real daring and started sneaking him into her house, well, that was something else. Dewey'd never been in a house like Lovie's before. It was bigger than Graceland.

And nicer, too, though he hated to say it. It was class. Which seemed kind of funny when he thought about it, big old water baby, splashing around with him in her giant tub. She was into kinky things he'd never even thought of, which was fun but he didn't exactly respect her the next morning. Actually he suspected she might have turned some tricks to get where she was, so it didn't weigh on his conscience that every once in a while he'd help himself to some pretty trinket that was lying around.

Yeah, screwing Lovie was pretty hunky-dory until that day, oh, it'd been about a month ago, they'd been floating around the tub, that Venus woman in the painting smiling down at them with that funny look like she knew something you didn't, and Lovie was raving on about her big party she was planning. That's all she talked about lately. She could hardly keep her mind on what he was there for, though sometimes the details of the party seemed to put her in the mood. Now that was weird. A woman who'd get turned on talking about hors d'oeuvres and gold cocktail napkins and who she was going to invite and who she wasn't. But she did—turned on like a light switch. She flushed all over, and the next thing he knew she was practically drowning him, and then she whispered in his ear, "I ought to invite *you*. We could dye your hair and you could dress up like Elvis. Wouldn't that be something?"

No, it wouldn't, Dewey wanted to say, but he couldn't because Lovie was practically smothering him. When he was on earth Elvis had a gutful of rich people taking advantage of him, parading him around their fancy parties, thank you very much.

Then she said, "Did I ever tell you we went to Milam School here in Tupelo together, me and Elvis? The kids all hated him. He was so weird and pitiful and poor. He was always pulling out that guitar and sucking up to the teachers. Sixth, seventh, and part of the eighth grade, before his family moved to Memphis, the teachers used to drag him from one room to another to sing and play. Kids liked to hear the songs, but they never liked *him*." She paused in her bouncing up and down on top of him and said, "I did, though."

"Oh, yeah?" Dewey managed.

Lovie was the only woman he'd ever known who could go right on with the program and talk a mile a minute too. It made him want to put a pillowcase over her head.

"I was his favorite junior high girlfriend. He said he was proud of me because I was elected Queen Beauty of the seventh grade. I mean, I was poor as he was, we were from the same neighborhood, but I was *pretty,* and Elvis said I could prove it—because I had that title. I noticed that afterwards, he always liked beauty queens with crowns. You want me to go put mine on? I still have it."

Wasn't that something? Lovie had been that close to Elvis. He wondered if they'd done it, nawh, probably not, junior high, they were pretty young, but maybe, he was about to ask her when Lovie said, still bouncing up and down, "So it broke his heart when I dumped him. I bet there's not many can say that they dumped Elvis. But I did. It got to be embarrassing, there I was, moving a little bit ahead, being Beauty and all, even though I was from Milltown. Elvis tagging along in his tacky clothes was reminding everybody of how poor we were, so I told him. I said, 'Go away. I hate your guts.' I didn't really, but he shamed me.'' Then, "Hey!'' she'd said to Dewey, who was still beneath her. "What's the matter, old son?''

For Dewey, who was furious, had gone limp. He pushed her up off of him and stepped out of that big silly tub filled with duckies, water toys, and him. Thought he was one of them toys. Just like Elvis. Use him. Suck him dry. Then she'd tell him, scoot.

So he dried off, dressed, stomped out—What are you doing? she was screaming. He never saw her again, at least not like that. Not until he got The Calling. And made The Plan. The Sacred Plan to Avenge the Presley Family Enemies in Tupelo. He'd written those words at the top of a page of notebook paper with this pen that wrote in gold he found at a fancy drugstore.

When he'd called her two days ago, said he had to see her, she was all huffy. Then she said, Okay, her husband was out of town anyway. Trying to sound exasperated, but she was faking, he could tell. He'd slipped into the house like he always did, after the help was gone. Slipped into her, then dropped fifty milligrams of Valium in her Diet Co-cola, gave it to her to sip when she'd worked up a good sweat. At that point, he could have dropped her in the tub, and that would have been that. But drowning wasn't part of The Plan.

The Plan was all-electric. Dewey hadn't even had to think about it. It'd come to him in a flash. Take a look at Elvis's motto, TCB, with the flash of lightning. That's what Dewey was doing. Taking Care of Business with Electricity. Electricity was perfect. It was a force of nature. It was just. And besides, Dewey, who'd fooled around with wiring, knew how to do it.

So, implementing The Plan, once Lovie was out-for-the-count in Valium Land, he laid her on her king-sized bed that she must have told him a million times came from some plantation near Greenville. Like used furniture was something to be proud of.

He'd left her snoring while he disconnected the main ground wire to the house. Then he took the ground wire from the whirlpool-motor branch circuit feeder and fastened it under one of the lugs for the timer that turned on the outside ground lights at six-thirty, off at ten. He reset the timer to come on at three-thirty, to make sure. When that happened, the housing of the whirlpool motor would be energized, which in turn would energize the #8 bond wire leading to the cold water pipe, which would zap the entire water system.

It'd been a piece of cake. Worked like a charm, too, the next day when she stepped in the tub. He'd read about it in the paper. Part Two of The Plan, Floyd Morgan, that was eating at his guts, but there was time to do something about that, after he started working out the details for the next part. Saving best for last.

And then he had to do that thing for Mary Ann. She got on his nerves, but since she'd dyed her hair dark brown, she was his Ideal Type Woman so he'd humor her. For now.

And then, there was this one other little matter he was thinking about taking care of, just for the fun of it—with Obie Vaughn and Shawn Magoo, those stuck-up impersonators who wouldn't know Elvis if he sat down beside them in a coffee shop and ordered biscuits and sorghum syrup and bacon, very well done please, in fact, burn it.

21

So?" said Sam into the phone. "How am I going to read your story, you keep calling me on the phone?" She and Harpo were trying to take a nap on a quilt-covered chaise in the tarted-up guesthouse at the Holcombs'.

"So," said Ollie, "we ran the license. Velma's trucker's named Dewey Travis, an independent out of Holly Springs, that's just north of here. Then we looked a little deeper, found the old boy's been in trouble now and again. Assault and battery a dozen times. Bar fights. Looks like he probably killed another trucker in a dustup last year, but the charges were dropped. As were a couple of assault raps from girlfriends who changed their minds. Man might not ought to be wandering around, much less have a trucker's license."

"Holly Springs is where Floyd Morgan the almost-electrocuted barbecuer's from too. Do you think that's interesting?"

Estella, listening in on the line, wondered what Floyd Morgan had to do with anything. He and his whole family were rotten scoundrels, had a lot in common with her Sonny, until old Floyd the lawyer seemed to have taken religion and left Tupelo about two steps ahead of a bunch of people who wanted to kill him. She'd heard he'd bought one of those big old pretty houses in Holly Springs that was on the Pilgrimage every year, Floyd probably pretending his family had lived there forever instead of buying it for cash he'd stolen from other people.

"Well, it is interesting," said Ollie. "The man who gives a ride to the woman who may or may not have lifted Velma Hightower's wallet is dirty, lives in the same town as a Q contestant whose cooker almost kills him. But does it mean anything?"

Velma Hightower. Now where had Estella heard that name before? Then she got it. She almost said into the phone, catching herself just in time, I'm gonna see Velma in a little while over at Dixie's, she's selling lingerie. You want me to warn her about this Dewey? Tell her y'all know who stole her wallet?

It'd taken Estella forever to worm the lingerie business out of Dixie, who wanted it to be a surprise, but Estella had explained that she couldn't come to the meeting and certainly couldn't *buy* anything now that she'd reduced her personal possessions so close to her goal, unless Dixie told her all about it. Then maybe she could chuck a few belongings out the back door before she went over with her checkbook. Dixie caved in, not wanting Estella to miss the meeting, especially knowing that Estella was mad with her for traipsing around in the yard last evening with that rifle. The very idea!

"How are you doing on Lovie?" Sam asked.

"Well, her husband's alibi checks out. He was definitely in Atlanta, which doesn't really mean anything since he could have set the murder up, or *had* it set up, before he left."

"I want to know about the lover."

Lover! Lovie Rakestraw? Estella thought, well, that goes to show you. You can never tell.

"We're going to be talking with everybody who knew her, see if we can come up with the man. And we're canvassing the neighbors, the neighbors' help, the Rakestraws' help again. Just keep hoping somebody remembers something. What we have from the scene are a slough of prints, a few hairs, some fibers. Looks like there were a lot of people parading in and out of her house. But then, word is she liked to show it off."

"Maybe she did that one time too many to somebody who was jealous."

Now that's a possibility, thought Estella. There were plenty of Tupelo ladies who thought Miss Lovie was too grand for her own good, though Estella doubted any of them would go to so much trouble. Most of the catfights in Tupelo were two women screaming at each other across their grocery carts in Blount's Supermarket. And if someone was really riled up, well, hot lead and quick draw were more Tupelo style than killing people in their tubs.

"In the meantime," said Ollie, "Grippa and I have the chief breathing down our necks. Hell, I've got as much on that dustup over at your house as I have on Lovie. Not that it's not important, of course, Harry winged and all . . ."

Estella held her breath.

Sam said, "Like what?"

"The bullet, of course. And its trajectory—well, it looks like we can figure a youngster pulling the trigger. Not Walter, Jr., 'cause we know where he was, and he's too tall anyway, but maybe one of his friends out to jerk Red's chain. Football players, high school, you know kids stick together."

"You mean the shooter's short?"

"About five feet."

"So since when are high school football players short?"

Shut up, girl, thought Estella. You're too smart for your own good.

"Okay, a student manager. A water boy. A little bitty cheerleader. What the hell do I know?"

The man was sounding pressed. Awful lot of action for a little town like Tupelo. "How tall was the woman Miss Estella saw out in the yard?" she asked.

"Five-four or so. Of course, Miss Estella was in her house, it was dark—"

"Full moon," Sam interrupted.

"Okay, but the woman was some distance away, and I'm not sure Miss Estella's eyesight is what it once was."

Now, wait a minute, Estella wanted to say, but she couldn't of course.

"Ollie, what was the woman wearing?"

"Hold up, I'm looking at the report. Jeans. Jeans and fancy red boots. Estella said this morning she was dressed up in a navy suit."

Sam tapped on the telephone receiver with a pen. Estella wanted to tell her to stop it. Then she said, "Ollie, let's run a couple up the flagpole."

"Shoot."

"One, Velma Hightower said the woman who stole her wallet was wearing jeans, Calvin Kleins, according to Velma, whose memory I'd definitely trust, and red boots with silver and white inserts. Now she was blond, but she could have dyed her hair, or be wearing a wig."

Estella was lost. *Who* were they talking about? Velma or somebody else?

Ollie said, "Well, now wouldn't that be interesting, the woman nabbed Velma's wallet at the snake farm cruises into town the same day with Dewey Travis, a potential bad actor, takes a potshot through Red's window—at who? One of y'all. But why?''

"Maybe that's what she did. But there's another way of looking at this. Ask yourself, who do we know who's short, about five feet, and had the opportunity?''

"I don't follow you.''

"Estella.''

Estella almost dropped the phone.

"And she wasn't in the kitchen when the shooting happened. Hell, I didn't even know she existed at that point—didn't meet her till the next morning.''

"So you're saying maybe she fired one at her own son?''

"Have you ever heard her talk about him? They have one of the strangest mother-son relationships I've ever seen. She bad-mouths him constantly, but she sleeps on the floor by his bed. I'd say it's because she doesn't trust him as far as she can throw him.''

"She sleeps where?''

"Yep. Can't you see her in little striped Brooks Brothers pj's curled up on a rag rug? And I bet when y'all questioned her about the shooting, it never occurred to you to suspect her because of who she is.''

There was a long silence on the line while Ollie and Estella mulled that one over.

Harry thought it would be a wonderment if Team Blue Pig didn't self-destruct.

Somehow he'd assumed that Buddy would be pleased that he and Slaughter had pulled the sartorial part of their act together. In fact, carrying the showmanship angle one step further, on the way back from Lucille's, while Slaughter was holding forth about what a fine-looking woman that Velma Hightower was, Harry'd been working on a little ditty for the judges. He'd already heard Slaughter singing along with Ray Charles on the radio, doing a fine falsetto on the bridges. And Buddy, well, judging from the little man's speaking voice, if he didn't have a bass that'd vibrate your wallpaper, Harry'd be surprised. Maybe one of them played guitar, which he couldn't with his broken arm. And he could teach the other one to play spoons real quick.

"So where's the good china, silver, crystal, and linen?" were the first words out of Buddy's mouth when Harry and Slaughter stepped into Team Blue Pig's HQ. "Didn't y'all stop by Estella's like I asked you?"

"You didn't say a word about that before," said Slaughter.

"Well." Buddy snorted. "I don't know what you think those outside judges are going to eat off of when they come roaming around. Paper plates?" He spit the words. "And we want to do something real special for the inside judges over in the judging tent. Thought maybe we could use Estella's great grandmother's Georgian serving platters, one of us carry the Baccarat candelabra. Now you're pretending I didn't tell you that?"

Harry thought maybe Buddy had been hanging his head over the smoker too long, was suffering from oxygen deficit. Not that there was enough oxygen in the air anyway, it seemed to be hotter and heavier by the minute. Then Harry noticed the small table and four chairs that had appeared in their assigned space along with a tiny platform which held a stand-up mike and a couple of blue-gelled theatrical spots.

"We're gonna make it a nightclub, Blue Pig," Buddy explained. "I'll sing, y'all be the waiters when the outside judges come around visiting."

"Only if we serving up *your* head," said Slaughter. "Like John the Baptist's—or somebody else's I might mention."

Harry didn't know what that last meant, but he jumped right in, said to Buddy, "Actually we're thinking along the same lines. Except what if we *all* sing? And this being Tupelo, I've been diddling around with the words to the King's 'Tryin' to Get to You,' you know, giving 'em a little Q twist. Like this . . .

> *I've been smoking over hickory*
> *Even threw in some mesquite*
> *I've been smoking night and day*
> *I've been turning all the way,*
> *Judges, hoping to get to you."*

Buddy didn't say a word, made a face like he smelled something nasty, and started stomping off in his little zoot suit beneath a voluminous white apron that looked like it might belong to Cooter Williams. Then he remembered something, stopped, and turned. "I know y'all don't care, but that whole hog's done on. I split it right down the inside of its backbone and put it in the cooker, belly side down. Now, while I take care of some things, y'all might want to try to keep it basted, it's not too much trouble." He shoved a bug sprayer that had been retrofitted with a stainless syringe into Harry's hands.

"What the hell is that? You sticking bug poison in the hog?" Slaughter sneered. "Furthermore, old man, you going to do some nightclub number to impress the judges, whyn't you ask me, since I *own* one?"

"A tonk is what you own. This is a classy place, and that is not bug spray, it's my basting sauce, and if you had the sense God gave a hoot owl, you'd shoot the pig with it all over about every thirty minutes." With that, Buddy whirled again and headed out, smacking straight into a Holly Springs Hogboy wearing a red Allis-Chalmers hat above his black cowboy shirt trimmed with rhinestones. The Hogboy, who was sniffing out the competition, had Cooter Williams in tow.

"Well, how y'all doing?" he said. "I'm Roy Clowers, son-in-law to Floyd Morgan—that's the man your ladyfriend gave the mouth-to-mouth to and saved." He was talking to Harry, but shaking hands all around. Harry noticed that Buddy seemed to change his mind about leaving, at least for the moment. Being a gentleman, and considering Cooter was an important inside judge, Buddy wasn't about to be rude or stupid.

"I'll tell you what." Roy stopped as Slaughter passed each man a beer. "It's a good thing that Miss Sam did what she did. If I had to go back to Holly Springs and tell my momma that Floyd kicked the bucket, well, the way she loves that old man, and them newlyweds and all, I know it of killed her."

"Newlyweds?" said Cooter. "My Lord!"

"Floyd says a man ain't never too old to change his ways and join the human race," Roy said.

"Floyd Morgan? Used to live in Tupelo? I remember that man," said Buddy.

Slaughter shot him a look: You *would*. But he kept smiling for the folks. Then reaching for a place to put down his beer, he knocked over the bug sprayer.

"What's *that?*" asked Roy.

"Our main secret weapon," Slaughter said quickly. Buddy turned, his eyebrows raised at Slaughter's singing a different tune. "Oh, yeah," said Slaughter. "Mr. Buddy Kidd, he makes one mean Q machine. This is only part of his artillery."

Buddy nodded, taking in the compliment. If it was

a compliment, not just part of Slaughter's shuck-and-jive Q routine.

"Yep," Slaughter went on, "my old man has the recipe for his basting sauce in a lockbox down in Jackson."

Did he say my old man? Harry thought he must have misheard.

"And the one for the eating sauce same thing, except up in Memphis. Yeah, my stepdad, well, ex-stepdad Buddy here, knows you can't be too careful with your recipes."

Stepdad? Is that what Slaughter said? Ex-stepdad? Did that mean Lucille had been married to Buddy? What the hell?

Then Buddy tossed in, not wanting Slaughter to have all the fun, "That way, they break in one, they still don't have the other. Pig ain't nothing without both sauces."

"Can you tell us just one little thing about your ingredients?" Roy begged, which was exactly what he was supposed to do.

Harry was still shaking his head. Buddy was Slaughter's stepdad? The same Buddy he was accusing of murder?

"Well." Buddy spit on the ground, which is what *he* was supposed to do. "I can tell you this, it involves a lot of blues."

"Blues?" said Roy.

"Yep. It's important that the pig you're smoking for whole pig has the right attitude when it goes to that Great Trough in the Sky. And the way you do that, you play the pig's favorite blues right there at the pig's last trot. It relaxes him, there ain't gonna be one speck of tension in that meat."

"And how do you know what that is, his favorite?"

"Well, it's a lot of trial and error. This particular

pig"—Buddy pointed at the smoker—"he was partial to John Lee Hooker. Lot of 'em though, they like a shouter, like Etta James."

"Is he putting us on?" Roy asked Cooter.

"Now why would I do you like that?" said Buddy. "Fact, I'll do you one better. I'll tell you the biggest secret of all."

"You ready?" Cooter asked Roy. The two men braced each other for the load of trash that was about to fly.

"Jack Daniel's," Buddy announced.

"You put bourbon whiskey in your sauce?" said Cooter. "Well, I'll be John Browned."

"I know them as uses Kahlúa, and then there's the cognac contingent. Then you got your black coffee folks—" said Roy.

"I didn't say I put it in the sauce," Buddy interrupted. "I said I use it." And then he stomped one small foot on the ground and pounded himself on the back.

That called for a round of shoulder-hugging and knee-slapping and another beer. And another couple of lies.

Then Buddy said, "You know, Roy, I don't mean to be rude, but the Floyd Morgan I remember, Cooter, you remember him too, you say he's *your* stepdad?"

"He is. And I know what you're about to say. You're gonna tell me he's the second meanest man you ever knew, the first being Red Holcomb. Am I right?"

Buddy laughed. "You got that one okay. Is he still mean?"

"Nope. He's still tight, has the first shiny new dime he ever made, but I think this brush with the angel of death might have even solved that. Y'all know he's almost electrocuted yesterday, police been sniffing around like they think somebody jiggled with his cooker, but I think they're barking up the wrong bush. Anyway, the point is, about ten years ago, Floyd fell out of a tree and broke his neck, and it changed his life.''

"He stopped being mean?" Buddy looked like he couldn't believe it.

"Man owned a lot of property," Cooter explained to Harry. "Owned most of Shakerag, the old—" And then Cooter stopped.

"Quarters, where we all lived," Slaughter rescued him. "Pitiful houses, falling down, he wouldn't ever fix a damned thing. You could freeze to death, holes in the walls, the ceilings, in the floors big enough a baby could fall through, no indoor plumbing, man didn't care unless you didn't come up with the rent, then you were out in the street, Jack. And it wasn't even paved.''

"Owned a bunch of East Tupelo, too," said Buddy. "Poor white folks over there. Man didn't discriminate in his mean. He was an equal opportunity Simon Legree. Plumb color-blind, except for green.''

"I hear that," said Slaughter. "You know, I remember Momma talking about how Floyd Morgan threw the Presleys out.''

"No," said Harry. "He evicted the Presleys?"

"Yep. He'd loaned Vernon Presley, Elvis's dad, the money to build that little house that Elvis was born in. You know, that one they've fixed up at the Birthplace?''

The men all nodded.

"And then Vernon got behind on the payments on the loan, which was something like two hundred dollars. Idn't that pitiful, but it was a lot then, especially to pore folks. Well anyway, Floyd took the house.''

"Floyd took the Birthplace?" Harry was incredulous.

Buddy laughed. "Well, you know, Harry, it wasn't a religious shrine then, when Elvis was a pup. Didn't people come from around the world to visit like they do now.''

''Now, Buddy, it ain't that many, day-to-day,'' said Cooter. ''It ain't like Graceland.''

''What about on the Deathiversary? Ooooohweeee. Look out!'' Buddy exclaimed. ''Now you have to admit, that's some folks.''

''The Deathiversary?'' asked Roy, who'd grown up in Arkansas.

''August sixteenth,'' Cooter explained. ''That's what Tupeloans call it, the anniversary of Elvis's death. Buddy's right, busloads of folks drive in here then. Tribute Week, they call it up in Memphis. Most of the fans hang out the whole time up there within spitting distance of Graceland like it was the Vatican, lighting candles, swapping lies, decorating their motel rooms, trading Elvis stuff. What comes here are mostly the Japanese and the English.''

''Some funny folks,'' Buddy said.

''They do these bus tours, book up all the motel rooms in advance, the salesmen—this is a big town for salesmen, the lonely ladies in this part of Mississippi, Alabama, Tennessee, come over and hang out at Bogart's in the Ramada, dance, drink, look for a little company—salesmen don't even stop in Tupelo Deathiversary week. Tupelo police turn out, let the Japanese take pictures of each other fingering their service revolvers. They arrest a few drunk Brits. An Aussie now and then. But that's just that week. Day-to-day? Like I was saying, it's pretty low key, the whole Elvis thing.''

Buddy nodded. ''Cooter's right. You do the Birthplace, Priceville Cemetery where his twin's buried, though nobody knows exactly where. I understand there's an old man out there makes a pretty penny pointing out the plot for the tourists, not that he knows either.''

Slaughter said, "Lawhon School in East Tupelo, Milam Junior High, Tupelo Hardware, where Gladys bought Elvis his first guitar, the fairgrounds here where he performed, that's pretty much the tour."

Harry was still shaking his head. He couldn't get over his afternoon. Just wait till he told Sam. Here he was, minding his own business, just hanging around barbecuing, and all of a sudden he was knee-deep in the miraculous.

He'd met Lucille, who turned out not only to have the leading collection of pre–August 14, 1958, Elvisiana in the western world, but to have *known* Elvis. He hoped she'd have some time before they had to go back to sit down and talk with him.

Plus, here he was *wearing* the King's very clothes.

And Sammy, without even knowing it, had saved the life of the man who repossessed the Birthplace.

Not to mention this latest scoop on Buddy Kidd and Slaughter Phipps.

Harry couldn't remember having spent a more interesting afternoon.

Dewey had picked up Red's little scarlet Lamborghini just as Red was making a left off North Gloster onto West Main. There was a train coming on the tracks that ran right across the middle of Tupelo's main intersection. Dewey was wondering, what if he pulled his bike in front of Red's little wop sports car as it straddled the track, then pretended to stall. He liked it. He could imagine Red's face as the train chugged closer and closer, blasting that whistle, trying to brake—but it wouldn't work. Red wouldn't know why he died.

He had to know why.

The others, Floyd and Lovie, well, he had said to Lovie, right before she passed out on her Valium-laced Diet Co-cola when he was at her house to wire the tub, the day before she died, he'd said, Who'd you think you are, breaking the King's heart? Those big old blue eyes had popped open and swarmed around for a second, trying to focus. Then he'd said, Do you know who I am? Do you, Miss Milam Beauty? Do you? Do you? Do you? Fear had flashed through her gaze for a minute, but then she'd moaned a little bit and conked out cold. He hoped some of that had come back to her before she died.

Floyd, he hadn't wanted to take the chance, he was such a wily old devil. It wasn't worth getting in the last lick, seeing as how it might boomerang. And look what had happened. He was right. The trick hadn't worked and Floyd hadn't died, and if he'd known who'd tried to do him, well, they'd already have yours truly chained to a wall waiting for the express shipment to Parchman.

He could do it right with Floyd next time.

But Red? Red Holcomb, the cherry he'd saved for the last bite, wanting to taste that sweet revenge in his mouth, no way that man wasn't going to know who was delivering him to the Devil. No way at all.

Now for a minute back there, Dewey had thought Red was going to turn in at the fairgrounds. But he didn't. That was good. Dewey didn't want to get mired up with those BBQ crazies right now. Impersonators. That was for later. Then Red had made a right onto Elizabeth. Dewey hung back, not wanting Red to pick up on the motorcycle. Not yet.

Dewey parked under a big pecan tree right on the edge of the fish hatchery property. That's where Red had stopped, at the Allen National Fish Hatchery, pulled the bright red car right in front of the big rambling white Victorian house with the green roof where the hatchery managers used to live. There was a pond across the road from the house, and it was into that pond that Red had heaved a wriggling croaker sack when Dewey walked up behind him.

"A good a way as any to kill a bunch of cats," Dewey said, taking the measure of the man. He was right, they were about the same size. Both of 'em with the bodies of retired jocks, slim-hipped, still bowed-up, but slipping in the area of the breadbasket. Dewey hadn't been up this close to Red since he'd begun implementing The Plan. Hadn't wanted to spook him.

Red jumped. "What?" Spit the cigar he was smoking right out of his mouth into the gravel.

"Cats. Good way to kill 'em."

Red's blue eyes narrowed. "Yep, would be. If it was cats."

Out in the shallow water, the burlap bag hadn't completely sunk. Shapes were still struggling in it. Then Dewey heard a dog yelp, and the bag disappeared. Neither of the men spoke for a long moment, stared up at the cumulus clouds gathering overhead. Red, who was wearing a tan riding jacket over a creamy shirt of wool challis, dark brown jodhpurs, and brown calf riding boots, took in Dewey's blue jeans and black leather jacket, the cheap red poly-mix cowboy shirt with the plastic pearl snap buttons, and said, "Do I know you?"

Dewey grinned. "Yes and no."

Red turned on his heel and reached for the door of the Lamborghini. "Then you'll excuse me now." He tossed the words back over his shoulder, not turning his head, so he didn't see Dewey take the six quick steps right up beside him. He didn't hear them either, even on the gravel. Dewey, who had studied karate for years, moved silently like a cat. However, Red did feel the two-inch barrel of the .38 Special that Dewey jammed into his spine right at the small of his back.

"Fuck up," Dewey said, "you ain't ever gonna trip the light fantastic again."

• • • • • • • • • • • • • **22**

So you're going to read it right now?" Ollie had said on the phone.

"Any minute." Then Sam snuggled deeper on the chaise. The more she and Ollie talked, the more she'd been looking forward to his story. Harpo was looking forward to her being still.

"Oh, Jesus," Ollie said. "What if you hate it?"

Did he think she wasn't afraid of that too? "Ollie, look. I'm not an editor. I'm a reporter. I'm not even a good judge for your fiction."

"Sort-of fiction. Some of it's true."

She told him to cool it. When she finished the story, she'd give him a call. She hung up the phone and picked up his manuscript. . . .

LITTLE MAN
A story by Oliver Priest

Slidell Peace was big for his age. At eleven, he already stood two inches over five feet and rolled the broad shoulders of adolescence. The beginnings of a mustache smudged his full upper lip. *Little Man* the whores in his daddy's Beale Street hotels called him when they pinched his brown cheeks to make him blush.

And oh, how they loved to make him blush.

"Little Man, he be coming into his own soon." Delilah, a high yellow woman, would wink across her bed at Loubella, the heavy-bosomed ebony whore who brushed her breasts against Slidell every time he passed.

"Sho nuff, child, that little pecker of his gone be standing up and your old thang gone be *paying* some attention." Then Loubella would lean her head back and her deep laughter filled the second-story room, found its way along the hall, down the stairs and out the front door. Slidell thought Loubella's laugh could probably be heard all the way down Beale, straight on past the city limits, across the Tennessee River, and half the way across the state to Nashville, where they made not just records but laws.

Slidell wondered about laws. Why were there laws against what Delilah and Loubella and the others did in River City Hotels Numbers Two and Three? People did the same thing, screwing folks they weren't married to, in Hotel Number One and nobody thought a thing about it. But the women who did the screwing there were called girlfriends or lovers or wives, instead of whores. From what Slidell could see, the screwing was pretty much the same.

The sheets sure ended up the same. Slidell was so tired of looking at the hotels' sheets he thought he was going to die.

He wiped a thin line of sweat from where it was dribbling down through his close-cropped nappy hair. Already he was bored enough to spit at the white mountains of double-bed sheets piled around him in the laundry room of Number Two, and it was only June.

"By the time school starts again, I'll bet I run two million damned sheets through the mangle," he'd said to his two little sisters the night before in their room where he was reading them a bedtime story.

"Slidell!" The nine-year-old Allison's eyes had grown wide, as if her pigtails were too tight.

"What?"

"Taking the Lord's name!" Her lips pursed just like their grandmother's who was a deaconess in the Sanctified Church back home in Tupelo.

"Let it go, Allison," Slidell said.

"Mamaw said the Baby Jesus can hear you anywhere and anytime. Ain't that so, Clarissa?"

Clarissa, her twin, nodded her head in agreement. Mamaw had told them that for sure. Papaw too, and he was a preacher who ought to know. "You gonna get in bad trouble, Slidell, when they find out about your trashy mouth."

"Yeah? Is that so? You think they gonna say something to me what with our momma living in a whorehouse?"

"Slidell!" Allison's eyebrows snapped up like a rubber band. "You know our momma don't live in no whorehouse."

"That's right. We live next door. But tell me this." Slidell drew back then, his hands in his pockets in a pose that cried out for a watchfob and waistcoat. "Where do you think all the money comes from that keeps you two little girls in shiny patent leather shoes and lacy underdrawers?"

Allison and Clarissa both watched their hands tracing patterns on the chenille bedspread.

"Don't tell me you don't know. Don't know where the money comes from and what they call our daddy?"

"Pigmeat," said Allison.

"Yeah. Unh-huh. And what else?"

"I call him Big Pig," said Clarissa. "But I heard peoples call him pimp."

"Clarissa!" said Allison. "You gone get your mouth washed out."

But Clarissa was already jumping up and down on the chenille bedspread, singing her chant. "Pimp! Pimp! Pimp!" she hollered.

Then their bedroom door flew open and smashed against the wall behind it. Filling the doorframe with his six and a half feet and three hundred pounds stood the man in question.

"Who you calling a pimp, little girl?" he thundered.

"You, Daddy!" Clarissa shouted, still bouncing up and down like a rubber ball. She grinned into the maw of the giant. "You!"

Pigmeat reached out with one hand and caught the little girl by her waist on an upward bounce. He held her face two inches from his, scowling.

Steam is going to pour out of his ears, thought Slidell. His goldwork is going to melt and flow and pour straight into Clarissa's mouth, open like a little bird's. And when that gold flowed, quick, quicker than the eye could see, Slidell was going to jump up under Pigmeat's chin and grab that diamond sunk in a gold casing in one of his two front teeth. Pigmeat said that diamond had once been at home in the navel of a French Quarter whore. Slidell would take that sparkler and hock it down the block at Smitty's Pawnshop and run off to—

"Why you calling me a pimp, you little snot of a girl?" Pigmeat's jowls shook in Clarissa's face.

"'Cause Allison did!" she squealed.

He snatched up Allison with the other hand. "And you, you measly pickaninny. What you got to say for yourself?"

"Slidell said—"

"Ah ha!" He tossed both the little girls from him as if they were tissues he was done with and in an instant had forgotten. "You!" he screamed at Slidell. "You, boy!" He backed Slidell into the wall with his great pudding of a stomach. "You call me a pimp, boy?"

Slidell was dizzy with fear. Pigmeat was going to tear his arms off.

But then the mountain began to rumble. And shake.

"You right, boy! You right! You looking here at Pigmeat Zachariah Jones, the biggest and baddest pimp in all the Delta!" At that Pigmeat began to laugh, his stomach yawing like a great steamer in heavy seas.

But Pigmeat was just getting wound up. He wiped the tears from his eyes and caught his breath. "The biggest dope dealer, and the smartest numbers man, and the mean-est, I say mean-est motherfucker—"

"And the sweetest man," their mother Luna finished for him as she slipped in the door as if she still, after three children, had her lean girlish figure, which she did.

She took the giant Pigmeat by the hand as if he were the fourth of those children and led him into the center of the room where she stood on her tiptoes and gave him a kiss, right about, Slidell figured, where that whore's navel diamond was still perched, right up there in that still-smiling mouth.

"You done saved the lives of these little bastards again, Luna." He winked at her. "I was about to chew them up and eat them for my supper." He paused and sucked on his teeth. "For an appetizer."

She pulled her man toward the door. "You children don't be troubling yo' daddy," she warned. Then she pushed him ahead of her, and for a count of one-two he eclipsed their earth, blocking out the sun of the globelight in the hall. Quicksilver, shining with the re-revealed light, Luna followed him. Now you see her, now you don't. Once more, their lightning bug Momma was gone.

Flitting, tasting this honey, now that, it was as if Luna needed a little vacation now and then from real life and would attach herself to a new man, happy and laughing, hanging on his arm and smelling sweet in whispering satiny dresses slipping, sliding like running water against her golden skin. Luna always rolled into a safe place, the pocket of a man who could afford her, could buy her those pretty dresses and a big fast car, in which one day she would jump with a pile of presents, when she got lonesome for her children, and she would roar down or up the highway, depending on wherever her latest man had taken her, and right up into her mother's yard, right into her zinnia beds because she knew it made her mad. Then Luna would carol, her words flung like the bright brassy notes her brother Slideman played on his golden trombone.

"Mommmmmmma," she'd call, dragging the

word out as if it were a whole song. "Momma, momma, I've come for my precious babies." Her children would drop what they were doing, drop their very forks as they raised to their mouths the food their grandmother had sown and reaped and canned and cooked as if it were nothing. They would fly to Luna's beautiful breast, the prettiest cleavage in the whole South, more than one man had been known to say. Her children would bury their faces in her bosom, and with hardly a word of good-bye, grab up a few things, "Don't bother, darlings, there's new clothes for you in the car," and they'd fly away.

Fun, child, what fun they had. How they laughed until they were breathless as the big heavy car, sometimes a convertible, would bolt down the highway, gobbling up the miles as if they were on the lam, as if it had been a hair-breadth escape, as if they had broken out of their grandmother's house just in the nick of time.

"Did you think I would forget you," Luna cooed, then snuggled them and sang along with the radio. Eventually, they'd fall asleep only to awaken, deep in the blackness of the night, to sudden bright lights and loud music, and a woman calling out, her voice like a red flag, "Ooooooooh, Luna, honey, is that you and those precious children. Lordy, girl, come on in here and get you all something to eat."

They'd awaken then, dumb and stupid, as if from a hangover from the liquor of excitement, and soft hands would come out and help them from the car and lead them into a room filled with a sharp smoky smell. Luna knew every down-home barbecue joint in the entire state of Mississippi, parts of Tennessee and Alabama, and the folks inside all knew her back.

Then they'd eat until they couldn't anymore, gnawing the sweet meat off the long rib bones, sopping up the pungent sauce with slices of soft light bread, washing it down with rivers of icy Coke from grease-smeared tall green bottles. They washed and wiped and peed in the bathrooms which were always somewhere out back and then piled again into the big car, all three of them in the backseat this time, tossed together like milk-drunk little pigs, mouths open, drooling in their sleep within minutes.

When they awoke, they would always be in beds somewhere Luna called home with someone they called Uncle or sometimes by his name depending on the man and his preference. There were always a couple of days when Luna would take them around, and everyone would ooh and aah over them, and they would have once again a whole new set of uncles and aunts and cousins and friends for the summer. Then Luna could tuck away and do whatever it was she did with her man, would play whatever role it was this one demanded or requested or begged of her, and Slidell would be the daddy for the girls.

This was the second summer they had spent in Memphis with Pigmeat, who Luna said was their *real* daddy—though Slidell didn't remember him all that well—and her true love, taking them all in. Slidell thought Pigmeat must be that, considering the gold Cadillac he'd bought Luna. Or that diamond ring, the stone almost as big as the one in his tooth.

How many tricks, Slidell wondered, did whores have to turn to earn his momma a diamond ring? How many times did they spread their legs on sheets like this one, stains here and there that wouldn't come out, for his new bike, the only ten-speed in all of Memphis the man at the store had said. And how many of those same sheets was he going to have to run through the mangle, he wondered, before he was through with this pile and could run upstairs where Loubella and Delilah had promised they'd wait for him.

He began to hurry then, zipping linen through the hot roller, carefully though, watching his fingers. He was always careful with the sheets.

"Boy, don't ever touch one before it's been washed and then touch your eye," Pigmeat had warned him. "You be careful unless you want to go blind."

Slidell most definitely did not want to go blind.

He rummaged through the heavy wicker basket before him now. Only four more sheets to go. The thick white piles he'd stacked on the broad table had disappeared as the maids came in and whisked them up on their way to clean and change the rooms.

The air in the laundry room was stifling. Summer in the Delta was hot enough without the blast of the driers and the hissing steam of the mangle in the bright yellow room. Sometimes Slidell imagined that he was trapped in the center of a gigantic egg, sunny-side up, its yolk fiery hot but not quite set from the griddle.

Finally it was over, the last starchy white inch of the last sheet was ironed. River City Numbers One, Two, and Three could roll on this Saturday night, safe in the knowledge that there was plenty of clean linen. Slidell pushed his chair back and walked over to a sink in the corner and dunked his head under the cold water faucet.

Pigmeat had said that running the pool hall was

going to be his next job. Slidell couldn't wait. Two summers in the laundry and he'd have gladly managed Hell if Pigmeat had asked him.

"I think you'll be big enough next summer, Little Man," was how Pigmeat had put it.

How big did a man have to be, Slidell wondered. What made him a real man instead of a little boy. Was it age, or the length of his body, the depth of his voice, the size of his cock—what it could do? Slidell already knew what his could do, that sudden hot spurt of pleasure his hand could bring him between a pair of these same white sheets.

It was time now. Slidell toweled his face, grabbed a fresh T-shirt and his book bag, and hurried up the backstairs.

"Who's there?" Delilah called in the coy voice of the eighteen-year-old debutante she'd never been.

Slidell knocked again.

"Why, Loubella"—Delilah's face broke into a wide grin as she opened the door—"Look what we have here."

"Sugah, sugah." Loubella rose from her bed and crushed Slidell's face to her incredible bosom. It was like drowning in hot foam.

Slidell turned then and crossed to a small wooden table, where he dumped out a pad and charcoals and seated himself on a straight-backed chair. He began to crack his knuckles.

"That's what he always do, Loubella, when he in a hurry. I guess he be ready to get down to business. Right, Little Man?"

Slidell nodded.

"Okay, chile. Who you pick today?"

Slidell stared at them for a long minute, as

if he'd never seen the two women before. He examined the sharp planes of Delilah's face, the cone-shaped proud breasts beneath her grass-green kimono. Then there was Loubella with the black African skin that she burnished with lotion to bring out its deep glow. Which one would he choose?

"Loubella," he finally said.

"Shoot!" Delilah pouted and turned to leave. "I think I'll go do my nails."

"You can stay," Loubella invited.

"No thanks." Delilah pulled the door behind her.

Loubella strolled over to the old record player, dropped on a record of Lady Day's which always put her in the mood. Then she turned, stood before the seated boy, her arms akimbo, her robe falling open. "Okay, precious baby, how do you want me?"

Slidell walked over to the bed and patted it. "Here, like this." He reached out a hand and took her robe as she shrugged it off, her shoulders revealing the rolling landscape of her naked black flesh. She sat where he pointed.

Slidell spread a knee here, moved an elbow there, turned her torso so that her blacker-than-black nipples aimed straight at him, then settled himself at the table with his charcoals and began to sketch.

He worked in silence for a long time, biting his bottom lip when Billie sang "Strange Fruit," which made him shiver.

After a while, Loubella began to fidget. "It's hot, sugah. You sure you don't want to take off your clothes too?"

Slidell frowned. He was having trouble with her left shoulder and her twitching didn't help.

"You want me to lick that sweat off your brow?"

Slidell lost his patience. "Shut up, Loubella! I'm trying to make you famous."

And then Loubella dropped her pose. It flew out the window with her laughter.

"Make me famous!" she cried. "Why, Little Man, Loubella be's famous already. From all Tennessee, Arkansas, Mississippi, mens come with ready cash money they can't wait to stuff between Lou and Bella." Then she grasped her two enormous breasts in her hands and lifted them, bestowing a kiss on the nipple of each.

"How many women you know who can do that?"

Slidell shook his head. None, but he was only twelve. Then he grinned at the woman. He wiped the charcoal from his hands on a handkerchief he'd stuffed in a back pocket. "Yes, but I can make you famous all over the world, Loubella. I can. And I'm going to."

The ebony-skinned whore looked into the eyes of the brown boy standing before her, the ever-so-slightly slanting eyes that gave him a look of mystery, and in them she saw a passion burning like she'd never seen in the eyes of any man, even all those who delved with their most precious parts into her sweet center.

"I believes you, Little Man." Her face was solemn. "I do."

Later that night, after Slidell had spent an hour or two with Pigmeat in the pool hall racking and stacking and keeping track of the beers and the balls and the saucers of pickled pigs' feet, he joined his sisters and his mother for supper in the dining room of River City Number One.

As usual, Luna was a vision. Tonight she was in a peach-colored sliver of satin that poured over her like water only to splash back and grab her beautiful behind.

"Don't you be looking at your momma that way," she teased. "You been drawing too many of them naked women."

"That's right," Allison spoke up. "And I think it's nasty."

"The only reason you think so, Miss Ironing Board," Slidell said, "is because you're jealous. Drawing you would be like drawing the Mojave Desert. Brown and flat as far as the eye can see."

"Momma!" Allison whined.

"Enough," warned Luna. "I don't want to hear no dozens tonight, children. Just eat your supper and leave each other be."

Then she passed the family-style platters of T-bones. She poured each of the children a small glass of wine, adding a couple of ice cubes and splash of water to the glasses for the little girls. Slidell watched her hand tremble. His momma was up to something. He'd seen the signs before.

"What you and Pigmeat doing tonight?" he asked.

"Why nothing, darling. He's gone hang around here like he always does, looking after things, and I'm going out with a couple friends."

"Where to?" Clarissa asked between gulps of watered wine.

"Not so fast, Clarissa." Luna took the glass from her daughter's hand. "Over to Bernice's to play a little pinochle. Maybe later we'll go have a little barbecue."

Slidell busied himself with his steak. He knew, as everyone did, of Luna's fondness for barbecue, but he also knew that sometimes she used the word as a euphemism for dancing and drinking and fooling around.

For it was Luna's determination never to miss a chance to grab at the golden ring. Why, you could never tell what might be behind that door, around that curve, over that hill. It didn't mean anything, sugah, it was all in fun. That was the philosophy that had given Luna three husbands in her twenty-eight years, many lovers, an occasional black eye, a lot of momentary heartache, but never a single second of serious regret.

"Bernice's, huh?" Slidell asked, putting down his knife and fork. Luna didn't say anything for a moment, then gestured to the waitress to clear and asked for desserts.

When the pie was on the table, she leaned over in his face and said, "Don't go laying your mouth on your momma, Slidell. A few hands of pinochle and a barbecued pork sandwich never hurt nobody." She gulped a cup of coffee and planted a kiss atop each of her children's heads. Then, in a flash, she was gone.

Slidell didn't know what time the screaming had started. He had been dreaming about nightfishing in a fast-moving river in a place as unlike the Delta as a place could be. There were high mountains, and it was spring, and there was still deep snow on the ground, its brilliant white aglitter with moonglow. Mrs. Shively, his art teacher, knelt beside him in a pretty red dress and whispered, "Imagine the colors in your mind, Slidell. Think of the silver skin, the blue, the brown speckles, the rose blush, pink as a baby's kiss, right at the throat. Color the trout to you, that's right, color it in your mind."

Slidell was concentrating on colors as hard as he could and they poured right out of his head and into the stream, and just as the trout began to jump into his outstretched fingers, the screaming began.

It was a high keening sound, spiraling up, out of human hearing. Soon the dogs would start to bark. There were no words to the sound, just notes of pure pain floating bright white in the black night of the hotel.

Then, as Slidell sat up and groped for his robe in the darkness, the words began.

"You fucking whore!" Pigmeat screamed. His words flashed like red neon.

Which whore had done what to anger Pigmeat? Then Slidell's logic rubbed its eyes and awoke. There were no whores in River City Number One.

"You touch me again, you son of a bitch, you *dead!*" Finally the woman's keening had found voice, his momma's words.

Slidell leapt out of bed and flew into the hall. There stood Luna and Pigmeat. Blood trickled from a corner of her pretty mouth, tracing a bright pattern down the bosom of her peach satin dress. Pigmeat slowly turned his massive head to stare with blood-red eyes at Slidell. With one huge paw he held Luna by the neck, pushing her against the wall. With the other he gestured at Slidell, waggling his fingers in invitation.

"Come on," he said. "Come on, boy, if you want to save your lying whore of a mother." Pigmeat's words slowed Slidell, but the adrenaline was still pumping. Steady like a drum. Steady as his heartbeat.

"Go 'way, son," Luna said without taking her eyes off Pigmeat's face. "Go on back to bed."

No way, Slidell thought. No way no man's gonna put his hands on my momma like that. He drew closer. "Let her go."

The fat man laughed in his face. His laughter smelled of cigars and sour whiskey. But he didn't loosen his grip. Then he shook Luna like a doll. "Yeah, I'm gonna let the whore go, son. All of you can get the hell out of here first thing this morning. Daybreak, I want to see all your raggedy asses out my door. You can pick up your new pap in the street. He be waiting."

"Momma, what's he talking about?" Slidell turned to his mother for an answer, but still she wouldn't look at him. He'd have to search elsewhere for an answer.

"I'll tell you, Slidell. She ain't going to. *She* tell you she got herself all fussed up in that shiny pink dress I bought her and stepped out for some pinochle with her friends. Same thing she told me. But I knew that ain't what she's been doing. So I gave her a while, just long enough to get herself situated with that pretty pink dress pulled up. Rutting like dogs, so hot they still wearing they good threads."

Luna turned and looked at her son then and shook her head No. But Slidell could see it in her eyes. Pigmeat wasn't the one lying.

"And you know where, boy? You want to know where your momma was two-timing this fat fool? Not in no bed. Nunh-unh. Not in no crib, like decent folks. There they was, the two of 'em, in the backseat of that big gold Caddy I bought her. Jism and barbecue sliding all over the seatcovers."

Then Pigmeat went on spinning the tale. How he'd snuck up on them and jerked Bug out of the car. Slidell could see it all, as if Pigmeat's words were a Saturday picture show. So clear he thought he could stop the story if he closed his eyes. But Pigmeat's words went on and on, and still he could see it. The mountain of a man smashing little Bug in the face. Punching him again and again till he didn't get up for more. Then opening the trunk of the golden Cadillac and throwing Bug inside. Luna's head snapping when Pigmeat slapped her. Her bottom lip splitting and the blood beginning to flow. Her right eye already swelling when Pigmeat stuffed her into the seat beside him and drove back home.

"I threw the son of a bitch out down there, boy. Then I planted my foot on his skinny behind. Everybody knows it now, son, that your momma is a whore, in the wrong hotel over here with me. Ought to be turning tricks next door."

Slidell's eyes fought a losing battle with Luna's. Hers kept running off, getting away. His slippery, will-o'-the-wisp momma who just couldn't stay put.

Pigmeat was still talking. "She's gonna take up with Bug. He be your new daddy, you see." He laughed then, proud of the damage he'd done the man. "Soon as she find his slinky ass done crawled off somewheres."

Pigmeat was right. Bug did become their daddy. But not exactly the way Pigmeat foretold.

By late the next morning, Sunday morning, when Pigmeat awoke, he had slept off all of the whiskey and most of his rage. Beale Street was quiet as a churchyard except for a couple of bluejays in a tree across the street arguing, Pigmeat thought, over who had the biggest set. Well, he'd proved who had 'em on Beale, hadn't he? That was for sure.

He rolled over and grunted. His right hand hurt, sore from the night before. But not nearly as sore as Luna was gonna be. He looked at her lying there still asleep. Her face was puffy, starting to darken into purple. It took a while, Pigmeat knew, for the full palette of battle wounds to blossom. And even longer for them to fade.

Wasn't it funny, though, how thinking about last night made him hard? He looked again at Luna sleeping naked on her back and reached out.

Two hours later Pigmeat was feeling fine. Luna understood what was what. He'd had a hot shower and was dressed in his favorite three-piece white linen suit. He'd ordered a breakfast of eggs, pancakes, and ham as he'd passed through the kitchen and was now carrying a mug of black coffee. He stepped outside to the porch of River City Number One. It was a fine day. He patted his mustache and sipped his coffee. Yes siree, a good day to be fat, prosperous, alive, and well-laid.

Pigmeat never saw Bug slowly slither out of the four-door Ford parked directly across the street. He heard neither the cock of the shotgun's hammer nor the twin shells fall into place. He did hear Bug call his name, and he turned with that special grace that some fat men have, in a fluent arc, with a look of expectation. The arc translated into a pirouette as the double blast caught him full in the neck and blew off his head. His body twirled one way, and his head bounced the other, both flying off the porch and landing in the dirt of Beale Street, but far enough apart from one another to cause all the immediate witnesses to begin to puke.

It was a couple of days before Memphis's

white powers-that-be decided that they had to do something about Bug. There was no hurry, just another nigger killing. But then, no, it wasn't. There was talk around the sheriff's office that what they really ought to do was take up a collection and buy Bug a plaque for having done away with the biggest whoremonger, drug pusher, and numbers runner in town, but though it might be appropriate, it wasn't kosher. A six months' vacation at a minimum security facility would have to do.

That was fine with Bug. The judge even gave him time to get his affairs in order, which meant that he and Luna could go ahead and marry instead of having to wait until he was released.

Luna was stunning in a dress of creamy camellia satin, almost white, but not quite. Her children stood up for her, Slidell in a new white suit. He'd outgrown the one he'd worn the wedding before. The two little girls fluttered in organdy ruffles of purple and pink.

Luna was especially proud of the ring Bug slipped on her left hand after she'd finished with the "until death do us part." She thought Greenburg the Jew had done a beautiful job, especially on such short notice, of melting and molding the gold into a setting that was delicate and light, the absolutely perfect counterpoint to the big diamond Pigmeat had flashed between his fat lips.

Of course, the mortician had had to pull all of Pigmeat's teeth for the diamond and gold, but given the divided condition of the corpse, his widow had felt they shouldn't have an open casket funeral anyway, and who knew the diff?

23

Mary Ann felt faint, and it wasn't just the heat. Girl, she said to herself, for not the first time in the past few days, get a grip.

But who could have imagined this? Nobody. Not in a million years.

For here she was, pretending she was Velma Hightower, sitting like the Queen of Sheba smack in the center of Dixie McClanahan's living room on the very middle cushion of her sofa slipcovered in yellow chintz. Lingerie samples tossed all over the place.

On one side sat a little old white-haired lady named Estella wearing a tiny navy chalk-striped man's suit, a white shirt, and a yellow and navy rep tie exactly like the one Carlin used to throw on the floor when he came off the road.

On the other side, Lucille in a great-looking purple velvet caftan.

Perched on one Wedgwood blue wingchair was another old lady named Alfreda. She was zipped up to her chin in a white jogging suit that said ROB THE ROOTER/CLEANS YOUR DRAINS in big red letters across her chest. Redheaded Alfreda, who seemed to be best friends with Estella, was also sporting the largest diamond solitaire earrings that Mary Ann had ever seen—which made Mary Ann think that maybe the jogging suit was some kind of joke.

The other wingchair was occupied by a hard-looking blonde (Mary Ann could have told her that shade was way too orange for her complexion, she ought to be highlighting anyway instead of doing her full head) in a black, white, and red Chanel suit looped with braid and buttons and tons of gold chains, including one with a gold cross with little pointy things that looked dangerous. Maxine Barnes, the suit-wearer, had a mouth on her that was dangerous too.

She'd just finished explaining to Estella, the little old dyke in the blue suit, at least Mary Ann thought she was a dyke, about her son being booked the night before by the Tupelo police for something that happened at a McDonald's with a man named Red. Mary Ann couldn't make heads or tails of her story. But finally Maxine Barnes said to Estella, "It was the last straw. I've had it with the son of a bitch."

At that, Estella drew up to her full height and said, "I know exactly what you mean, Maxine. I feel the same way myself, but inasmuch as I am his mother, I would appreciate it if you were a little more careful about what you call him. Only because that makes me the bitch, if you get my drift."

"My apologies, Estella. Would you prefer yellow-bellied sapsucker?"

"That'll do nicely, thank you."

Which made Mary Ann wonder. Did dykes have children? Not ever having known one personally, Mary Ann wasn't sure. Actually, once she got Carlin's insurance money, she was thinking she might drive out to San Francisco and see if she could find herself some. Dykes, that is. It had occurred to her more than once that since all the men she'd ever known were such losers, it was an area she might look into. She wondered if any of them came in cute. But, wait, yes, she knew they did. There'd been that news clip on TV on the Gay Freedom Day parade in San Francisco, and leading it was this bunch of women, Dykes on Bikes, and some of them were right pretty. They were riding motorcycles exactly like the girl in the Calvin Klein Jeans advertising insert. Mary Ann was wondering if there was some kind of trial period you could go through to see if you liked it, being a dyke, then she was thinking maybe she'd been watching too much Sally Jessy when the French doors into the dining room swung open, and that's when she felt faint.

The woman who trundled in looked like a hippo in a dress of peachy gauze who'd just gotten up from the Thanksgiving dinner table. Except, lose the gut, she favored Mary Ann enough to be her younger sister. Gave Mary Ann chills, it was so weird.

"Hi!" She came right up to her and stuck out her hand. "I'm Dixie McClanahan. So nice of you to be with us this evening."

Nice for who, Mary Ann wondered. And was this really the woman with the rifle she'd seen out in the yard last evening? Sure it was dark, but who could miss that belly? Well, there was that hedge . . .

"Dixie!" That was Estella. "Sit down. You make me nervous."

"I'm not sick, Estella."

"You know," said Maxine, "my Walter saw you pulling out of the club parking lot the other day, and he said he was gonna call the Mercedes people and tell them they ought to send somebody out to take a picture of you in that little SL coupe. He said it was a kind of testimonial to the way they balance those cars that it doesn't flip over when you make a left turn."

"Now Maxine," Dixie said sweetly, "don't you know I consider the source when I hear things like that? And Walter, well, really, you know how he sneaks into the employees' dressing room at the country club and sniffs their underwear? Why that cute little cocktail waitress was saying to me the other day—"

"Dixie McClanahan, watch your mouth!" That was Lucille, who seemed to have an interest in Dixie not getting her head bashed in.

"Lucille," said Alfreda, "as the senior member of *this* club, I guess I ought to let you in on the rules. One is you can say anything you want to as long as you don't draw blood. Another is nothing ever leaves the room."

"I don't want to know any of your rules," sniffed Lucille. "You never invited me before. You only let me come tonight because you had to, I'm the one who brought the lingerie lady."

"We wanted to protect you," said Dixie, who'd worked her way onto a straight-backed dining room chair. If she sat on anything low or soft, her back hurt, and besides, she couldn't get up again, sort of like being a turtle flipped over on the road.

"Protect me from what?" said Lucille.

"Protect her from what?" Mary Ann asked the same thing at the same time, then clapped her hand over her mouth. She hadn't meant to speak out loud.

"The Club," Alfreda explained to the two of them, "and I do not mean the old country club, was organized right after Red Holcomb bought our medical records at auction, our very personal medical records. Bought them from Dr. James Ireland, who moved away. You, Lucille, had better sense than to go to him in the first place, so we didn't see any point in getting you mixed up in this thing—not knowing whether we might all end up in jail before it was over.''

"That's right," Lucille nodded, ignoring the part about jail since the likelihood of a bunch of white society ladies ending up there was extremely remote. Not unless they took to shooting cops in the middle of Main Street at high noon. "My momma spent half her time delivering babies that old Doc Burma Ireland, Dr. James's daddy, took credit for, I never had any use for either one of them."

"Dr. Ireland was an OB-GYN man," Dixie said to Mary Ann.

"Is this the same Red who's your son?" Mary Ann asked Estella. "The one, if I understood what you were saying, that her son"—she pointed at Maxine—"tried to shoot at the McDonald's?"

"That's the one." Estella smiled. "That's my Red. Except I call him Sonny."

"It was the same reason," said Maxine, "I mean, the medical records thing was why Walter, Jr., *my* son, was threatening Red. He never intended to shoot him, just to scare him, because he knew how upset I was that Red, that son of a yellow-bellied sapsucker—and by son I refer to his pa, Estella—is sitting around running his greasy fingers over my personal medical information. I'll tell you, ever since this thing began I've been so upset I could hardly eat."

"Well now, Maxine," Dixie started, then thought better of it.

"Sonny is the very same one," said Estella, "who we were supposed to scare yesterday evening with a little sound and light show, courtesy of me. But Walter, Jr., had those plans of his own that threw my timing off, and then—" she turned and stared at Dixie—"some other people couldn't remember that they were supposed to stay in their house."

"Was that you—" Mary Ann began.

"That *was* you," Lucille said to Estella. "That was you out in the yard last night jawing with Dixie right after that gunshot, nearly scared me to death. I thought Dixie was dead, I was going to have to run out there and C-section those poor babies."

"That *was* you carrying that rifle," Mary Ann said to Dixie.

All the other women turned and stared at Mary Ann—who realized she'd screwed up. Big time.

Then Dixie leaned forward, as much as she could with the twins sitting on her lap, and sweetly asked Mary Ann, "And which bush were you hiding behind, Mrs. McClanahan?"

24

Isn't she something?" Sam whispered to Floyd Morgan. On stage Elvira, the tall skinny purple-haired female Elvis impersonator with the punk hairdo, had just finished her version of "Don't Be Cruel." The fairgrounds crowd was on its feet.

"Uh-huh," Floyd agreed. "Only I'm not sure from exactly which planet. And I'm about to die in here from the heat."

Elvira, in her white-spangled jumpsuit with the sequined eagle on the back, *was* pretty strange. But then, all the contestants were. Some bad and strange. Some good and strange. But definitely out there where the air was thin.

Sam had wanted Floyd to see if he knew Dewey Travis, and taking Floyd to the Elvis preliminary judging seemed to be the easiest way to find out.

She'd wanted Harry to come too, but Slaughter, Lavert's cousin who looked a lot like Lavert and kissed her hand when Buddy introduced them, said Harry had gone on a little scouting tour pretending he was an outside judge from New York City. That way he could wander, taste everybody else's ribs, and because the competition thought he was a Yankee and didn't know diddle about pig, nobody would pay him the slightest bit of attention.

Up on the stage Elvira, who was nothing like Elvis except for his moves, was saying, "I want y'all to know that I speak to the King every night in my dreams, and he tells me that he loves y'all for coming to these events." The crowd gave itself a loud round of applause.

"He loves y'all for keeping his spirit alive." She threw a teddy bear into the crowd, and two fat women collided and bounced off one another jumping for it. "You know," Elvira continued, lowering her voice, "people ask me what I do with the money I make performing Elvis. Well, I make a lot, and here's what I do with it!" With that, Elvira threw a handful of what looked like gold coins out into the audience.

Floyd, who was pretty good for an old man, snagged one. On one side there was Elvira's face, on the other side the King's. Floyd bit into the coin and grimaced. Junk.

"I do the same thing Elvis did with his money!" Elvira proclaimed. "I give it away!"

"Not to me you didn't," Floyd grumbled.

"Did you know," Elvira continued, "that Elvis paid more income tax than any other single person in the entire history of the United States?" She threw another shower of coins into the crowd. "The King never invested a cent. The King didn't need to stash his riches away in tax shelters and stocks and bonds."

A man up front sailed a dollar bill airplane back at Elvira, who caught it in midair and tucked it down the front of her snow-white jumpsuit of lights.

"All right!" The crowd liked that.

"The King didn't sit around in some stuffy old bank vault clipping his stock coupons." Elvira flashed a brilliant smile and tagged another green airplane. This one was a tenner, and after tucking it down her cleavage, she reached over and kissed its pilot, who'd crawled halfway up on the stage.

"The King knew the secret of success! All those Cadillacs, those wheelchairs, the hundred thousand bucks he gave to charities up in Memphis every Christmas!" Elvira tossed another handful of fake coins, and in return an air force of green filled the stage.

"That's it! That's it!" she called, arms wide, white cape spread, her bosom proud with legal tender. She turned her back and flapped her arms and the multicolored sequined eagle flew. "The more you give, the more you receive!"

"Now that is something!" said Floyd as people threw money with both hands. "That is truly something! That woman's got her act down better than Jimmy Swaggart."

"Catch your breath, Floyd," said Sam. "Your Holly Springs neighbor's up next."

"Mrs. McClanahan? Why, what do you mean? I thought that was *your* name. Me, I'm Velma Hightower." Mary Ann was speaking to Dixie while her eyes were sliding around the room searching for exit signs.

Let's see, she could jump up, make a dash for the front door, hope there wasn't one of those complicated locks like she'd seen on TV that people up in New York used to keep out the burglars and crack dealers, but even if she made it, her rental car was up the street at Lucille's. So grab your purse, girl, make sure you got your keys, kick off those red high heels, though God knows she'd hate to lose them, but it was better than losing her hide, these women looked like they were about to reach over and snatch it clean off—

"Mary Ann," said Dixie. "Are you okay? Do you want a drink of water?"

"I'm fine, thank you." She was beginning to stand, about to try her fifty-yard dash. "But I'm afraid you've made a mistake. My name's—"

"Sit down!" Lucille thundered, then reached over and grabbed her by both shoulders and pushed her down so hard Mary Ann thought she might leave some of her polka dots on the slipcovers.

Then Lucille turned to Dixie. "So is that why you were asking me if she looked like you, this lingerie lady, whatever her name is?"

"Well, I'll be. She does, doesn't she," said Maxine. "Enough to be Dixie's sister, that is, except she's not big as the side of a barn. Do you think y'all are related?"

"Only if you think sleeping with the same man makes women kin," said Dixie. "Which would make a whole bunch of us more or less sisters, wouldn't it?"

The women stared at one another for a minute. Then Maxine Barnes said, "Well, I for one do not have a clue what you're talking about."

"Honey," said Dixie, "are you sure you want to go into this in front of everybody? Taking into consideration that cute guy I passed your name along to at the Snake Pit, that'd make us—"

Maxine reached right over and clamped one bediamonded hand across Dixie's mouth, waggled the forefinger of the other. "Girl, you say another word, I'll choke the life out of you right here without giving it a second thought."

"I really can't imagine what Dixie means, women sleeping with the same men," Alfreda complained to Estella. "I think that's terrible."

Estella said, "Alfreda, wake up and smell the coffee. You think your fella hasn't been cleaning the drains of half the old women in Tupelo? You been hanging around too much with that Martha Jane of yours. She's making you stupid."

"Well, I never . . ." Alfreda sputtered. "Never thought I would live to see the day you would say such a hurtful thing to me, Estella. I don't know what's come over you. I think it must be your own guilt. We know how you go on about sleeping on the floor beside Red's bed, modern-day Christian martyr looking after her only son, but if you must know I have my own ideas about whose bed you've really been napping in."

Mary Ann couldn't wait to hear who that was, the little old lady semi-dyke was tiptoeing through the tulips with. Her upstairs maid, maybe?

"We always knew you had a sweet tooth for chocolate, Estella," Alfreda continued. "Not that I blame you. He is an awfully cute old man. And spry."

"What!" Lucille wheeled and lowered her head right into Estella's face. Mary Ann thought Lucille looked like a big brown bull who'd snatched off the matador's purple velvet cape, thrown it over her back, and was about to stomp the bullfighter into mashed potatoes. If she was Estella, she'd be scared to death. Actually, she *was* scared, but since the women seemed to have their own axes to grind, she was clutching her bag, slipping off her Dorothy-red shoes, making ready to haul butt, boogie full tilt on down that road, and she didn't mean the one to Oz either. She just wanted to find a way to get the hell out of Tupelo, pronto. Or at least back to the Ramada and Wacko Dewey, they could lay the Big Nasty on Miss Dixie here who'd then for sure hand over the money, then she'd stiff Wacko, blow on out to the Coast. Now that was her plan. Right this minute.

"Wait, wait, wait." That was Dixie holding one hand high in the air like a grammar school teacher. "Now, ladies. Let's simmer down a minute. Talking about the little boys, our hormones have tilted our brains. And you"—she lowered that hand and aimed a finger at Mary Ann—"can forget your red hot getaway. Do you understand what I'm saying, Mrs. McClanahan? Mrs. Mary Ann McClanahan? Stay put or we'll tie you to a chair. Don't think we won't. We're desperate women here."

"That's right," said Maxine. "Desperate to recover our personal records from that snake in the grass Red Holcomb—and I for one would like to teach him a lesson he won't forget. Like blowing him to hell. Burning him at the stake. Drawing and quartering might be interesting. Or, Estella, do you think maybe he has an iron maiden in one of his warehouses we could put our hands on?"

"Don't even talk to me," said Estella. "I was doing like we planned. I was going to shoot through the window, turn out the lights, and then when I flipped them back on, there'd be this big sign in the yard that said RED HOLCOMB! POP THE PAPS OR DIE! Outlined in flames, maybe. Sonny's daddy was a closet Klanner, he'd know what the fire meant. Of course, that might have been too subtle. I was considering going ahead and shooting him dead."

"That is the craziest thing I ever heard," said Lucille.

"Besides, it's not what we agreed on at all," said Dixie. "Pop the Paps! Good Lord, Estella, do you mean Pap tests? That's ridiculous. It was supposed to say, Free the Tupelo Women's Medical Records. And that's it."

"And *you* were not supposed to be traipsing around in the yard with a rifle, Miss Priss!" said Estella.

"Well, I'm sorry, but I couldn't help it," said Dixie. "I couldn't stand those barking pups anymore. The rifle was to scare Red if he came out and caught me dyeing them."

"You dyed his dogs?" said Mary Ann.

"Bright red," said Dixie. "Carmine, it said on the package."

Mary Ann liked it. That was the kind of thing she might of thought of herself. "And then what'd he do?"

Before Dixie could answer, Maxine asked Estella, "What happened with those pups, anyway?"

"They're gone," said Estella, shaking her head. "I fear the worst. I tried to get Ollie Priest to come and rescue them."

"Well, I feel real bad about that," said Dixie. "But what I don't understand is why you went and told Ollie I was out in the yard with a rifle. Why'd you do that, Estella?"

"Because, child, I had to throw the suspicion off me, and who's going to arrest a woman eight months gone with fatherless twins?"

"These twins are not fatherless," said Dixie.

"Well, they most certainly are," said Estella.

"Just because their father's dead does not mean they didn't have one," said Lucille, coming to Dixie's defense.

"Hmph," said Estella.

"What do you mean hmph, you little old hussy?" said Lucille.

"I mean, Lucille Phipps, that first off you ought not to go around calling me names. I have not been doing what Alfreda accused me of. Though I don't know why you'd care if I did. If you wanted Buddy Kidd back, all you'd have to do is crook your little finger."

"Hmph," said Lucille.

This thing was getting more and more complicated, thought Mary Ann. It was better than *As the World Turns*.

Estella continued, "And second, as far as the father of those twins is concerned, what I'm saying is that living right next door, I know what I know and I see what I see, and you, Ms. Lucille Phipps, ought not to go asking any questions you think you might not want to know the answers to."

"Now, Estella," Dixie jumped in like she didn't want Estella to say another word, "instead of our talking ugly to one another, I think we ought to get back to Mrs. McClanahan here."

Uh-oh. And just when Mary Ann thought they'd forgotten all about her, she could grab her samples and skidoo.

"What I want to know is exactly who the hell is this woman?" said Maxine Barnes. "And why the hell is she at our meeting? I mean, she has cute things"—Maxine reached over and fingered a bustier of gold lamé—"but when I need new undies, I put Walter on a plane, we buzz up to New York, grab one of those private dressing rooms at Henri Bendel. Have ourselves a good time playing dress-up."

"Now *that* is an interesting idea," Dixie said. "Maxine, honey, I didn't know you had that much imagination. I bet Walter looks cute as hell in lace."

"Shut up, Dixie—after you answer my question."

"Okay. Okay. *This*—" Dixie pointed a finger right in Mary Ann's face. "This is Mary Ann McClanahan from Fairhope, Alabama, who was married to Carlin at the same time I was. Except I was married to him first, which means she wasn't at all, at least not legally."

Well, shoot, thought Mary Ann. The woman knew the whole thing, there wasn't much she could do to argue with her, was there? So she sat there trying to decide how to hold her mouth. Which didn't last long because it didn't take half a minute for Estella to be right up on her peering in her face.

"Mary Ann, is that your name? Is that true?"

Mary Ann nodded.

"Dixie McClanahan, how did you know all this, and why didn't you tell me?" Lucille was pissed, Mary Ann could tell.

"Well, my God, Lucille, I thought once you saw her, you'd get it, and when you didn't, I thought maybe I'd imagined the whole thing. But then I called my private detective, and he said I was right. This is Mary Ann McClanahan, all right. The real thing."

"Private detective?" Mary Ann couldn't help herself. "You had somebody tailing Carlin? And me?"

"Oh, yes," Dixie nodded. "Will Rakestraw, he's my lawyer, when I told him I wanted to divorce Carlin because I knew he was stepping out, not to mention doing a whole lot of other stuff I'd rather not talk about, he said, Honey, you watch out. That sucker's going to try to take every dime you've got. We have to outsmart him, so he found me a private investigator."

"So you knew about me all the time?" Mary Ann couldn't get over it.

"Just for the past year, year and a half."

"Well, why'd you let it go on so long?" Maxine was outraged. "I'd have killed the sucker right out."

Then Dixie turned and gave Mary Ann a little smile—which made Mary Ann wonder exactly where that PI had been and what did he know and when did he know it. Like, had he been on their camping trip to the Smokies?

Dixie said, "You know, my first husband, Stuart the Great, his estate was very complicated. There was so much property and scads of investments, and when Carlin came along and I fancied I was in love with him, well, you know in the heat of passion, women do some pretty foolish things.''

"Like you added his name to some of those deeds?" asked Mary Ann.

"Would you listen to this woman?" said Dixie, laughing. "You hear what's going through her mind? What she's wondering is, if Carlin's name was still on them, and she was married to Carlin, even though the marriage was illegal, is she entitled to any of it? Am I right, Mary Ann? Tell the truth."

Mary Ann did have the grace to blush.

"A true sister under the skin," said Dixie. "Which is exactly the point I was making earlier, ladies. You sleep with 'em, some of it rubs off. Or maybe it's that they keep finding the same woman over and over. I've noticed that, haven't you? A man divorces a woman, then goes out and finds her twin. Not that Carlin went to the trouble to do the divorcing part—"

"What I want to know," Lucille said to Dixie, "is exactly how long ago you stopped sleeping with Carlin."

"Why, Lucille!" said Dixie.

"Don't Lucille me. I'm getting the drift why you never mourned the sucker a single second, not that I would have either, but is he the father of those twins—or what?"

"Eight months ago, if you have to know."

"So you're saying he could be?" said Estella.

"Yes, Miss Nosy Next-Door Neighbor. That's what I'm saying."

"But not necessarily?" said Estella.

"Estella," said Alfreda, "what the hell difference does it make to you? You're as bad as Red, poking around in our private business. Sticking your fingers in places they have no right to go. You're holier than thou about narrowing your earthly possessions to one hundred, but I'll tell you what, Missy. You number those facts, secrets people don't want you to know you're always snooping around collecting, they're *worse* than possessions. And a lot more harmful. You don't watch out, people are going to figure out that Sonny may be the most hated man in Tupelo next to his dead daddy, but it wasn't his daddy alone those mean genes came from.''

At that Estella Holcomb burst into tears. It was something to behold, thought Mary Ann, a little old lady dressed up in a man's suit bawling her eyes out. Maybe she wasn't a dyke after all. Or did you have to give up crying rights when you gave up men? There was a lot about this business to know.

"I'm so sorry," Estella sobbed. "I didn't mean— I don't know what's wrong with me—Sometimes I just—"

"It's all right, honey." Lucille reached over and gave the little old lady such a big hug for a minute Mary Ann thought she was going to take her on her lap and sing her a lullaby.

"*I'm* sorry," said Alfreda. "I love you, old girl." That made Estella cry all the harder, and then Alfreda started up too.

"Now, now, now," said Dixie. "Maxine, I'm sorry I was ugly to you."

"Me too," said Maxine, but Mary Ann didn't think she sounded very sincere.

"Time! Let's blow our noses and kiss and make up and go on with the business at hand," said Dixie, like it wasn't only her house but also her show, which Mary Ann had pretty much thought since Dixie walked in. "Now what we want is our records back from Red. Am I right?"

"Right," the women chorused.

"And what Mary Ann here wants is the hundred-fifty-thousand-dollar life insurance policy she'd be entitled to if I hadn't been married to Carlin first. Am I right, Mary Ann?''

Mary Ann nodded. She hated it that this woman knew so much about her and she didn't have a clue what was happening here. It was really getting on her nerves. Making her feel like a fool. Like she was outclassed by some country club lady. Again.

"So here's the deal," said Dixie. "I move we exit the Red Holcomb business, ladies, and turn it over to Mrs. Mary Ann McClanahan whom I will personally reward with an amount equal to the life insurance if she recovers our records in twenty-four hours starting right now." Dixie was looking at her watch like she was serious.

"Second," said Maxine.

"All in favor."

The vote was unanimous, including that of Lucille, who didn't even have voting privileges, but who cared?

"Now what makes you think I'd want to do that?" said Mary Ann, who was thrilled to pieces that she might get her hands on that one-fifty after all, but had absolutely had it with being pushed around.

"Well, Miss Velma," said Dixie, with a look in her eye that told Mary Ann this wasn't even *close* to her trump card, "you do what you want to, but I think what with one thing and another you've been up to lately you'll find this arrangement more comfortable than the accommodations in the Tupelo pokey."

• • • • • • • • • • • • **25**

However, Dewey didn't follow Elvira the female Elvis impersonator on stage. The emcee announced that their next contestant, Dewey Travis of Holly Springs, had been unavoidably detained by a group of fans who'd mobbed him coming out of a men's room at a local cafe, mistaking him for the real thing alive and well and back home in Tupelo. Dewey would be a little late.

"That's it. I can't stand it in here any longer." Floyd stood. "I've got to get back to my ribs."

It was sultry. Sam had sweat running down inside her cotton sweater. But she held on to Floyd. "Now just wait. I want you to see if you recognize him. Maybe he's been hanging around your house, waiting to sabotage your cooker. Maybe you've seen him. Maybe you know him."

"I don't care who he is or what he did." Floyd stood up just as the emcee was introducing Shawn Magoo, a fat man with a piglike face in a black jumpsuit trimmed in gold who immediately started bleating a sappy version of "Danny Boy." Sam could tell Shawn thought he was God's gift. "I know you and the police have got this wild hair about somebody doing me in, but I'll tell you what. The time for that was long ago when I used to be a mean cuss. Now, I'm a changed man. I'm a sweetheart. Call up my new wife and ask her.''

Magoo was waving his fake diamond rings and jabbering about how busy he'd been being famous in the past six months. ''On second thought, maybe I'll go with you,'' said Sam. ''Just for a minute.''

As she and Floyd stepped off the bleachers and onto the dirt hard-packed by generations of fidgety children, broncos, and show cattle, a motorcycle roared up in the twilight. The rider, swathed in black leather from neck to toes, was wearing one of those Darth Vader helmets. A gold lightning bolt flashed above the smoked face mask.

Sam knew she'd seen this picture before, this exact one, just about this time of day, and even when the man lifted the mask and she realized it was Dewey, that wasn't it. It wasn't just the knowing it was Dewey. She'd seen the whole darkly dangerous image before, she just couldn't remember where and when. Was it yesterday? Yesterday was such a jumble. . . .

Dewey ambled up to Sam and Floyd and extended a hand. ''Howdy,'' he said. ''How y'all? Y'all enjoying the contest?''

''We've been waiting for you, Dewey,'' said Sam. ''Heard you were detained by a bunch of overzealous fans.''

Dewey drew a circle in the dirt with his boot. ''Well, I don't know about that. Is that what they said?'' He gave them a shy grin. ''I was just taking care of some business for my brother.''

''Your brother still live here in Tupelo?'' asked Sam.

Dewey didn't say a word.

Floyd said, ''Where do you live, son?''

Sam smiled at the "son." That's what she called Harry. Now here's Floyd, pushing eighty, using the same term for Dewey, who had to be in his mid-fifties.

"Used to live here. Now I live in Holly Springs."

"You don't say. Me too. Both places."

"That's mighty interesting, idn' it? Small towns, you'd think we'd run into each other before now." Dewey smiled.

"You'd think," said Floyd.

"Well, listen, I hate to be rude, but I got to go on inside, get up there and do my thing. Nice to meet you, Floyd. Good seeing you again, ma'am. I'll see *you* later." He winked and he was gone.

What the heck did that mean?

Floyd was shaking his head. "I never saw that man before in my life. Not that exact one, anyhow. But I'll tell you, that Dewey Travis, idn't that what you said his name is? If he's not a Smith or a Mansell, Gladys Presley was a Smith from out of the Mansells, my name isn't Floyd Morgan, and I'm not the man who used to own the Presleys' little house over on Old Saltillo Road. Now they call it Elvis Presley Drive."

Sam stared at him. "You did?"

An hour later, everyone else had gone home, and Dixie and Mary Ann were sitting up in Dixie's big bed drinking iced tea. Both of them wearing long flowing nightgowns of white cotton batiste, Dixie's.

"He wasn't very good, was he?" Dixie was saying.

Mary Ann giggled. "You mean in the sack?"

Dixie waggled her eyebrows.

"Well, sometimes when he just came off the road, I'd say he'd hit a five."

"Uh-huh," Dixie sighed. "A six, maybe, if you got him stoned."

"Y'all do grass?" Mary Ann was finding there was no end to the amazements. Here she was snuggled up telling secrets like she hadn't since pajama parties in Juvenile Hall in New Orleans when she was a teenager, but with a genuine member of the Junior League *and* a country club. Wasn't that something? Furthermore, Carlin had been married to a woman who not only looked like her, but was everything she wanted to be. Used to want to be, that is. Before she became a girl desperado. And here she was finding out Mrs. Junior League had a touch of girl desperado in her too.

"Oh, yeah. Sometimes. I used to do all kinds of stuff. I was kicked out of Alabama for being a hellraiser. Never went to class, I didn't do anything but drink for two solid years."

"Really?" Even though Mary Ann had never gone to college herself, she knew that when Dixie said Alabama, she meant the university, not the state.

"Yeah. But then I got hold of myself, went back to Memphis, did the whole Queen of Cotton routine. Stuart the Great, that's my first husband, was up there visiting some geezer had more money than God and we met standing out in somebody's yard drinking gin and tonics. He was twenty years older than me, already a semi-famous doctor down here, I was three sheets to the wind being just as cute as I could be telling him stories about when I was in school, how we used to steal cars, me and my fraternity brother friends, I was the sweetheart of Chi Phi, and once we held up a bank."

"You did?! *My* first husband was a bank robber. Isn't that something?"

"Was he any good?"

"You mean in the sack?"

"No, silly. Doing stickups."

Then they almost fell off the bed laughing. They'd

switched to champagne, Dixie having decided that the twins were old enough to have a little nip. Hell, they're almost big enough to vote, she'd said, popping the cork of the Perrier-Jouët.

Mary Ann said, "He was a *terrible* bank robber. The second job he pulled, he gave the note that said *Stick 'em up and put all your money in this bag* to a woman teller he'd gone to high school with. She just waited till he left, called and told the police exactly who he was, they came over to the house and threw his butt in jail. But he was hell on wheels in bed, I'll give him that."

"So was Stuart the Great. *And* he had the greatest sense of humor. Plus he thought I was the best thing since sliced bread. We sort of had this double life. I mean, people here in Tupelo thought it was scandalous anyway that Dr. Stuart Hardy, who'd never been married, came home with me, young enough to be his daughter. But we did all the right things, in public. He did the doctor things and I did the Junior League lady things and then we'd come home and get naked and a little crazy and sit around and eat brownies and make love all weekend."

"Dixie, I think you're drunk."

"Why, am I scandalizing you, darling? I thought *you* were the bad girl."

"Well, I am. It just amazes me that—"

"That I'm bad too? Honey, didn't anybody ever tell you about appearances being deceiving? Besides, I wouldn't think that a woman who'd killed her husband and then came after his wife for the insurance money would—"

"Now I didn't *exactly* kill Carlin."

"That's not what my PI said."

"Well, was he there?"

"No. But he knew that two of you went camping and one of you came back. You, putting out this story about Carlin falling off some rock. See, I, knowing Carlin and what a worm he was and how every once in a while he'd get tooted up and think that the way to make his point was with his fists—"

"Did he hit you, too?"

"Just once. After that, when he got that look on his face, I'd pull out a stack of one-hundred-dollar bills and start counting. I told you Stuart the Great was bucks up, didn't I? Carlin got the message. He'd go down to the basement, pound his head on the cement floor or something. I'll tell you, hon, he *wanted* my money. Now tell me all about killing him." Dixie licked her lips.

Mary Ann looked around the bedroom. Was there a little tape recorder running in the bedside table?

Dixie said, "I know what you're thinking. If it'll make you feel better we can go outside and sit out in the middle of the yard. I'm not going to turn you in, Mary Ann. I'm *proud* of you. I just wish I'd had the nerve."

Well, if she put it like that. "I guess you know Carlin and I went to the Elvis Hall of Fame in Gatlinburg. It'd taken me weeks of begging to get him up there. But that was my plan. I was going to drag him away from home to this deserted place, like some remote campground in the Great Smokies, and then I was going to shoot him with my second husband's, the dirty cop's, gun which I knew could never be traced."

"And then what?"

"What do you mean?"

"Well, what was your story going to be?"

"Oh, that Carlin went off to take a whiz in the woods and he never came back. See, what would really happen is I'd take him on a hike, sweet-talk him off the path, and shoot him. Then I'd report that he went off to peepee and that was it. I waited and waited, but never saw him again. Some crazy deranged person stalking the Smokies got hold of him.''

"You weren't going to make up some tale about how they broke into your tent and tied you up first?"

"No, no, no. That's how you get caught. Making things complicated. What I think is you keep it as simple as you can, and just play it by ear. Things work out. You'd be surprised."

"And you wanted to kill him because—"

"Because? Because he was Carlin! Jesus Christ!"

"No, no, I know what you mean. I just wondered if there was some, well, you know, some huge horrible thing he did that set you off."

"Well, I'll tell you, that morning when he put his cigarette out in his eggs and started raving about how stupid women are—right after I'd been telling him about this article on Jessica Lange living the independent life. Doing what she wanted. Saying she'd just always gone done the road full tilt. I think that was it. Just one mean put-down too many."

"Was it that article in *Vanity Fair?*"

"Yes, indeedy. You saw that? The issue that had that little Calvin Klein Jeans magazine in the plastic bag with it? With the girl on the motorcycle?"

"Mine didn't have the jeans magazine. Is she the same girl as in those ads? That pretty one with the dark hair?"

"Yep."

"When I see those, I'll tell you, I just want to go buy myself a Harley. There's this guy at Wild Dog Cycles up in Ashland, that's in Benton County, he has some old Harleys that'd give you palpitations. But can you see me on one now?" Dixie poked at her belly. "Wouldn't I be a sight? But now, go on. You're in the Smokies, then what?"

"Well, Carlin and I pitched our tent in this deserted

place just like I planned. Or rather, I pitched the tent.''

"Carlin never was handy.''

"Not to mention lazy. Anyway, so I hauled him off on the hike, which took some doing, but once we got started he wanted to do his He-man routine.''

"Did he take off his shirt?''

"He wanted to, but I wouldn't let him. I thought it might be hard to explain later when they found him. But he's jumping over logs. Scrambling up these big old rocks. And of course I've got to do it all too.''

"Of course.''

"So we're up on this humongous rock that hangs way out over this valley, and I think, well, maybe instead of shooting him—because then I'm going to have to do something with the gun, and I've never been too crazy about blood, and I know from watching TV they can do all these lab tests, and gunpowder leaves traces on your fingers—I think, maybe I'll just push him off. It's about a mile down to the bottom of this valley, and I really want to get the hell off the rock, it's making me weak in the knees. Then Carlin says something about me being a whiny wuss, and I said *he* was the wuss, and then he called me that word that I just absolutely hate.''

"I know the one.''

"So I made a really rude comment, and he hauled off to hit me. Then, before I a got chance to push him or shoot him or do anything, he put everything he had into that right cross—and I ducked. I'll tell you, the momentum behind that thing, he would have taken my head off if he'd connected, but instead, he just flew right off into the wild blue yonder.'' Mary Ann paused, remembering. "It was absolutely beautiful. I wish you could have been there.''

"Oh God!'' said Dixie. "I'd loved to have seen it.'' They sat thinking about Carlin, circling slow and like a buzzard all the way down. Then Dixie said, "Were you disappointed, Mary Ann?"

"You mean because I didn't get to push him or shoot him, like I planned?" She nodded. "Yeah, sort of. I mean, I really *wanted* to kill him. I got to where I could taste it."

"Well, Red Holcomb, the son of a bitch next door, the one who bought all our medical records you're going to get for us? You can pretend he's Carlin if it'd make you feel any better."

26

Red Holcomb *was* right next door, but not anywhere that Dixie would have imagined.

Most of the time, when she thought about him, which she tried not to because it always ruined her day, she pictured him sitting in his study, which was chockful of rare books and prints, volumes of Dickens, Trollope, Mark Twain, that were worth a fortune. Framed letters with signatures from Confederate generals Robert E. Lee and Stonewall Jackson, as well as President of the Confederate States of America Jefferson Davis. Papers and books and maps and globes and unopened boxes of correspondence from the famous and near-famous that remained to be catalogued. Dixie imagined Red sitting amid all that wordy clutter fingering the ever-so-personal records of the women of Tupelo as if he were fondling their silken underwear.

But Red wasn't there.

Sometimes Dixie imagined him in his bedroom with the records, Red sitting up in the middle of the same cast iron single bed his daddy had slept in as a boy—along with two bedwetting brothers. The Holcombs had been poor, sharecroppers for generations, before Red's father Arvis began to make a toehold buying and selling things. Among his other pleasures, Arvis had liked to kill, and the heads of local deer and bear and wildcat that loomed from the walls of Red's bedroom were Arvis's. The newer ones were Red's. Red had shot wildebeest, zebra, lions, antelopes, leopards, and cheetah in Kenya. He'd also laid claim, illegally, to protected elephant, gorilla, and rhino. The thought of all those poor dead animals staring down glassy-eyed at Dr. Ireland's gynecological notes with Red in his pj's or, even worse, naked, made Dixie squirm.

But Red wasn't in his bedroom.

Neither was he in the sprawling attic of the house, which was stacked with repossessed bedsteads, velvet Victorian loveseats, chifforobes, Grand Rapids dressing tables from the forties with wavy circular mirrors, a knotty pine hope chest stuffed with cross-stitch day-of-the-week tea towels and tatted curtains and table linen for twenty-four all handworked by a bride whose groom-to-be had perished in a flash flood. When the bride-who-never-was was sixty-four, Red had foreclosed on her house. When she killed herself, Red had helped himself to the furnishings since there was no one else to claim them.

Nor was Red in the guesthouse—the very sharecropper cottage where his daddy'd been born—sifting through his guests' suitcases, jewelry cases, dresser drawers, checkbooks.

Red Holcomb was where Dewey Travis had left him.

Alone. Well, almost alone.

In the dark.

Tied with rope to a straight-backed chair.

And Red was scared. He'd never really been frightened of anything in his life, except being poor like his daddy'd been, but he was plenty scared now.

He hadn't been, at first. Not even when Dewey, who'd introduced himself right off like he was proud of what he was doing, had stuck the .38 Special in his back and said, Get in the car and drive us back to your house.

Red'd been mad.

Mad that the peckerwood had sneaked up on him like that.

Mad that the peckerwood with the black hair and the sideburns, Jesus, one of those crazy Elvis imitators, had had the audacity to start telling him, telling *him,* that he was going to hand over old Doc Burma Ireland's medical records. He sounded just like one of those old women who thought he wanted to know about her privates had been yammering at him on the phone for weeks.

Mad that the peckerwood laughed, *laughed,* when Red said the records wouldn't be of any use to him, he wouldn't understand the medical language.

Then the peckerwood said, The ones from January 1935 would be *real* useful.

That was when Red's rage started to chill a little. To cool. To congeal into fear. Because that was when he understood that the peckerwood knew what was in those records, and a man who knew that might be willing to do all sorts of things to get his hands on them.

Like tie him up and lock him in his own storm cellar with a little company that rattled like dry leaves in a darkness that was cold and thick and deep. And terrifying.

"I really didn't think we'd win," said Harry. "I mean, lookit, I told you from the beginning that the Japanese were this year's cookoff's guests, and I think it's the polite, not to mention the politic, thing to do Toyota-plantwise, letting 'em win ribs, which is only the first round. And they really were good, those sumo ribs. I tasted 'em when I was spying around and I'd be proud to claim them.''

The big boat of a pink Cadillac was gliding along the country road in the gathering dark. Sam was driving, heading out to the Elvis Presley Lake and Campground. She and Harry hadn't seen each other since early morning, and Harry'd said yes indeed he'd like to hear the Jesus bikers' music and the singing, take a break from the Q for a while, they could tell each other about their days. He'd go back later—that is, if this storm didn't hit too hard and wash them out. Somebody had to sit all night with the whole pig, and spell Slaughter and Buddy.

"Idn't it something," Harry said, "Sammy, slow down a little bit, you'd pick somebody and I'd pick somebody for Team Blue Pig, and they'd turn out to have been stepson and -dad to one another?"

"Slaughter and Buddy? You're kidding."

"And they don't get along worth a damn, though maybe they're doing a little better."

"What's the problem?"

"At first Slaughter just kept saying Buddy was a murderer, with no details. I gather it has to do with Slaughter's real father, something about a shooting when Slaughter and Buddy and Lucille Phipps, that's Slaughter's momma who I got these clothes from, all lived up in Memphis in a Beale Street hotel."

"You've got to be kidding! That's who the people are in Ollie's story." Sam took both hands off the wheel to explain about Ollie wanting to write, asking her to read his work. "I love the story, it's about these people named Bug and Luna and their son Slidell—and *they* live in a Beale Street hotel, and whorehouse. The story's told through the thirteen-year-old Slidell.''

"Is it about the murder?''

"In Ollie's version, Buddy blew this man Pigmeat's head off with a shotgun in the middle of Beale Street. Pigmeat would be Slaughter's dad.''

"Sammy, come on. Buddy? How do you know the story's true?''

"Ollie said it was based on truth. I haven't been able to reach him on the phone to talk about it.''

"Well, I'm sure it's an exaggeration. I mean, I wish you could have heard those two when we started playing for the judges this afternoon. It was like they'd made music together for years. Slaughter grabbed my guitar, he was Muddy Waters all over again. And Buddy? He sings, you want to shoot yourself.''

"Unh-huh. I bet. I wonder if he served time.''

"Sammy, you've got murder on the brain. Me, I'm just here to cook some pig, have as good a time as possible with a busted arm, win a prize, maybe see my name in the paper. Get us home before you get so deep in this murder business I have to leave you, don't see you again for eons.''

"Ollie's in the murder business. I'm just poking around a little trying to help P.J. and Velma Hightower since P.J. was nice enough to—That's it! That is it!'' She slapped herself in the forehead. "Dummy! I'm such a dummy, Harry. I just realized where I saw Dewey Travis before. Dewey's the Elvis imitator I was telling you who gave a ride into Tupelo to the woman who stole Velma's wallet. Ollie says he's been brought up for assault several times, murder once, though the charges were dropped. Anyway, he has this lightning bolt on his motorcycle helmet—''

"Didn't you say he was a truck driver?''

Sam shook her head. "He is, but he's got a Harley, and that's who I saw last night, Harry, in the Elvis

McDonald's parking lot. That was Dewey on the Harley, I thought had picked up Harpo and was making off with him. Instead of P.J. See, my instincts were right the very first time I laid eyes on him. So what was he doing at the EP McDonald's?"

"Buying a Big Mac, probably. And giving a woman a ride into Tupelo is not tantamount to murder, Sammy. Neither is looking at your dog—which, by the way, he did not steal. And what do you mean a lightning bolt?"

"A gold zigzag." She traced it in the air with her right forefinger. "And some letters I couldn't make out. I was so crazy looking for Harpo, but wait. Today, I got a closer look." She closed her eyes.

"You're driving, Sammy."

"Hold on. T. C. B. That's what I saw."

"Taking care of business. That was Elvis's logo, his motto."

"Well, I guess that would make sense. Dewey being an Elvis imitator." Sam paused. They were passing the house where Ollie had pointed out the storm cellar in the yard to her. The way the wind was rising, one of those might come in handy tonight. Maybe they should have stayed in. "There's an awful lot of Elvis around this weekend. I told you that Floyd Morgan said he used to own Elvis's birthplace."

"Wait a minute. He did more than that. I met his son-in-law this afternoon who said Floyd evicted the Presleys from that house. Loaned Vernon the money to build it, and when he got behind on the payments, tossed their butts out in the street. You saved the life of the Presleys' Simon Legree. Sam. Sammy. Honey, you have to put your foot on the gas to make the car go."

She ignored that last, turned to him. "Not more than an hour ago, when Floyd and I were talking to

Dewey, Floyd said he'd never seen Dewey in his life, but that he looked like he had to be a Smith or a Mansell, Gladys Presley's folks. Now what do you think about that?''

"Well, that's the side Elvis resembled, all right. Looked like a bunch of them. I've seen pictures. Great uncles. Aunts. Great-grandfather Mansell. Lot of dark soulful lookers in that crowd."

"And Dewey Travis, this shady character who looks a lot like Elvis would at his age, I swear, Harry, I wish you had seen him, is driving around on a Harley. Didn't Elvis ride Harleys?"

"Sammy, hon, where're you going with this? Getting a little carried away, are we?"

"With this lightning bolt and a TCB thing on his helmet, just like Elvis. Now here we go. Now we've got Floyd Morgan, who threw the Presleys out in the road, almost killed in an attempted electrocution. Am I right? And Lovie Rakestraw *was* electrocuted. All while Dewey's in town. And what is a lightning bolt but electricity?"

"Now who's this Lovie again?"

"The one who was zapped in her tub, Harry. I think Ollie's right. There is a connection—this electricity business. I've got to get to a phone."

"Yeah? Well, what did Lovie Rakestraw have to do with Dewey? That's what you're saying, isn't it, that Dewey comes to Tupelo and electrocutes these folks—or in Floyd's case, tries to? Okay. He did it. You sure you don't want to throw the potshot at Red into this too?"

Sam narrowed her eyes. "Well, now—"

"Okay, what's Dewey's motive?"

"Elvis. He's one of those Elfans gone wacko. Or some kin, Elvis's cousin. Think about it. Floyd took Elvis's house. Zap! Floyd's history. Lovie did something, I don't know yet. Zap! Okay, now you want to know why Dewey's just now getting around to it. You think I'm nuts, don't you?''

"I think maybe sitting in the car with a man wearing Elvis's old clothes has worked some kind of voodoo on your brain waves."

"I don't know. But I can't wait to get Ollie on the phone." Sam was fairly bouncing up and down on the leather seat. "Ollie's going to *love* my theory. Even if it doesn't wash, don't you think it's a great idea anyway? It'd be dynamite in his book. The man's definitely got to write a book." Then she heard what Harry had said. "No kidding? Really Elvis's clothes?" She turned to look. "Where'd you get them?"

"Eye on the road, babe. Slaughter took me over to his momma's house, Lucille Phipps I was telling you about, she lives right up the street from Red off on this little cul-de-sac, she runs a mail-order genuine Elvis clothing business."

"Uh-huh. You believe that, I have a bridge I'd like to sell you."

"No. For real. Listen to this. Lucille's mother was a friend of Gladys's, in fact, Slaughter said his granny *delivered* Elvis, but he made that part up. I'm sure there was a doctor who delivered him and Jesse Garon, I'll check it out in one of our books when we get back to Red's. But anyway, Lucille's mom did Gladys some favors when they were all dirt poor, and Gladys left a whole bunch of Elvis's old stuff to her when she died. Her mom gave it all to Lucille." Harry fingered the lapel of the pink jacket. "Like this. Tailored by the Lansky Brothers of Beale Street, Memphis, Tennessee. The genuine article."

"You think it's going to help you win whole hog?"

"Well, it helped us come in second in ribs. Which is like first American."

"Harry! You didn't tell me that! Right behind the Japanese? That's great!"

"Yep, yep, yep. Now I'm ready to listen to some Jesus biker gospel, maybe pick up some tunes for Blue Pig tomorrow afternoon."

"P.J. said they had guitars and drums, and somebody over from Waco plays saxophone. Velma said they had some a cappella singing too."

"Velma. That's the wife of P.J. who rescued Harpo, right? I met her today."

"You did? Where?"

"Over at Lucille's. She came in while Slaughter and I were there. Nice-looking woman. Slaughter was flirting with her. I think it pissed off his momma, Lucille. I'm not sure why."

"Slaughter was flirting with Velma? Really?"

"You sound surprised."

"Well, I wouldn't exactly think Velma was his type. I caught a glimpse of him this afternoon out at the fairgrounds, and we're talking hunk material, Harry. Sweetie."

"Well, Velma's pretty nice looking. Not in *your* league, of course."

"Are we speaking of a two-hundred-and-fifty-pounder in a polyester pants suit with dark brown hair piled up on her head like Marie Antoinette? Five-foot-six, forty-five or so?"

"Five-foot-four, one-twenty, curvy, lots of dark curls, little red suit with white polka dots, red high heels, I thought Slaughter was going to slip one off and drink a beer out of."

"That's not Velma. *That* is the woman who stole Velma's wallet, the one who was standing out in front of Red's house last night when the shot was fired, the one Dewey Travis gave a ride into Tupelo to after he blew her off into a snake farm. Now, what I want to know is, is she some kind of gun moll for Dewey? Is she like Bonnie to his Clyde or something?"

"Sammy, you've left me in the dust."

"You *met* her. God, I can't believe this. I'm running around town like a chicken with my head cut off looking for this woman, chatting up Dewey, trying to get Floyd—who doesn't care if he dies or not as long as he can cook some Q—to ID him."

"You want to know where Velma is, or at least the woman who calls herself Velma? She's going to be at Lucille's this evening selling lingerie. Why don't we call Lucille, you could talk to her about this woman, I could ask her about Buddy and the shooting business. Sam, Sammy, you want to slow down? You're about to drive right through that gatehouse. Honey, we're here."

"Harry, my dearest sweet backseat driver know-it-all boyfriend." She patted him on his cast. "How'd you like to try for two?"

"Oh, I forgot to tell you," Dixie said to Mary Ann. "Estella was listening in on the phone next door at her house and there's a woman named Sam who's a writer or a reporter or something and her boyfriend Harry who're here for the cookoff staying over there with Red, and anyway, Sam, the woman, is talking to Ollie Priest, he's a detective, on the phone. Did I tell you Ollie came here looking for you today? Asking Lucille and me about you?"

"No! Why?" Mary Ann's heart did backflips. Was it the meat packer in Miami? The salesman in Boca? Or the Velma Hightower thing? God, she *knew* she shouldn't have used the woman's credit card, but she couldn't use hers because she hadn't wanted any trace of Mary Ann McClanahan in town if she'd had to do—do she didn't know what to Dixie. *Now* that didn't matter, Dixie didn't even care, but so what? It was already too late. They were going to throw her in the pokey for a plastic offense.

Dixie said, "Oh, you know, sometimes Estella makes me so mad. She wanted to throw suspicion off herself about shooting at Red, and she knows they think it was her, something about the trajectory of the bullet and her being short, so she had told them she saw you standing out in the yard last night."

"But how did she know who I was?" Mary Ann wailed. This wasn't even fair.

"Well, she didn't. She didn't know Velma or Mary Ann or whichever, then. She just described what you looked like and your boots."

"Oh, God. I didn't think about them. I guess they stand out."

"Well, red usually does."

Mary Ann sighed. "So what'd you and Lucille say?"

"Practically nothing. I warned Lucille not to. Lucille didn't know who you were, of course. But I thought I did, and I didn't want you to get in trouble."

"Dixie, if you don't beat all. And here I did it to myself trying to sneak around you."

"You should have just walked up to the front door and said, I'd like to have my hundred and fifty thousand, pretty please."

"And you'd have said sure and handed it to me."

Dixie laughed, showing pretty white teeth. "Well, almost. But the other thing that Estella told me tonight in the kitchen, I almost forgot, is that when she was eavesdropping on the phone on that reporter and Ollie, one of the things Ollie said is that the man who gave, well, she thought it was Velma, but you said somebody gave you a ride into town?"

"Yes?" Mary Ann realized with a jolt that for the last few hours, she'd forgotten all about Dewey.

Well, she could forget him for good now. She certainly didn't need him. She'd pulled this whole thing off all by herself, without a man, just like she'd intended to do in the first place. And Dewey was too weird, anyway. He made her nervous. He'd *liked* the idea of Plan B, scaring Dixie with those—Oh, Jesus. She'd clean forgot. She had to get ahold of him before he did that.

"Estella said that Ollie Priest said the man is dangerous. That he'd killed somebody, or almost killed somebody. I don't know if you've seen him again, but I thought you ought to know."

"Dewey. His name's Dewey, and he *is* weird. He said he'd killed a woman, but I thought he was kidding. Like *we're* kidding about killing Red. I mean, I'll get y'all's records for you, but I wouldn't—" She wouldn't kill anybody, not really. But Dewey? Dewey'd probably *like* it. Why hadn't she given this whole thing more thought earlier, before it got out of hand? Now she had Dewey roped into it, he was crazy, and she didn't even know where he was or what he was up to. Well, at least he hadn't grabbed Dixie earlier when he saw her at the fairgrounds. But wait a minute.

"Who?" Dixie was saying, looking like she might throw up. "Who'd you say gave you a ride?"

Mary Ann brushed the question aside. "Listen, Dixie, were you out at the fairgrounds earlier today?"

"No! Now did you say this man's named Dewey or not?"

"Jeeztz Louise! Are you impatient? Dewey, Dewey Travis. He's a trucker. His tire blew and knocked me off the road into a snake farm. That's where I met the real Velma. But wait, earlier today Dewey said he saw *you* out at the fairgrounds. He said you're writing a story about him or something."

"I don't write, Mary Ann."

Then they turned in bed and stared at one another.

"I bet Dewey thinks you're that reporter you were telling me about, that Sam. What does *she* look like?" Mary Ann hoped she was wrong. God only knew what Dewey was up to, and she didn't want this reporter woman snatched up by mistake.

On the other hand, maybe she was overreacting. Dewey could have forgotten about the whole thing. He could be off on some Elvis trip of his own. Yelling Shazam! at folks, showing them his blue T-shirt with the lightning bolt. There was probably nothing to worry about. Probably not.

"I've never seen her," Dixie said. "Now, Mary Ann, let me make sure." She took Mary Ann's arm. "Are we talking about a man named Dewey Travis who looks like an old Elvis? Is great in the sack?"

Then Mary Ann started to laugh. "Oh, no. Don't tell me we both slept with *him* too? Him and Carlin? Oh, my God!"

But Dixie was shaking her head. "It's not funny, Mary Ann. Jesus! Why didn't I think of this before? Oh, criminee. It's because I didn't want anybody to know. I put him out of my mind on purpose, and now look what's happened. It could have. It probably did. Oh, shit!" Dixie raised a hand to her mouth.

"What are you talking about, Dixie?"

"Lovie Rakestraw. She's been sleeping with him too. Jesus! Oh, my God, my God. When I think about that—I laid him off on her. I just saw him that once, I was mad at Carlin 'cause I caught him screwing this eighteen-year-old girl who works down at the dime store. So I said, What's good for the gander is good for the goose, son. It was right about then I told him he was going to have to change his ways or change his address. Anyway, I jumped in my car and drove right over to Bogart's and picked me up somebody.

Boy. I did that all right. Picked me up more than I bargained for, I can tell you that.''

"So you're saying you fixed Dewey up with this Lovie woman?''

"Yeah. I did it just that once with Dewey, he didn't even know my name, and maybe a month later I ran into the both of them at the Fast Lane one day, not together, but you know, anyway, she's making Oh-my-goodness-what-do-we-have-here? noises. Lovie's always been so jealous of me she couldn't see straight. I never did a blessed thing to her either, till that day. I just wasn't in the mood to play her silly little games. I can't stand people who are never happy with what they have, and it's bad enough I had to play bridge with her, so I said, Here, you want him, take him. He's great. Except maybe I was a little ruder.''

"Yeah? Sounds okay to me.'' Mary Ann was still amused. She couldn't get over the coincidence. Carlin *and* Dewey.

But Dixie wasn't laughing. "Is Dewey still here in Tupelo now?''

"Sure. He's been staying with me at the motel. You know, he's so crazy, he thinks he looks so much like Elvis, he's entering that impersonators' contest.''

Dixie still wasn't laughing. "And you're saying he's cool? Who gave you that shiner?''

"No, I would never say that about Dewey. Probably we'll turn on *America's Most Wanted* and there'll be his picture. But this?'' She pointed at her eye. "We were asleep, and I was dreaming about snakes, and—it was an accident.''

"Well, Mary Ann, I don't think it's any accident Lovie Rakestraw's dead.''

"A man who plans ahead.'' Dewey had nodded at the wall phone in the storm cellar after he'd finished tying up Red. "I like that." Then he'd pulled a yellow-handled screwdriver out of a leather tool belt. He'd fiddled with the receiver while he talked. Red squirmed, but his trussing held fast. "Now, I can't be coming back here to see if you've changed your mind, I've got things to do. Besides, the neighbors'll start calling the six o'clock news, telling 'em they've spotted Elvis out in the side yard. So, what I've done is hooked up this sound-sensitive electric gizmo they use for paraplegics. To answer, you just yell—actually try *Woof!* real loud." Red hadn't wanted to but the .38 Special is a very effective persuader, so he'd woofed. "See, now you've got dial tone, because there's nobody on the other end of the line. If you knew how, you could dial out, send for help to come and get you out of this mess. But you don't. Red? Red? Are you listening to me, man? Stop staring at them. They ain't going nowhere. That is, unless I push this button." Red had held up a little black box that looked like the remote you might use with your TV or your VCR or one of those beepers men wore on the golf course and in suburban movie theaters to make themselves seem important. "If I push this button—" His big thumb had hovered and teased. "I can be standing outside, oh, as far away as my bike parked on the street, and it'll release the magnetic catch on the door of their box. Then it's haul ass for higher ground, if you can, that is." Dewey had given a little tug to the ropes that pinioned Red. "They're pretty excited. I popped 'em with a little shot of amphetamine—read about doing that in a story about a man killed a whole bunch of people out west. Neat, huh?"

That had been earlier. Now the phone rang. Red barked like a dog and there was Dewey on the other end saying, "See? Isn't that something? Now, Red. You thought about what I need?"

"I have." Red's throat was so tight he could hardly get the words out.

"Can't hear you, man!"

"Yes! I said yes!"

"Everything? No tricks?"

"Anything. Tell me what you want. Elvis and Jesse's birth certificates. Jesse's death certificate. What else?"

"There *ain't* no death certificate for Jesse Garon! Jesse Garon ain't dead!" Dewey slammed the phone down and the sound precipitated a frenzy of rattling in the dark storm cellar.

It continued for what seemed like an eternity in the pitch black, and though Red knew the box was still locked, he could feel the creatures crawling all over him. And he could smell them.

He remembered the smell from his childhood when he and his daddy had been out in the woods cutting briers and had stumbled upon a den, and his daddy had gone to chopping and yelled at him to run. Run, boy. It was the smell of the poison, his daddy'd said when the twisting and killing was all over. Made you feel right queer. Red Holcomb hadn't cried since then, since he was four years old. Till now.

Harry hadn't seen so many fat white people screaming and clapping with religious fervor since the last time he'd been in the Superdome with a bunch of Saints fans and a few thousand cases of beer.

But those folks didn't fall out in the aisles and start talking in tongues, and most of them weren't wearing motorcycle jackets.

These folks were growing stranger and stranger, and it was hotter than Hades in this tent. Harry wished Sam would come back from the phone. He'd heard enough to know there weren't going to be any licks he and Blue Pig could use.

The preacher, a tall, skinny guy with blond hair down to his shoulders, was done up in white leather with silver studs and lots of long fringe. Striding up and down the speakers' platform, sweating and screaming that the fires of damnation would make tonight's heat feel like a blast of air-conditioning, he looked like a mix of the pictures of Jesus that Harry had seen in Sunday school, Wild Bill Hickok, Greg Allman, and Richard Brautigan.

"Tell the Lord Jesus that you love him right now!" screamed the preacher. And a whole lot of people did. Real loud. "Don't wait until tomorrow. Tomorrow you might not be here!"

That was true, thought Harry. Take Brautigan. He'd met him once in a bar in Livingston, Montana, filled with drunk macho writers and drunk macho would-be writers and drunk writer groupies. Harry, who'd been as drunk as any of them, had walked up to Brautigan, whom he recognized from his book jacket photos, and said, "I think you're a mighty fine writer, and I'd be proud to shake your hand." Brautigan had said, "That's the first nice thing anybody's said to me in about five years." A month later Harry had read in the paper that Brautigan had shot himself in the head.

The people around Harry now were jerking with the spirit, juking with the spirit, talking in tongues with the spirit, and he was just about to go looking for Sam when she grabbed his good arm.

"I got three offers to run off with fat Jesus bikers to the Promised Land, but I told them I was spoken for," she said.

"Good woman. What'd Ollie say? Did you get him?"

"Yeah. He thinks I've been listening to too many choruses of 'Got My Mojo Working.' But on the other hand, he said he'd send somebody over to Lucille's about the Velma impostor because she might lead them to Dewey who—you're not going to believe this part, Harry. Ollie got a call from the people at the National Crime Information Center. Remember I said he'd done that check on Dewey when he ran his license? It seems that right after that, the Fort Lauderdale Police put out an APB on him. He's wanted for suspicion of killing a woman down there. A woman who collected Elvisiana, Harry."

"Sweet Jesus! I guess you were right." But then he stopped, his mouth open, staring at something behind her. "Would you look at that?" He turned her around.

"What? What are you looking at?" And she was too hot to care. Outside, the wind was coming up strong, and still it was sticky. "Let's go, babe."

"Sammy, what do you think that guy with the green suspenders is doing up there?"

"Why, that's P.J. See that woman carrying the other side of the box? That's Velma. See her? Now does that look like the woman you met this afternoon?"

"Not a bit. But what do you think they have in that box? Why's he holding it out from him like that? You want to try to get up closer and see?"

"No, I want to get the hell out of here, take a cruise by Lucille's. Maybe get a look at this Velma impostor, if the cops haven't already grabbed her."

"Oh, my God, Sammy. Look." Harry pointed at the stage.

"Holy shit!" Then Sam couldn't look away, even though she felt like she was going to faint. Or throw up. Or both. "Harry," she said, her teeth clenched, her face scrunched up, "I really hate snakes."

"I know you do, hon. I do, too. Let's git."

But they didn't move, mesmerized by the slow writhing of the six feet of snake P.J. was holding in each hand, his arms wide, twelve feet of snake if you added it up.

"They're king snakes, right?" Sam was hoping. A king snake was what your daddy always said it was when you were a little girl and came in crying about the terrible thing out in the garden. He'd tell you that to calm you down, then, when you weren't looking, grab his shotgun.

"Be still!" the white-blond preacher commanded, sweat pouring down his face. "Be still and hear the voice of the serpent!"

The crowd did a freeze-frame right in the middle of their churning, waving, howling, rolling, and in the silence Sam heard the buzz of the diamondback rattlers. Seeds of destruction shake shake shaking in a dry gourd held overhead by a madman. It was a sound you only had to hear once. It'd freeze you in your tracks.

"And these things shall follow them that believe. In my name shall they cast out devils!" screamed the preacher.

"Amen," said the crowd.

"They shall speak with new tongues."

"Amen!"

"They shall take up serpents!"

"Do Jesus! Praise the Lord and His Holy Name!"

"If they drink any deadly thing, it shall not hurt them!"

"Shall not hurt them! Shall not hurt them that believe!"

"They shall lay hands upon the sick!"

"Yes, Lord, yes."

"Oh, yes Lord. Yes. Yes."

And then a woman began ululating. Speaking to the Lord in a new tongue. She stood in the aisle writhing, dancing with the snake from a distance. But drawing closer, her arms outstretched. Reaching. Yearning.

Her fingers working, anticipating the feel of the wrist-thick serpent. She had stars in her eyes. She was breathing hard. You could see the rapture.

Then P.J. began to speak. "Oh, Lord. We thank you for the gift. Thank you for the gift. Thank you for the gift." The snakes writhed and twisted in the air.

"Out of here," Sam said.

"And we curse! We curse! We curse the name of the monster who came into our sacred place and stole Thy blessed serpents!" said P.J. "Took Thy agents of salvation! Desecrated Thy ceremony of redemption! Blasphemed Thy temple! Leaving us only these two agents of Thy love."

"And at the same time," said the white-blond preacher, raising his hands. They floated upward. "At the same time, we forgive him."

"Yes, we do."

"Do Jesus."

The volume dropped. The words were low, almost seductive.

"Milk of the Lord. Kindness of the Lord."

"We forgive him, forgive him, oh yes!"

"Amen. Forgiveness *is* the Lord."

"We forgive him. We do."

Do, do, do, do, do. The refrain echoed in Sam's ears as she and Harry stumbled out of the tent into a wind-scorched night that felt like the breath of hell.

Down in the storm cellar, Red Holcomb said over and over though there was no one but the serpents in the box to hear: Anything. Anything. Everything. I'll give you everything. Just please, somebody, anybody, get me out of here. *Now!*

It had seemed the simplest way to keep them both in one place. Shoot them in the foot. After all, a man couldn't watch two people at the same time *and* tell them a story.

And Dewey really needed to tell Shawn Magoo and Obie Vaughn the story. That's why he'd gone by the fairgrounds, where he knew they'd be, the two of them working the crowds who'd come to walk around, sample Q, and shoot the bull. Vaughn and Magoo, the other two finalists in the competition, would be wearing their Elvis getups, signing autographs, chatting folks up. Acting like big deals. Feeding off the King's memory like greedy ghouls. Dewey wanted them to know, not just with their minds, but in their blood, in their bones, down to their very protoplasm, that pretending to be the real thing was an abomination in the eyes of the King. It was a sin.

So he walked up to them, each hanging out at a different end of the fairgrounds as if they'd staked out territories, as if it were theirs, this hallowed ground onto which Elvis the child had climbed the fence many a time to smell the hotdogs and candy apples, ride the Ferris wheel and merry-go-round with nickels saved or snitched, watch the snake charmers, the tattooed ladies, the daring young men who rode their motorcycles around and around and around the sheer walls of a pit.

This was the same place, the stage, the very spot, where the raggedy ten-year-old Elvis had stood in the 1945 Mississippi-Alabama Fair and Dairy Show children's singing contest—in the very same grandstand where Miss Tupelo and Miss East Tupelo were picked along with Miss Mississippi and Miss Alabama—and Elvis won second prize, five dollars. A fortune.

It was the same spot to which Elvis had come eleven years later in the fall of 1956, crowned in glory, fresh from the filming of *Love Me Tender,* to sing for twenty thousand hysterical fans. They tore their hair. They tore the buttons from his shirt. They tore their neighbors' arms from the sockets just for the chance to get one foot closer to the rocking and rolling homeboy whose records the local radio station wouldn't play for a long long time because they sounded like "race" music, black rhythm and blues.

It was this precious ground that Shawn Magoo and Obie Vaughn, fat and smug and smirking, disgusting pretenders to the throne, dared to tread as if they had felt even one day of Elvis's pain. As if they had suffered even one moment of his humiliation at the hands of the snobs of Tupelo, of Memphis, of the world at large who thought he was some kind of freak. Nonbelievers who didn't know that the King was born with the sound, the moves, that brought together black and white old-time religion, black rhythm and blues, white country, rock, Johnnie Ray, Little Richard, sex, life, ecstasy, naughtiness, juvenile delinquency, charm, high humor, wet heat, Mr. Death, and, at the very buckle of the Bible Belt,

Jesus Christ Almighty. Elvis turned musical history on its ear. He brought millions screaming out of their seats. And yet, they wouldn't play him in Tupelo until the rest of the country, the rest of the world, was absolutely electric with the sound of his name.

Oh yes. Elvis was indeed a prophet without honor in his own land.

People in Tupelo mistreated him. When he was a boy. When he was a man. And even now, they defamed his memory.

Dewey Travis knew all this. Part of it he knew from reading every book ever written about Elvis. And part of it he knew because it was his story too. The very same pain flowed in his veins. The same blood. The blood of Presleys and Smiths and Mansells. The blood of a soldier of the Revolution. French Norman. Scots-Irish. The blood of a Mansell who fought the Indians under Andrew Jackson—and then married a full-blooded Cherokee, Morning Dove White who was Elvis Aron and Jesse Garon's great-great-great-grandmother. The blood of survivors of the Mexican War. Survivors of the devastation of black-vomit yellow fever. Survivors of the Tupelo Battlefield, one of the very last of the War Between the States. Survivors of tuberculosis. Survivors of Prohibition and gun-toting revenuers who'd just as soon shoot a man as burn his still. Survivors of share-cropping and poverty and pain-racked childbeds.

"See this?" Dewey screamed, pointing at a spot in the grass of the Priceville Cemetery. It was almost dark, but there was an eerie light left in the western sky as the hot wind rose higher and higher. A canopy of strange round clouds filled the southern sky like a ceiling hung with thousands of breasts.

"See what?" Shawn Magoo was rolling around among the graves, moaning and carrying on about his foot. Just as Dewey thought, a big crybaby. "What do you want us to see before we bleed to death?'' The man was almost hysterical

"I want you to see the spot where they say Jesse Garon's buried. Where they put him in a shoe box tied with a red ribbon.''

"But there's no marker!'' Obie Vaughn wailed. "There's nothing to see. Won't you *please* take us to a hospital?'' Obie was inching his way over behind an angel-topped monument. As if he could hide from Dewey and his .38 Special.

"Of course there's no marker. They were too poor. Now here's what I want you boys to do.'' Dewey had pulled two shovels from the back of Red's pickup truck he'd borrowed. Red wouldn't be using it today.

"Dig our own graves!'' Shawn was crawling around in the cemetery grass now, bumping up against Lellar Mae Wilson, Lummus Poteet, Velcie Eugene—none of whom protested. Tears were rolling down his face. "Why? Why are you doing this to me? What'd I do?''

"You can be the winner of the contest, if that's what you want,'' said Obie Vaughn, his big blue eyes darting around for an idea, anything to placate this crazy. "You can have the trophy. We don't care, do we, Shawn?''

"No. Unh-uh. We don't care at all. We'll be happy to give it to you.''

"Shut up and dig. Right there!'' Dewey pointed at the spot where Elvis's twin was said by some to be buried.

There was a place marker for Jesse Garon at Graceland, out by the swimming pool alongside Grandma Minnie Mae, Gladys, Vernon, and Elvis. But there was nobody home under that marker. Everybody knew that.

And Dewey was out to prove that there was nobody home here either. No dead twin. Nothing. Nothing at all. Because Jesse Garon had never died.

Now there it was. There was the secret. The biggest bestest darkest secret of the universe. Jesse Garon Presley, identical twin to Elvis, alike in every single way, was alive and well in Tupelo.

"Dig! Dig now!" Dewey stepped back and waved the .38 Special. He fired one shot into the air. Forgetting their pain, the two men dug.

All the while, the thunderheads rolled in from the south. The last golden rays of light slipped from the western sky, and one fat drop of rain landed on Dewey's face. Then another.

He turned his face to the heavens and began the story that he'd brought Shawn and Obie to hear. But he didn't address it to them. He was talking to heaven.

"Momma," he said, "sweet Momma. Sweet Janice. I thought you were my momma all these years. It was only August when I was sitting beside your bed, Elvis singing 'We Call on Him' on the radio, saying we call on him when storm clouds gather, just like tonight, boys." *Now* he was talking to Shawn and Obie, "If I were you, I'd do some calling on Him too." Then he went back to his little chat with Janice. "I was back home in Jasper, over in those rolling Alabama hills at our little house in the piney woods, fences all around draped in kudzu. It was hot. Hotter than tonight. I'd driven that rig thirty-two hours straight to get there, trying to get to you, to hold your sweet hand, listen to your breathing, knowing any one could be your last on this earth before you found your heavenly rest. And, bless your heart, that's when you told me the truth.

"Or as much of it as you knew. You told me my birth certificate wasn't real. It was a fake you'd paid a dollar for on a back street in Birmingham. You told me you didn't know my real name, or the names of my real parents. You'd been standing in a dry goods store in Jasper when this really sweet-looking young woman with a soft round face, dark hair, and sad eyes came and stood beside you at the counter holding this little baby about a week old wrapped in a raggedy blanket.

"And you said, Oh, what a pretty baby! And the woman'd asked, Do you have one of your own? And you said, No, I want to, but it doesn't look like me and my husband, Wyatt, can. I love children so much, it's about to break my heart.

"The woman said, I bet you'd make a good mother. Which made the tears come to your eyes, and so you went on pretending you were looking at the material you were about to buy to make Wyatt a new shirt because you hated for a stranger to see you cry. When you turned back around, the baby was lying there in that raggedy blanket on the counter beside you. And the woman with the sad eyes was gone.

"An hour after you told me that story, sweet Janice, while Elvis was singing 'Amazing Grace' on the radio, you breathed your last, and you were gone. And I was all alone."

Metal clanged on metal. "We're hitting something here," said Shawn. "Dewey? Dewey? We're hitting something."

"What do you mean?" Dewey jumped over to the shallow hole, still holding the automatic. "It must be a rock."

"No, it's not," said Obie. "I think it's some kind of little metal box. Maybe a baby's casket." Then he bit his tongue.

"It's not a baby's casket!" Dewey raged. "There ain't no baby casket in here!"

Shawn and Obie both hobbled back from the little

grave. Dewey may not want anything to be there, but there it was, as plain as the nose on your face.

"Jerk that thing up here!" Dewey shouted. "Hurry up. Get it up before that rain gets bad."

Thunder rolled in the southern sky. Five seconds later, lightning streaked the heavy gray clouds.

Shawn stumbled forward and worked his shovel under the edge of the little box crumbly with rust. Then he squatted down and pulled it out. Rain splattered on the tin surface.

"Do you want me to open it, Dewey?"

Dewey wanted to open it himself, but he couldn't drop the gun. "Do it!" Then he growled, "I bet it's just some crap kids buried, playing around the graveyard. Kids ought to be whipped. Ought to know better. Ought to have some respect."

Shawn eased the top off. The hinges were long gone from what appeared to be a little lockbox, like a cash box no more than two feet long, a foot wide. Lightning flashed again, and in the illumination the three men saw a tiny skeleton. Shawn dropped the box and tried to run. Dewey aimed and shot Shawn Magoo square in the back of the neck, and he fell, facedown, into the wet sod.

Obie froze. "I won't tell anybody, Dewey. Honest I won't. I won't tell them about Shawn. I won't tell them about you finding Jesse Garon."

The second bullet flew like a little bird right into Obie's open mouth and out the back of his head.

Dewey knelt down beside the box and picked up the crumbling paper on which someone had written a poem to a little girl born still. A love child, much beloved, named Dollie. The spidery words began to run in the rain.

Dewey leaned back on the heels of his motorcycle boots and raised his face to the sky, opened his mouth and shrilled the scream of the victorious. "I *knew* I was right!" he shrieked to the roiling sky. The clouds were flying now. The air scorching. "I knew, Momma Janice. I knew, sweet precious baby. I knew it in my heart always! And now it's time to tell the truth! It's *Revelation Time!*"

28

"Good Lord have mercy!" said Estella as Sam came banging in from the garage through her kitchen door. "Child, you are soaked to the bone. Where on earth have you been?"

"I just dropped Harry off at the fairgrounds. He and Buddy ought to be along after they shut things down, if they're not washed away in this deluge."

"Well, get in here and dry yourself off." Estella reached for a towel.

"I will, Estella, as soon as I go and see about Harpo. He's probably out there shaking to death in all this thunder and lightning. Then I've got to get over to Lucille Phipp's."

"You don't need to be doing any such thing. Honey, they're issuing tornado warnings on the TV."

"Well, this is important." Sam stopped for a minute, puddling on the tile floor. "But I guess I can call her."

"You most certainly can, as soon as the phone comes back on. The phone lines are down."

"Then I've got to go. There's this woman pretending to be another woman named Velma Hightower—oh, Estella, it's too long to explain now. But wait a minute, what am I talking about? You saw her, standing out in the yard last night. About the time of the gunshot.''

"That's right." Estella squirmed. And then she made a decision. "Are you sure her name's Velma?"

"I *know* her name's not Velma. But whoever she is, she may be in cahoots with this character named Dewey Travis who—well, he's a bad actor. Estella, I just don't have time right now." Sam threw open the back door. It slammed back against the house.

"So you think *she's* dangerous too?" Estella yelled, grabbing raingear and following Sam into the backyard. They fought their way through the gusts toward the guesthouse.

"Well, if she's not, she could be in danger." The wind grabbed Sam's words and tossed them in the top of a pecan tree.

Oh, hell, thought Estella. Things had gone and gotten so complicated. Here they'd cornered Mary Ann McClanahan into stealing Doc Ireland's medical records away from her Sonny, and now not only was he nowhere to be found, but Sam was about to muddy the waters with this Velma business—she never had gotten straight what that was all about—and they did not need this damned tornado right in the middle of things, thank you very much, Jesus.

"You really think so? What'd this Dewey person do?" Estella dumped a torrent of water off the top of her Australian bush hat in the shelter of the guesthouse porch.

"Just a minute." Sam opened the living room door. "Harpo, Harpo, it's all right, sweetie. I'm here."

The little dog, who had spent the afternoon sitting on the top of the sofa staring out into the side yard, bolted past Sam out the door, hopscotched across the swampy yard, and made a beeline for the door of the storm cellar, where he sat and barked and barked and barked.

Lucille wasn't at home anyway. Ten minutes before the patrolman Ollie sent over had pulled up in her yard and five minutes before the lines went down, Dixie had called. "Lucille, could you come over here, please? I know it's terrible out, but Mary Ann and I seriously need some advice."

"It's not those babies is it?"

"The babies and I are fine. Mary Ann and I have been sitting up in bed talking about old times—"

"Yours and Carlin's and hers and Carlin's? Sounds disgusting to me."

"You want to stay over there and bad-mouth me on the phone, or you want to come over here and get the straight skinny, help us figure out what we ought to be doing about the father of my children who—I hate to say this, but it's possible he might be a murderer, Lucille."

"Oh, hell," Lucille said, hanging up the phone. Well, at least it was an area where she had some expertise.

The grassless earth of the fairgrounds had turned into a muddy bog. The WELCOME TO TUPELO DAYS AND THE THIRD ANNUAL INTERNATIONAL BARBECUE COOKOFF banner had blown across the road. And though phone lines were out, the electrical power was still on, and in the bobbing light of a fixture high on a pole, Harry and Buddy and Slaughter were struggling mightily.

"Cooter said to pack it all in," Slaughter yelled to Harry through the wind as he lugged his cute little chairs toward the hearse. "He said the cookoff's over."

"We could load the smoker onto the trailer and

haul it back to Red's garage. Keep that pig going."
Harry, who'd changed out of his Elvis togs and back
into his jeans in the car, was ankle-deep in mud, but
unwilling to concede defeat.

"Son," said Buddy. "Let it go. We took second,
that's first American for the ribs. That's all there's
gonna be. Next year we can go for the gold."

"Next year, humph," grunted Slaughter. "Who's
gonna be this *we* next year?"

"Why, me and you and our main man here,"
Buddy said.

"Ain't gonna be no you and me again," said
Slaughter.

"Now, wait just a minute, guys," said Harry, duck-
ing out of the way of a flying table. "I'm tired of y'all
sniping at each other. That never solves anything.
Now why don't y'all just sit down and talk about it?"

Slaughter cocked an eyebrow. "You got your
Ph.D. in psychology along with musicology and pig,
Dr. Zack?"

"No. But I know that whatever problems y'all
might have had in the past, and I think I've got an
inkling of what—"

"You don't have jack shit about our situation."
Slaughter spat into the wind and jumped as a piece
of blue and white tenting almost blew him over.

Then a giant bolt of lightning split the sky and
struck a pine tree a block away. They could feel the
thunder's rumble in their guts.

"Holy jehoshaphat!" said Buddy. "If we're gone
squabble, I think we ought to do it inside."

"I'm with you, Buddy." This was getting scary.
Harry grabbed Slaughter's arm. "Let's leave all this.
The only thing I care about's the smoker, and it's not
like it can't be replaced. Myself, I'm not so sure."

As they turned toward Buddy's hearse and Slaughter's Riviera, the lights of the grandstand suddenly

flared up like a white blaze in the night. The lashing rain was backlit. Then loud-speakers squalled, a guitar twanged, and a country voice ground out the opening words to "Hound Dog." Thunder rolled and lightning ripped the sky.

The hair stood on the back of Harry's neck. He looked into Slaughter's and Buddy's eyes and saw the wonder bounce back. That was Elvis, sure as shooting. Without a word, they turned and ran as a man through the pouring rain and tearing wind to catch the King's homecoming. It was return engagement time.

The little dog and five women stood in a semicircle before the storm cellar door: Sam, Estella, Dixie, Lucille, and—

"Who exactly are you anyway?" Sam reached for the hand of the brunette in the yellow slicker whose name Estella had half-swallowed. This had to be the Velma impostor.

"Oh, hell," said Mary Ann. She shook off Dixie's frown. "I'm Mary Ann McClanahan from Fairhope, Alabama. And you must be that newspaper reporter. Listen, I'm glad we found you before Dewey got hold of you. For some reason, Dewey, that's Dewey Travis who—well, it's a long story—thinks you're me." Knowing what she knew about Dewey now, Sam shivered at the thought. "It's kind of confusing, but I think it'll all be okay. We've decided we ought to go have a little sit-down with the police."

"I think that might be a good idea," said Sam, who still didn't have all the players straight. Just a few minutes ago, Estella had started trying to explain about Dixie McClanahan who lived next door, something about her husband Carlin, recently deceased, when the three women had burst out Dixie's back door, headed for the little red Mercedes. "Y'all come on over here. I think I've found Sonny," Estella had hollered. So here they all stood, drowning. Could Mary Ann be Dixie's sister? They looked a lot alike. But that wouldn't make sense because they had the same last name. And if Mary Ann was Dixie's sister, what was all this Velma business?

Now a voice poured out from the storm cellar. "Help! Help! Get me out of here!" So that was what Harpo was barking about. Sam couldn't believe it. Usually the little dog took to the bathtub when it thundered in the next county, and here he was rescuing, well, that was definitely the voice of Red Holcomb coming from the storm cellar. No doubt about it. Now how did Red get himself locked in there?

Harpo, so soaked that he looked like a little white rat, barked again, then stared up at Sam. So there. She took one step toward the cellar door when Estella shouted, "Keep back!"

"But, Estella—"

"He's mine," said Mary Ann.

"Please get me out of here! Now!" Red pleaded. "That crazy bastard—there's *rattlers* down here!"

Damn! thought Sam. P.J.'s rattlers. *Dewey* took them and locked Red Holcomb up with them. But why?

Lucille took Dixie's arm as she reeled back, holding her belly. "Are you all right, honey?" Lucille asked. Dixie nodded.

Wasn't that a shame, thought Sam, the woman's husband dead and her big as a house, had to be twins—any minute.

"Rattlesnakes!" Red screamed. "A box full of rattlers!"

"Now, Sonny." Estella yelled at her son through the double doors. "If they're in a box, they couldn't be hurting you. Just calm down."

"Mother! Is that you? Get me the hell out of here!"

"Go for it," Estella said to Mary Ann.

Sam stared at the women. What the hell? The man was locked in a storm cellar with rattlesnakes and they were playing games. But then, she thought about it for a minute, the man was Red.

Mary Ann squatted down right at the door and shouted. "Red? Red, this is Mary Ann McClanahan. You don't know me, but the women of Tupelo whose medical records you have? Well, they've—"

Sam shook her head. So *that* was it. Those records Ollie had told her about.

Red shouted, "He's got this remote control thing! He'll punch it and the box'll open! Quit jabbering, damn you to hell!"

Mary Ann looked at Estella, who just shook her head. Sam had to give it to her, her only son down in a hole with a bunch of rattlers, Estella could still muster up disgust at his bad manners. Then Estella said, "Do you believe that nonsense? Remote control? Hogwash if I ever heard it."

And she was right. Dewey had faked that part.

"Now, Red," said Mary Ann, "shut up and listen here. What we want is your guarantee that you'll return the medical records, all of them, the second we open this door."

"Records?" screamed Red. "You can have anything you want! Just get me out!"

Mary Ann turned to Dixie and gave her a thumbs-up. "Anything?" she said to the door.

"Anything!"

"He'll promise you the moon and the stars," said Estella, shaking her head. "That doesn't mean he'll do it."

Mary Ann turned to her. "How much would you say he's worth?"

"Five, six million, maybe more."

"Really? Wow!" Mary Ann's hair was stringing

and rain poured off her nose. Still, she was pretty. "He ever been married? Have any heirs?"

Lucille said, "Woman, you thinking what I'm thinking you're thinking, I'd think again. You don't want to marry this sucker. You don't want that. Not for all the money in the world."

"Well," said Mary Ann, leaning back on her heels. Red, three-inch spikes sinking into the mud, which reminded Sam of those fancy red boots Velma had said Mary Ann was wearing back at the snake farm. When she was blond. Who was it Velma said Mary Ann reminded her of blond? Mary Ann said, "I don't know about that. Here I am a fresh widow, excuse me, almost-widow. Bored to tears with the lingerie and aloe vera business. Just free as a bird. And deserving of some creature comforts."

"Jessica Lange," Sam blurted.

They all stared at her, except Mary Ann, who turned and gave her a dazzling smile.

Sam said, "Mary Ann, I don't know him all that well, but I don't think you ought to consider marrying a man, no matter how much money he has, who doesn't respect women. Who's a racist. Who doesn't even give a rip about his own dogs. I think he's disgusting. Excuse me, Estella."

Estella shrugged her tiny shoulders in her Burberry. She couldn't agree more.

"Goddamnit to hell! Are you bitches nuts?" That was Red.

Estella spread her hands wide and shook her head.

Mary Ann pulled her little pearl-handled Colt from her purse and gave it a professional gunslinger twirl. "Well, you know, girls, there's more than one way to keep a man on the straight and narrow. If he's made a bunch of promises, signed on the dotted line, and then goes back on his word, well, if I was married to him and that happened and some night he fell off a rock or down a hole or something, well, I'd be sitting pretty, wouldn't I?''

Sam wasn't sure why or what or where or when or who had strung it up this way, but it seemed to her that Mary Ann McClanahan was already sitting in the catbird seat. The rest was details.

"I am the man. Duh, duh, duh, duh, duh. Yes, I am the man." Dewey stood center stage. Legs spread. White light poured on his face. Rain drove into his mouth, down his sideburns.

"It's him," Slaughter whispered. "I know it's him."

Harry wasn't so sure. "Come on." The three of them waded right up to the foot of the stage, to the very place where thirty years ago teenagers had slapped and screamed and begged and pleaded and sweated and shoved to gain a toehold, an inch of ground, to see the young crown prince come home.

"It's not him." Buddy made a face. "He's too old."

"Man! If you don't beat all." Slaughter was exasperated. "He'd be fifty-seven!"

"King wouldn't age," Buddy disagreed. "King'd always look to me like he did when he come back here and played. I remember that. You don't. You too little."

"And I have come," Dewey screamed. *Come, come, come,* the sound system reverberated. "I have come to claim my crown! Claim my brother's kingdom!"

"What does he mean, his brother? Elvis got no brother. Brother's born dead," said Buddy.

"Jesse Garon," Harry breathed, staring up at Dewey. "That's it. This is the man, this is that Dewey Whatsisname Sammy was talking about, and

he thinks he's Jesse Garon. Dollars to doughnuts!''
Harry forgot the part about how he was dangerous.

"Damn if he don't sound like Elvis though," said
Buddy. "Ain't that something? But what's he doing
here singing in this tornado? Think the man's crazy?
Hey! Hey, you!" Buddy sloshed closer to the stage.

Twanggggggaduh sang the electric guitar.

"Old man," Slaughter yelled at Buddy, "get away
from there. Leave that man alone. You don't know
nothing from nothing anyway, be bothering him."

Dewey sang, "They're all gonna be there." It was
a song with a gospel sound Harry had never heard
before. "Gonna be there at His feet. Just like mine."

"Don't know what?" croaked Buddy at Slaughter,
his little black face an angry fist beneath his fedora,
which didn't make much of a rainhat.

"Don't know jack about the Presleys, I'll tell you
that, you think Jesse Garon was born dead," said
Slaughter.

"Who says he wasn't?" Harry wheeled.

"Momma. Momma says *her* momma, Granny, who
delivered those twins said both of them were just as
fine as wine. Two boys looked like they were gonna
be identical."

"Boy's crazy," said Buddy. "Both of y'all's crazy.
Him up there and you."

Dewey clutched the microphone with both hands.
"All these years. Oh yes, *years* of darkness and pain.
But the sunlight is here!" He raised his palms into
the rain.

"Man's nuts," Buddy nodded. "Crazy as a loon.
Just like you, Slaughter, you believe that story you
telling."

"You calling my momma a liar? You putting your
mouth on my momma?"

Harry wasn't sure whether to step in or step back.
Considering his broken arm, he went with the latter.

"I am saying that that is not the truth. Lucille sometimes chooses to bend the truth to fit her own needs," said Buddy Kidd.

He ought to know, thought Harry. He was married to the woman. Assuming that that part of Ollie Priest's story was true. Buddy'd know her in a different light than her son.

Dewey sang, "Days of travail are gone. Sunshine days are here. We'll be sitting in the garden soon. Singing in the garden. Loving in the garden."

Slaughter shook his curls, which had mushroomed into a damp cloud atop his head. "Momma says, and Momma don't lie about stuff this serious, that there was a white girl, an unmarried teenager, who lived next door to the Presleys over on Old Saltillo Road. Her house's not there anymore. Granny delivered her little baby girl, a stillborn, a day before the Presley twins. Old Doc Burma Ireland didn't even know about that child. But he came to check on Gladys after Granny'd done all the birthing. All doctors did for the poor folks was the certificating, make it legal. And what they'd done was—"

"Now you gone tell us some old trash about switching babies," said Buddy, shaking his head.

"I am, 'cause that's exactly what they did. Presleys couldn't afford to feed themselves, much less raise two children at the same time. Those folks were desperate." Slaughter was standing facing Buddy with his back to the stage, leaning right into the old man's face.

Now Dewey was singing "An American Trilogy," a syrupy concoction of "Dixie," "Battle Hymn of the Republic," and "All My Trials," that Elvis recorded in his last years. It made Harry wince. Then the "hush little baby" phrase caught his attention. But no, no getting carried away, Slaughter's story was preposterous. Couldn't be. Unh-uh. No way.

300

"Gladys and Vernon already had that dead baby girl wrapped up in the shoe box their pitiful little neighbor had kept her in next door, didn't want to let her baby girl go. They had her in their house when Doc Ireland came, showed her to the Doc, and he made out the death certificate for Jesse Garon, that's what they said they'd named him. And that was that. They did it because they were too 'shamed to let anybody know what they were gonna do."

"And so what happened to this Jesse?" asked Buddy, his voice thick with sarcasm.

"Momma says old people who know, over in that East Tupelo neighborhood, they say the Presleys gave him away. Nobody knows for sure."

At that Dewey Travis swooped down over the lip of the flooded stage and dragged Slaughter up by the scruff of the neck. He pressed his .38 Special to Slaughter's head and said, "Don't you ever say that again, you son of a bitch. Don't know. *I* know. I know *exactly* what happened. And now's the time to tell the whole world. So you hear me? You hear me good?" He was screaming right in Slaughter's face as yet another boundary fell in his mind. "The King is alive in Tupelo!"

It hadn't taken Mary Ann very long to realize that marrying Red wasn't what she wanted. But that didn't mean she didn't have a wish list.

"A million dollars," she yelled down at him. Then she turned. "Dixie, you can keep that hundred and fifty, honey. Though I appreciate it. Red here's gonna take care of me."

"A million?" Red choked. Then he said, "No problem."

"Are you sure now, Red? I don't want you having second thoughts." Mary Ann tapped the Colt on the cellar door.

"And another half million for the ASPCA," said Estella.

"Did you hear that, Red?" yelled Mary Ann.

"Momma, are you nuts?" he screamed.

"I know what you did with those precious pups, Sonny. Just remember, Mother knows everything."

"Okay! But get me out!"

"I think that children's program up in the projects could use a half mil, easy," said Lucille.

"What do you say, Mr. Holcomb?" Mary Ann was using her sweet voice on him now.

"You're killing me! Killing me!" Red screamed.

"Well," Lucille raised her voice so Red could hear her, but kept her conversational tone, "honey, I'd say, you just do what you want to do. You want to say no, that's fine. But then, I ain't the one down in that hole with those rattlers bound to jump out of that box on top of my head any second. You ever seen anybody snakebit, Red? Whoowee, I'll tell you. I saw a child once, stepped in a den, that child's head was swole up as big as a pumpkin. Green, it was too."

"Jesus loving Christ! *Yes!*"

"And I've been thinking I'd like to have my own little house again," Estella said. "One I can run all by myself."

"What about Buddy?" Lucille sniffed.

"Well, sugar plum, what about Buddy? Don't you think it's about time you quit being so stiff-necked and took him back? I do. You know you love that man."

"I do not."

"Then why'd you have those children with him?" asked Estella.

"Now, Estella, you of all people ought to know human women don't seem to be any better than the animal kingdom at deciding about that," said Dixie.

"You speak for yourself, Miss Dixie." Lucille thumped Dixie's belly like it was a ripe watermelon. "Now we gonna stand out here forever, drown like turkeys don't have enough sense to close our mouths in the rain, or we going to find us some police and do what we said we'd do about the father of these babies? 'Fore he goes and does somebody else wrong."

Wait a minute, thought Sam. *Who* was the father of Dixie's babies?

Red had had it with words. He was just screaming now. Screaming and crying. Sam thought it was sort of pitiful and said as much.

"Oh, hell," said Estella. "Let's let him out. Mary Ann, you keep that little gun trained on him, we'll get him inside, make him sign some things."

"Too bad I left my notary seals at the house, but we'll just hold him till the storm's over, I can get 'em," said Lucille.

"Okay," said Estella. "But before we do, there's just one thing I want to clear up. Lucille, you know Buddy's long ago told me the story about how the two of you married when y'all's just kids, had Slaughter together, then divorced while you're still carrying the little girls. Buddy said he'd played the fool then, slipping around, it was his fault."

"Lucille," Dixie said.

"Just a minute, sugar. I want to hear what this crazy old white lady's saying."

"You kept all three of y'all's children. When you went and told the children that Pigmeat up in Memphis was their daddy—and they were too little to know the difference—Buddy said he wanted to die."

"Lucille!" Dixie was more insistent, but Lucille shushed her as Estella continued.

"Then Pigmeat was treating you so bad and sniffing around those little girls and you got scared and

begged Buddy to come up and help you. Fell in love
with him again, first sight, y'all making love, Pigmeat
caught you, beat you both, threatened to kill the kids,
Buddy shot him dead. I told Buddy he did the right
thing. He said he thought so, he'd do it again. Except
he'd want Slaughter to know the truth. Slaughter hat-
ing him so, thinking Buddy'd killed his real dad, was
the reason y'all broke up the second time. Isn't that
right?''

"Lucille!"

Dixie was urgent, but Lucille paid her no mind.
She didn't turn her handsome face away from their
gaze, though Sam suspected that not all the water
running down her cheeks was rain. "I was young at
the time," Lucille said. "I was confused. But once I
made my decision to tell them Pigmeat was their pa,
I couldn't keep going back, now could I? Say, No,
hon, *this* one's really your daddy. Or maybe I meant
this one." Then she stopped and stared at Dixie.
"Sweetie pie, what you want? You feel okay?"

"Well," said Dixie, "I feel about as fine as I think
a woman can who is about to give birth standing out
in the yard in the middle of a tornado."

"Let him go!" Buddy screamed.

"You get back!" Dewey's eyes rolled. "Now get
back unless you want to see this boy's brains spat-
tered all over the stage!"

It wasn't the time to tell Dewey that he shouldn't
call Slaughter boy. But Harry didn't know what it
was time to do, except close his eyes and wish this
all away. Crazy man with a gun point-blank at Slaughter's head. There weren't a lot of options here. It was
time for a miracle or for some real creativity. Yes!
Creative bull was one of Harry's specialities.

"Jesse?" Harry floated the word out softly as a
mother's kiss across the foot of the stage.

Dewey's head jerked up.

"Jesse? I'm Harry Zack. I'm sure you've heard of me. From Nashville? I'm here scouting talent. I've been producing some of the younger names." Harry grabbed for a couple. "Travis Tritt and Trisha Yearwood. They're good. But who would have ever dreamed, not me, not in a million years, I mean seeing *you* here tonight up on that stage, listening to those sounds, I tell you, man, I am devastated. Wiped out. I mean, you want to do it, just give me a chance, we're gonna be shameless about making you bigger than anybody's ever been. We're talking beyond platinum. We're talking beyond stardom. Man, we're talking intergalactic!"

Dewey had been kneeling all this while, Slaughter pinned on the flooded stage, the gun at his ear.

"He's straight," Slaughter said to Dewey. "The dude's changed the face of musical history. Zack's a kingmaker, man."

Buddy stared at the man holding his son and slowly slipped his right hand down the side of his leg while dropping to his left knee. Since the time he'd served in a Tennessee jail for popping Pigmeat, he'd never been without a piece in his ankle holster. Never used it, but, well, the world being what it was—and now lookahere.

"I'd sure like for you to do another song," said Harry. "You do 'That's All Right, Mama'? My all-time favorite. We could rerecord that, man, do it simple with just a couple of old guys, exactly like you did it for Sun Records, it'd be triple platinum before we could say Fuck Colonel Parker."

Dewey laughed, rain streaming down his face. "I always hated that old bastard. Screwed me six ways to Sunday."

"Out of jillions," said Harry. "That's not gonna

happen to you. Nothing's gonna happen to you but good times, blue skies."

"You think?" And then Dewey seemed to forget about Slaughter. He stood, the .38 Special still in his hand but held loosely like it was a brightly colored scarf he was about to throw to the crowd. Then he dropped it and reached for his guitar.

Slaughter leaped free from the stage. Buddy pulled his .25 Beretta from its holster, but Harry grabbed his arm. Wait. Though he didn't know what they were waiting for.

Then, as if on a signal, the three men started backing away from the stage, stepping backwards as fast as they could. Lightning was crashing all around them in the hard-driving rain.

"Play it, man," Harry called. "Play that guitar."

Dewey hit a chord. His lip curled. A black forelock fell in his streaming face. His eyes closed. His mouth opened and "It's All Right Mama" poured out into the storm. His left leg, anchored by toes that never left the stage, shook to the mean beat. His whole body trembled with the words. The sound was ecstasy. Pure gold. The man was flying higher than Superman or the angels ever flew. He was Elvis. He was nineteen years old, July 5, 1954, doing take after take, sweating out his big chance, busting his cherry big time in the Sun Records studio. Backed by the hard-driving bass of Bill "Blackie" Black's bass and Scotty Moore's red-hot guitar. It was the very sound that, the first time you heard it, you would stop your car. Get out in the middle of the road and shake your head and say, That's it. That's the sound I've been waiting for all my life. It was the sound that burned into your guts, reached into your heart, and made you ache at the same time it gave you hope. It made you long for something, for possibilities—you weren't sure quite what.

Back, back, back, Harry and Buddy and Slaughter kept backing up, open-mouthed and amazed but making tracks from the hot black magic. Off in the distance sirens screamed as Ollie Priest and the Tupelo Police Department and the federal agents who'd joined the chase closed in on their quarry.

Then a mighty bolt of lightning slammed the stage like God's own hand. The power scissored and zigzagged. The energy raced through the pools of rainwater and danced around the top of the microphone in a halo of St. Elmo's fire and played crazy crazy crazy music up and down the strings of that electric guitar, and Dewey Travis or whoever he was, he shook, he rattled, and he rolled. And he was gone.

Dixie, lying on her kitchen floor on a soft tumble of blankets, gasped, "Oh God, I can't do this. I just can't do it."

Lucille had never delivered a baby before, much less two who were in God's own hurry, who couldn't wait for doctors or hospitals, but acted like they were in a race to get here this Sabbath morning and tap their way to Sunday school.

Lucille said, "Sure you can, sugar. We're almost there. You're doing fine. Beautiful. My momma'd be proud of you. Proud of me too. Okay now, now breathe, deep breath, easy as sliding down the banister, I can see the top of a head. Here it comes. Breathe shallow. Don't push. Easy now. Here we go, sugar plum, sweetie pie, little baby. Come to your Aunt Lucille."

Sam, holding Estella's hand, had to remind herself to breathe. She'd been present for plenty of people leaving this earth, but this was her very first birthing, and all of a sudden she found herself crying like a fool.

Mary Ann kneeled by Dixie's head and wiped her

brow. "Come on, girlfriend," she whispered. "Take it easy. Piece of cake. I did it twice. You can do it too."

Dixie grinned up at her, then grimaced, then screamed long and loud and louder and longer, and a tiny baby girl with big brown eyes, a cloud of dark auburn curls, and skin the gold of light coffee said Hello, world.

Lucille stared at the child and gasped, "What on earth?"

Outside, the storm, which hadn't turned into a tornado after all, began to wear itself out. April rain fell softly on the roof.

No sooner had Sam and Estella wrapped the perfect little girl in a white cotton blanket than her identical twin sister arrived on the scene wailing like a fire engine.

Dixie gathered both her daughters to her breast. "Aren't they little dolls? Couldn't you just eat them up? Huh, Grandma?"

Lucille stared at her. "Who are you talking to?"

"You, Lucille. Aren't they just gorgeous? Gonna be heartbreakers. Knock the socks off this old town."

Mary Ann clapped her hands. "Thank you, Jesus, they're not that crazy Dewey's. Or Carlin's, puke, pardon my French."

Lucille rocked back on her heels. "Dixie McClanahan, are you telling me that—you calling me Grandma—you mean my Slaughter is—"

"It looks like it's turned out that way, doesn't it?" said Dixie. "Doc Ireland said it might, the timing and all. Dewey just that one time, Carlin once in a blue moon." She paused for a long moment and smiled like she was thinking about something that tasted good. "And Slaughter."

"Well, Lord have mercy, Dixie," said Lucille. "Didn't you ever hear of being careful?"

"I was. Well, sort of. Accidents happen, and I didn't think I could get pregnant anyway. Don't fuss at me, Lucille. I feel like I've been run over by a truck. Besides, I was *so* mad at that rotten Carlin. Dewey was a bad mistake, but Slaughter's awfully cute. Don't y'all think he's cute? I bet Mary Ann thinks he's cute."

Mary Ann and Sam and Estella laughed. And the babies wailed in unison.

Lucille said, "Y'all hush! All of you girls! I have to think about this a minute. Take it all in."

But Lucille couldn't stop the grin that was breaking across her pretty face like sunshine after the rain—which would be happening pretty soon. It was only an hour or two until dawn in Tupelo. Tupelo, Mis'sippi.

SARAH SHANKMAN

SAMANTHA ADAMS NOVELS

"MS. SHANKMAN HAS GREAT FLAIR FOR
CARICATURE AND WRITES WITH WIT AND HUMOR...AN
AMUSING FEMINIST EDGE ... A GOOD READ."

—THE NEW YORK TIMES BOOK REVIEW

THEN HANG ALL THE LIARS

FIRST KILL ALL THE LAWYERS

NOW LET'S TALK OF GRAVES

SHE WALKS IN BEAUTY

THE KING IS DEAD

HE WAS HER MAN

ALL AVAILABLE
FROM POCKET BOOKS

POCKET
BOOKS

436-04